THE MASTERMIND

ZARA COX

Boldwood

First published in Great Britain in 2025 by Boldwood Books Ltd.

Cover Design by JD Design Ltd.

Cover Images: Ren Saliba Photographer and Shutterstock

A CIP catalogue record for this book is available from the British Library.

Paperback ISBN 978-1-83678-947-5

Large Print ISBN 978-1-83678-946-8

Hardback ISBN 978-1-83678-945-1

Ebook ISBN 978-1-83678-948-2

Kindle ISBN 978-1-83678-949-9

Audio CD ISBN 978-1-83678-940-6

MP3 CD ISBN 978-1-83678-941-3

Digital audio download ISBN 978-1-83678-943-7

This book is printed on certified sustainable paper. Boldwood Books is dedicated to putting sustainability at the heart of our business. For more information please visit https://www. boldwoodbooks.com/about-us/sustainability/

Boldwood Books Ltd, 23 Bowerdean Street, London, SW6 3TN

www.boldwoodbooks.com

To the reader who see the signposts for Morally Grey City and immediately step on the gas, this one is specially for you!

1

CESARE

The first and golden rule of the Salvatore family was simple.

Famigghia above all.

But the second rule was equally as sacred and the most practised on a day-to-day basis.

Don't. Get. Caught.

Didn't matter if it was lifting a Benjamin from your *Nonno's* wallet while he dozed in his favourite wingback chair after one too many Scotches or you were smashing kneecaps underneath the Long Island Expressway.

For the most part, I, as the oldest male of my generation of Salvatores, lived by that rule and made sure I enforced it on my younger siblings.

Hell, if we could have emblazoned it in place of the Salvatore name on the family crest that hung on the wall behind my grandfather's desk without it being fucking obvious, we would have.

I didn't plan on getting caught today.

So I carefully cycled through my options as I flexed my fingers on the wheels of my Formula One race car on the start-finish straight of the Monza race circuit, for once in my life wilfully shutting out the roar of the adoring *tifosi*.

'I asked you a question,' I snarled into the radio connecting me to the pit wall, blinking away the red haze I could feel descending.

Yes, I had a white-hot temper. And sure, everyone on my crew and in the pit lane knew about it. But I also had legendary control, a trait significant enough that my grandfather, Orazio Salvatore, head of the Cosa Nostra and much-revered Salvatore crime family, had bypassed his own son, my father, to hand me the coveted position of Underboss.

Except it wasn't a role *I* coveted.

Except it wasn't a role I could refuse without dire consequences.

My engineer remained silent. Fury built as I crested the apex of Curva Grande, my eyes narrowing on my target – the car in P1.

Telltale static chirped right before another voice came on. 'You've been given a ten-second penalty,' Rafaelle, my brother, said.

If he thought he could mitigate my anger by being the bearer of bad news, he was dead wrong. My nostrils filled with rage and internal combustion engine fumes from the cars in front of me. 'Repeat that.'

A resigned sigh. 'You heard me, Cesare. The official stewards' conclusion is that your overtake move endangered another driver.' There was an edge in his voice that said he too believed the penalty was bullshit.

Added to the great pile of bullshit that'd been shovelled our way with increasing frequency lately, we'd passed the point of it being sheer bad luck.

And that was a situation I intended to do something about.

'Where's my engineer?' I asked my brother, even though we both knew why he'd delivered the news instead of Brazzo, my race engineer.

I wasn't above shooting or maiming the messenger. And this infraction was right up there with the worst of crimes. A ten-second penalty with eleven laps to go and being in second place would mean my chances of winning had gone from high possibility to zero.

'I'm here, Cesare.' To his credit, the man's voice only shook a little. 'If you brake later at Lesmo, we can gain a tenth to—'

'Don't tell me how to drive, shithead,' I seethed as G-forces flattened my helmeted head against the headrest in the steep Parabolica curve. 'Just give me the tyre life deltas.'

The moment he finished rattling off the data, I stomped on the throttle and breathed out, re-engaging control and letting my wrath recede to the to-be-opened-later box at the back of my mind.

The *tifosi* – Italian Formula One fans so zealous they'd earned their own moniker – sensing blood, roared when I took half a second off the leader in the next lap.

The thrill of the hunt raised my temperature from simmering to a steady boil.

Another crackle of the radio set my jaw into granite. 'Do not fucking speak to me unless—'

'Cesare,' a softer voice interrupted. Bibiana, my sister and chief strategist. 'At your current lap times, you'll finish 10.5 seconds ahead of fourth place. A podium finish in third place is better than nothing. If you keep your head.'

She had a mind-boggling head for numbers and a calculating mind that secretly terrified me at the best of times. That she also used that mind as an investment analyst to turn millions into billions for the Salvatore family was the only reason Orazio had allowed her to join Furia Racing, the Formula One team I'd risked life and limb to turn from dream to reality.

The dream now hung in serious balance because finishing anywhere but first, especially if the top step was taken by the scarlet-red car in the lead, would drive Orazio into another days'-long ranting I could do without.

'Is second a possibility?' I asked Bibi, even though I guessed what her answer would be.

'I'm sorry, but no. It'll be close but we'll run out of laps before that can happen.'

'Fuck!'

Despite her sound analysis, I couldn't stop myself from flooring the pedal. The one thousand horsepower beast responded like a dream, harvesting every last kilojoule from the power unit, edging me closer and closer to my nemesis as the laps dwindled.

From the corner of my eye I saw the *tifosi* rise to their feet as the grandstands whizzed by. Sparks flew behind my race car in a shower of light. We'd gone too aggressive with the ride height and my tailbone was definitely feeling the effect of the carbon-fibre floor scraping the ground, but I didn't care. Good thing I was fit and used to sustained pain. An ice bath after the race and a few cognacs and I'd be right as rain.

As to whether I would escape unscathed from Orazio's disappointment without him implementing the ultimatum hanging over my head was another matter.

Jaw clenched tight, I winced through correcting an understeer at the Ascari chicane and rounded Parabolica just in time to see the scarlet monstrosity of Mancinelli Racing streak past the checkered flag to win the race.

I stabbed my radio. 'Tell me we made it?' I snapped.

'Yeah, we're 11.2 seconds ahead of fourth,' Brazzo confirmed. 'Take away the ten seconds and we're cool,' he added, as if I couldn't do the math.

Third place. A spot I actively detested. It was two steps down from my rightful position. And it was a place that was also becoming far too familiar. Suspiciously so.

'Rafa?'

'*Sì*, debrief in an hour.'

I exhaled and manoeuvred the racing green and black car into its resting position, confident my silent command was understood. On days like today I was glad my brother and right-hand man was equally as ruthless, if not more so.

With my dreams of wresting the Salvatore name from a bloody and gruesome history into a semblance of respectability, I would need every ally I could cajole, threaten and blackmail into subservience.

* * *

The continued roaring of the *tifosi* drowned out the blows of my fists pummelling the shit stain whining incoherently for his life on the floor. The wild Italian fans were rabid on any given day. But when one of their own won and another occupied the podium in Monza, the spiritual home of motor racing? The atmosphere was off the charts.

There would be partying into the night in Monza and around the country.

Unfortunately, unlike the past three years straight, it wasn't a Salvatore mounting the top step and basking in the adoration of the thousands who flooded the racetrack after the chequered flag fell.

My fury after being forced to stand next to Narciso Mancinelli, watch the cocky, snot-nosed kid smirk and fidget his way through the national anthem and all but shove the first-place trophy under my nose was at boiling point. No doubt there would be images splashed all over the newspapers by nightfall stoking the juicy private and public race and family rivalry. Wondering how I was taking the threat of being deposed by a driver ten years my junior.

Yeah, that shit ended tonight.

The smell of motor oil, hot tyre blankets and naked terror filled the air as I leaned over the man attempting to curl into a foetal position. His thin jumpsuit didn't protect him from the stomp of my boot on his ribs.

There was a vein of recklessness in my actions tonight. For one thing, I was meting out punishment not in a secluded spot far from prying eyes, but in the back of the Furia Racing Team garage in the pit lane, where a dozen team motor homes and hospitality suites filled with people risked someone stumbling onto my little impromptu tête à tête with the snivelling weasel.

The extra muscle that permanently shadowed every Salvatore from my grandfather down were dutifully guarding the various entrances, but still, with phone cameras everywhere these days, few things remained truly secret for long.

I didn't care.

Not when everything I'd worked so hard for was on the line. When my fickle grandfather was growing restless, making noises about it being time to 'abandon that shitty little pipe dream'. As if that same dream hadn't cleared the Salvatore Organisation a cool half a billion last year in legitimate sponsorship and another billion through a few shrewd laundering schemes.

Frustration drove my fist into flesh already pulpy from my beating, and I barely felt the wince as my knuckles jarred against bone.

Another gasping appeal for mercy only made me madder. 'You know what you need to do. The pain stops if you give me the names.'

'Easy, brother,' an amused voice said from beside me.

I turned to meet dark cognac-brown eyes. Rafaelle took a step back at my fierce look, his hands rising in mock surrender while his lips twitched.

'You think this is funny?' I seethed.

'I'm just saying you'll ruin your hands and unless you plan to keep your gloves on all weekend at the next race, someone will notice your handiwork. Do we even know for a fact that something's going on?'

'I've been telling you for weeks that we have a mole,' I snapped. 'Possibly several of them. Cos these fucking rats always travel in packs, don't they?'

Rafaelle's easy charm vanished. Death slid into his eyes, easing my black mood to have his full attention. 'You know this for a fact?'

'Fist has been looking into it. He caught this one with a burner. Connected a few dots, found some fresh cash in his account and shook him up a little before he brought him here.' I kicked the piece of shit, then glared at my brother. 'Before a month ago, when was the last time we lost three races in a row? Or finished outside the top five?'

Rafa's brows bunched, then he shook his head. 'Never.' He looked down at the whimpering asshole, then sighed. 'Fine. But let someone else have a go with him.'

Relinquishing control didn't come easy to me. Never had. Which was why I was determined to make Furia Racing work. It was my ticket out of a mobster's shortened destiny at the end of a fired gun or a slit throat.

And it had been working like a dream.

We were a relatively young team on the Formula One racing circuit. But we'd entered with a proverbial bang and quickly made our mark by securing our place at the top of the pile, aided by not so clean money funnelled from our various Salvatore concerns.

Everything had been going swimmingly. Or as smoothly as a Sicilian mafia operation could go these days. Until the Mancinelli fucking Family decided to muscle in where they weren't wanted.

But that was the story of our lives, wasn't it?

The Salvatores and the Mancinellis. The real-life unoriginal Romeo and Juliet tragedy, locked in war and hatred over a long-dead woman.

We'd been the bane of each other's lives for almost three quarters of a century. Our violent friction was well-documented and even celebrated since the Salvatores held the record for coming out on top. That tally tickled Orazio no end, hence his feral need to keep controlling everything.

When it came to sustaining vendettas, he was firmly in the win-at-all-costs-or-die-trying camp. He'd made damned sure that unwavering principle was drilled into every one of us before we turned five.

'Go on. It's my turn.' Rafaelle shooed me away, moving in without permission.

I gritted my teeth and let go of the weasel's lapel. Snatching a spotless handkerchief from my pocket, I cleaned the blood off my knuckles and paced away as my brother crouched next to my soon-to-be-dead ex-employee.

Rafa didn't use his fists to shut the man up. Hell, he looked weirdly entertained, watching the fucker cry and snot all over himself. I didn't hear what he whispered in the idiot's ear, but the already pale man went as white as a sheet. Then he started blubbering even faster.

Arms folded, I suppressed that flash of unease I experienced when I watched my brother at work.

Every male Salvatore had done a stint in the US military. Some bullshit character-building plan Orazio Salvatore had read somewhere and decided to instil in his family. I was a marine for exactly one tour before my father yanked me out. Rafaelle did two tours with a special ops team he still never spoke about. We all suspected whatever skills he'd been trained to utilise contributed to his deadliness. Even I was occasionally afraid to turn my back on him, and he was the one person I trusted above any other in the world.

I watched him hook the tips of his fingers into the weasel's cricoid cartilage and squeeze, that same placid expression on his face. The pain would be excruciating. The lack of oxygen terrifying.

'You're about thirty seconds away from dying,' Rafa informed him casually. 'Besides the two names you've given us, is there anyone else involved in your little operation?'

The man mouthed *no, no, no*, attempting to shake his head while wrestling free from Rafa's chokehold. Realising he couldn't, naked fear surged in his eyes, right before the stench of ammonia filled the garage.

Rafa hissed and sidestepped the spread of piss before it touched his polished Prada wingtips. 'Crap. He's telling the truth. He knows fuck all.'

At age thirty-one to my thirty-two, Rafaelle had been my shadow since before we hit puberty. We'd sliced and diced, pummelled and buried enough assholes to know when an interrogation was a lost cause.

I returned to the traitor's side and leaned over to look into his florid face. 'Do you have life insurance?'

'W-what?' His eyes were bloodshot from Rafa's treatment and my punches, but they blinked rapidly to meet mine.

'You have a wife and two kids under five. A man

should make thoughtful contingencies for his family before he passes, especially when his job description includes other dangerous side gigs besides just 'hospitality,' don't you think?'

'I... I... Please, Boss. I didn't mean to. I just... The money was...' He quit talking while he was ahead in favour of staring imploringly up at me. If only I had an ounce of the mercy he sought. But nobody toyed with my dream and lived. Especially a dream the Mancinellis were horning in on like the fucking parasites they were.

'You didn't answer my question. I suggest you do it quickly. I'm not in the mood to stand here inhaling the fumes of your piss. Are you a snivelling, lying little piece of shit who doesn't take care of his family and betrays his employer for a few thousand dollars or not?'

The misery that drenched his face gave me my answer.

I straightened and stepped back.

Umberto 'Fist' Lazlo, my head soldier and second cousin, so nicknamed for his thick fists and his absolute obsession and macabre glee with pounding everything to death, met my gaze. I gave a single nod as I walked past him.

'Please, Don Cesare! Please, have mercy! I'll

never betray you a—' The sound of bone shattering cut off his pleas.

Rafaelle and half my soldiers fell in behind me, the other half staying to help permanently silence the man. As a rule, we didn't kill indiscriminately but neither did we hesitate when the occasion called for it. He was a rat who'd secured a job in my team's hospitality department for the sole purpose of feeding information to our arch enemies in Mancinelli Racing.

We found out two races ago but played a waiting game, hoping he'd lead us to bigger fish, because the more damaging problem we had was in the sabotaging of our car's performance, which led me to believe the true culprits were in my aerodynamics and data analysis team. Two crucial areas within any racing team because without accurate data, we were fucked.

Short of firing them all mid-season – a fucking nonstarter – I was stuck with my ass hanging out until the traitors were found.

My phone buzzed for the hundredth time as we reached the parking lot. I ignored it.

'You know you have to talk to him sooner rather than later, right?'

'You think, Captain Obvious?' I snarled.

Rafa's amusement only increased. Years of taking out whatever range of moods we happened to be in on one another had hardened him to my volatile temperament. I slid behind the wheel of my Furia Falco and punched the ignition.

The roar of the supercar immediately eased a layer of my foul mood. Technically, the car wasn't licensed for road use yet, but it didn't hurt to be the Underboss of a Sicilian-American crime family with several police chiefs' phone numbers on speed dial. Especially when you contributed millions of euros to their election campaigns.

As I eased out of my parking spot, Rafa's own phone buzzed. I started to smirk at his grimace, but it stalled when he smiled again. It wasn't our grandfather trying to reach me through him. Not yet anyway.

'It's the twins. They say the fuckers are at the club, crowing about their win.'

'The whole team?' I asked casually, but in my chest, something primal stirred. A different feeling to the bloodlust I'd just left behind. The kind of thrill derived from flirting with danger when you should know better.

It was just as strong, equally lethal. And it was reserved for one person.

'Yeah,' Rafa confirmed. 'The keys players at least. Led by Narc-Fuck.'

I felt his stare drilling into the side of my face but kept my gaze on the road.

Narciso Mancinelli, or Narc-Fuck as Rafa and my twin younger brothers liked to call him, was a cocky little shit, but in the grand scheme of things, he barely made a blip on my radar, not unless he was standing, undeservedly, on the top podium that belonged to me.

No.

When it came to the Mancinelli clan, my energy and focus were reserved for the top players. And at the top of that pile, with a very special place on my shit list, was one person.

The eldest of Bonafacio's grandchildren.

Maddelena Mancinelli.

2

CESARE

Half an hour later, and my mood had plunged further south.

Frustration bit deep, pounding in time to the music blaring from the speakers in La Miraggio nightclub. My gaze swept back and forth on high alert for anything and anyone out of the ordinary as I awaited Rafa's return.

So far he'd cornered three key Mancinelli Racing crew members and discreetly taken them out back for a 'quiet word'.

Nothing.

I was already riled up from the stupid shenanigans of the Mancinellis crowing about their race win like it was the second fucking coming.

But that wasn't what was eating at my insides like battery acid.

She wasn't here. You'd think she'd jump at the chance to rub my face in it like her uncle Stefano, currently well on his way to being high and hammered, and feeling bolder by the second as he ventured closer to my VIP section, laughing and pointing like some stupid puppet while his audience laughed.

I ignored his drunken sneers and caught Rafa heading my way. The subtle shake of his head made me curse under my breath.

Had it been a mistake coming—

The thought stalled when the small crowd parted. And I saw her.

She'd arrived without fanfare and almost slid under my radar.

Bitterness and that slow sizzle of electricity that always attacked me whenever she breached my thoughts tossed my mood deeper down the toilet.

Rafaelle dropped into the seat next to me, then followed my gaze. 'Yeah, meant to tell you. Hot Tits has arrived.'

My teeth ground and I shot him a glare. 'Watch your fucking mouth.' That was *my* name for her. No one else was allowed to use it. And if anyone found that fucking weird, it was their problem not mine.

Rafaelle returned my glare with a smile before his gaze shifted sideways. 'You want me to take care of him or have Fist do it?'

I read his lips more than heard the question but I knew he was referring to Stefano. Ignoring him had made him bolder, and I could hear raucous laughter to my right.

The twins, Dante and Lorenzo, five years younger and almost as zealous about racing as I was, were equally fucking pissed off at the scene unfolding before us. And by my silent order not to crack open a few Mancinelli skulls the way they were itching to. Coming third had riled us all up but descending into mayhem would get us nowhere.

That said, maybe my earlier thought was right. Maybe we should've stayed away, tackled this differently.

Nah, who the hell was I kidding? I thrived in mayhem.

And that state was being greatly exacerbated by having to watch *her*, writhing on the dancefloor in that fucking red cocktail dress, right in my line of sight.

'Just say the word,' Rafa encouraged, drawing my gaze for a split second.

At times like these I envied his ability to remain calm, no matter the circumstances. There was a reason he was nicknamed The Silent Assassin. You didn't see or hear him coming until the knife had slid between your ribs and he was walking away with a smile on his face. I'd seen him do it often enough.

I was almost tempted to ask him to do it one more time to the idiot grinding his small dick against *her*.

Maddelena. The girl who'd left... something... an indelible mark I couldn't rid myself of all these years later.

But no. *She* I intended to take care of myself.

My phone buzzed, another summons from Orazio. Continuing to ignore him wasn't the best course of action. But I wanted some answers before the inevitable confrontation.

The de facto head of the Salvatore family hadn't used his fists to make a point for at least a week. But that glorious reprieve was about to break, most likely on my face, if I didn't find answers for him.

I'd taken many a black eye and bruised rib in my stride over the years. Rafaelle too. But the old man, that fucking cunning fox, had wised up to the fact that his two oldest grandsons lost their minds when his fists were directed at their youngest brothers. Or even worse, on Bibiana. If I didn't answer soon, that was where he would refocus his ire.

I looked over to my left, to where the twins were staring at one another, engaged in that silent twin speak that frequently drove me up the wall.

They looked as sullen and perplexed as I was furious.

Dante, the second driver in my racing team, had gone from a consistent one-two reign on the podium alongside me to now finishing outside the top five in the last few races. His anxiety levels had gone through the roof lately, only his twin gluing himself to his side keeping him on an even keel.

We'd had every engineer, strategist and aerodynamicist on the Furia Racing Team scratching their heads as to what had gone wrong before we'd concluded that there was nothing wrong with our racing car. That it was outside influences adversely affecting our team.

If I couldn't find answers from the Mancinelli stooges, then I was headed straight for the top.

I eyed my brothers, read every version of their barely bridled patience. Dante was a slightly less icy version of Rafa, while Renzo rivalled me in the hot-head stakes. I could tell he was about to blow from the way his knees were bouncing and the loud cracking of his knuckles.

Dante shot him a 'chill' look that earned him a sneer. 'We look like chumps, sitting around with our thumbs up our asses. We should...'

I stopped listening, my fixation on her seizing my attention.

As with every time I'd seen her... except that night when my warning had well and truly riled her, *as intended*... Maddelena Mancinelli looked fucking flawless.

The quintessential Sicilian beauty.

Her skin glowed with the kind of health and vitality that didn't come from creams or endless pampering but from Mother Nature's grace and favour.

Old Man Mancinelli may be nicknamed El Topo, on account of his rat-like features, but by some stroke of genetic genius, all his offspring had escaped being saddled by his fugly DNA.

Every last one of his daughters, and even the idiot Narciso, had inherited their grandmother and mother's striking good looks.

It killed me that I could never take my eyes off her when she was in the same room. That something about that one and only close encounter an eternity ago had imprinted her on me in a way I couldn't scrub off, no matter how I tried.

And I had tried.

Women in all shapes and sizes had graced my bed since I hit puberty, eager for Salvatore cock, if only for the chance to boast about it to their friends and family. It didn't hurt that mine was impressively miles above average, too.

Dozens of women. And yet that itch behind my breastbone remained.

Maddelena Mancinelli had helped herself to something vital of mine in those stolen moments out on the field in the Middle of Nowhere, Connecticut.

Like the kind fucking Romeo should've known better than to risk with Juliet?

Fuck no. There was no forbidden love, or even hate – that was reserved for the fuckers messing with my dream – here. But there was... something.

Something I intended to get back, or die trying.

I let all of that show on my face, and I saw the moment she clocked me from across the dancefloor. The moment she saw it, too.

Her stunning blue eyes widened a fraction and the hand clutching her glass trembled before she got control of it. The dumbass she was dancing with took one look at me and left her high and dry on the dancefloor, a move she acknowledged with pursed lips and a fierce glare my way.

I ignored the glare, for now, my attention on the glass's bubbly contents.

When the hell did she start drinking?

I knew for a fact El Topo had a list a mile long of all things forbidden where his granddaughters were concerned. Just as I knew at the top of that list, etched in blood, was the warning to stay away from us Salvatores, on pain of severe punishment.

And yeah, drinking was in the top ten.

As if she read that thought too, a corner of her mouth lifted, a challenge issued.

'How long are you two going to keep eye-fucking each other? I'm getting fucking pregnant over here.'

The twins burst into laughter, the thick tension easing a fraction before ratcheting right back up.

'Rafa...'

He didn't heed the warning in my voice. 'I'm just saying, there's only so much of the sex fumes I can take before shit gets weird, you being blood and all. Either do something about it or shut that shit down.'

I managed, barely, to drag my eyes from her to scowl at my brother. 'Whatever the fuck you think you see, you're wrong.'

He opened his mouth. I held up my hand. Mutiny flashed across his face before he clamped his mouth shut. I didn't fool myself into thinking this would be the end of it, though. My brother was dogged if nothing else.

Another skill he'd honed in that super-secret part of the government he refused to divulge, no matter how much liquor I poured down his throat.

'You have a job to do. Whatever it takes to find the mole, do it. I want them dealt with before the next race. Understood?'

He didn't answer immediately. But he got the gravity of my order. And honoured it with a two-finger salute a second later.

My phone buzzed again. And again. And again.

Another burst of raucous laughter from across the room, loud enough to be heard over the thumping music, drove the twins to their feet. Un-surprisingly, they'd reached the end of their tether.

'We've had enough of this shit. Either we break some ribs, preferably that *pezz'i miedda* Narc-Fuck's, or we leave. Which is it going to be, brother?'

I leaned forward, elbows on knees, clenched fists dangling between my legs. 'Go home. I'll follow shortly.'

Rafa's eyes narrowed. '*Frate...* whatever you're

thinking is probably not a good idea,' he muttered for my ears only.

My gaze lanced back to her, my insides spasming as if someone had shot a Taser into my belly. Relentless echoes of bodies touching, writhing, exploring in the dark unravelled through my brain. My fingers twitched. I bunched them into tighter fists. 'Maybe not, but when have you known that to stop me?'

Rafa sighed. 'Just make sure you're well-equipped for hazardous weather in case you fall through that thin ice you're skating on, *si*?'

I didn't answer, but my clenched jaw spoke volumes for me.

He jerked his chin at the twins, who left without another word, leaving behind the bodyguards stationed strategically in the room.

Electric volts rippling through me surged higher when I rose to my feet.

And started across the room towards my target.

3

MADDELENA

The first rule for a Mancinelli woman was unbreakable.

Stay away from the Salvatore men. Or else!

It'd been drilled into my sisters and me from birth and enforced with many a backhand from Mancinelli men if we so much as *thought* about breaking that rule.

But the team was riding high from our third straight win. And winning, especially in Monza, the birthplace of Formula One racing, was like winning every single lottery in the world.

When that happened, there was only one place worth celebrating or you might as well stay home. La Miraggio.

Podium positioning wasn't something we'd needed to worry about in the past since we'd been nowhere near the podium, never mind winning a race. And while I'd been disappointed for the team in previous seasons, as the consigliere of my family's assets and CEO of Furia Racing, in charge of managing the hundreds of millions of dollars that flowed in from both legitimate and more... creative areas of the business, I couldn't very well stay in my hotel room tonight of all nights.

But Christ, how I'd wanted to.

Because I'd suspected that *he* would be here. And I was right.

I could feel the burn of his hatred from the VIP lounge where he sprawled amongst the velvet cushions with the indolence of a panther.

I raised my glass to swallow a mouthful of champagne someone had thrust in my hand. But just like most people reacted when Cesare Salvatore was in the same room, I knew I would choke on it. That my body would refuse the simplest commands.

Case in point – my maddening inability to look away.

So I saw the moment he rasped a command and his brothers and a handful of soldiers made their way to the entrance and left him alone.

With any other man I would've raised my expensively trimmed eyebrows at the sheer lunacy of leaving himself vulnerable in a roomful of vicious, cutthroat Mancinellis. To the last man, I knew each of them carried a blade, a gun or a knuckle-duster. Some all three.

But Cesare Salvatore demonstrated not a single ounce of vulnerability.

He met my stare, dominated it until I shivered with the urge to self-preserve, to lower my gaze. Then, only when he was satisfied that his deep intimidation had caused the fractures he sought did he rise, an exquisite marble statue coming to life.

With every step he drew closer, my breath knotted tighter in my lungs.

The heir to the Salvatore throne had turned heads since he grew height and muscles in the summer of his fifteenth birthday. Those muscles had been honed on the football field of the nauseatingly expensive Calmonte Catholic Academy in New York City. Then studiously maintained by taking an active part in physically suppressing any challenges to his birthright. It was an open secret that to tangle with Cesare Salvatore, his brothers or any of his soldiers on a dark street corner was to never see the light of day again.

His breathtakingly good looks were passed down from both his parents, borrowing the square, movie-star heartthrob jawline and piercing charcoal grey eyes of the Salvatore men, and the sensual mouth and haughty cheekbones from his late mother.

At six foot three, he towered over most men in any room, but with the dark silk shirt, darker jacket and pants and thunderous fury rolling across his face, he was a force-five tornado, hellbent on inflicting maximum damage to anyone who dared to cross his path.

It wasn't surprising therefore that even with my soldiers twitching to reach for their guns, and many members of my family tensing at the very visible threat, everyone still gave him a wide berth, allowing him clear passage to where I stood at the bar. No one had forgotten the humiliation of being trounced in our last two skirmishes. Least of all my grandfather.

It was why tonight's win was especially sweet. Why the celebrations were particularly wild. And why no one wanted it ruined.

'If you're here to toss about more threats and warnings, save your breath,' I pre-empted before he could speak, fighting the shock sheeting through me that Cesare planned on speaking to me. It'd been well over ten years since our last direct interaction, after all. 'Narciso told me you didn't take our win well. At all.'

The corner of his mouth ticked up, but it wasn't from amusement. He'd been practically combusting during the podium celebration. It hadn't helped that my little brother hadn't held back from rubbing his face in it.

Standing on the ground beneath the iconic Monza podium, I'd willed time to fly by before Cesare gave in to his worst impulses and pounded my baby brother into the floor.

I'd seen him do it to others many times in the past.

Including that night.

The memory was seared into my brain.

Growing up, I'd thought that as second-generation children of a mafia family brought up in America, they'd be less... aggressive.

Watching nineteen-year-old Cesare Salvatore pounding into a coma the boy who'd dared to brush up against my ass, then following that up with almost killing my best friend's brother for the simple crime of being our driver and protector that fateful night, had taught me different.

And it hadn't even been that he'd done it because he was interested in me. Oh no. He'd made his scathing feelings clear that night when he'd discovered his mistake. He may have battered the poor boy with his fists, but me he'd battered with his words.

From then I'd earned myself the dubious title of Most Hated Mancinelli.

I clenched my fist around my glass of untouched champagne as he stepped far too close, saturating me with the scent of smoked wood and wild thunderstorms.

That my first, unchecked instinct was to step closer, bury my face in his throat or his wide chest and just... breathe him in was appalling and bracingly disturbing. So I was eternally grateful when my knees obeyed my command to remained locked, my body as still as I could maintain it in the presence of a feral predator.

I wished I could say that was an exaggeration. The smouldering glare I'd sustained from across the room for hours now bore down on me with naked fury and dislike.

'Enjoying your win?'

'Any reason why I shouldn't?'

'Absolutely,' he breathed. 'It wasn't earned honestly, and you know it.'

Anger stiffened my spine. 'Any win that isn't achieved by Furia Racing must be manipulated somehow, is that what you're saying?' I tossed back.

He stared at me in silence, his gaze drilling deeper. I couldn't help myself. I slowed my own gaze to trail his face, over the fierce slashes of his dark eyebrows, past the silky fans of his eyelashes to the chiselled cheekbones and severe jawline, ending at the sensual dark red curve of his mouth.

That mouth had haunted and titivated thousands of my dreams. I hated and desired it in equal measure, a secret I intended to take to my grave.

'What?' I snapped when the silence stretched my nerves.

'I'm trying to work out if you've developed a good poker face or if you're really that clueless. There was a time when I recall you weren't so skilled at hiding your true feelings,' he mused.

'I was a teenager. And if my memory serves, you hadn't quite gotten a handle on that infamous Salvatore temper. Oh wait, what am I talking about? You still haven't, have you?' I was belly-dancing with ten-foot-high flames. Any minute now I was going to be devoured in an inferno.

He didn't fall for my taunt.

Cesare inhaled, slow and steady, his broad chest

expanding until it seemed to fill my vision. Control locked into place as smoothly as a gear shift on his powerful racing car. Pivoting slightly, he dropped an elbow onto the bar countertop, his body relaxing as he studied me like a specimen beneath his microscope.

'Believe me, sweetheart, when I truly lose control, you'll know about it.'

The silky-smooth warning of danger tunnelled through me, straight between my legs in a shockingly invasive caress I couldn't bat away.

My thighs clenched as I scrambled to drag my brain from images of a wild, out-of-control Cesare Salvatore. In my bed. Pinning me against a wall. Bending me over a table.

'Are you going to get to a point anytime soon? You're harshing my vibe. And in case you haven't forgotten, my kind isn't supposed to mix with yours. Somebody might just tattle to your precious *Nonno*. Then where will you be?'

Anger flashed across his face, but he throttled it almost immediately. 'Anywhere I fucking want. I'm a grown man. And leave my grandfather out of this.'

A flash of bleached-blond hair darted across my vision and I almost groaned when its owner cut through the crowd, making a beeline for me.

'Come to offer your congrats? Only I don't think I heard you give it over the sound of the *tifosi* roaring my name,' Narciso said with a full smirk and twinkling eyes, right before throwing his arm around my shoulders. 'Is he bothering you?' He didn't bother to keep his voice down. A few heads turned our way, tension rising.

Under normal circumstances, I would've welcomed my baby brother interrupting an unwanted conversation. But my heart lurched with fear for him beneath the livid gaze Cesare slanted him.

'Fuck off, *picciruddu*,' he growled. 'The grown-ups are talking.'

Ciso's face reddened. He was about to lose his shit. Unfortunately, the Salvatores weren't the only ones cursed with violent tempers. Another reason I needed to end this conversation asap.

Besides, while I was sure I could talk myself out of confrontation with my father and grandfather, especially if I exaggerated how sorely the Salvatores were taking their loss today, a prolonged conversation with the enemy wouldn't be as easy to explain away.

I held out my glass to Ciso. 'Get me another one, please? This one's gone warm.'

I was his big sister and if nothing else, respect

had been bred into us, so he didn't tell me to piss off to my face, but his eyes said so loud and clear. Snatching the glass from my hand, he stalked to the other end of the bar.

'You let him disrespect you like that?' Cesare snapped, narrowed eyes trailing Ciso.

I stepped in front of him, visibly blocking his ferocious gaze. 'You leave him the fuck alone, Cesare. I mean it.' As the oldest, I was a mama bear when it came to my siblings, especially since our mother had become a husk of herself for reasons shrouded in family secrets. As lethally dangerous as Cesare was, I wouldn't hesitate to take him on if he threatened my loved ones.

His head snapped back to me, nostrils flared and eyes darkened dramatically. 'I don't remember giving you permission to use my name,' he said, his voice low and infinitely lethal.

I hadn't used it since that night almost a decade and a half ago. Except in my helpless dreams when my traitorous hand snuck between my legs and I woke in a sweat, poised on the precipice of yet another thwarted climax. 'This isn't the Dark Ages. If you don't want to be addressed when we're speaking, feel free to stick to your side of the room.'

'You're playing a very dangerous game, sweetheart.'

A shiver sizzled through me. 'Now who's taking liberties?'

His mouth twitched again but his eyes remained lava hot, smouldering with their promise to devastate. 'You have the nerve to talk to me about taking liberties when you're playing dirty?'

A cool breeze washed over my neck. Sore loser or not, the look in his eyes was deadly serious. Cesare Salvatore hadn't spoken directly to me in years. That he'd crossed the room to do so tonight, in full view of his family and mine, with Vesuvius-hot feuds and bodyguards who even now watched us with hands hovering near their weapons, was gravely significant. 'I'll say it again. I have no idea what you're talking about.'

A muscle ticked in his jaw. 'You have until the next race in Azerbaijan. Hand over the mole and stand down whichever official you've got in your pocket tossing penalties my way and I may consider drawing a line under your little shitshow.' He stepped forward and leaned close. His breath washed over my ear and the most vigorous shiver yet juddered through me. This close, I know he didn't miss it. That he didn't really care about his effect on me. Yet my belly clenched in shame as he continued. 'Don't, and I'll make your life hell for the rest of the season. And *that* will be just the start.'

Shock replaced the lustful shiver as I watched him wander back to where he'd come from. He jerked his head at Rafaelle, the other terrifying Salvatore.

With the same height and build and only eleven months separating them, people often wondered if the brothers were fraternal twins. Granted, they were thick as thieves and often one was never far behind the other, Rafaelle tending to trail his brother in his rightful place as Cesare's second.

Together they turned heads, in fear and the kind of morbid fascination reserved for ruthless, beautiful predators. But somehow, my eyes always skidded past Rafaelle to his brother, my breath always catching at the first sight of the heir.

'What the fuck did he want?' Ciso grumbled, returning with my champagne. 'And why the hell did you send me away?'

I didn't want to hurt his pride by telling him Cesare would eat him for breakfast and barely remember the meal afterward, so I took the drink and took an unwanted sip to buy myself time to digest what Cesare had said.

A mole.

Bribing race officials?

What the fuck?

'Maddie?'

I pinned a smile on my face. 'We're having a great night. I didn't want him to ruin it.'

Scepticism narrowed his eyes. 'Then why tolerate him in the first place? I came over because it didn't seem like you were in a hurry to tell him to fuck off,' he said, suspicion joining the scepticism.

'Think about it. What do you think would've happened if I had?' I nodded to where a drunk Stefano swayed on his feet, surrounded by a few more Mancinelli lieutenants and a gaggle of the race bimbos who gravitated to power and fame like vultures to carrion.

The product of my grandfather's third wife, my uncle was only five years older than me and a complete hothead who gave shoot-now-ask-questions-later a whole new meaning. 'With them in that state, do you want to end the night with a body count and a trip to jail we'll need to explain to Nonno? And a possible summons to the race authorities?'

He frowned. 'Of course not, but—'

'Let it go, Ciso.' I firmed my voice.

His mutiny lingered.

Knowing there was a fifty-fifty chance he'd ignore me, I gulped down another mouthful of champagne and set the glass down. 'I'm heading back to the hotel. Don't stay too long, yeah?'

I felt his brooding gaze all the way to the door. The two bodyguards assigned to me peeled themselves from the shadows and fell into step beside me. I didn't acknowledge them, nor did they me.

I learned the lesson the hard way not to trust or confide in the men my grandfather chose to guard me after a horrifying showdown the night I came face to face with a Salvatore for the first time. Men who were supposed to guard me had turned on me on a dime to save their skins, leaving me to my grandfather's weeks-long wrath and a painful reminder of our family's number one rule.

Bitterness churned through me at the memory of that night and of the control exerted on me since then, especially when my *other* flaws rose to the surface like unwanted sludge.

I was a grown woman of thirty-one and yet I'd had sex only a handful of times in shadowy places with faceless men whose names I didn't recall. My father believed I was a virgin, taking pride in assuring my grandfather when the subject of 'organising a husband for me' came up. It would have been hysterically funny if it wasn't desperately sad and pathetic.

So I dragged my mind from it as the armoured SUV rolled to a stop and my bodyguards ushered me inside.

Our carefully vetted hotel was only a mile away. The well-oiled machine that was the Mancinelli mafia *famigghia* had booked the whole floor so there would be minimal cross-pollution with unapproved guests.

When we arrived, I barely took note of my surroundings or the usual gaping audience that I tended to attract with my burly bodyguards wherever I went.

Thankfully, this was Italy and in a luxury hotel people tended to think they were in the presence of some overblown celebrity instead of what I really was – the granddaughter of one of the most notorious members of Cosa Nostra to ever come out of Sicily in the last century.

I made it to my hotel suite with very little fanfare, ignoring all but the most important texts pinging on my phone from my sister, Sofiya.

A little rabbit told me tonight's celebrations were… interesting?

I groaned under my breath.

For a family that ran an organisation that thrived in the underbelly of society, we sure were shit at keeping secrets.

Or maybe the more accurate assessment was my sister's ability to pry secrets from stone. Her uncanny gift of telling truth from lies, bullshitter from traitor, had become an invaluable asset Bonafacio relied on more and more. Lately she'd been more absent than present at our home in Upstate New York. My enquiries as to why had earned me a sharp rebuke from my father and stone-faced silence from my own sister. Not gonna lie, it'd had hurt a little. Okay, a lot. It had raised my suspicion that either Sofiya really didn't want to be close to me as I dearly wanted, or that Bonafacio was succeeding in driving a wedge between us for his own purposes.

Is it worth asking where you are?

I hedged in answering her question, partly through worry, partly because I needed time to parse through my own thoughts.

Nowhere interesting

The reply was laughably predictable.

> Nothing interesting over here, too.

Yes, I was a little annoyed by her non-answer. Annoyed and worried.

> *Eye roll emoji* Answer my
> question, Mads.

Or I'll go digging myself.

While it'd taken me a long time to accept the inevitability of my surname and birthright, Sofiya had acclimatised to being the daughter and granddaughter of a gangster long before she'd hit puberty.

There'd been no need for me to protect her as I did my two other sisters because she'd toed the line from the moment it was shown to her with a cunning dexterity that left me speechless and a little terrified. Because Sofiya was *always* three steps ahead. Despite her being my little sister, I had no idea what her end goal was. She was the one most comfortable in Bonafacio's shadow and it'd made me wonder if it was the reason for the distance between us.

She doted on Narciso though and I was guessing that was where she'd gotten the info tonight.

Sore losers being sore. Nothing to
worry about. Promise.

I held my breath, hoping she'd drop it. She didn't answer for several minutes. Then another dreaded ping arrived. Grimacing, I read it.

Cool. Thinking I'll join you in
Azerbaijan. Thoughts?

She was testing me, feeling me out. Probably on Bonafacio's orders?

I'd known since I could walk and talk that my father, uncle and the smattering of cousins all jumped to my grandfather's bidding, but I'd believed I stood between my siblings and Bonafacio's absolute control of their lives.

Lately, with Sofiya's activities and secrets, I wasn't so sure I'd succeeded.

Telling her to stay away would have been as good as shouting from the rooftops that something was going on. Having her come would be asking for another set of eyes on a situation I wasn't sure was a problem yet. And if Sofiya thought Narciso was under threat from the Salvatores, who the hell knew how she would react?

I paced my hotel room, pressure building behind my eyes as I considered my response.

I had two weeks before the next race. I could go home, head her off at the pass. But... she was a resource I may well need by then, if I hadn't gotten to the bottom of things myself. With a sigh, I surrendered to the inevitable.

Sure, it'd be good to see you. x

I watched the speech bubble pulse for five seconds, then disappear.

Shaking my head, I tossed my phone on the bed, then finally allowed myself to replay my conversation with Cesare.

I was 99 per cent sure his trigger finger was itching for retribution after losing the race to us.

But he'd seemed dead certain of his allegation. And as much as I was unwilling to admit it, I came from a family who stopped at nothing to win.

It didn't even hurt that the men in my family would go over my head as the official Mancinelli family's consigliere to make a damning decision to bribe our way into a championship. The end result was the only thing that mattered, especially when pitted against the Salvatores.

I stepped beneath the shower, Cesare's threat ringing in my ears.

But then, in my vivid imagination, the tenor of his voice changed, his meaning taking on a different, more sensual timbre.

I'll make your life hell for the rest of the season. And that will be just the start.

My nipples pebbled under the cascading water, the promise of more forbidden interactions with the Underboss of the Salvatore Organisation sending ripples of danger-edged delight through me. Bracing one hand on the wall, I squeezed my eyes shut as the other hand slid down my belly to the hot, pulsating place between my legs.

I moaned when I breached my puffy lips, unsurprised to feel myself already wet and slippery. My shaky gasp blended into the hiss of water as I toyed with my over-sensitised clit.

The shape of his mouth, the sensation of his breath on my neck, the glorious headiness of his scent. The promise of fury and shattered control in his eyes.

And always... always... *that kiss.*

The one that had set us on a path to hell. A taste of the forbidden blended perfectly with danger.

All it took was remembering the feel of his Salvatore mouth on my Mancinelli lips, his outlawed tongue sweeping in to stroke mine, my middle finger sliding deep into my pussy, and I was unravelling.

My choked moans filled the shower as I came hard enough to feel my heartbeat pound in my ears. To accept that I was still, all these years later, hopelessly addicted to Cesare Salvatore. To the last man on earth I should be thinking about, never mind lusting after.

The enemy heir who could spark a war with a snap of his fingers.

4

MADDELENA

The Past

'Ciara, I'm really not sure about this,' I whispered as my best friend dragged me towards the barn-like building in the middle of nowhere.

Her fingers tightened around mine in response as if she was worried I'd bolt. She would have been right.

'What were you thinking?' What I really should've asked was what was *I* thinking? Because this idea, which had 'ill-conceived' stamped all over it to start with, was now bullet-ridden with 'worst idea ever'.

'Relax, Maddie,' she admonished. 'Besides, if we

didn't do this, you would be stuck in your bedroom, having the worst birthday ever.'

'But at least I'll still be alive. You know what will happen if my father or my grandfather catches us?'

'Yeah, my father will stand right alongside yours as they skin us both alive.' She said it with a flippancy that made my heart lurch. Because I wished I could say she was joking. There were strict parents, and then there was Matteo and Bonafacio Mancinelli.

Recently they'd been making threats about sending my sisters and me to some mountain convent in Sicily. I was convinced it was partly why I'd agreed to this escapade my best friend had talked me into.

As a newly minted seventeen, some could have said I was a late bloomer on the rebellion front. One of those was Ciara, who couldn't believe her luck when I'd agreed to her sneaking me out tonight for a surprise event. Emphasis on the surprise. Because if I had known *this* was what she'd planned, I probably would've chickened out.

My ill-advised heels sunk into mud and I groaned. 'At least you could've told me what I was wearing was wildly inappropriate,' I grumbled, slanting her a glare.

Her beautiful smile flashed in the dull lights strung around the field.

'That would've given away the surprise. Trust me, babe, your mind is going to be blown by what I have in store for you.'

The dark, ominous building loomed even larger and scarier as we got closer.

'Seriously, Ciara, where are we?' I asked, a little worried. All the dire warnings my father and uncles had drilled into me since before I was out of diapers crowded in my brain as I looked around. Visions of being kidnapped and thrown into some hell hole just to get back at my family reeled across my brain. 'And how long are we staying here?'

'Don't you trust me?' came the classic blackmail technique of all best friends.

I rolled my eyes. 'You know I do.'

Ciara's smile returned just as the door to the barn cracked open. 'Then get ready for the best night of your life.'

A mountain of a man appeared out of the darkness and glared at us for a half-minute before he jerked his head.

'Hand over your phones over there.' He pointed to a shadowy corner. 'You can pick them up on your way out.'

I felt a quick surge of helpless relief. Neither my father or the minders I'd successfully ditched could reach me if my phone was turned off, at least for the next hour or so.

I could toss off the shackles of my dubious birthright for a short time and actually enjoy my birthday, even if turning seventeen meant I was one year closer to the horrible and inevitable fate my father and grandfather had set out for me. Marrying me off at the first opportunity so I could be bred like a heifer.

Ciara's hand tightened around mine and she pushed me into the large gloomy space. It took several seconds for my eyes to adjust to the darkness. To realise what I was looking at.

Hundreds of bodies. Heaving back-and-forth, all wearing headphones.

We were at one of those silent-discos-in-the-dark, which was all the rage.

Despite my deep reservations, my excitement built as I turned to Ciara. She was Cheshire-cat grinning, satisfied that she'd blown my mind.

'Happy birthday, bestie.' She threw her arms around me. 'And don't worry, my brother is on alert to let us know if the old dogs discover we're not really having a sleepover at my house. He's waiting down the road to drive us back when we're ready.'

Relief whistled through me. 'Really?'

She nodded. 'Really. I told you, I've got your back. Now come on. Drinks first, then we get some serious moves on!'

She seemed familiar with the set-up, and I wondered how many times she'd been here. Although we were best friends, her home life wasn't anywhere near as strict as mine, despite her whole family working for mine.

Ciara's parents were childhood sweethearts who'd married for love. I was old enough to know that marriages were hard but that a little love went a long way. The acute absence of it in my own home put its presence in other homes in great relief.

Ciara's lucky mother had her father wrapped around her little finger, and my best friend had learned to manipulate that same advantage from the crib. The result of which was that she got away with murder on a nauseatingly regular basis.

It was only because her father was a trusted lieutenant that she hadn't been forbidden from hanging around with me. That could all change tonight if we got caught.

Worry threatened to resurge as she handed me a

cold glass with contents I couldn't see. Sniffing it, I smelled the alcohol. I should've protested but I was already breaking so many rules tonight. What was one more? I took a tentative sip. Sweet, but with a kick that made me choke.

Ciara laughed, slapped my back and handed me a pair of over-the-ear headphones. 'Come on, drink up. It's time to get our groove on.'

I sipped more of the drink, a little surprised to see it wasn't so bad and went down easier once I got used to the alcohol's burn.

I finished it, set the empty glass down and slid on the headphones.

It felt like it was written in the stars when the last strains of Rihanna's 'Disturbia' gave way to 'Paralyzer' by Finger Eleven. Two of my favourite songs back-to-back? Ciara's grin widened at my delighted screech.

Elbows locked, we rushed to the dancefloor.

An hour of this was almost worth being caught. But just for extra protection I sent a quick prayer to Saint Nick to protect this particular child from her grandfather's wrath before I threw myself into the moment.

Time and reality slithered away.

At some point, Ciara pushed fresh cocktails into my hand and I dutifully hydrated.

I was near euphoric and drenched in a fine sheen of sweat when a hard body slammed into me, knocking me off balance. Several more bodies joined the cascade effect, flashing terror through me at the thought of falling and being trampled beneath hundreds of dancing feet. My arms windmilled as I pitched forward. But before I could scream, hands snatched me upright then dragged me free of falling bodies.

The centre of the dancefloor was pitch-black, but I felt the power throbbing from my impressively tall saviour.

'Thanks,' I gasped before I remembered he – and I knew it was a he because I was plastered to his hard, chiselled body – couldn't hear me with our headphones in place. But whoever he was, he smelled incredible in that cross between woodsmoke and a dawn sea-breeze that some genius found a way of bottling to make millions while making women drool.

Besides, unless I was tangled up with a seriously butch chick with a stubble, then my rescuer, whose hands had begun their own expedition over my body, was rampantly male.

The thin material of the cocktail Lycra dress I'd let Ciara talk me into borrowing from her wardrobe heated up under his exploration, and it felt as if he was touching my bare skin when his hands slowly tracked up over my hips to settle on my waist.

He squeezed slowly, as if not wanting to scare me. Or maybe that was just the way he liked to seduce.

Whatever it was, my breath slowly strangled in my lungs, my body lifting itself up onto my tiptoes, just so I could strain closer to him. To breathe in that intoxicating smell I wanted to drown in. His breath hissed as his hands stopped just beneath my breasts.

I swallowed, self-awareness impinging on the moment. People had returned to their dancing, the brief toppling incident already over. I'd lost track of Ciara, and to be honest I wasn't sure I wanted my best friend to stop what was happening right now.

This felt illicit, decadent in ways I'd only dreamed about late at night, when I watched risqué movies on my portable DVD player.

My thoughts stalled when he commanded my attention once more. Unlike me, he had no qualms in dropping his head to my neck, breathing me in. I was wearing my favourite perfume and it thrilled me that he seemed to like it.

He muttered something I couldn't hear against my neck, and I shivered at the feel of his mouth brushing my skin. I hoped he was saying I smelled incredible.

I strained to see him in the dark, frustration biting at me when I couldn't. His hands dropped to my ass, and he pulled me closer into his body, snatching a gasp from me when I felt the thickness behind his fly.

I knew all about sex. I lived in a mansion within a compound full of men who loved to brag about their exploits. So while I was a virgin, I knew the ins and outs of sex probably more than I should have done.

He was thick and hard, and my thighs clenched in shocking response to his virility. His head dropped once more, and I swore I heard him growl right before he muttered something else.

I shook my head to indicate I had no clue what he was saying. Then I sensed his frustration just before he lifted my left headphone.

'Come outside with me.'

The sound of his voice shot a million volts of electricity through me.

Not because it was sexy, and trust me, it was the sexiest sound I'd heard in my life. Not because that rasped demand feathered his breath on my ear, a sensation that somehow tunnelled straight between my legs, setting off a dampness that shocked and thrilled me.

But because I recognised that voice.

I should've snatched myself out of his iron grip and fled right then. It wouldn't have been difficult to lose myself in the darkness amongst the sea of gyrating bodies. Especially when he took one hand off my hip on the way to capturing my hand.

But between one blink and the next, the window of opportunity had closed. At least that was what I told myself as I followed him, feeling a quiet awe as the crowd parted for him.

Once we broke through the writhing bodies, I realised three things.

First, my saviour and captor had no clue who *I* was.

Second, going outside with him would reveal my identity and put me in extreme danger.

And thirdly, and shockingly most importantly, I wanted to stay exactly where I was without him learning the truth. *Ever.*

The faint outline that I could see of his broad, quarterback shoulders and powerful neck made me groan under my breath. I didn't need to see his fallen

angel dark good looks or merciless eyes to remember how utterly hot he was. I saw it in the hallways of my private school and on the football field
several times a week.

His dry callused palm slid against mine and I
gasped at the friction.

Trepidation climbed up my spine, but it was
soon overtaken by the promise of excitement. *He
didn't know who I was.* And as long as I stayed inside
in the dark and kept my mouth shut, he would be
none the wiser.

I squeezed his hand. He stopped. His gaze bore
down on me, trying to decode my intentions. A moment later, my headphones were plucked off and
tossed aside.

'You don't want to go outside?' he asked.

I pressed my mouth tighter and shook my head.
Then squeezed his hand to confirm my silent wish.

He seemed to debate for a fraction of a second
before he was changing course, dragging me to the
left side of the warehouse, away from the door and
the bar where Ciara had gotten our drinks. Again,
the crowd seemed to part for him, but this time I
knew why.

He was the most feared and revered boy in
school, with a vicious temper he didn't bother throt-

tling on any given day. Unless you were part of his inner circle, everyone from the principal to the janitor gave him a wide berth.

So what the hell are you doing letting him lead you to goodness knows where?

Common sense, and a healthy dose of belated fear, made me squeeze his hand again. He paused and I sensed his gaze searching mine in the dark.

Then those strong hands were wrapping around my waist, lifting me off my feet.

A second later I was pinned against the wall, and my oblivious saviour, Cesare Salvatore, the firstborn son of my family's worst enemy, was kissing me.

Full, sensual, *forbidden* lips I'd tried my damnedest never to stare at when I was unlucky enough to encounter him in the hallways of Calmonte Catholic Academy seared over mine, pressing, sliding, then parting before his tongue swept in, urgently seeking mine.

My senses reeled so hard I saw constellations. My fingers curled into the expensive stretch of his leather jacket as my legs tightened around his waist. He rolled his hips into me, and I gasped.

Holy fuck. Holy fucking heavenly saints and celestial angels!

I should've hated every second of this. Should

have regained my senses and run as fast as my feet would carry me. This wasn't just dangerous behaviour. It was beyond insanity and definitely homicidal.

I'd been around long enough to hear my grandfather's bitter recounting of how Cesare's grandfather, Orazio Salvatore, had mercilessly slain the woman he loved simply because she'd spurned his attention in favour of another. That it so happened that the other man had been my grandfather, and thereby locking the former best friends into eternal enmity, would've been almost cliché if I didn't know the stark body count left in the wake of the decades-old Salvatore–Mancinelli war.

And here I was, clinging to the Salvatore heir, begging to become the next casualty. A whimper escaped me, a puny little sound that came nowhere near expressing the turbulent feelings cascading through me.

Reading it as perhaps a request of reprieve, his mouth freed mine, trailing kisses to my ear. 'Fuck, aren't you a sexy little thing.' Deft fingers brushed my nipples and he chuckled with triumph and satisfaction when I jolted with fresh arousal. His lips brushed mine, then returned for a lingering taste. 'I know every hot piece of ass within a fifty-mile radius. So where have you been hiding this glorious body, hmm?'

I didn't need to clench my teeth or squeeze my lips together to stop myself from speaking. My tongue was tied into knots from the expert way his hands and mouth were tuning my body. Another shockingly weak cry left my lips as he caught my nipples between his fingers and squeezed.

'Not going to tell me?' Dark, sexy laughter rumbled from him, stunning me.

Cesare Salvatore smouldered and snarled and answered wrongs with his powerful fists. All while wearing a devastating smirk with one of those expensive Mayan cigars he favoured hanging from one corner of his sexy mouth.

He *never* laughed. Not even when he was with his fellow jocks and the pretty chicks who followed him around like a rabid hive.

So it felt like a sacred and wild privilege to hear it. Smoky and mysterious with a hint of a breeze, just like the aftershave that clung to his skin.

'It's cool. I love a good mystery. But if you're going to tell me, better do it before I'm balls-deep in this tight pussy. I'd hate to offend a beautiful girl by calling her Hot Tits when I'm pounding her.' The hot, almost feral lick of my lips as he said that showered me with fresh shivers. His large hands closed over my breasts, and he groaned long and deep. 'And if you want to be a good girl and return the favour you can call me—'

'Salvatore? Holy shit! *Maddie?*'

My name was a horrified screech uttered by a poleaxed Ciara, who held up a glowstick she'd evidently conjured up from somewhere so she could locate me in the dark.

Every organ in my body threatened to shut down as my brain screamed *noooooo*. I half-toyed with the possibility that he wouldn't have recognised me if Ciara hadn't said my name right after his. That he would've simply snarled at her to fuck off as he so often did with girls he deemed beneath him. But everyone knew Ciara Paolini's one and only friend at Calmonte Catholic Academy was Maddelena Mancinelli.

Cesare's head swung sharply from Ciara back to me.

He jolted like he'd been shot. Then he turned into a column of steel.

I didn't even recall when I'd unwrapped my legs from around his waist, and I deeply resented the wall for holding me up when I wanted to sink through it and disappear to the bottom of the world.

The click of a lighter sounded far too close to my face a nanosecond before a flame danced into life three inches from my nose. My yelp of fright was ignored as the flame zoomed closer. For a terrifying second I was paralysed by the notion that he intended to set me on fire. To watch me burn just for shits and giggles. I pressed my spine into the wall but even that infuriated him.

His free hand slapped the space next to my head, his body now half-caging mine. I could've wriggled away but I knew in my bones I was better off not setting him off harder than he already was. That, like captured prey, I needed to remain still, if not play dead.

Three feet away, Ciara was equally immobilised, but not by fear, although there was plenty of it in her wide eyes and her gaping mouth. But it was another Salvatore brother holding her still as the firstborn held the lighter in front of my face, his piercing eyes searing unholy fire at me.

'What. The actual. Fuck?' The flame was dangerous enough, but his voice was an acid-drenched steel blade held against my skin. Burning and flaying.

His eyes scoured my face, dropping repeatedly to the mouth he'd just ravaged, the swollen mouth now throbbing in sync with my frantic heartbeat as disbelief built and built and built in his face. And alongside it, an emotion that terrified me even more. Pure, unadulterated loathing.

'I'm going to ask you once. Do not even think about lying to me. Understand?' The blade cut deeper. There were a thousand ways he could slay me with that voice alone.

I swallowed and nodded, aware that the burning lighter had caught the attention of the clubbers. That an audience was forming around us as people nudged each other and pointed.

'Did you know who I was?' Cesare breathed.

Every vital organ in my body dropped to the floor then slithered out of harm's way. My gaze darted to Ciara, whose eyes were now plate sized. She started to shake her head at me, urging me to deny, but Rafaelle dropped his head and whispered something into her ear. She swallowed audibly and froze in place.

'Hey!' A single snap of fingers close to the flame made it dance. Made me jump. 'Don't look at her. Look at me,' he ordered. 'Answer me.'

Fear and regret drummed through my veins. 'Yes.'

Cesare Salvatore didn't move. Didn't blink.

Didn't speak right away. But I felt the weight of generations-old condemnation slam into my shoulders, then drag me down until I was splayed in the filthy warehouse floor at his feet.

Then, from a great height, I heard him speak. 'You just sealed your fucking fate. One way or another, you'll pay for this.'

5

MADDELENA

Present Day

The knock when it came on my hotel room door almost two weeks later wasn't surprising. I'd been expecting some form of contact from Cesare since he dropped his ultimatum in Monza.

I was worn out from waving away questions about what I was doing talking to the Salvatore heir in the nightclub that night. Only years of practice had saved me from crumbling beneath my grandfather's third degree once Stefano had snitched on me at the first opportunity.

I didn't divulge that Cesare had accused us of sabotaging or that I was expected to hand over the culprit in a matter of days. Years of watching my family's hair-trigger response to even the most benign threats had taught me the men in my family were very much cut from the all-haste-no-brains cloth.

Telling my father and grandfather would be the same as brandishing a red rag in front of a bull. Bonafacio lived, breathed and salivated at the smallest chance of bringing down a Salvatore in whatever way, shape or form he could turn fantasy into reality.

Ordering a handful of our soldiers to take down one or two of theirs for the insult of accusing Mancinelli Racing of underhanded tactics – although he would proudly crow about it himself with zero shame were that the case – would be as easy as tossing back a shellful of his favourite Sicilian oysters.

Things had been relatively calm since we started winning races. The ticks were in our favour, and for now Bonafacio was happy just to rub his success in his enemies' faces, something he'd been doing in our private clubs back in New York City.

While I knew it wouldn't last for much longer, I was reluctant to upset the status quo. I'd needed to be meticulous in my investigating. Which regretfully meant that it'd been treacle-slow going.

Even as Nonno's consigliere, a role he'd handed reluctantly to me as a show of power and in direct response to Orazio Salvatore naming his only grand-daughter a chief strategist and accountant for the Salvatore empire, I was mostly a figurehead, given information on a need-to-know basis. If Bonafacio had deemed it prudent to win Formula One races through subterfuge, bribery and sabotage, I would be the last one to know.

On account of my flaws.

Digging would land me in serious waters if dis-covered, an act my grandfather would see as a be-trayal, even if I didn't intend to be stupid enough to reveal I was doing it on Cesare's ultimatum.

To be fair, I wasn't. Not entirely. Because contrary to my expectation, since the absurd decision was floated of starting Mancinelli Racing team to 'show those *pazzo* upstarts how it's really done', I'd grown to love the thrill of motor racing. And no, I would never admit, even under torture, that it had anything to do with Cesare Salvatore's open adoration of the sport.

Since that night at the silent disco – when I'd had to watch him batter not one but two boys – including Ciara's poor brother for bringing me to the disco, and managed to somehow not die myself at the hands of the Salvatore heir – and in the almost decade and a half since, I'd learned to suppress any desire to willingly look at, think of, or speak about anything to do with Cesare.

Sure, with Bonafacio's rabid obsession for his enemy's family, avoiding Cesare completely was near impossible. And once I'd started attending the races, seeing him in his race suit, his mile-wide shoulders, tapered torso and tight ass cutting across the paddock and pit-lane had been unavoidable.

But I'd kept any direct confrontation to near zero.

For his part, he'd looked right through me like I was thin air each time our paths crossed. And absolutely no one was informed about the shocking electric tug in my middle on the rare occasion his cold, charcoal-grey eyes slashed across my body.

I sucked in a breath now as I approached the door, furiously working out how to play this. For a second I was irritated that Sofiya, after almost threatening me with her arrival, had texted yesterday to say she wasn't coming after all. No explanation as to why. Sure, a part of me was relieved because, seriously, the less eyes on me right now, the better.

That the thought immediately conjured up charcoal-grey eyes set within a fallen angel face that felt almost X-rated was a secret I had no intention of revealing. Ditto for the slow sizzling rushing through my veins as I opened the door.

The person who stood there sent fresh trepidation up my spine.

Fist.

Cesare's personal killing machine with his soft voice and dead eyes.

'What do you want? And how did you gain access to my floor?' As with every hotel we stayed in during racing season, we'd booked out the whole floor of the luxurious Claremont Hotel in Baku and paid extra to have exclusive lift access to this floor made on a strict limited-to-family-and-trusted-personnel basis.

'The Boss wants to talk to you.'

I glanced past him, my heart jumping into my throat.

But Cesare wasn't behind him. Instead I was greeted with the sight of my men sprawled on the floor in the hallway. My eyes darted back to my visitor before debating how quickly I could sprint across the room to the gun I kept in my nightstand.

'I wouldn't do that if I were you. They're just taking a short nap,' Fist said, his low voice completely belying the streak of violence I knew lurked just beneath his gentle giant demeanour. He'd been Cesare's shadow long before the Salvatore heir had stepped into his rightful mantle. Being the head soldier for the Salvatores wasn't just a job for Fist. It was a lifelong calling he'd embraced dark heart and shrivelled soul. Just as his father had for Orazio. 'It's up to you whether you want to make their condition permanent,' he finished, eyes resting steadily on me.

'And me? Have you been ordered to make my condition permanent too if I resist?'

His headshake was neither belligerent nor offended. It was a calm response to my un-calm question. 'Not at all. Like I said, the Boss wants to talk.'

'Then why isn't he here himself?'

'He would prefer you come to him. I'm here to facilitate that.'

'I was about to have dinner.' I was stalling, delaying the inevitable as much as I could.

Eyes as dark as a wormhole flicked to the sterling silver room-service trolley, and he nodded. 'I can see that. And I apologise.' But he intended to do fuck all about it, his small shrug said.

'Can I at least get dressed?' I gestured at the belted bathrobe I'd changed into on arrival from the racetrack. Although I knew this meeting was hanging over me like a dark cloud, I'd half-hoped, foolishly, that it would dissipate over time under its own steam. That Cesare would conclude it wasn't worth threatening annihilation over some assumed conspiracy.

Apparently not.

Fist hesitated for a moment, then nodded. 'Sure.'

Deciding I wasn't a great threat, or he could easily handle whatever threat I posed, he stepped into the hallway without shutting the door, his back turned respectfully.

I didn't bother contemplating escape. For one thing, I was on the thirty-seventh floor. For another, Cesare would find me.

If not today, then tomorrow during first or second practice. Also, I was a consigliere, damn it. He might scare the shit out of me, but I wasn't about to visibly cower before him.

I'd buckled beneath his fury once upon a time.

Never again.

Sliding on my favourite dove-grey jumpsuit –

because it boosted my confidence, and my sister Jacinta called it my Boss Lady Suit – I re-tied my hair in a tight bun and slid my feet into three-inch heels. I hadn't taken off my make-up when I returned from the team meeting, so I snatched up my purse. Then stopped. My gaze went to the nightstand once more.

Bringing my gun was prudent. But... was it even worth it?

I'd be amazed if Cesare's people didn't pat me down and relieve me of it. And even if they didn't... was there a scenario where I saw myself shooting the Salvatore heir?

I bit my inner cheek, now wishing Sofiya was here. Among her many talents was sharp, accurate shooting. The memory of her coldly aiming her rifle and downing a buck in the woods near our Connecticut family home whistled across my brain before I shook my head free of it and turned my back on the bed.

The Mancinellis and Salvatores had clashed many times over the years over many issues, but I didn't really see Cesare killing me over a suspected mole within my racing team.

And if that thought was more in hope than expectation, I guessed I'd find out soon enough.

Stepping out and seeing how effectively Fist had

immobilised my soldiers, I grimaced. Heads were going to roll for this. But that was tomorrow's problem.

I was relieved when the elevator reached the ground floor and I saw Fist had left these soldiers alone, even though their eyes widened when they saw the giant striding one step behind me.

'Good evening, Doña, we going somewhere?' one soldier asked.

I curbed a grimace at the hollow honorary title. 'I am. You're not. I have some business to take care of. I'll be back in an hour,' I said briskly, not slowing my stride.

Roberto, the oldest and most senior of the secondary team, stepped closer with a frown. 'We really should come with—'

'I've given you an order, soldier.' I hardened my voice. 'Do I need to repeat myself?'

He slowed his roll, although mutiny lurked on his face. 'Uh, well, no, if you insist, Doña,' he said.

The knot in my middle eased a fraction but didn't dissipate altogether.

There would be a reckoning, or at the very least a few questions needing answering. Unless I managed to turn the debacle upstairs to my advantage.

Ignoring Fist's hulking presence behind me, I

paused and faced Roberto. 'You might want to check on your buddies upstairs. And I suggest you keep whatever you find there under wraps. You don't want to find yourselves suddenly unemployed, I don't think? Or for word to get back to my grandfather about your levels of incompetence?'

Now he froze, his mutiny morphing into mild anxiety as my words sank in. If any of them planned to tattle to my father or Bonafacio about my little late evening excursion, they would be equally in the shit for their abysmal performance tonight.

His gaze remained on me for a beat or two before he turned and barked orders at his men. They were rushing towards the elevators when I walked out the front entrance with Fist.

The drive ended three short streets away, at the equally stunning Soraya Baku Hotel. Not nearly enough time for me to reach deep inside for the yoga technique I used to steady my breathing.

Instead, I had to rely on years of hiding distress from the men in my family who loved to pick on the weak.

I was almost thankful Fist wasn't the conversational type, having seemingly lost interest in me as I hurried to keep up with his giant strides across the foyer to the private elevator that whisked us up to the Presidential Suite.

The actual suite was at the end of a long corridor with small anterooms dotted with a dozen soldiers.

A female soldier, built like a Mack truck, stepped forward as we approached, then conducted a very thorough search, including an X-ray of my heels. It would've been amusing if not for the imposing, gold-handled double doors standing ominously before me, behind which I knew Cesare waited.

The second I stepped back into my heels, Fist swept the doors open and stood to one side, giving me a clear view of Cesare Salvatore.

He prowled towards me, a breathtaking vision in navy.

He was wearing a dark navy shirt open at the throat, exposing a hint of his intricate tattoos, with his sleeves folded back to display deliciously brawny tattooed forearms, darker bespoke tailored pants that hinted at lean hips and powerful thighs. Polished Italian shoes.

His impact was immediate and catastrophic, and it took serious composure not to stumble back from the force of it.

'Any problems?' he asked Fist while he conducted a head-to-toe scrutiny of his own, his eyes lingering for a fraction longer on my breasts and hips.

The head soldier stared unblinking at his boss. 'Nah. Her security could use some serious upgrade, though. It's almost as if someone doesn't care that any schmuck can walk in and have access to her with minimum fuss.'

Fist ignored my glare as Cesare's eyes narrowed. After a moment, he nodded. 'Noted. Thanks.'

'Sure thing, Boss.' He left as silently and stealthily as he did everything.

Cesare's focus hardened on me. The power of his stare blazed like a dozen suns. 'Is that true?'

'What are we talking about, exactly?' I hedged.

The ink on his arms rippled beneath his expensive cotton shirt, impatience dripping off his body. 'Don't play dumb. Is someone slacking on your protection? Before you rush to answer that, remember I was able to cross the room to where you stood in the nightclub with very little opposition while your soldiers stood around with their thumbs up their asses.'

'That was to prevent senseless violence because even you aren't dense enough to start shooting in a nightclub full of civilians.'

His eyebrows rose. 'Be very careful who you call dense, *duci*,' he warned softly.

Duci. Sweetheart.

The endearment ping-ponged through me, seeking a soft place to land. A soft place I was *absolutely not* going to allow.

'Why have you summoned me here? I have nothing to say to you.'

He didn't respond right away. He strolled to the large drinks' cabinet set on the far side of the massive living room, poured himself a shot of MacCallan 21, then flicked me a glance. 'Drink?'

'No. Thanks.' My gaze flicked to the door once more, before giving up, not relishing a dozen guards dragging me back here to continue this meeting.

Instead I moved into the room, my gaze lingering on the large French doors that led to a terrace with stunning night-time views of Baku City. Then back inside, over the banquet-like dining table. And the silver trolley standing beside it with multiple covered dishes.

Cesare stoppered the bottle, then, crystal glass dangling from his fingertips, he strolled over to the wide sectional and sank into it. 'Take a seat.'

I shook my head. 'I'd rather stand. I'm not going to be here that long.'

He sipped his drink, and I tried to keep my eyes off the roll of his Adam's apple as he swallowed.

Tried. And failed.

'You seem to be under some misapprehension about what's happening here. Either you think I was kidding or you know I wasn't but are still not taking me seriously. Which is it?' he asked, his voice all silk and muzzled terror.

'If I said neither, what then?' I dared. Far too foolishly.

Despite his careless sprawl, he was barely bridled. A restlessness skulked just beneath the surface, ready to unleash vicious claws and shred me to pieces.

If I'd had to guess, I'd have said the last two weeks hadn't been easy for him. Perhaps he'd even suffered some consequences of losing to a Mancinelli. Like mine, Orazio Salvatore wasn't known for being the warm and fuzzy kind of grandpa.

It staggered me how two men who'd been best friends as teenagers loathed themselves so viciously now. How they'd infused that hatred so effectively in the blood of their offspring. All because of a dead woman no one had ever even met. I'd often wondered how she would've felt about this vendetta in her name had she lived. Whether she would be flattered, romanticise it even, like some movie star gangster's moll would, or be horrified by all the death in her name.

I knew firsthand how the whole family cowered beneath Bonafacio's legendary rages when things weren't going his way. How my two youngest sisters had often cried themselves to sleep from sheer terror when they were younger. The two fake molar implants I'd needed after taking a beating meant for my sister Jacinta were testament to his ferocious temper.

Cesare's nostrils flared now. 'You're not foolish enough to have not bothered looking into the situation.'

I wished I could look away from him. But then I would never turn my back on a leopard, so I was fully justified keeping my eyes where they were. Right? 'Fine. I investigated it. There's no mole.'

'Bullshit,' he replied smoothly, his low, deep voice reaching across the room to wrap around me. Hold me in its thrall.

'What makes you so sure, anyway?'

'Some chump whose name I never bothered to learn,' he said, then he allowed himself that half-twitch of a smile that had so fascinated me. Once upon a time. 'And the fact that you Mancinellis haven't had an original thought about anything.

Ever. So excuse me if I find it hard to believe you'll have the balls to be innovative enough to improve your piece of shit engine. Especially when I know every single engineer in your team isn't capable of the leaps you seem to be having.'

His use of the past tense for the snitch was deliberate. My stomach dutifully hollowed at the raw violence in his voice even as my hindbrain rejected what could possibly have happened to the guy.

'Even if what you say is true, what makes you think the sabotage is coming from us? It won't come as news to you that you're not the most beloved person or team in the paddock. Not everyone is a giggling fan of the great Cesare Salvatore.'

Every last trace of amusement vanished. He jerked forward so suddenly, I stumbled back a step, then cursed under my breath for the vulnerability when faint dizziness washed over me. I saw him clock the misstep. His eyes narrowed as his gaze swept over me.

'You're not foolish enough to have forgotten the warning I gave you all those years ago, are you?' he asked, again with that low, deadly voice.

I swallowed, clenching my fists when the wave of dizziness returned. *Shit, shit, shit.* I should've taken the time to eat a chocolate bar or a piece of fruit.

My gaze flicked to the door.

He saw, and his face clenched tighter. 'Give it up. You're not getting out of here without giving me answers, Maddelena.'

Very few people called me that. My mother, when her fear spilled over and she clutched her rosary tighter, her eyes imploring or seeking salvation that never came.

I will pray for you tonight, Maddelena.

You should come to church with me, Maddelena.

I warned you what happens when you challenge your grandfather like that, Maddelena. Look at you now.

Her voice didn't send my insides into freefall as Cesare Salvatore's did, though.

'You're not a very good liar, Maddelena,' he continued. 'And it looks like you've only gotten worse over the years.'

Shit. I bit the inside of my cheek. My only option was to remain silent.

'Tell me who you think it might be.'

I snorted. 'And watch you tear through my team like a shredder through paper? Fuck no.'

His head tilted a fraction, and the light above him bathed his glossy hair and five o'clock shadow in soft light, highlighting his raw, panty-melting hotness. 'What makes you think I won't do that anyway?'

I struggled to regain my focus. 'Because you want to keep racing. And like it or not, you're in a legitimate organisation with rules even you can't evade.'

The corner of his mouth lifted. 'You think I won't find a way to get what I want?'

The sense that the question entailed more than finding a mole was strong and visceral enough to douse me in shivers.

'I've already uncovered one more culprit,' he added.

Shock jolted me, propelling my feet closer to him before I even clocked I'd moved. 'You have?'

'Hmm.' He took another lazy sip of his drink. 'I had an interesting conversation with the official who gave me that ten-second penalty at the last race. Specifically about the quarter of a million euros that magically appeared in his wife's Swiss bank account the morning of the race. And the fact that he resigned the very next day citing non-existent health issues.'

It took every ounce of composure to keep my jaw from sagging. Was he lying? Because if he wasn't... if his allegations were true...

I started to shake my head, then stopped when a

wave of dizziness surged through me. Frantic, I reached for the back of the sofa closest to me.

Cesare charged across the room, his hands grasping my arms, preventing me from dropping in a shameful heap at his feet. Much like he had that first time. 'What's wrong with you?' he barked.

I barely managed to suppress a gasp as his touch seared me. As memory crashed like two meteors colliding.

Cesare Salvatore was touching me for the first time since that night in a field in Connecticut. Since he'd whispered filthy things in my ear, believing he was saying them to a stranger.

Since he'd recoiled in furious horror when he'd realised he'd just made out with his enemy's grand-daughter.

6

MADDELENA

He shook me once, his brows turning darker shades of black thunder. 'I asked you a question.'

'I'm hypoglycaemic.'

Displeasure flattened his mouth. Then he was wrapping his long fingers around my elbow.

Heat sizzled up my skin, the calluses on his fingers, which I knew were derived from his punishing sessions at the gym, snagging decadently on my skin.

'What are you doing?' I demanded, hating the slight wobble that had nothing to do with fear and everything to do with my hyperawareness of Cesare Salvatore.

'You were about to have dinner when Fist came to you.'

'Yeah, so?' My gaze strayed to the untouched tray set on the cart.

'I ordered you another meal,' he said.

I forced a huff, ignoring the curious softening in my belly at the gesture. 'Do you seriously think I'm going to accept food from you? Or anything else for that matter?'

A furious muscle rippled through his jaw. 'You need to fucking eat or you'll pass out and yet you refuse my offer?' A hard glint lit his eyes. Then he was marching me across the room. 'Let me put it another way. You have very little choice, sweetheart. We're not done talking. So you either risk passing out and leaving yourself at my mercy to do whatever the fuck I want to you, or you eat the food I ordered for you so we can get to the bottom of what I want to know.'

He released me once we were at the dining table, but not before I felt his fingers drag down my arm, almost... linger.

I shook my head, sure I was hallucinating the very brief, puzzling caress. Because when I looked at him, his arms were crossed, his face a mask of immovable granite.

'How do I know this isn't poisoned?' I challenged, not heeding the warning to bite my tongue.

'You're not important enough for me to go to the trouble,' he snapped.

Shit, that stung. But I'd stood up to powerful bullies, even when it was ill-advised. Even when it reduced my poor mother to tears and much intercession on my behalf in church.

'Then what am I doing here? Because the way I see it, I'm the only one you think you can push around and keep what you think is happening a secret. Because what? You think you have some sort of leverage over me?'

In one lithe stride he'd closed the distance between us.

He was tall. So imposing and towering I had to tilt my head up to meet his eyes. Then I was compounding my dire situation by breathing him in.

His scent had changed subtly from when he was a teenager. The base notes of woodsmoke still lingered, but on top of that, instead of sea breezes, he smelled like furious thunderstorms. The kind that lured you outside, impossible to resist, even though the possibility that you could be struck down by sizzling lightning was real.

'Not think, sweetheart. I *know*. I have eyes and ears everywhere. And I know for a fact you haven't said anything to anyone either, including your own family. So fuck yes, I have leverage. Which means you'll give me access to you whenever I want to discuss this.' He yanked out a seat without taking his steaming gaze off my face. 'Now sit down and eat. Because I sure as fuck won't catch you the next time you swoon like a goddamn Victorian virgin.'

I cycled through the dozen self-defence moves Sofiya had taught me, then discarded them all one by one.

Cesare Salvatore was twice my size, which in itself wasn't the problem because the bigger they were the harder they fell, right?

Except I'd seen him in action more times than I cared to remember. And every one of those times, my stupid brain had inputted the ruthless violence he'd meted out to some poor idiot as well as noting the hypnotic symmetry of movement. The way he could anticipate and block lines of attack as if he was some kind of sorcerer.

With my weakened state, he would probably laugh his head off if I tried to attack him. Not to mention, Fist was lurking outside.

Either way, I wouldn't get very far.

So I sat. Plucked the silver cloche off the nearest plate. And barely managed to bite back a groan.

The steak was cooked to perfection. Medium

rare with enough hints of pink to remind me I was a failed vegan. The fries were fat and golden. I was startled by the tiny silver container of sea salt sitting next to the plate, though.

Cesare Salvatore knew how I liked my fries?

Unbidden, my gaze slid to his.

He was watching me with the same predatory stillness that sent a few more waves of trepidation through me, mixed with the kind of absurd anticipation one felt at the beginning of a rollercoaster.

Then my belly grumbled loudly at being kept waiting. Face heating and to cover the sound, I picked up the pristine cutlery, sprinkled a pinch of salt over the fries, and dug into the steak.

At my first bite, he pulled out the adjacent seat and sat down. He picked up a bottle of red wine, and when I shook my head, he swapped it for mineral water, which he poured without asking.

'How long have you suffered with hypoglycaemia?' he asked after he'd set the glass down next to my plate.

I continued cutting into my steak – which lived up to its promise by tasting obscenely sublime – without looking up. 'Are we exchanging pleasantries now? After your man rendered my men unconscious instead of doing the civil thing and calling up to my room to ask for this meeting?'

'Would you have come willingly?' he countered.

I swallowed without answering because we both knew I wouldn't.

'Exactly,' he muttered. 'Answer me, Maddelena,' he breathed after another minute passed.

'Since I was fourteen,' I muttered.

His eyes narrowed. 'That why you were always hanging out with the vending machine at the school cafeteria?'

I forgot to ignore him and blinked in shock. 'You noticed?'

'I refer you to my previous statement.'

'Which one?' My dizziness from low blood sugar had receded. A different kind of dizziness – this one a complete byproduct of having him so close, so focused on me, took its place. 'You claiming to know everything about me – clearly wrong since you didn't know about the hypoglycemia till now or you having eyes and ears everywhere. Also false, by the way, or we wouldn't be here in the first place.'

He didn't answer. Merely jerked his head at my plate. A lock of hair fell down his forehead, adding to his scarily hot as hell package. It really wasn't fucking fair.

I carried on eating until my belly protested its fullness. Then I set down the cutlery. It was the best meal I'd had in a long time, but hell if I was going to disclose that.

'Any other symptoms besides the dizziness?'

'What are you, my doctor?'

His nostrils flared, then he drained his glass. 'I always wondered why El Topo made you his consigliere and not that idiot Stefano. Looks like you have some spine after all, *si*? That should make things... interesting.'

I wanted to snap at him not to call my grandfather that. Nonno had cut off body parts of upstarts who'd dared to use that disparaging nickname. But I didn't bother. Cesare would probably have been amused by that.

'Or not, seeing as I don't plan to be as accommodating next time as I was tonight,' I replied.

One eyebrow arched, raising his insane hotness several more notches. 'Wanna place a bet on that?' he asked.

'No. I don't gamble. I make accurate calculations that reap substantial benefits.'

I dabbed the corners of my mouth with the starched napkin and dropped it next to my plate. Now I had nothing to occupy my hands with or keep my gaze distracted, compulsion dragged my focus back to him.

'Then tell me, *in your calculations*, who in your opinion is the mole? Which one of your employees is stupid enough to have weaselled their way into my team to feed you information, Maddelena?'

I pushed the chair back and rose, telling myself walking across the room to snatch up the purse that had fallen during my dizzy spell wasn't putting vital distance between us.

Ping.

My heart stuttered. With very few friends – none who would contact me out of the blue especially knowing it was a race weekend – the only people who would try to reach me was my family. My fingers moved to the clutch's opening only to see Cesare plucking his own phone from his pocket.

Ping.

He read the screen and displeasure spasmed across his face.

'You should see to that,' I said, forcing my feet towards the door.

Still sitting, he pivoted towards me, his gaze slowly sweeping my body. 'You know if I don't get a name, I'll have no choice but to put you in my crosshairs, right?'

Why the hell did that low-voiced threat make my nipples hard? Light a fire so deep in my pelvis I had to clench my thighs and withhold a moan?

'Give it up, Salvatore. All that's happening here is you're being beaten at your own game. I know it's hard when you discover not everyone is an adoring fan, ready to drop to their knees for you and your overblown ego.'

Ping.

He ignored this one, rising to approach where I stood. 'Oh, you'll end up on your knees one way or the other, Maddelena. And since I'm a betting man, I'm willing to place a wager on you absolutely gagging for that when it happens.' He jerked his chin at the door. 'Fist will drive you back.'

Almost on cue, the door opened behind me, the giant soldier waiting with his long arms crossed in front of him.

He was dismissing me like I was a common little nobody. Much the same way he'd done back in high school for years. Until that night.

I watched his broad back and the ripple of muscles beneath his shirt as he scooped up his phone and activated it. Did he remember every detail of that night like I did? Or did he dwell only on the violent parts?

What the fuck did it matter?

I followed Fist back down the hallway and into the lift. Again, he ignored me, his long no-nonsense strides when we reached the lobby telling me he wanted this task to be over almost as much as I did.

My insides churned, fuelled by disgruntlement and anger and weird arousal.

Just to be contrary, and to claw back some power, *dammit*, I changed course and stopped at the front desk. The receptionist looked up with a bright smile that wavered a little when she saw me. Whether she recognised me, or if it was due to the unholy light probably burning in my eyes, I shrugged it off.

'I've just had a room service meal delivered to the Presidential Suite. Can you tell me what the charge is, please?' I asked, aware of Fist hovering three feet away.

She blinked, then frowned as she tapped the keyboard. 'Umm, including the red wine, a charge of six hundred and sixty-seven US dollars has been added to the room bill.'

There was nothing special about a billionaire mobster buying me a five-hundred-dollar steak. Both our families were obscenely rich, and I was used to the finer things in life. And yet, I couldn't stop my belly fluttering in secret, unwanted delight.

Cesare could've insulted me with a shoe-leather-textured twenty-dollar steak and a withered salad without breaking a sweat. He hadn't. Because...?

I shook my head and slid my black Amex Centurion across the counter. 'Charge it to my card, please.'

'Oh... but—'

'Can you do it right away, please. I'm in a hurry.'

With a puzzled nod, she hit a few more keys then put through the transaction. I slid my card back into my purse. 'Can I borrow a paper and pen?' When she handed the items over, I scribbled my note and folded the paper. 'Have this delivered to the suite's occupant, if you don't mind.'

She took it, placing it on a tiny tray. Her gaze darted to Fist and she swallowed before nodding. 'Of course, madam. Right away.'

I rode the wave of triumph all the way back to my hotel and long past changing and sliding into bed with a tiny smile on my face.

Then I felt it all crumble when less than an hour later, I heard a noise at the door. Sliding out of bed, I approached cautiously to find an envelope lying on the polished hardwood floor. Trepidation moving through me, I picked it up and opened it.

Something fluttered to the floor, but I was more

caught up with reading the words within the folded piece of paper.

The note I'd written, so neatly and concisely, mocked me.

I don't accept free meals from Salvatores. I pay for my own dinner.

Because beneath it, scrawled untidily yet bold and dominating, was Cesare's response.

Too bad. Your payment has been reversed. See receipt. And my advice? For your own sake, don't ever fucking try this again.

I snatched the receipt from the floor and bunched both scraps of paper in my fist, torn between feeling thwarted and excited at the thought of future interactions. Tossing it away, I stalked back to bed and yanked the cover up to my chin. Glaring at the ceiling, I vowed that the next time I clashed with Cesare Salvatore, I would come out on top.

And stay on top.

7

CESARE

I watched the streetlights of Baku grow sparser as we headed northwest out of the city.

'How far is this place?' I asked Rafa, who sat beside me in the armoured SUV driven by Fist. Behind us, three similar vehicles filled with our soldiers followed.

This meeting was the reason I'd cut my encounter with Maddelena short. That and the sense that I was wasting my time since she intended to stick to her bullshit narrative.

'We'll be there in about a half hour,' he replied.

I nodded, relieved I had a little time before I needed to slip into my underboss skin. While the blood of the Cosa Nostra ran through my veins, it was a fucking pain in the ass balancing two lifelong destinies on a full-time basis.

But since this was how I'd sold my shiny deal of walking two paths instead of one to my grandfather, I had no choice but to stay on that tightrope. One slip and Orazio would yank away his goodwill without a second thought. He was still spitting nails over my coming third two weeks ago.

I winced as I replayed our conversation when I'd finally answered his call after leaving La Miraggio.

'You're fifty-four points behind that little *pezzi*. At twenty-five points for first place, you know that means more than two full races where he doesn't place in the top ten for you to get back on top, *sì*?' he'd ranted, as if I couldn't count.

Orazio had a way of pointing out the obvious as a riling technique. As a way of emphasising your failures or stupidity. I knew that. We all knew it, and yet it was a sharp arrow that didn't fail to land a bull's eye every single time.

You know you totalled your mother's car with that stupid stunt, sì?

Yeah, Nonno, I was right fucking there, behind the wheel when the bumper 69'd the oak tree.

My fingers had curled around my phone as I

fought to remain calm. 'I know that, *Nonno*. I'm fixing it.'

'Oh yeah? How? By standing two steps down on the podium and glaring your way through our sacred national anthem?' He laughed then, a full-belly laugh as if he was being entertained at the Comedy Club. Then he'd sobered with chilling swiftness. 'This wasn't what you promised me, Cesare. *Winning* was what you promised. Yet here I am, like a piece of shit being dragged through the mud by your failure. Salvatores do not get dragged through the mud, *capisci*?'

'*Capisci*,' I'd echoed, bypassing the fact that I'd delivered on my promise for two years in a row and made us a shit load of money in the process.

His exhale was loud with a distinct rattle, the effects of years of sucking on cohibas and guzzling bourbon showing more frequently as he approached his eightieth birthday. 'You need me to make some calls? I know the Minister for Transport over there. He owes me several favours.'

Fuck no. The last thing I wanted was for Orazio to catch a whiff of any suspicious activity or gain a foothold into my dream. He would bulldoze his way into what was still a manageable situation and blow it out of proportion. 'No, I don't, *grazii*. I have things under control.'

He'd grunted. 'See that you do, *niputi*. Because I want that one-forty million.'

It didn't matter that he couldn't personally claim the prize money that came with winning the Formula One Constructors' Championship. That it was strictly for the development of next year's race car. Orazio acted like losing it would be tantamount to having it stolen from his personal bank account.

'...a man's word is his life's blood. You swore an oath.'

My jaw gritted at the third reminder. My promise may as well have been written in blood.

Two point five billion in five years in lucrative deals had seemed like an achievable goal when I'd presented my plan to my grandfather, knowing that the lure of it would sway him into allowing me to achieve my dream of becoming a race driver.

And it'd worked. Especially when I'd sworn heaven and earth to fulfil my underboss duties alongside this new venture. I hadn't told them that this was my ultimate aim – to pull the *famigghia* out of organised crime and into something fully legitimate. Yeah, that would've earned me several broken bones and another spell scrubbing toilets. Or worse.

'And I will deliver, *Nonno*. You have my word,' I'd said.

He'd read me the riot act for another five minutes, then ended the call. But not before summoning me back home after the next race. I'd already used the excuse of chasing Salvatore Organisation business in Sicily to not return home to New York after the Monza race, so I knew better than to even try it again.

I could delay my return by a day or two but no longer than that. And to make that inevitable confrontation a little more bearable, I needed answers.

Especially when my meeting with Maddelena hadn't yielded anything more than the inkling that she wasn't being entirely truthful.

Predictably, my mind sprinted back to when she'd walked through the door tonight.

Already detesting the sizzling impatience going off under my skin like irritating little fireworks, some part of me had hoped she would've lost some of her allure in two short weeks.

Fat fucking chance.

Sure, that jumpsuit had covered more than the cocktail dress revealed, but all the curves, hills and valleys had been in plain sight. Begging to be rediscovered and explored.

Even watching her eat a steak had turned me on. *Jesus*, I had it bad.

I'd needed a quick detour to the bathroom to rub one out before meeting Rafaelle. And I had a feeling I would need to do it again before the night was—

'At any other time I'd leave you to daydream about Hot Ti—' Rafa barely managed to stop himself from stepping on that landmine, but his unrepentant grin dared me to kick his ass for the misstep. 'I mean Maddelena.'

A growl built in my chest anyway. And fuck me if it wasn't absurd how territorial I was getting about the woman who I freely admitted now was embedded deep beneath my skin.

Cristu, how truly fucked was I if I couldn't stomach hearing her name from another man's lips, even if that man was my own brother.

'But I need you to get your head in the game. These Azerbaijani motherfuckers are twitchy as fuck. Dying in a worthy battle is one thing. Being taken out for the simple reason of being distracted will greatly shame me, *frate*. So much so I might not attend your funeral. So do me a solid, *si*?'

Spoken in jest but I knew he was deadly serious about every word.

I slapped his shoulder and nodded. 'My head's in the game.' Then I repeated it once more to myself.

The man we were going to meet was relatively medium fry in our operation. But a fifteen-million-dollar deal was still nothing to be sniffed at. It was a trickle that contributed to the steady stream that turned the wheels of the Salvatore empire, which was what Orazio had told me, with several swings of his fist, when I'd dared to question how much money was enough as a know-it-all twenty-year-old.

The lesson hadn't ended there.

I'd been sent to the sleaziest strip club we owned somewhere in the armpit of Jersey City. Made to work alongside the janitor three hours every night for a month, cleaning overflowing toilets and floors sticky with fluids I was too repulsed to investigate, then handing over the pittance I'd made to Orazio. He'd gleefully hand it over to his accountant to be added to the heaving Salvatore coffers. To this day I knew to the exact number what my contribution had added to my family's wealth.

Two hundred and seventy-nine dollars, six cents, after taxes.

For a month's work.

It was a lesson well-learnt that the accumulation of wealth was the number one goal of the Salvatores.

I'd been somewhat heartened to learn though that there were *some* lines Orazio wouldn't cross when it came to making money – the buying and selling of children. Most everything else was up for grabs.

I blocked Maddelena from my mind as we arrived at our destination in Sumqayit.

The isolated collection of warehouses bordered the banks of the Caspian Sea. Leather-clad soldiers dotted the front of each warehouse, their numbers growing as we rolled towards the largest warehouse in the middle of the surrounding structures.

Its doors were thrown open, a line of men spread out at six-feet intervals.

Fist parked and glanced around, then nodded for us to alight.

The man we were here to meet, a short, stocky guy wearing gaudy rings named Yalcin Kamirov, stood in the middle, watching us with beady eyes as his men patted mine down and relieved them of their sidearms.

Rafaelle bared his teeth at the man who approached him, letting loose his unhinged grin until the man hesitantly stepped back.

Then my brother made a show of unholstering his gun and handing it over. Everyone present suspected – and I knew – he had another one secreted somewhere on his body, but they didn't dare to push him further.

Kamirov had more at stake in this deal than we did, although I suspected he would attempt to strong-arm me as part of some old-school gangster shitshow he had to perform.

He started by waving imperiously at one of his minions once we were seated in a damp-smelling office inside the warehouse, him behind an obscenely large desk with his chair jacked all the way up so he was eye-level with me.

A tray of premium Russian vodka and three shot glasses were placed before him.

He poured then snapped his fingers. 'Come, let's drink to new partnership!'

I shook my head. 'Not for me, thanks.' Expecting the usual suspicion and paranoia that came naturally to people in our shady line of business, I preempted the encroaching bullshit with, 'I never drink during race week.' Clearly a lie since I'd indulged in my favourite cognac only an hour ago. But also because I loathed the taste of vodka, even the premium label he'd clearly shelled out for to impress me.

I much preferred top-level Scotch like Mac-Callan. Or the excellent *vinu russu* produced on the

Salvatore vineyard we owned in Northern Sicily. A place I hadn't visited in far too long.

Rafa drank his shot.

A layer of violence receded from the space and Yalcin nodded enthusiastically, distracted by a shiny new subject. 'Ah, yes!' He tossed back his shot, poured another, then pointed a fat finger at me. 'I watch your races. That is interesting business model, no? A racer and gangster? I wish I had your talent, but even if I did' – he laughed and slapped both ring-strewn hands over his heaving belly, then laughed harder as it jiggled beneath his offensively cheap polyester shirt – 'I cry if I have to give up my nene's *djiz biz*, yes?'

'That's probably wise,' Rafa agreed with a grin. 'You find your lane, you stick to it, I say. Saves slashed throats and broken bones.'

Confusion shortened Yalcin's raucous laughter as he tried to work out if Rafa had just insulted or threatened him. Behind him, his men twitched, equally confused.

Giving up after several seconds, Yalcin's eyes switched to me. Accurately read my need to get the fuck on with this.

'Əvət! So, I was thinking, in spirit of future relations, we renegotiate original price slightly, yes?'

The muscle above my left cheekbone twitched. 'No. We will not be doing that,' I replied. 'The original price stands.'

Yalcin exaggerated a grimace. 'You have not even heard my counteroffer.'

'Don't need to. We had an agreement. There will be no deviation from that. Fifteen million for three consignments of your favourite toys. Renegotiations are not part of the deal. Fresh negotiations, however, I'm always open to.' I pulled myself out of my lazy sprawl so there would be no mistaking my deadly intent. 'Fair warning though. If those future negotiations include you thinking you can leverage a certain competitor of mine in the hopes of cutting a better deal, I'd save you the trouble and tell you now, you will be cut off without further warning.'

Because our feud was a widely known thing, there were those who thought they could use it to pit us against the Mancinellis. Those idiots soon learned their lesson.

I rose from the chair as Rafa reached for another shot glass and tossed back a second helping of vodka. Setting it down with a click, he rose too.

'The Turks have been begging for us to cut you off and give them your order. They're willing to pay 25 per cent more than what you're paying.' I leaned over the table, bringing myself into Yalcin's space, trying not to gag at the fumes of vodka and stale sweat rolling off his body. All around the room, fingers edged closer to belts and holsters. I ignored them all, my eyes drilling into him. 'Maybe I'll jump on my plane and head over there after my race on Sunday. Maybe I'll stop next door, pay your Armenian neighbours a visit, tell them a spot has suddenly opened up on my customer list.'

Barely ten seconds passed before Yalcin waved his fat fingers. The tension eased a layer, but I wasn't done.

'The next time you think of threatening me with the Mancinellis, I'll have my brother deprive you of a few of those rings, with your fingers still attached to them. *Capisci*?'

Mutinous fury rolled over his face, and his mouth worked in preparation to mouth off some more.

The muffled pop to my right made Yalcin jump in his seat, his eyes widening in shock as his head swung towards the sound a split second before a scream ripped through the warehouse.

The runner closest to Rafaelle who'd made the error of breaching my brother's personal space clutched at his left knee, babbling in terrified Azerbaijani as blood spilled between his fingers. All around us, guns cocked in a symphony of impending violence.

'What is meaning of this?' Yalcin yelled.

I smiled. 'That was for wasting my time. Don't worry, Rafa didn't hit anything vital. Your man will walk with a small limp for the rest of his life but' – I shrugged – 'at least he'll live to tell stories about it, yeah?' I nodded to the tablet on his desk. 'Let's finish our business, shall we? I have a busy weekend.'

He scrambled to pick up the tablet and activate the screen. Ten seconds later, Rafaelle's phone pinged. He pulled it out and checked the screen before slotting it back into his pocket.

The Salvatore Organisation had just added fifteen mil to their coffers. That should make Orazio happy for, like, ten seconds.

I finally straightened. 'Next time, let's meet in New York. I'll introduce you to a juicy steak that will blow your mind.'

Lies. I had no intention of ever meeting Yalcin Karimov again. He'd overplayed his hand, revealed his weak underbelly and shown he was nothing more than a figurehead with a bloated ego to go with his bloated body. From now on he'd be dealing with a medium-ranking lieutenant while I went after bigger fish in Turkey.

We exited the warehouse and Sumqayit with zero fuss after our guns were returned.

'Call the Turks. Arrange a meeting.'

Rafa frowned. 'You were serious about going over there?'

I shook my head. 'No. Make it somewhere neutral. A month from now. After the US Grand Prix but before the race weekend in Mexico.'

'You want to hand Orazio a fat new deal on home soil in addition to a possible race win in Austin or to save being skinned alive in case we don't.' He nodded approvingly. 'I like it.'

But...

I heard the unspoken word loud and clear.

'What? Spit it out.'

'But... you know nothing's gonna save you when he finds out you're fucking around with Maddelena Mancinelli, right? I mean, nothing short of you telling him all these... secrets meetings you've been having are a prelude to you slitting her thr—'

My gun was in my hand and buried in his throat before he'd blinked. 'Finish that sentence. I fucking dare you,' I said with gritted teeth, hugely alarmed by the cold sheets of ice washing over me at the thought of Maddelena being harmed.

Dark caramel eyes he'd inherited from our mother regarded me with zero concern for his safety. 'You've just proven my point, *frate*,' he murmured.

From his position behind the wheel, I saw Fist's eyes flick to me, then return to the road.

With my free hand, I hit the privacy screen separating us.

Fist was as loyal as they came, but even I wasn't sure I wanted him to overhear what I had to say to my brother.

Rafaelle watched the screen until it reached the roof, then raised his eyebrow at me.

I flicked my gun's safety back on and returned it to the holster beneath my left arm, a little shaken. It wasn't the first time I'd threatened a family member with a gun. Hell, it was almost a rite of passage in my family. In Orazio's book, you weren't truly a man until you'd handed down your first pistol-whipping.

But it was the first time I'd been confronted with the unsettling possibility that my intent wasn't entirely hot air and bullshit. That the thought of anyone – myself included – harming Maddelena in any way tossed a red haze of unhinged fury over me.

'Talk to me,' Rafa pressed softly.

I realised my fingers were trembling slightly where they rested on my thighs, and I clenched them into fists.

'She's...' I ploughed my fingers through my hair, gripping a handful tight enough to make my scalp burn. 'I'm not sure what she makes me feel but... it's not... insubstantial.'

Rafa's eyes narrowed. 'You're saying you have a thing for her? Like some weak *West Side Story* bullshit you're going to let pass through you like a badly made cannoli or the more serious Godfather Three kind that'll earn you a bullet between the eyes and plunge us all into a shooting and poisoning spree?'

I laughed, a little alarmed that the fucking *Romeo and Juliet* analogy kept circling back to kick me in the balls. If Rafa could see it after just two meetings with Maddelena, how long before everyone dropped their own interpretation on things? How long before fresh vendettas were hatched by two bloodthirsty old men in the name of family honour?

Was I better off coming at this thing from a different angle?

The sucker punch to my gut gave me the answer I needed. And the answer to Rafa's question. 'Fucking hell if I know what the fuck I'm feeling, but it won't fucking go away.' *And I didn't feel inclined to let it.*

He raised his hands slowly, pre-empting an attack. 'At the risk of you going through with shooting me, why don't you just fuck her and get it the hell out of your system?' He shook his head in bewilderment. 'I mean, if you ask me, I'm hella shocked you've waited this long to go through with what you threatened her with in that warehouse. Maybe all this is... pent-up bullshit for her misleading you back then?' His gaze probed deeper. 'Is that why you didn't do anything back then? Because it was more than just a dick-dip-and-bounce thing?'

I shrugged. 'Maybe,' I hedged, but the itch beneath my breastbone and the heavy stone in my gut screamed *yes.*

That, like it or not, Maddelena had bewitched me that night and whatever strain of witchcraft she'd used on me had only intensified since. *Were* we falling into some macabre, modern-day Romeo and Juliet bullshit? Feeding off the danger because of the sheer homicidal lunacy even the thought of pursuing anything with her would birth? Was that why I hadn't gone through with making her pay, because I was a little terrified the feelings she evoked in me went beyond just retribution?

Or did I know I would need to find a fucking counter-spell to release myself from said lunacy but hadn't found the antidote yet?

I wasn't about to say any of this to Rafa of course because I wasn't some emo sorority chick high on ayahuasca bleating on about star-crossed lovers and witchy spells. And I couldn't promise I wouldn't shoot him this time if I said something stupid and he laughed.

But whatever it was, it'd started before she and her family threatened the dream I held sacred above all else. She'd dragged herself into the orbit I'd hedged on allowing her to occupy.

So... maybe Rafaelle was right. Not handing out retribution back then made me weak when I was nothing but.

Fuck her, get it out of my system.

And if it fails? Romeo and Juliet didn't exactly walk off into the fucking sunset, and you enjoy breathing, no?

I was a master at pivoting and improvising. I'd had to be as the son and grandson of the powerful Cosa Nostra.

My fingers drummed on my thighs as I stared out of the window. The lights of Baku City were coming back into view. Roadblocks were fully in place to cordon off parts of the city that would turn into the racetrack. I should be concentrating on FP1 tomorrow.

Not the way she looked. The way she smelled. Hell, even the dainty way she ate her steak was fucking hot. And fuck yes, those hot tits.

I didn't get a chance to see them, play with them and taste them all those years ago.

Porca troia, Rafa was right. She fucking owed me. My nails dug into my thighs as my cock thickened and jerked in eager agreement.

Hitting the button of the privacy panel, I felt Rafa's curious gaze as it descended once more.

'Fist, change of plan. Drop me off at Claremont Hotel.'

'Nah, ignore that order, Fist,' Rafa countermanded.

'What the fuck?' I growled.

'You got away with invading her territory once tonight. Fist laid out a few of her soldiers. You'd be walking through two loads of soldiers with wounded pride, with the possibility of one trigger-happy schmuck itching to put a few bullets in you before you can reach her.'

'I'd love to see them try,' I snarled.

'Oh, they're cum-brained enough to try at some point. But let's not make it easy for them, *si*? You concentrate on getting through first and second practice tomorrow and let me work out the logistics.'

Impatience clawed through me. Now that the seed of seducing myself free of her had taken hold in my brain, I wanted to get the show on the road. But my brother was right. While I'd been confident Fist could handle the task I'd set him, I knew we'd ruffled Mancinelli feathers. Between that and Rafaelle blowing the kneecap off Yalcin's minion, perhaps we'd tested the Almighty enough for one night.

I slammed my head against the headrest as Fist turned left towards our hotel instead of right towards Maddelena's.

Rafa slapped me on the shoulder. 'You've waited over ten years. What's another twenty-four hours?'

8

CESARE

'The latest upgrades seem to have made the improvements we need.'

'*Seem* to have?' I echoed, my voice projecting what I really thought of the bullshit assessment. The team meeting had barely started and my gut was already churning.

Brazzo, my chief engineer, curled into himself and darted a furtive glance at me.

He was an engineering nerd, plucked from the research bowels of a luxury sports car manufacturing company and onto the frontlines of a dynamic racing team. The man had zero charisma and was terrified of his own shadow. But he was highly intelligent, when he wasn't cowering beneath my gaze. Usually, I left Bibi to deal with him, but the stakes were too high to coddle the fragile sensibilities of my engineer.

I felt Bibi's glare. I glared back. *What?*

Cut it out, hers replied.

I sighed. 'Go on,' I encouraged Brazzo, despite sensing I wouldn't like what he said next.

Free Practice One had been a little above uneventful. Sure, the new parts we'd brought had made the car sing. But that song was just above mediocre at best. An overture when I wanted the aria.

'It tallies with what the wind tunnel predicted. We saw a total benefit of three-tenths of a second at four different corners of the circuit. The specifics are on the printout in front of you.'

Renzo picked up the sheet, eager to devour the raw data, while I ignored it. 'I drove the car for the better part of an hour this morning. I know exactly what it feels like. What I want to know is why didn't the upgrades bring us closer to the Mancinelli car?'

The other engineering crew fidgeted in their seats, none of them eager to leap up with an answer. But I knew.

'Let me guess. Because they brought the exact same upgrades we did and have seen greater gains?' My buzzing phone had appraised me of those facts long before the dedicated pit lane reporters had creamed themselves in announcing it to the world. 'So the goddamn janitors around this place know more about what our competitors are doing than you fucking lot?' I seethed.

Bibi sighed, her sharp gaze imploring me to cool it.

Fuck that.

If I was staring down the barrel of another shitty race weekend, I was most definitely going to spread the hurt around. I barely felt the sting from the hands I slammed down on the table.

I took a little selfish comfort in the flinches that rolled around the table, though. 'I'm done fucking around with this bullshit, so I'll lay it all out there. We have a mole feeding vital information to our competitor. From our work in the wind tunnels, to what upgrades we have in the pipeline, to our race strategy, to what everyone on this table is having for breakfast tomorrow.'

Shocked gasps rippled around the room. I watched everyone carefully, but dammit, either the culprit was very good or I was barking up the wrong tree in the wrong forest.

Bibiana's jaw dropped right before cold fury billowed from her eyes like an avalanche. Her expression promised endless retribution.

'If the mole is in this room right now, know that I've known what you've been up to for weeks now. My advice to you – turn yourself in. I might just let you—' Bibi loudly clearing her throat pulled me back from making a publicly incriminating threat.

Don't get caught.

I clenched my fists on the table. 'You might think you have a credible reason for taking this path. You do not. You're just making things worse by making me hunt you down. So the ball is in your fucking court.'

Stunned silence followed the ultimatum I hoped came as a bombshell to all but one or two people. I knew it would spread like wildfire through the crew in minutes, so I texted Rafaelle to watch out for suspicious behaviour. When I tossed my phone onto the table, Renzo was staring at me, his raised eyebrows lost in the sweeping hair slanting across his forehead.

I shrugged.

'Right, meeting's over. Let's start prepping for FP Two, everyone,' Bibi said through barely clenched teeth. 'You too, Renzo,' she said when he remained sitting while everyone hightailed it out the door to get out of firing squad range.

The moment he shut the door behind him, she rounded on me. 'What the fuck, Cesare! Why would you blurt that out there without speaking to me first?'

'It was a spur-of-the-moment thing,' I replied with zero regret. 'At the very least it should shake things up a bit.'

'Shake things up? You're going to have people out there walking on eggshells and afraid to do their jobs in case you point a finger at them.'

'Unless they're a bunch of pussies, and I don't think I managed to build a team from scratch and win two championships on the back of pussies, they have nothing to worry about unless they've done something wrong.'

She surged out of her seat and paced to the door before spinning back around, anger bristling through her tall frame. 'Jesus, even you're not naïve enough to think that just because you tell them there's nothing to be afraid of, they'll automatically stop shitting themselves? You strike the fear of God into them just by walking down the damn corridor.'

'Good. I should. I'd like to think they joined this

crew because they wanted to be part of something exciting,' I countered.

'And how fucking excited do you think they are about being called snitches?'

'At the risk of repeating myself, if they've done nothing wrong then they don't need to worry, *si*?'

She pinched the bridge of her nose and I felt almost sorry for her. Almost. She wasn't the one headed home to face Orazio's wrath, wondering which bone he would break this time in his rage.

'Rafa said you were making progress in locating the mole. How is that going?'

I raised my brows. 'How do you think?'

She shook her head. 'It still doesn't justify you scaring the bejesus out of them. Most of them are good, talented people.'

'A little fear goes a long way in reconsidering a bad idea. Tell me you didn't think twice about rebelling because you knew the old man would skin you alive if you were found out?' At her crossed arms and pursed lips, I continued. 'Tell me the only reason you haven't gotten around to telling him and Orazio to fuck off with the plans they're cooking up for you even as we speak isn't out of fear?'

She paled and, yeah, I hated myself a little bit for pulling that card.

As the only female offspring of my generation of Salvatores, she had it three times as hard. Her astonishing IQ had earned her a seat at the table but not a voice the older generation liked to hear. And since the not-so-small incident of a shot-to-death-multiple-times-under-mysterious-circumstances husband had left a huge question mark over her head, she was even more ignored than the wives and girlfriends.

Back in New York she was treated worse than a sidepiece. She was a near pariah. She'd found a place within my racing team and earned the respect sorely due to her.

'You dare to bring that up? Throw it in my face?' she muttered, her voice tight with the strain of unspoken trauma and deadly secrets.

I sighed and rounded the table, approaching her with caution.

Like me, she had the vicious Salvatore temper. Raising my hands, I tried to look conciliatory. 'Sorry, Bibi. That was below the belt.'

She didn't immediately throat-punch me when I reached touching distance, so I pushed my luck and pulled her into my arms. She remained stiff and unyielding for a full minute before her arms dropped.

Sliding them around my waist, she sniffed into my shoulder. 'What the fuck, Cesare,' she repeated.

I hugged her tighter. 'I know. I'm a fuckwit.'

She waited a beat. 'And?'

I sighed again. 'And I'm in a shitty mood because I've been summoned.'

She pulled back to look into my face, her eyes shadowed with past ghosts having risen to the surface with my unthinking comment. 'Orazio?'

I nodded. 'And since it looks like the top podium isn't going to happen this weekend either...' I left the rest unsaid.

She grimaced. 'He's going to tear you a shiny new one if we don't get him this championship.'

'Tell me something I don't know.'

'I think Brazzo is erring on the side of not wanting to overpromise and underdeliver. There's at least another tenth to be shaved off at Turns Five and Six, and Eleven and Twelve. I might get you close enough to secure third place in Quali tomorrow. And we might get lucky and those two idiots will take each other out at Turn One.'

My teeth clenched so tight my jaw cracked. 'How the hell are we discussing third place like it's the golden pinnacle of our achievements?'

She stepped back from my fury, frustration clear

in her own face. 'Until you find the mole or get to the bottom of whatever the hell is going on, we have to work with what we have. I'll strategise the hell out of the race plan tomorrow and give you as much advantage as I can.'

I gathered her close again and dropped a kiss on her forehead. '*Grazii*. I know you will.'

She held my gaze for another few beats before she nodded. Watching her walk stiffly away, I felt another pang of regret for dredging up memories she'd probably buried deep.

About to follow her out, I paused when my phone pinged.

My heartbeat stuttered for a split second before I remembered I hadn't given Maddelena my phone number so she wouldn't contact me this way. The only other person I wanted to hear from was Rafa, telling me that miraculously, my outburst had worked and he'd collared the traitor.

That hope was dashed too, because it wasn't a text alert.

I frowned, staring at the app I didn't recognise. What the fuck?

I was meticulous about what I downloaded onto my phone. As a rule I didn't keep incriminating shit on my device that could come back and bite me in the ass, especially since the feds had had a hard-on for the Salvatores since Orazio stepped foot on Ellis Island. With the passage of time, they'd only gotten more desperate to pin something on us to put the brakes on the obscene wealth we were amassing.

So far only a handful of careless soldiers had been caught in their snares. Because most of us knew better than to open sketchy-looking apps.

I squinted at the pulsing logo on my screen.

The picture was of an... owl? Black with shiny feathers and soft glowing yellow eyes. Wracking my brain, I came up short on what it meant.

About to delete it unopened, I stopped when Rafaelle walked in.

'You sure set the cat amongst the pigeons, eh, *frate*?' The king of deadly mayhem grinned as he crossed to the buffet spread out on the far wall and helped himself to a Sicilian ham stuffed bagel. 'I'm sorry I missed it.'

'I take it nothing's shaken out of the tree?'

'Not so far,' he replied, taking a huge bite.

I beckoned him. 'Get over here, take a look at this.'

I tilted my screen towards him when he reached me. He stared unblinking at the app. 'What the hell is that?'

'Fuck if I know. It just appeared on my phone two minutes ago.'

'You think someone's fucking with you?' His grin disappeared, replaced by deadly focus.

I stared at the app for a long moment. 'It'll be the height of ballsiness to send me something like this and assume I'll be stupid enough to just open it, no?'

He nodded after a brief hesitation, then set his plate down and tugged the phone from my hand. 'It's almost time for FP2. You need to get ready. I'll take a picture of the logo and run it past our tech guys. See if anything pops up.'

I headed for the door. 'If it doesn't, delete it. I don't want it on my phone any longer than it needs to be.'

'Sure thing.'

9

CESARE

FP2 was a shitshow, the only crumb of salvation coming from Bibi, who kept her word and optimised every advantage to help me reduce the time deficit to Narciso's car.

But half a second off his lead with Renzo three-quarters of a second behind was still too much.

I left the racetrack in an even filthier mood than I'd arrived in.

Rafaelle waiting in my hotel suite when I entered didn't improve things. I craved a shower, a rage-abating jerk-off session, and a juicy steak. Necessarily in that order.

But I pushed my wishes to the back of my mind when I read his face.

'What?'

'The tech guys came up empty.'

I bit back a curse and the urge to demand what the hell we were paying them for. They were pretty damn good. Most days. When they weren't strung out on molly and chasing college-grade pussy.

'So you deleted it?'

'Yeah,' Rafa said. 'But then fifteen minutes ago it popped back up.'

I froze. 'What?'

He held up the phone. Sure enough, the owl with the yellow eyes was back. I dragged my fingers through my hair. 'Swear to God, I'm this fucking close to shooting someone in the balls, just for shits and giggles.'

'You and me both,' Rafa quipped.

We both stared at the pulsing logo.

'Gimme that.' I snatched the phone from him, stared down at the screen for ten seconds. Then sucking in a breath, I stabbed it.

'Fuck! What did you do that—'

We froze as the owl blinked, grew in size, spread its wings and launched off an invisible perch. The 3D image filled the screen with black feathers, which subsequently exploded in a shower of green source code.

'Whoever is behind this has a flair for the dramatic,' Rafa observed dryly. 'And not in a fun way. Owls creep me the fuck out.'

I silently agreed. My slightly elevated heartbeat returned to normal when my phone didn't explode in my hand.

The source code drained away, leaving a smattering of letters behind, which then rearranged into a simple question.

WANT HELP FINDING YOUR MOLE?

Rafaelle tensed, his eyes darting to mine as a message box popped up at the bottom of the screen.

I typed:

Who is this?

The cursor blinked in and out for a full minute. Then the screen went blank. Another handful of seconds, my home screen was restored with no sign of the logo.

'I think you just pissed off your fairy god-hacker.'

I stared at the screen, caught between fury and hope that Rafaelle was wrong. That I hadn't just blown the first solid lead I'd been granted.

But... was I really desperate enough to trust some faceless keyboard warrior who'd popped up out of the blue?

I glanced at my brother. 'You think this is the result of what I threatened at the meeting? That someone has known all along and kept it to themselves?'

He shrugged. 'I don't know, man. But on the off chance you haven't pissed them off, are you going to chase this? What if they're just fucking with you?'

I exhaled, my mind racing. Just as the logo flared to life. I hit it without hesitation this time. The same question shimmered into being.

WANT HELP FINDING YOUR MOLE?

Teeth grinding, I typed:

Yes

The answer appeared immediately. My fingers tightened around the phone as I read it.

HOLY MAMA HOLDS THE KEY

Fuck.

Rafa frowned. 'Holy Mama?'

Mary Magdalene. 'Maddelena,' I breathed.

'*Figghiu ri buttana*,' Rafa muttered.

No. She wasn't that great a liar. Was she?

My fingers flew over the keyboard.

Bullshit. If you want to help, stop wasting my
time and tell me something I don't already
know.

Rafa's hand clamped over my wrist before I could
send it. 'I'll ask again. You sure about this?'

I paused. 'I already know she's involved
somehow but I don't think it's her doing the dirty
work. I think she's either covering for the real culprit
or deliberately choosing not to investigate. Either
way, all I'm doing is cutting through the noise to get
quick confirmation. If this is some *pezz'i miedda*
yanking my chain for funsies, I'd much rather know
soon so I can use the time to find them and impress
some manners into them.'

His lips flattened, then he released me. I hit the
send button. The screen dissolved again.

We waited. And waited. After ten minutes I
tossed the phone onto the coffee table. 'Fuck this
shit. I'm going to take a shower.'

Rafa didn't reply.

An ice bath had restored my weary muscles after second practice, but those things were more torture than refreshing. I let the hot water soak into my muscles and bones until the tips of my fingers started to prune.

The urge to masturbate had greatly diminished. Especially with my brother within hearing range. Once I'd towelled off, I pulled on a pair of joggers and a black T-shirt and strolled out of the bedroom.

Rafa was finishing a cognac.

'Anything?'

He shook his head. 'Nothing yet. Want me to stay?'

I checked the time and shook my head. We both needed a good night's sleep in preparation for Free Practice Three and Qualifying tomorrow, even though I doubted I'd get any decent sleep tonight. But there was no reason for us both to wait around. 'Nah. Leave it with me. I'll take care of it if they come back.'

He set his glass down and rose. 'Cool. Call if you need me, but only if it's strictly urgent. I have a Goth groupie in serious need of deliverance tied to my bed.'

I grimaced, but not without an ounce of jealousy.

'*Cristu*, keep that shit to yourself.' My hankering for racetrack groupies seemed to have taken a dive along with my race performance. But I had a strong suspicion the former had a lot to do with Maddelena Mancinelli.

His sociopathic grin back in full, irreverent force, he sauntered out.

Needing air, I strolled outside to the terrace. With a compulsion I couldn't fight, I turned east in the direction of her hotel. Even on foot I could be there in under ten minutes.

It was a little past dinner time. Would she have eaten or was she neglecting her meals again the way she had in high school?

When I'd seen her hovering near the vending machine back then, I hadn't really given it much thought. It had been irritating as hell to notice her in the first place when I would've given anything for a reprieve from the reminder of the bitter feud between our families.

I'd had an earful of it at home on the regular. I didn't need it dogging my steps in school, too. I'd signed up to play football and lacrosse – against my father's wishes because he deemed it a waste of valuable time – just so I could lengthen the time I was free of the burden of being Cosa Nostra. Pretend I was just another Sicilian-American football-and-pussy-loving teenager.

Maddelena's presence had been a constant reminder.

A burr under my skin long before that night in the warehouse.

And then the discomfort had morphed into a... yearning.

Hands braced on the terrace wall, I groaned low and long. Then I yanked my phone from my pocket. The absence of the owl logo chafed too, but I brushed it away and hit the number on my speed dial.

He answered on the first ring. 'Fist. Need you to take care of a thing for me.'

'Sure, Boss. Shoot.'

I relayed what I needed, then hung up, my mood fractionally better.

Whatever tomorrow held in store, it would end the way *I* wanted it to.

10

MADDELENA

The promise of my soft, luxurious bed so ridiculously early on a Saturday night should've been pathetic, but I didn't care. The bone-deep weariness weighing me down made me fairly confident – *please, God* – that I would pass out the second my head touched the pillow. If for any reason that didn't happen... well, I planned other ways to ensure a good night's sleep. I needed a little – okay, a *lot* of – reprieve.

With Narciso taking pole position and the team out celebrating, I wouldn't be disturbed tonight. *Please. God.*

Dropping the towel I'd used to dry myself into the hamper, I grabbed a fresh one to towel my newly shampooed hair dry as I padded naked from the bathroom.

'Hey, sis, what's occurring?'

I froze, then jumped with a screech and lashed out with the towel, adrenaline powering my heart rate into fight mode before recognition kicked in.

A soft chuckle came from the shadowed figure reclined in the armchair next to the balcony doors.

'What the hell, Sofiya?' Darting back into the bathroom, I snatched the robe from the hook, punched my arms through the sleeves and tied the belt with more force than necessary. Was I annoyed that my plan to sleep naked and possibly utilise the vibrator in my nightstand had been thwarted?

Maybe. Okay, *yes*.

Exhaling my irritation, I re-entered the bedroom.

She was sitting cross-legged in a yoga pose, dressed in dark grey leggings and a soft chunky grey sweater, elbows propped on her knees.

Sofiya usually wore her hair short, severe and slicked back. It struck me how long it'd been since I'd last seen her when I saw that her hair had grown enough to be knotted on top of her head and she had auburn highlights streaking the usual jet black. Besides a brush of mascara, she was make-up free, her natural beauty on full display.

She returned my scrutiny, her eyes tracking me across the room.

'When did you get in?' I picked up the hairbrush on my nightstand and ran it through my hair. I needed something to dissipate the adrenaline coursing through me. Something to distract me from the unsettling realisation that for a split second, I'd hoped my unwanted visitor was Cesare, not my sister.

'In time to check in and catch Ciso take pole position,' she answered.

My eyes darted to my phone. Quali ended three hours ago, and I'd been back in my hotel room for nearly an hour. 'You've been here over four hours and didn't bother to let me know?'

She had the grace to look away, but there was no sign of contrition when she looked back at me. 'It was a long flight. I wanted to relax a little.'

'You've seen Ciso though, of course.'

A flash of guilt lit across her face, but it disappeared far too quickly to make a meaningful impact. 'Yeah. He said you were busy with crew meetings so we hung out for a bit after he was done with his media duties.' Uneasy silence lingered for a moment before she tilted her head a fraction. 'So, another potential win on the cards. Must be pissing off the

Salvatores no end, huh?' Her eyes drilled into me as she asked the question, and I sensed there was more to her words. And to her visit.

I shrugged. 'I don't really concern myself with the Salvatores' feelings.'

Her gaze didn't relent. 'I heard a little rumour in the paddock tonight.'

I stiffened, then forced my shoulders to relax. 'Oh yeah?' I was sure I could talk my way out of my visit to Cesare's hotel suite last night. But I didn't relish it.

'Apparently the heir blew his top at his team meeting yesterday morning. Announced there was a mole and that heads would roll unless the traitor came forward?'

I'd heard the same rumour. Which was why I'd imagined he'd contact me again. And no, the sensation in my belly wasn't disappointment.

I set the hairbrush down and met her gaze. 'I heard that too. So?'

Her eyes narrowed. 'So.' She dragged the word out. 'Was that why the heir was hanging around you at the nightclub two weeks ago? Because if things are escalating—'

'Why are you really here, Sofiya?' The unsavoury secrets I sensed she was being forced to keep on behalf of Bonafacio and the family I could take. The distance it'd created between us even though we weren't close to start off with hurt, but I could deal with that too. What I wasn't going to stand for was her probing into my business. Especially when said business was dangerous and could earn me worse than a beating if I didn't tread carefully. I hated to even think it, but I wasn't entirely sure I could trust my own sister. And *that* hurt, too.

She spread her arms out in blatantly false nonchalance. 'What? I can't turn up and watch my brother kick some Salvatore ass on the racetrack? Bonafacio is beside himself with glee, by the way, so kudos to you all, I guess.'

'You guess?'

She rose lithely to her feet. I swallowed another wavelet of jealousy.

Sofiya was as slender as a prima ballerina but with exaggerated curves in all the right places. And at five eleven, she was also the tallest of the Mancinelli women. She'd been first in line when athletic talents were being handed out, winning netball and hockey championships, as well as high school track and field.

I wanted to think her athletic ability to go toe to toe with him was what made her and Narciso so close, but I knew it was because my sister just wasn't a girl's girl type of sister. Hell, she wasn't a people person, period. And that was before the burden of being Bonafacio's... whatever she was. Confidante?

'I also spoke to Stefano tonight.'

I grimaced. Our father's half-brother was a menace and a nuisance at the best of times. An oops byproduct of Bonafacio's tryst with a stripper that had ended up in a third, very acrimonious marriage, Stefano was born a pariah and had been desperately trying to fit in since he'd drawn his first breath.

At thirty-six, he was caught between generations. With my father and aunt treating him like the unwanted family pet, and Bonafacio not having any defined use for him, he'd been pawned off as part of Mancinelli Racing just to get him out of New York.

He'd been the first one to spring to mind when Cesare first raised his accusation. But with his short fuse and overblown sense of his own importance, openly confronting Stefano with a charge like that would be like tossing a lit match into a fuel tank, so I'd needed to be circumspect.

'I'm hoping we haven't been stupid enough to actually do something like this at all or without covering our tracks properly?'

'What did Stefano say?' I asked, evading the direct question. For now.

Sofiya turned from snagging a bottle of water from the fridge. 'He said, and to quote, "I would give my left nut to know who the mole is, so I can triple whatever he's getting."' She wrenched off the plastic cap and took a gulp. 'And you know how he gets when he's marinating in jealousy.'

Pursing my lips, I nodded. 'He's not the mole, if there is one,' I said.

'He's not. Besides, he doesn't have the brains or balls to orchestrate something like that. Not without a fuckload of help from someone more... astute.'

My gaze searched hers harder, even though I suspected I'd fail at reading her unless she wanted me to. 'Is that why you're here? Do you know something I don't, Sofiya? Or are you here to play amateur detective? Because if it is, I can do without another headache to manage.'

She took a longer sip. 'I told you, I'm here to support the team for the weekend. But... if anyone chooses to throw their weight around or something interesting kicks off, I'd hate to miss it.'

The shards of cold steel in her voice sent several shivers down my spine.

I pushed steel into *my* voice when I answered.

'I'm CEO of this team, Sofiya. You don't do anything without running it by me first, is that clear?'

Her eyes remained on the cap she was screwing back on the water bottle. And when she raised them, they were disarmingly neutral. 'Sure thing, sis.'

I told myself that had to be enough.

But the heavy ball of dread in my belly remained long after she'd left.

11

MADDELENA

Even before I surfaced from the restless sleep I'd fallen into an hour after Sofiya left my suite, I knew this visitor wasn't friendly.

'Your security are a bunch of dumbasses I ought to put right out of their pathetic miseries.'

For the second time in three hours, I screeched as the living daylights were scared right out of me. But this time I didn't freeze. I dove towards my night-stand to retrieve my gun... and found empty space.

'Looking for this?'

I pivoted towards the voice, my breathing choppy and loud in the silence as I surged onto my knees, primed for flight.

In the light coming from the French doors and

curtains I hadn't pulled completely because I didn't like sleeping in pitch darkness, I caught the dull glint of my Beretta resting on his knee.

'What the fuck are you doing here?' I croaked.

'I'll get to that in a minute. First, I should say I love the fact that you sleep in the nude,' he said, his voice deep and dangerously sensual.

Heat surged, rough and immediate, through my body. Then I gasped when I realised said body was partly on display, the covers having dropped off in my rush to grab the gun now in Cesare Salvatore's possession.

I double-fisted the duvet and yanked it back over my body. But it was too late. The sensation of his eyes on my skin coupled with the lurid dream of him he'd just so rudely interrupted, and the fact that he was here at all, in my hotel room, blended into a soup of lust heavily laced with peppery danger – which seemed to be just what my treacherous body craved – and turned my nipples hard, my pussy damp and slippery.

Casually, he set the gun down on the coffee table beside him and flicked on the floor lamp. Having Cesare bathed in light instead of lurking in the dark should've been a marginally good thing. I could see my enemy a lot clearer. Read his intentions better.

But all my stupid brain could compute was how indecently gorgeous he looked in another all-dark getup with a camel-coloured holster strapped over his shoulders. The butt of his gun peeking beneath his left torso and the glimpse of tattoos at his throat, chest and arms ratcheted up the danger levels, and my fists tightened on the covers.

He looked utterly delicious, and my fingers yearned to trace the ink and the rough texture of his five o'clock shadow, beg for it to graze my inner thighs on his way to eating me out and sending me to heaven. But then hell would inevitably follow, because while he might send me to heaven, discovery by my family would definitely send me to hell if I kept up with this insanity.

My breath shuddered out as I tried, and failed, to drag my gaze from his. 'What do you want?'

'I told you I'd get to the bottom of this.'

Fear overtook lust. I fought to regulate my breathing.

Cesare was right in his assessment last night. Lying didn't come easy to me and I almost wished my instincts weren't blaring with the strong warning that there was something shady going on in my team. That even the engineers were a little surprised with how well we were doing.

His gaze pierced mine from across the room. 'It's time to come clean, Maddelena. Last chance.'

I shook my head. 'My answer hasn't changed. I don't know what's going on.'

He sighed. I dragged my eyes off him, just to give my brain cells time to rejuvenate, and glanced at the door. I wasn't going to bother asking him how he'd gotten in here. No doubt Fist had wreaked havoc again on his behalf.

But I was definitely having serious words with my men.

Sofiya was one thing. Cesare getting through a second time was unacceptable.

'Yeah, you should really do something about that. Because I'm going to be supremely pissed off if it happens again a third time,' he said, accurately reading the direction of my thoughts.

My eyes widened. 'You want my people to take you out the next time you try to gain access to me?'

His lip twitch was chock full of conceit. 'I'd like someone to at least try. It took Fist less than three minutes to lay them all out. I didn't even need to get involved.' His head tilted. 'Maybe I should take care of that for you,' he mused.

'What? Hell no.'

After a moment, he shrugged. 'Sure, I'll leave it

for now. We've agreed you'll give me whatever access I need anyway.'

'I didn't agree to anything remotely close to—'

He held up his hand like a king ordering a subject. My teeth set hard. 'I'm not rehashing old ground with you.' His leg dropped and he leaned forward, elbows on knees.

The force of his aura pushed me back onto my knees, the heels digging into my ass reminding me that a two-inch quilt was the only thing between my naked body and Cesare.

'Your sister's turned up,' he said, almost conversationally.

My spine stiffened. 'So? She's here to support her family on what's going to be another one-two win for the team.' I crossed my fingers beneath the duvet, praying I hadn't just jinxed us.

'Is that so? It's a little curious that the only Mancinelli family member without a clearly defined role should turn up out of the blue at this race, especially when she hasn't been to a single race all year, don't you think?'

It would've been scary how much he knew about my family's affairs if I didn't know mine were equally rabid about knowing the ins and outs of Salvatore business. 'You should see a doctor about that overactive imagination of yours. And while you're at it, get some help for those obsessive tendencies too.'

His teeth gleamed in the dark, and even though I knew he wasn't amused, the transformation on his face snatched the air clean from my lungs.

Jesus, he was breathtakingly sexy.

'Bluff and bluster won't get you out of this, *bedda*. You know something is going on, even if you're genuinely blind to it. Are you?'

My skin tightened as the urge to deny it swept over me. But, dammit, I couldn't commit to the lie. And I knew the second he saw that.

He exhaled slow and steady. 'Good, now we're getting somewhere.'

Rising, he crossed the room to the drinks laid out on the cabinet. Examining it in detail, he plucked a bottle of Louis XIII Cognac from the selection and poured a finger.

'Drink?'

My glare drew another amused twitch of his mouth.

Drink in hand, he turned and leaned his hip against the cabinet, his gaze sweeping over me in blatant appraisal.

'Let's cut through the bullshit. Have you directly

or indirectly given the authority for someone to infiltrate my team?'

'Regardless of what you think, I have a top-class team of engineers and aerodynamicists who've built an exceptional car.'

'By copying almost frame by frame from mine,' he replied. 'But I get that most teams steal from the best. Imitation is the sincerest form of flattery, after all. But you didn't answer the question, Maddelena.'

I hoped the relative darkness covered my shiver when he said my name with that rough timbre. I scrambled to recall his question, then shook my head. 'No. For the hundredth time, I haven't given anyone approval to spy on your team.'

He stared at me for an eternity, then nodded. 'That doesn't take you out of my crosshairs, but I'm prepared to take a different tack when it comes to dealing with you.'

Outrage dimmed my arousal. 'Excuse me?'

'No, you're not excused. But we'll get to you in a moment. First things first. Make sure your sister stays out of my way.'

I frowned. 'Why would you want Sofiya to...?'

His eyes narrowed on my face, and I caught a hint of surprise before it disappeared. But with it, I sensed that I'd missed something. Something he thought I knew? Maybe about Sofiya's true role?

'Second. You come when I call. You ignore my call, even once, and I break my silence and let your family know you're helping me find the mole in your own team. I expect they're not going to be happy about that?'

'What next? You expect me to service you in bed, too?'

Dear God, Maddie, you did not just say that!

A feral glint lit his eyes, but he grinned and again I felt the blow to my solar plexus. 'No, baby, that's a bonus you earn for doing what I say.'

I huffed to hide the chagrin tumbling through me. 'You're delusional.'

'And yet your nipples are hard. I bet your pussy is wet too. Should we find out?'

I clutched the duvet tighter, knowing for damn sure he couldn't see his effect on me unless he had X-ray vision. 'Fuck off.'

'No, baby, I'd rather fuck you.'

My breath puttered to a stop.

My eyes locked on his and he... he wasn't joking.

I shook my head, but the image of me pinned beneath Cesare, that beautifully inked gladiator's body, and the thick cock whose imprint I still remembered all these years later, pounding into me wouldn't dissipate.

His wicked laughter writhed through me like live electricity. 'You're thinking about it, aren't you?'

He strolled over with measured strides, the glass dangling from his fingers. He stopped a foot from the edge of the bed, studied me with sizzling ferocity. 'Do you want me to fuck you, Maddelena? Finish what you started in that warehouse that night?' His voice was a husky rasp, shrouded in hot, dangerous promises.

I swallowed so hard, a cringe-worthy *glurrk* sound left my throat. 'No. Absolutely not.'

'Liar.'

My thighs trembled with the urge to remain in place in the middle of the bed. 'Finish whatever you have to say and leave. I have an early start tomorrow and a race to win.'

His gaze dropped to my death grip on the clump of sheets. 'So damn sure of yourself, aren't you?'

I started to shrug but the gesture froze when he slowly lifted his glass and took a sip. 'Do you always drink before a race?'

'Usually? Nah. But looks like you've driven me to drink too.'

A small bark of disbelieving laughter fell out before I could stop it. 'Yeah, right.'

'You don't think so?' I watched, helplessly and completely mesmerised, as he dipped two fingers into the amber liquid, my eyes widening when he reached out and swiped the alcohol over my lips.

Before I could stop myself, my tongue darted out and licked the liquor. It was no more than a drop or two and yet it flooded my system with warmth and insane intoxication, gathering a moan in my chest I barely managed to hold back.

'I'd like a token to seal our new deal, which for the sake of clarity I'll repeat. I call. You come. Or else,' he said, his eyes fixed firmly on my wet mouth.

'A token? Like... a handshake?' *Or a kiss?*

His gaze grew hot and borderline feral as it trailed over my face and shoulders to where my chest met the duvet. He took a step closer. Held out his hand.

Hesitant, because I didn't trust Cesare Salvatore further than I could throw him, which was not far at all, I held out my hand.

He captured it, wrapped his bigger one around it. Then the bastard jerked me up with a merciless yank that unbalanced me. I fell into him with zero finesse, partially dislodging the sheets covering my body once more.

Me knowing and him guessing I was naked beneath the quilt was one thing. Having it confirmed raced flames over my skin. 'Cesare! What the hell?'

He caught me easily as I scrambled to keep my dignity. But beneath the frantic tussle, I felt his stillness, the wave of hyperawareness that came with the insane attraction I felt around this man.

'That's the second time you've used my name,' he murmured, his delectable mouth far too close to mine.

My face and body heated up faster. 'I figure I'm due since you use mine with liberal abandon. Let me go!'

He ignored me and there was something baffling yet exhilarating about being pressed against his body and him showing absolutely zero interest in ogling me as most men would. Cesare seemed entirely content with reading my face while resisting my efforts to extricate myself with insulting ease.

That was, until he spoke. 'Do you always sleep in the nude, Maddelena?' His voice was thick, a touch slurred.

Only then did other things impinge on my senses.

He was hard. *Insanely so.*

Blood surged through my veins as his hips rocked against me, pushing the imprint of his arousal into my bare belly. Much as he'd done that night. His arm was still a cage of iron around my waist, but his fingertips moved ever so softly against my ribs, covering my skin in goosebumps.

'N-no,' I whispered before I wondered why the hell I was answering him.

'Why tonight?'

Because I was hot. And horny. And I needed easy access to pleasure myself while thinking of you in your delicious race suit. Or dressed in all black. Or naked. With a cigar hanging from the corner of your mouth and a sexy smirk on your face.

I pressed my lips together, refusing to answer.

His head canted lower, his mouth hovering tantalisingly close to mine. All I needed to do was reverse the push into pull and I could close the gap, turn memory into reality.

'I still think of the way you wrapped these beautiful legs around me that night, you know that?' he muttered.

Surprise, and growing lust, pounded through me, arrowing straight between my clenching thighs.

'Y-you do?' Why the hell did I sound like a damn sacrificial virgin?

'Hmm,' he growled. 'At the most inconvenient fucking times. Like while I'm navigating Eau Rouge, and every scrap of my concentration is needed, and yet I'm wondering if those legs that pinned me so sweetly... were the legs of a traitor.'

Like a blast of ice water in the face, his words shocked me out of my base emotions. But something else instantly captured my attention, freezing my flight.

The gilt-edged mirror hanging on the wall across the room. My head snapped to the left, my shocked wide eyes staring at the image we made.

His tall, dark frame against the white covers and my smaller pale body was so stark, so... entrancing, I couldn't look away.

Cesare turned too. The unabashed hunger blazing in his eyes, despite his harsh words, dragged a moan from me before I could stop it. While my top half was completely bared and pressed against his torso, the covers were half-draped over my lower half.

But the top curve of my ass, my tousled hair, his arm pinning me, my splayed hands on his chest par-tially hiding the globe of one breast, the arousal I couldn't hide blazing in my eyes... *Everything* was on display. And the more we watched one another, the thicker and deeper the river of lust grew.

'You can't look away, can you? You like how well we fit together, *bedda*?'

A strangled, incoherent sound left my throat.

The distinctive click jerked my focus downward, my eyes widening in horror when I saw his phone in his hand, aimed at the mirror. 'Oh God! Y-you took a picture of me?'

'Of us,' he amended.

I fought to scramble away from him, but the arm banding me tightened, keeping me plastered to his front. His still, *very aroused*, body.

'What for? To... to blackmail me?' I wasn't sure why a lance of hurt impaled my middle.

Just because the sight of my body made Cesare Salvatore hard didn't mean I had stopped being the enemy. Or that he owed me any leniency for the crime he believed I was in the process of committing against him. And yet...

'Now, there's an interesting thought.' The tip of his nose brushed my cheek but his mouth remained infuriatingly absent, making me crave it more on my skin. 'But for that to be anywhere near effective, I'd have to actually make the photo public. And I promise you, *bedda*, any man who sees you like this I will gut from throat to balls.'

I was drowning in the sheer feral insanity of that throatily worded threat of unspeakable violence when he took a long inhale of my neck. I sagged against him, my blood surging even faster through my veins as he finally placed his lips at the juncture between my neck and shoulder.

And he licked me.

Oh God. The feel of his tongue was incredible. I wanted to experience it... everywhere. My hands clutched a handful of shirt and felt the tensile strength of his pecs shifting beneath the cotton. Overcome with need I couldn't contain, I dug my nails into him, felt him tense for a moment, before he exhaled harshly.

His mouth, warm and firm, travelled from my neck to my jaw, then completed the tiny distance to my earlobe. He caught the delicate skin between his teeth, the bite sending fresh sparklers that immediately threatened to turn into fireworks.

'Still want me to leave?' he breathed in my ear.

This was madness. He'd come on a fishing expedition and all I was doing was baiting myself onto his hook. I ought to send him on his way. Tell him... 'N-no... Yes.'

Low, dark but strained laughter feathered the shell of my ear, and dear God, I *whimpered*.

'You don't sound sure about that, *bedda*. And look at you, your nails are digging into me so hard, I'd have to pry you off to leave.'

Eyes heavy with drugged desire slid to the mirror and I gasped again at the image reflected. The sheets had slipped, taking any semblance of decency away. Now my ass and thighs were on full display and all Cesare needed to do was look down to see my painfully budded breasts.

Which is exactly what he did in the next instant when he loosened his hold.

And pushed me back onto the bed.

12

CESARE

Fuck me.

Fuckmefuckmefuckme.

My blood rushed so fast south it left me light-headed and ridiculously grateful I was propped up against the side of her bed. Otherwise I would've folded like a soft pretzel at the sight of Maddelena Mancinelli splayed on the rumpled sheets like my every Christmas and birthday wish rolled into one.

Her shapely legs hadn't fallen open and she'd kept them tucked together – much to my regret – when I'd tumbled her backwards. But she wasn't rushing to cover up her tits in some overblown display of coyness.

So I could feast on those glorious blush-rose

peaks, caught in the vicious teeth of arousal heightened even more by the mix of innocence and siren.

She gnawed on her bottom lip as she watched me with those wide, sexy, alluring dark blue eyes.

'Do you have any idea how fucking gorgeous you are? How insane it drives me to want you like this?'

She made another of those infuriatingly sexy sounds, a cross between a whimper and a moan. Her supple thighs rubbed together and her nipples tightened, straining harder, and so damn gorgeous my mouth watered. Lowering a hand to my fly, I gripped my cock, grimacing, when I felt a spurt of pre-cum dampen my sensitive crown.

My irritation with the hacker's silence had driven me from bed an hour ago. Coupled with Narciso snatching another pole position, frustration had bubbled over and I'd been driven from my suite when my prowling had got on my own nerves. I'd left my hotel room with no particular destination in mind until I'd found myself in her hotel lobby.

I'd thought, fuck it, if I was suffering, she needed to suffer too. And possibly give me some answers, including why her sister, the one with the shadowy history, was in Baku City. There were whispered rumours about Sofiya Mancinelli that warranted we keep a sharper-than-normal eye on her.

And I'd handed that task over to Rafaelle.

I couldn't deny that my head had driven me here as much as my cock even though I hadn't thought our conversation would end this way. Although if I was being honest, the second I saw she was naked under the covers, a substantial part of my brain had leaked out of my ears.

I gripped my dick again and reached for my fraying control. 'Open your legs, *bedda mia*. Show me that pussy I've waited a fucking decade and a half to see,' I grunted like a heathen.

Her eyelashes fluttered, her eyes drifting down to half-mast. I realised she was staring at the hand I was stroking over my cock, those puffy lips still caught between her teeth.

She wanted me, but she was fighting her instinct, her reality.

I almost felt sorry for her because I was in the same position. For whatever reason, the cosmos had decided that Maddelena Mancinelli and I would be furnace-hot for each other without considering the potential consequences.

And fuck me, right in this moment, neither was I.

My breath strangled in my lungs as she slowly, excruciatingly, parted her beautiful legs.

My first sighting of her pussy made me want to

recite every gratitude Sunday school prayer I had learnt. She was beautiful. Her slit was wet and pink, the thin triangle of hair above it neatly trimmed. Saliva surged in my mouth with the need to taste. To devour.

She stopped when her knees were a half foot apart. I fought the feral urge to grip them and nudge them wider. To keep going until she was fully exposed to my hungry gaze. But I took it slow, dragging my fingertips from her ankles to her calves to circle the top of her knees and back again.

She squirmed in the bed, her eyes darting between my fingers, my face, and my cock.

On my next circuit, I trailed my fingers down the middle of her upper thighs to the curve of her hip. A soft moan popped out, and I had to clench my teeth to stop from falling on her and *taking, taking, taking*.

She was so fucking soft, her creamy skin like a warm lure of silk. I had the insane notion that I could stroke her skin forever.

Her belly dipped beneath my exploration and then quivered as I circled her belly button on my way up to the bottom curve of tits I'd touched once and spent fucking years dreaming about.

Her heart thrummed beneath my fingertips as I splayed them over her flesh.

'Your heart is racing, *bedda*,' I muttered. 'Out of fear or excitement, I wonder?'

Tiny sparks lit the eyes that flicked up at me. 'I'm not afraid of you,' she whispered huskily.

I smiled. 'No? Perhaps that's where we've all gone wrong?'

I closed my hand over the firm mound of her right breast, unable to stop the thick groan that left my throat at the sublime feel of her.

It was the perfect, glorious handful, but I knew if I gave in to the urge to taste them, there would be no walking away. So I toyed with her nipple, gloried in the arch of her back as she continued to squirm beneath me.

With my other hand, I pried her knees further apart, then when she gave another of those delicious sounds, I straightened, my brain rebelling against depriving myself of those beautiful tits.

Instead, I dropped my gaze between her thighs and groaned again. 'You're so fucking wet. Is this what you needed? Did you slide into bed naked so you could tend to this naughty little pussy?'

The blush creeping up her neck into her face, and the slide of her gaze away from me, told me the truth. I laughed. 'I'll put that on the list of things you will do for me while I watch, Maddelena,' I vowed.

'It's almost funny how you think I'll just fall in line with whatever you want?' she dared.

I dragged my eyes from the mouthwatering cunt to her flushed face. A part of me loved that she was mouthy. That she didn't know when to back down, even as her hips rolled in search of relief. It sure would make for some interesting clashes ahead.

'Fall in line or not, I'm going to eat this beautiful pussy now, and you're going to let me, aren't you, *bedda mia?*'

Her face contorted a little as she fought with herself and lost the battle, a moan overtaking her as I closed my hands over her delicate ankles, yanked her to the end of the bed, then trailed my fingers down her inner thighs and stopped short of my main goal.

'Beg for it, Maddelena.' My voice was a fucking mess, my cock screaming for relief. Relief I planned on denying it, much to my own dismay.

At her stubborn silence, I dropped to my knees, my hunger building so wild that I feared for my own sanity. I channelled all that into depositing kisses along the same path my fingers took, then taking a huge, gulping, sniff of the most beautiful pussy I'd ever seen.

'Fuck, you smell incredible. You'll taste even better, I bet.' I dropped a whisper of a kiss on her mound. She jerked then made a sound of frustration. 'But you don't get to come until you beg for it.'

'Cesare...'

'That's a start.'

Her eyes squeezed tight. 'Fuck you.'

'And here I thought we were making such wonderful progress.'

'Fuck. Please,' she whispered, almost inaudibly.

I could've insisted for more, made her scream the word until her throat hurt. But I was at breaking point, the need to throw the last dregs of common sense out the window and fuck her into that bed until we both passed out so damned insistent that I intended on rewarding myself twice as much for clinging to the plan firming at the back of my mind.

So I thumbed her neat little slit open, groaned at the tiniest hole I'd ever seen on a woman, and gave in to the feral urge.

Predictably, she tasted fucking heavenly.

Ambrosia mixed with the faintest tartness that reminded me of the limoncello I'd overindulged in one summer in Sicily. I'd paid the price for it, as I suspected I would pay the price for my obsession with Maddelena's beautiful cunt.

But now, as I did back then, I had no intention of

stopping, no intention of holding myself back from this sublime feast. The sound she made as my tongue flicked over her engorged clit was like the best aria from the greatest performer on earth. I ate her out like she was my last meal and when I managed to drag my gaze from her delicious core, the sight of her heaving breasts and her open-mouthed look of wonder nearly sent me over the edge.

I circled my tongue over her tight hole, groaning deep at how tight she was. When her gasping breaths grew erratic, I knew she was close. Moving my tongue higher, I slid my middle finger inside her.

A wave of despair washed over me because, *santo cielo*, she was tighter than a drum. Either naturally, or because she hadn't indulged in a while. The knowledge sent electricity zipping down my spine, tightening my balls with the need to fuck. I probed her to the knuckle then, at her needy cry, I curled my finger as I flicked my tongue faster over her clit. Wetness gushed over my finger as her hips chased her pleasure.

'Please,' she whispered a little louder.

'You want to come, baby?'

This time, there was no hesitation.

Her head bobbed as she buried her fingers in my hair, her hips rolling faster. When another wave of wetness crested my tongue, I lost it. With uncouth desperation, I stroked her as I ate her out, a totally disarmed part of me wondering if this was the first time – after having mastered the art of cunnilingus in many backseats as a teenager without once feeling this out of control – I would blow my load just from eating a woman's pussy.

My effort was rewarded five seconds later with the most beautiful shout before her legs closed around my ears, convulsions ripping her apart as she climaxed.

Ambrosia and tartness gushed into my mouth, and I happily devoured it, the obsession intensifying until I was lost beneath the certainty that this path I was taking would define me in ways I couldn't name.

But hell if I was going to step off it.

* * *

Maddelena

Holy mother of all holies.

The symphony of light and colour that had accompanied the best orgasm of my life trailed away, and I fought to pry open my eyes. When my weak efforts resisted, I allowed myself another half minute. Just to breathe.

To contain my wonder before I came across like the absolute ingenue I felt right now. But I couldn't help but be awed by what had happened.

No one had gone down on me like that.

And I had the strongest suspicion that the set of circumstances that had brought me here to this moment meant that no other experience could match it. I almost regretted that, but the tiniest sliver of common sense finally kicked in.

I opened my eyes and saw Cesare rising to his feet. His mouth glistened with my juices, and the bulge behind his fly was even thicker. My mouth watered.

Whether regret would come in the morning or I would accept this as the culmination of what had started in that warehouse, I refused to contemplate right now.

If this was to be a one-and-done thing – and I failed to see how it couldn't without all-out war breaking out between our families; hell, even *this* risked everything – then I planned on being fully present, on holding back the fallout for as long as possible.

So when Cesare leaned over me, fusing his

mouth with mine in a filthily melding of lips and tongue and the taste of my surrender, I moaned like a whore in church, raised my arms and wrapped them around his neck.

He lifted me like I weighed nothing, the punishing regime required to maintain the optimal physique of a Formula One race driver on full display. Without breaking the kiss, he resettled me against my pillows.

Then he stepped back, a pained expression on his face, and... pulled the covers over my body.

I blinked in confusion as he took several more steps back, even though his gaze remained pinned feverishly on me.

He was leaving?

The question must have shown on my face. One corner of his mouth lifted, but then a ping from his pocket distracted him.

He reached for his phone, and whatever he saw on there hardened his face. He turned away, then paused to look me over once more.

Vulgar hunger mingled with cold fury before he throttled it. 'To be continued, *duci belleza*. That you can count on.'

13

CESARE

'For someone facing imminent dismemberment, you're entirely too zen for my liking.'

I let my gaze linger wistfully for a moment on the private jet we were swapping for one of the three sleek matte black Sikorsky S-76 helicopters Orazio had commissioned last year after seeing it in *Succession*, his favourite TV show.

To my eternal regret, he'd adopted several unpalatable traits from that show.

Sighing as we lifted off from the private terminal in Teterboro Airport in New York, I turned to Rafaelle.

His eyes narrowed. 'Come to think of it, you've

been pretty chill considering you came second in the race yesterday. What gives?'

Silently, I handed over my phone. He scrolled quickly through the neon-green message thread and glanced sharply at me.

'Fuck. That's why you were texting with those questions last night?'

'Yeah.'

He read through the messages again. 'You think there's some teeth to this?'

I shrugged. 'No fucking idea. But I'm going to use it to buy myself some time for you, Bibi and me to dig into it, ideally before we turn up at the next race,' I said as I took my phone back and read through the messages.

For some reason, most likely the hacker fucking with me, they no longer disappeared immediately. Sometimes they stayed for half an hour. Sometimes two hours. This latest thread had remained on my screen all the way across the Atlantic.

It started last night just as I was rethinking the lunacy of leaving a blissed-out Maddelena to her dreams when I could have been balls-deep in her tight cunt. And in a way, the messages had set my big head straight as my little head had promised the worst case of blue balls in the history of mankind.

I'd stormed out with Fist guarding my back, my fingers flying over the screen.

For reasons still beyond me, my mysterious hacker had seemed in a mood to answer questions. Starting with one I'd asked before.

Who the fuck are you?

Nightowl.

A *duh* eye roll wasn't even worth the effort.

Why are you helping me and how do I know you're not feeding me bullshit?

That had pissed him off and he'd disappeared for half an hour, returning when I was back in my hotel room, mourning my disappeared wood and wondering if I could get it back in time to rub one out to the memory of Maddelena's incredible taste and scent.

His next message, when it came, smothered enough thoughts of sex to redirect my brain power north instead of south.

TRY SEARCHING THROUGH THE WILLOW

'The fuck?' I'd muttered, my feet frozen in the middle of the hotel room.

What the hell is this? I don't have time for a motherfucking easter egg hunt!

Tossing my phone on the bed after that because I'd suspected this 'Nightowl's' cat and mouse game would mean silence for another few hours, I'd been surprised when the ping had arrived as my phone was bouncing on the bed.

I'd snatched it up.

W.I.L.L.O.W.

Growling my frustration, I'd paced for ten minutes before throwing in the towel and texting the siblings group chat.

The name Willow mean anything to anyone?

The chorus of no's hadn't lifted my mood. Nor had the ribbing about karma and the consequences of forgetting the names of chicks I'd banged coming back to haunt me.

The temptation to tell Nightowl to shit or get off the pot had been strong, but I'd managed to control myself.

In a last-ditch attempt, I'd sent one last text to the trio of MIT students we supplied free molly and a cool ten grand a month retainer to be at our beck and call to dig info for us.

Their response just after midnight had been eye-opening to say the least. And kinda obvious when spelled out. *The fucking Russians.*

My first instinct had been to call in every favour owed and start fresh tabs if necessary to get to the bottom of this as soon as possible. But common sense and the need for caution had stayed my hand.

If the cause of my woes really had ties to who I believed to be Willow, then we were dealing with a whole new level of threat.

And if Maddelena was somehow tied up in it too...

The rush of alarm and tension coiling through my middle at that thought had dried my mouth. Considering she was a very bad liar and we both knew it and yet she persisted in stating her innocence, had she been forced to deny any wrongdoing out of fear or genuine ignorance? And which other Mancinelli knew, if at all?

The possible new players were cunning enough to have slipped a mole right under her nose.

The notion that I was searching for excuses for her didn't escape me. But curiously it didn't bewilder me as much as I thought it would. Which in itself was... nuts.

But in the hours before morning, what had puzzled the fuck out of me was the hope that she truly wasn't in with the fucking Russians. Because if she was... what Rafa had said in the car on the way back from the meeting with Yalcin about me needing to slit her beautiful throat?

Unfortunately, that was a possibility that had grown exponentially real. And potentially out of my hands.

Even if it was the last thing I wanted.

* * *

The Salvatore Estate in Fallbrook in the Lower Hudson Valley came into view from the left side of the chopper windows, and my breath hitched. Originally set in sixty-seven acres of prime real estate, Orazio had spent decades buying up the surrounding mansions and countryside until we now owned over five thousand two hundred acres.

At the last valuation, it'd been estimated to be worth over three billion dollars.

Just another reason the various government agencies were creaming themselves to find a reason to snatch it from under us. And the reason Orazio had made sure he had past, present and future generations of politicians and law enforcement officials firmly in his pocket.

It had everything from four swimming pools, a bowling alley, stables, shooting range and full golf course, to underground bunkers the size of three football fields – in case of the nuclear attack Orazio predicted was imminent – and a miniature cathedral where we were all required to attend mass on religious holidays and family occasions.

Beside me, Rafaelle tensed as we swooped over the mausoleum where several loved ones were eternally resting. Including Isabella Salvatore. Mama.

Security was stationed at seven different points around the compound, and soldiers and attack dogs patrolled with military precision, armed to the teeth with the latest in armament of the mostly illegal kind.

The air was brisk and fresh when we alighted and I chose not to vocalise that I would've preferred the fumes of New York City that still managed to rise up to my fifty-fifth luxury duplex in Lower Manhattan. Or any fuel-laced air pumped from hybrid engines in any pit lane in the world for that matter.

Bibi, the twins and a handful of soldiers landed two minutes after we did on an adjacent helipad.

Another of Orazio's paranoia-fuelled orders was that no more than two of his grandchildren were ever to travel in the same vehicle at any time in case of an assassination attempt. Since the twins refused to be separated and Bibi grumbled about travelling on her own, she'd called 'fuck it' and jumped on the jet and chopper with the twins. It was a toss-up as to whether Orazio would lose his shit over that, but I was hoping she didn't catch any heat since he would be directing his rage at me.

We all had a tough dinner to get through tonight and she'd been through enough.

I felt for her as I watched her wearily trudge the short distance from the helipad to her wing of the sprawling mansion.

The twins peeled off to the hunting lodge they'd unofficially commandeered on their twenty-fifth birthdays, even though for Orazio's sake they spent enough time in the main house to fool him into believing they still lived under his roof.

The moment we stepped into the grand foyer,

Rafaelle slapped me on the shoulder and headed down the right hallway. To the kitchen. His favourite place in the house.

Because it had been our mother's favourite place.

It was a ritual he never broke whenever we returned to Fallbrook, no matter what. I suspected Rafa would storm through fire or a category-five tornado, risk life and limb to rescue Matri's beloved pots and pans if it ever came to it.

I hoped it never did because I sure as fuck wouldn't let him.

No matter how badly her terrible death had shattered all of us, but especially him, life was worth infinitely more than a handful of crockery.

And yes, I got that there was a certain irony in my thinking when I willingly risked my own life every time I slid behind the wheel of a Furia Racing car.

His footsteps trailed off and I exhaled, letting the very rare silence wash over me. Lifting my head, I stared up at the rotunda and the fancy mosaic Orazio had had some Sicilian painter etch into the domed ceiling.

Somewhere up there, all our names were inscribed onto scrolls and saints' robes and arrows carried by fat little winged cherubs in a celebration of family, Catholic benevolence and love.

A ludicrous lie.

The Salvatores hadn't known peace since a woman named Valentina Baglioni had met her mysterious end in a dirty alley in Palermo on Valentine's Day some six decades ago.

Her name too was up there, notably closer to Orazio's than even my grandmother's.

I dragged my gaze from the ceiling as footsteps approached.

Fabiana, the housekeeper, and as close to a surrogate mother as I was allowed without Orazio deeming it mollycoddling, smiled. 'Cesare, welcome home.'

'*Grazii.*'

'Your *papa* and *Nonno* are on the golf course with Bagio and Pietro. They will be back in an hour. Dinner is at the usual time.'

I allowed her enveloping hug and a kiss on both cheeks before, predictably, her eyes moved past me, searching.

I smiled ruefully. 'He's in the kitchen. You should get in there before he rearranges everything.'

'*Diu miu.*' She shot off with a yelp and a swift sign of the cross, and I turned towards the stairs.

If I was lucky, I would be left alone for an hour.

Just about enough time to solidify my defence before the Sword of Damocles swinging over my head fell.

14

CESARE

Dinner at Fallbrook was a formal affair.

The men were required to wear bespoke three-piece suits, the women tasteful dresses from the selection of handpicked Italian designers who were in Orazio's good graces. Dozens scrambled to be on that list just for the exponential clout it afforded them. What the public didn't know was that being on that list cost them a nice slice of their annual revenue.

'Magnanimous' wasn't a word my grandfather was familiar with.

I arrived first and took my place opposite the space where my father would sit, to the left-hand side of the head of the table.

Rafaelle strolled into the dining room with Bibi on his arm, muttering something in her ear that made her roll her eyes. Her make-up was expertly applied but I could still see the faint bags under her eyes.

Hopefully the ball I intended to set rolling tonight would help us find our quarry quickly and she could get back to the usual challenges of evading Orazio and Papa's clever traps.

Whatever Rafa said as they neared the table made her giggle, triggering my smile.

Rafa pulled out her chair and she took her place two seats down from me, before he claimed the one next to me.

'I'm guessing the wives won't be in attendance,' Bibi said, eyeing the remaining place settings. She meant the wives of my uncle Bagio and Pietro, who were normally considered senior enough to eat with us.

'Doesn't look like it,' Rafa replied.

She sighed. 'Fuck, I'd hoped this would be a nice family dinner without the ritual grilling.'

Rafa grinned. 'Nah, sis. If you have any skin left after the old man is done with you, you can have the aunties whisk you to the country club spa in the morning for a "Prosecco and dermal rejuvenation".'

He said that last bit in the Barbie imitation of Pietro's wife.

Just as Pietro walked in.

Bibi tucked away the middle finger she'd been aiming at Rafa and dutifully greeted our uncle, offering her cheek for a kiss.

Then Pietro shot a searing glare at Rafa. 'Don't know what you're so cheerful about.' His gaze swung to me. 'You're about to experience your grandfather's full wrath.'

'Thanks for the warning, Ziu. But it's really not necessary. I'm inflammable and unflappable. Which is why I occupy this seat.'

The reminder of my superior rank stung, as I fully intended it to.

The first time I'd heard the phrase The Three Stooges in reference to Orazio Salvatore's sons had been in middle school. I'd patiently learned the meaning behind it, then waited for the pimply faced kid who'd dealt the insult to my father and uncles and rearranged his facial features in the art supply room.

Sadly, the connotations had proved correct, borne out by Orazio bypassing his own firstborn – and appeasing him with a token consigliere role he'd never utilised – to hand the underboss role to me, and never promoting Pietro and Bagio above the roles of mid-level capos. Even the twins were ranked higher than our uncles.

Pietro's attempt to stare me down started and ended within ten seconds, as did his disgruntled muttering when footsteps approached.

Renzo and Bagio entered first, followed by my father and the head of the family and the Salvatore Organisation.

As one, the men stood next to their chairs, arms clasped respectfully as Orazio Salvatore entered the room.

At just under six feet tall, he hadn't attained the height he'd passed down to his sons and grandsons, who all edged him by two or three inches. For a time, he'd secretly worn shoes with lifts, then inexplicably gave up the ruse.

But secret lift or not, Orazio possessed an electrifying presence. I'd seen grown men piss themselves without a single word spoken by my grandfather. And on a visit to the Old Country years ago, more than one elderly woman had hurriedly made the sign of the cross upon seeing him.

With his neatly combed grey hair, which retained an impressive amount of black, and expertly cut Tom Ford suit gracing his trim body, he looked younger than his years.

Until he moved. Then the telltale signs of age showed in his stiffer spine and laboured breathing.

Orazio loved to refer to himself as a spry seventy-something. But no matter how physically sub-par he might have been, his bark still packed a considerable punch.

As I discovered the second he rounded the dining table to his place at the head and turned livid grey eyes on me.

'When the fuck were you planning on telling me Mancinelli and his inbred spawn have been sticking their diseased peckers into our business?' he bellowed right in my face.

Bibi flinched but kept her gaze on her plate as the men retook their seats. Renzo's fingers drummed on the table, a condition that either meant he was jonesing for a smoke or he'd taken something to take the edge off. I cringed inside because right now I occupied Orazio's full attention, but it was only a matter of time before he caught that faraway look in Renzo's eyes. The look he'd baffled everyone with since his seventeenth birthday. The look he completely lost only when he was driving a race car.

Dante refused point-blank to talk about what the

fuck was up with his twin, and we'd all stopped ask-ing. As long as whatever secret he was keeping wasn't a danger to himself or the family, I would let him keep it. For now.

I focused on my grandfather as one of the staff hurried over with Orazio's favourite red wine and poured. I didn't bother to ask him how he knew. Not after bellowing about it at the team meeting on Saturday.

I waved away the offer of wine. 'I told you I was taking care of things. And I believe I have.'

'You *believe*?' he sneered. 'Did you not also *believe* you finishing in third would never happen again?'

Pointing out that I had finished second, not third, would earn me a backhand. I knew that as I knew the back of my own hand. So I cut through the bull-shit. '*Sì*, we have a mole. But if the information I've received is correct, the problem is bigger than that.'

He froze, his eyes narrowing. 'Explain.'

I sucked in a short breath. The repercussions if I was wrong would be monumental. It might cost me the deal I'd made with Orazio.

But my gut told me I was on the right path.

'I believe someone is attempting to destabilise us through the Mancinellis. I hope I'm wrong but if I'm not, we have bigger problems. We might be facing a scenario where Mancinelli didn't do this on his own. That he might be seeking help from the Russians.'

The grenade bounced across the length of the dining table, peppered with mutters of '*miedda*' and '*figghiu ri butana*'. Then it detonated with a slam of Orazio's fist on the table.

I felt a piercing gaze and darted mine right to meet Bibi's. Her wide eyes fired silent questions at me.

How long have you known? Why the fuck didn't you tell me? Fuck you, frate.

I responded with a brief look of apology before turning back to Orazio.

'How long have you known this?'

'My suspicions were raised last night. I received enough corroboration this morning.'

'Corroboration is not enough. You better be 100 per cent sure of yourself before you go throwing around accusations like that, boy. We took a big hit the last time we clashed with those *stronzos*.'

'I'm sure,' I said, offering up a silent prayer to all the listening saints, and a vow to hunt down Nightowl and deliver a slow, excruciating death if it turned out this wasn't the Russians and I'd been led on a dangerous wild goose chase.

'It makes sense,' Rafa said, propping me up.

'Their second driver came out of the blue with up-wards of a hundred mil to buy the seat. And sure, he's got some talent but nowhere near what the crop of Formula Two drivers have got to offer. Those fuckers are trying to haul themselves to the top by dragging us down and messing with us long enough to snatch the championship.'

'And I have people digging into it. I'll know if this is their entire game plan or if they're hoping it's an-other gateway after we kicked their asses last time,' I added.

We hadn't escaped completely unscathed. We'd lost good men and good, seasoned soldiers in our year-long clash with the Russians five years ago.

'But you're sure it's Liv Ivanovski and his crew behind this? Not some other outfit?'

The question came from my father, the first words he'd spoken to me since entering the dining room.

Unlike his brothers, he'd accepted my elevation above him with grace if not open pride. And it may have had something to do with the life-altering re-ality of my mother – his childhood sweetheart – being slaughtered, shattering any ambition he'd har-boured. The last true Salvatore battle Giacomo had participated in was our clash with the Russians, when mired in grief and hungry for revenge, he'd personally slaughtered several of our enemies.

After that, he'd just... caved in on himself.

I watched him with a mixture of sadness and empathy now as I nodded. 'As I said, it's being looked into, but yes, I'm as sure as I can be in this moment.'

It had been the tiniest of tenuous links. One casually tossed my way and halfway to being ruled out at the tail end of my conversation with the MIT hackers. They'd cross-referenced Willow with every crumb of information on the Mancinellis and their racing team including Stan Paul, the new driver they'd acquired at the start of this season. It'd tossed out a rambling list, at the end of which was the Russian word for willow. *Iva.*

It'd been like catching sight of a single flare of a match in the middle of a cyclone.

Your brain suggested it was a million other things, but your eyes insisted it was what it was. By the time my jet took off, the link had firmed.

Liv Ivanovski. *Iva.* Willow.

And he was either using the Mancinellis with their full cooperation or slithering his way into Salvatore business in the hopes of toppling us through our enemies.

Either way, I intended to crush him, once and for all.

'Just like El Topo, to lie with other vermin and believe that he will better me in any way.' Orazio lifted his glass and gulped a mouthful of wine. Then he pointed a finger at me. 'I want your plan of action laid out for me by noon tomorrow.'

I cleared my throat. 'With respect, *Nonno*, that's not how I'm going to handle it.' And I wasn't going to. Probably because he would cut off both my hands if I told him my plan of action fully involved Maddelena Mancinelli. And my cock.

Another ripple of shock travelled down the table. Even Rafa stiffened.

'*Scusi?*'

'As and when I confirm that Ivanovski's intentions reach beyond my... *our* racing team, I'll discuss our next steps with the *famigghia*. But if he's only coming after Furia, then I prefer to deal with him my way. That is what we agreed after all, was it not?' I asked evenly before he could release the thunder and lightning brewing in his eyes.

His mouth worked for endless seconds while everyone held their collective breath.

At the first sign of the turbulence dissipating, my belly slowly unclenched. But I braced for the furious finger in my face once more. 'The second you dis-cover otherwise, you report to me. *Capisci?*'

'Understood.'

'Thank fuck. Can we eat now? I'm starving,' Renzo grumbled, unfortunately redirecting the storm towards himself.

'And where the fuck is your shadow?' Orazio barked at Renzo. 'Did he not get the message that this was a family dinner?'

'More like a firing squad,' Renzo snarked under his breath.

Fresh thunder rolled across Orazio's face. 'What did you say?'

'Nothing, *Nonno*. I think he's taking us coming second and sixth a little hard. That Bellarussian fucker Paul drove me into the wall and Dante sprained something when he punched a wall. I think.'

'Oh yeah? What's he doing about it beside hiding in his room and crying like some pussy over a little sprain?'

Giacomo shifted in his seat. 'Don...'

'*Silencio!*'

I knew better than to show emotion for his treat-ment of my father. That would anger the old man more. So we all pretended not to notice our father cave in on himself a little at the berating.

'Probably rejoicing that he doesn't have to starve to death.'

I groaned inwardly as Orazio's gaze snapped back to me. 'He drove your brother into a wall and you still think we need to *wait and see*?' he snarled.

'Yes. I do,' I replied with a harder tone, and glared a warning at Renzo.

I withstood another long, searing stare from Orazio, every inch of my skin tensed in preparation to fight my corner. And just like last night, there was no explaining the undeniable notion that the foundation of my reasoning for taking this path involved Maddelena.

After a full minute, Orazio raised his fist. But it was to summon the staff hovering just outside the dining room doors.

Tempers settled. Delicious food was served. I made conversation. I ate.

But I was searingly aware of every second that passed brought me one second closer to the next time I was alone with Maddelena.

15

MADDELENA

From my quiet corner on the SkyPark observation deck of the Marina Bay Sands Hotel, I looked down at the Singapore racetrack. I wasn't sure how my security had managed to cordon off the quiet spot for me considering this was one of the most popular features of the hotel, and I didn't much care. The sultry temperature and cold cocktail with the sights and sounds of the vibrant city at my feet was the perfect way to end an imperfect day.

I should have been relieved that after two breaches of security they had finally got their act together. It didn't even matter that half of them had been swapped over, probably due to several demotions and a few fist-to-jaw reckonings in the two weeks since the last race.

It didn't matter because the next breach to occur would be from me. A mostly willing participant.

My phone buzzed with a new text message. They had been arriving all day long from Cesare, with hard questions about his mole, to which my every answer sounded highly suspect, dropped me deeper into a pit where my guilt seemed unquestionable.

My own clandestine probing had confirmed what Cesare knew and I had suspected. That somehow a different agenda had been carefully laid within the Mancinelli racing team. One I'd been deliberately shut out of.

Every question he'd asked that I hadn't been able to competently answer – because surprise surprise, my access to vital information had suddenly been blocked, or said information seemed to have vanished into thin air – shamed me.

The final straw had arrived halfway through the week, when I'd been preparing – silently relieved – to leave New York for Singapore.

All week my grandfather had swung from the high of his certainty that – despite there being seven more races to the end of the season – we would win this year's championship. Hell, he was already planning exactly how big the celebrations would be.

But what disturbed me most was the frequency with which he'd pursued his other new favourite subject. Dropping names of eligible men he'd loved to see as sons-in-law into our conversations.

After one such reference aimed squarely at me, Narciso had smirked, his gaze shifting from a departing Bonafacio to me. 'Careful, sis, I think Nonno Bona is planning a triple celebration with marrying you off as the cherry on top of the two crowns I'm going to win us this year.'

The grunt of pain that followed had diverted my attention to Sofiya to find her watching me with a carefully neutral expression.

'What was that for?' Ciso grumbled, rubbing his calf and glaring at Sofiya.

'I think it was for talking about your older sister as if she's a side of mutton in a butcher's shop,' I'd snapped.

He'd had the grace to flush with shame. 'I said cherry, not mutton,' he'd muttered. 'Cherries are nicer.'

But his words had burrowed deep, trailing white-hot vapours of fear behind it.

If Bonafacio was getting over his fear of losing

his precious moneywoman, then I was fucked. Because it meant he'd either found my replacement, or worse, a husband who he believed he could control just as ruthlessly as he controlled every member of his family. But unfortunately, spineless men who cowered before El Topo tended to take out their frustration on their wives behind closed doors. The thought of finding myself in that position was the very definition of hell.

'And you shouldn't count your chickens just yet, Ciso,' I'd added.

That warning, admittedly couched in a little spite, hadn't appeased me for long. And it had earned me a hooded glare from Sofiya for threatening her precious baby brother, closing the door on the idea of asking her if she knew the details of Bonafacio's plans.

By the time I'd decided to track her down to ask her anyway the next morning, she was gone. Narciso had shrugged his ignorance when I'd asked if he knew her whereabouts. My father had smirked and said, 'She's doing her part to safeguard the championship. You stick to doing your part to ensure the money is flowing in the right direction, *si*? And plan for every contingency. We can't afford any mishaps this close to the end.'

'What does that mean? What contingencies?'

He'd waved me away impatiently. 'Nothing, nothing. Your grandfather will let you know if anything is needed from you.'

And that had been that. I arrived in Singapore with a million more questions hanging over my head than I'd gone home to New York with.

The perpetual churning in my belly spun faster as another text arrived. But it wasn't a question this time.

Lose your security.

My heart jumped into my throat, but the sensation chasing it was neither fear nor concern. More like the feeling you got when you're hovering over the first plunge on a rollercoaster, knowing your breath was about to be snatched clean from your lungs and your stomach would be smooching your spine. And welcoming the thrill it would bring. But hell if I was going to make this easy or blindly follow his intentions for me.

Not happening.

I felt his seething irritation and dominance from how quickly the words popped up.

Lose them. Now. Temporarily.

Or this time Fist will disable them
PERMANENTLY.

Start with the old fucker who's
been leering at your tits for the last
ten minutes.

I swivelled on my barstool, my gaze darting to Roberto, and sure enough, despite his left eye still being swollen half-shut from the beating he'd taken for dropping the ball, his right one was firmly fixed on the cleavage exposed by my white bustier top.

At my glare, the tops of his ears reddened and he glanced away.

Rising, I leaned over the railing. Another text pinged.

Now, Maddelena.

I can't just tell them to leave.

Why the fuck not? They work for
you, not the other way around.

I rolled my eyes. Just like a typical dominant alpha male to be completely oblivious to the glaring differences in gender power dynamics.

> I'll let you think about that for a minute, shall I? Does your sister go where she pleases without security?

A half minute passed before he responded.

> Point taken. But the instruction still holds. Do I need to remind you of our agreement?

Yes, please. I clenched my thighs together at the memory of how he'd sealed his wishes.

As I swallowed, my gaze darted over the sparkling horizon, past the stunning Supertrees, the fifty-metre-tall vertical gardens in the Gardens By The Bay. I'd strolled through the Hanging Gardens to acclimatise and fight jetlag. And still I'd laid in bed, wild anticipation keeping me wide awake at the possibility of Cesare breaking into my hotel room once more.

He hadn't.

Now my secret yearning was crooking his finger,

and I was fighting it. Even though I knew deep down I was going to do as Cesare commanded.

If for nothing else, to find out what he knew.

And if anything else happens? Like his mouth ending up between your legs?

Gauging where my other guards were positioned, I sucked in a breath and pulled up the hotel's spa services. One advantage of staying in the most expensive suite in a luxury hotel was that its management bent over backwards to accommodate your every whim.

My call was answered on the first ring.

'This is Miss Mancinelli in the Presidential Suite.'

'Yes, of course. How may I assist you, ma'am?'

'I'd love your Asian massage. The full works. But not in my suite. Can I have a private session in the spa?'

'Of course. When would you like to attend, ma'am?' the eager voice asked.

'Within the next half hour, please.'

'Certainly. The staff will be on hand to welcome you whenever you're ready. Shall I send your personal butler down or—'

'No, I won't be needing him, thank you. I'll see

you shortly.' I hung up and ignored my trembling fingers as I texted.

> I have a three-and-a-half-hour window. Starting now.

He answered immediately.

> The Merlion Suite. Five minutes.

A deep trembling seized my whole body as I turned away from the breathtaking view and headed for the private lift that serviced my suite. Roberto and the other bodyguards fell in behind me, one hurrying to summon the lift. I stepped inside when it arrived but waved Roberto away when he went to hit the button for my suite.

'I'm going to the spa. You can come and check it out and make sure it's secure, but I don't want you hanging around, scaring the customers.'

He frowned. 'We will blend in, Donã, no problem.' His tone suggested anyone who had a problem would be dealt with.

I raised a sceptical eyebrow. 'You think so? With that shiner? I like this hotel. I'd like to come back and stay next year.' I hardened my voice. 'You'll check it out and wait for me back in my suite. I'll let you know when to come and get me if you're that worried.'

They exchanged wary looks I ignored. I was putting them in a precarious position, but I reasoned this temporary discomfort by taking them out of the equation was better than the alternative of risking Fist dealing with them.

The trio of smiling staff waiting for me with a tray of refreshments didn't blink an eyelash when they saw the burly soldiers with me. And they kept smiling all the way through Roberto and one other guard peering into corners and cupboards and satisfying themselves there was no threat lurking behind the tall ferns and oriental screens.

I waited, clutching my glass of iced mineral water, for a full three minutes after they left, then crossed to the desk.

'I'm sorry, but there's been a change of plan. I have to step out for a little bit. Apologies for the inconvenience. I'll pay for this treatment anyway and have my butler reschedule?' I signed the receipt and tossed in a hefty tip that produced wider smiles and a flurry of bows that trailed me to the empty executive lift.

The ride to the designated floor rushed by far

too quickly with each floor sending a louder roar in my ears and sweat to my palms, until I feared I was going to pass out from the surge of adrenaline-fuelled excitement.

The doors swung open.

An impatient Cesare reached in with both hands, wrapped them around my waist and yanked me out. My head spun as he hoisted me high like I weighed nothing and marched down the wide corridor. I was thankful for the dizziness for blurring the faces of the soldiers scattered round the suite.

'Legs, waist. Now,' he rasped in my ear.

I'd suspected our text exchange had riled him some, but looking into Cesare's exceptionally hot face, I saw something else. Feral, uncontrolled hunger. That had nothing to do with the snitch he still hadn't caught – as far as I knew – and everything to do with me.

The thrill intensified as he stopped in his tracks. 'Everyone. Get the fuck out!'

The snarl was barely decipherable. But the men and women understood. From the corner of my eye, I saw a massive shadow – Fist – step forward.

'Boss, maybe you should—'

'Now!'

Feet scurried away as we entered the suite

proper. And between one breath and the next, the door was kicked shut and my back met a textured wall.

Charcoal-grey eyes framed by lush dark lashes women paid good money for seared me. 'I believe I gave you an instruction.'

My eyes dropped lower, to the thinner slash of his upper lip and sensuous curve of his lower, inhaling sharply when his grip tightened fractionally around my waist.

'Do what you're told and you might be rewarded,' he murmured, all arrogance and dark, dominant promise so confident of his power.

Entirely justified apparently, because my black palazzo pants-clad legs rose and wrapped around his waist almost of their own volition.

'Tighter,' he bit out, his breath washing over my mouth, making it tingle.

I eagerly complied.

He groaned.

I moaned.

And just like that we were back in that dark warehouse in Connecticut, anticipation thick and heavy as he pressed his way deeper between my legs. Rolled his hips and imprinted his thick, engorged cock against my hungry core.

'Oh God,' I gasped, my arms flying around his neck, terrified of this intense, long-awaited replay being snatched from me.

He leaned closer, pinning me with more of his hard-packed body. 'Do you know how fucking insane you've driven me with the memory of how you taste, *bedda*?'

Unintelligible sounds rattled from my throat, my head heavy with the surge of dizzying desire. It dropped forward, seeking another refresher of his mouth on mine.

But he reared back. 'Uh huh. Not yet.'

'Why not?' I cringed at the faintest whine in my voice. 'What's the point of all this if you're not...?' I trailed off, my face heating with the need rocking through me.

'If I'm not going to unwrap you and gorge like a motherfucking Neanderthal the second I have you?' he finished.

Another moan shivered up my throat. Because that was *exactly* what I wanted. To be devoured until there was nothing left.

White-hot eyes raked over my face. 'Because first you're going to tell me how much you've missed me, too.'

Too? Cesare had missed me? If it was true, why

was he admitting it? If he was lying... was this a trap? A power play of some sort?

'Look at you, tearing yourself apart over whether this is some trick,' he hummed.

I licked my lips as his deliberately hovered closer, teasing me. 'You would do the same in my shoes.'

His gaze rested at the pulse beating in my throat for several seconds before he shook his head. 'Nah, baby. There are some things I don't fight even if it doesn't make sense. This' – he rolled his erection over my ever-dampening sex, the seam of his jeans hitting my clit at the perfect angle and making me shudder against him – 'I've accepted as one of those things. Don't make me ask again.'

Did I miss him?

Was water wet? Hell, forget water. Did *I* get wet and achy with need every single time I thought of him? His mouth between my legs, his long clever fingers pushing inside me, stretching me, tormenting me with the prelude of what the massive rod between his legs would do to me?

'Yes.' The word shivered from the corner of my soul, a place I'd never cared to examine. Because every single wish that resided there was forbidden, every yearning an act of treachery. To my family. To my savage history. To the love for Valentina that Bonafacio swore had been the purest kind. To all the soldiers who'd died in the avenging of that love.

But watching the transformation that my single admission brought to Cesare's face, it was almost worth it.

And when he grunted and cursed under his breath, then swooped down to finally capture my lips with his, *almost* turned into certainty.

His tongue breached my lips like a heat-seeking missile, licking me like I was the ambrosia of eternal life. My hands clawed and clung as tightly as my legs, delirium thickening my blood as the magic of his kiss completely overwhelmed me.

But just when I thought, with shocked surprise, that I could actually come just from being kissed by Cesare, he raised his head. A trail of spit joined our lips and I gasped when he flicked his tongue out and licked it.

Drunk on the decadence of it, I swayed towards his mouth, but he reared back further, denying me.

'Liv Ivanovski, is he your secret partner?'

My head swam as my body screamed with the deprivation of pleasure. 'What?' I asked dazedly.

'Answer me, Maddelena.'

My eyes widened. 'I... You can't... Is this why...?'

His eyes hardening dried up my line of questioning. 'No,' I whispered.

'No he's not or no you don't know?'

I scrambled to locate my brain cells. 'Ivanovski... the Russian head of the Solynik Clan?'

The fingers in my hair tightened, angling my face up to dig into my gaze. 'You know him? You've met with him?'

'No!' I shook my head, the need to emphasise my answer pressing down on me. 'Not personally, but his name has crossed my grandfather's lips once or twice... back when you were...' I frowned, the fog clearing a little more. 'What do you mean, is he my partner? Is he the one you think is behind what's happening?'

His hold tightened another notch, then eased, his fingers massaging my scalp as he maintained the pressure of his gaze. 'You wouldn't be lying to me, would you, *bedda*?' he queried without answering my question.

'No, I wouldn't,' I breathed. 'Are you going to tell me what this is about?'

'*Cristu*, you really don't know, do you?' he muttered, almost to himself.

Almost with relief.

16

MADDELENA

Unwarranted shame kicked through me and in that moment I wasn't sure who I hated more – my family for keeping me in the dark or Cesare for dragging my ignorance into the light in such an underhanded way.

Both sensations were equally dismaying enough to loosen my grip on his waist. To attempt to uncoil myself from—

'What the fuck do you think you're doing?' he grated.

My breath hitched at the flare of temper in his eyes, but my own anger built.

'This is why you brought me here, isn't it? Now

you have your answer. I had no hand in this and I don't have a fucking clue who does.' I slammed my hands against his rock-hard chest. He didn't budge. 'Let me go.' I hated the hitch in my voice, the bigger one in my chest.

I'd allowed him to seduce me into mindlessness so he could pump me for information. He was leaving me high and dry when I wanted a very different sort of pumping. Even if it was heinously forbidden. Even if it could trigger a fucking war. For a dizzying moment I wondered if this was how past illicit lovers had felt, standing on the precipice, staring danger in the face. Unwilling to turn back.

Juliet Capulet. Anna Karenina. Isolde.

'Cesare.'

His nostrils flared and I recalled how much he enjoyed me using his name.

'No fucking chance. Especially not now.'

Before I could ask what he meant, he was kissing me again.

His vigour was intense as the hand on my waist rose to close over my breast. He groaned, moulding me with rough caresses before, with a grunt, he yanked down the top of my bustier.

Heated eyes dropped. 'Fuck, you're even more

luscious than I remember,' he slurred. He flicked his thumb over my budded nipple, sending shudders of delight through me.

'Legs, Maddelena,' he prompted, biting my lower lip in wicked punishment.

I tightened my legs around his waist, happy with the realisation that he wasn't stopping after all, relief and need tearing through me in equal measure when I felt him where I wanted him most.

'You know how long I've waited for this?' He licked the sting from my lips, then nipped them again. 'Now every time we fuck, I'm going to take you up against a wall at least once, until the madness you stoked is gone.'

I thrilled at the 'every time we fuck' but chose to remain silent on the subject. It was now a blatant and undeniable fact that I was weak when it came to Cesare Salvatore. That I was circling the depths of an unfathomable kind of hell if this came out. But already I was priming myself for the next time. And the next.

And if Bonafacio was truly plotting to marry me off despite my flaws, then I intended to gorge my-self on—

I yelped at the not-so-gentle pinch of my nipples.

'*Duci.*' It was a snapped endearment that shut off my unwanted train of thought.

I blinked.

'I'm going to give you one guess on how I feel about you being distracted by anything besides what's happening between us right now.' Without waiting for an answer, he stepped back, disentangling us so my feet dropped to the floor. 'Strip.'

The growled command went straight to my pussy. My hands shook as I attacked my pants, nearly ripping the zipper. When they pooled at my feet, I kicked them away.

Cesare devoured every exposed inch, his breathing a little erratic when he lingered longest on the stretch of silk and lace framing my hips and cupping my damp centre.

He licked his lips and dragged his eyes upward as I reached beneath my left arm and lowered the zipper. The stiff, boned bustier parted and fell away.

And for the first time in my life, at the grand old age of thirty-one, I was caught beneath the naked hunger of a breathtaking man.

It was almost as if fate had planned things this way.

My first was a disastrous fumble in the backseat of Ciara's boyfriend's borrowed Toyota after an even

worse double date. It'd left me never wanting to repeat the experience.

Then, after the harrowing night of bloody carnage that had left devastation in its wake, sex had
been an ineffectual way to cope that had left both
parties deeply disappointed. Unfortunately, I'd re-
boarded that broken wagon and repeated the cringe-
worthy experience a few more times before finally
throwing in the towel and accepting that the kind of
sex I saw in movies and read in books was a complete hoax.

So, right here and now, basking in the fiery focus
of a very aroused Cesare Salvatore, the most breathtaking man I'd ever known, felt like dancing in pure
sunshine after a cleansing rain. And if there was
more pleasure in store – please, God – then I was
about to have my mind blown *in the best way*.

'Finish, baby.' He jerked his head at my panties.

My breasts swayed with my movement as I
hooked my fingers into the sides of my panties and
tugged them down.

'Fuck,' he rasped.

He attacked his own shirt, instantly distracting
me with the unveiling of inked bronzed skin lovingly
etched with swirling patterns, a Sicilian inscription I
intended to read... later, all encasing a mouthwa-

tering eight-pack. Courtesy of a brother who needed to keep himself in prime health for the same reason Cesare did, I knew not every man could achieve the coveted eight-pack.

'You like what you see, *bedda*?'

'Yes.' There was really no point playing coy or pretending he wasn't an exceptional, mouthwatering specimen. Virile and masculine. And with the massive bulge pressing so aggressively against his fly...

Yeah, I was saving embarrassment for when my inexperience inevitably filtered through because even now, I wasn't sure what to do with myself. All I knew was that I wanted to lick every inch of Cesare's skin.

A smug grin curved his lips as he caught my eager gaze on the belt he was releasing. The sound of his zipper lowering flooded my mouth with drool so fast I flushed.

'I would give my pinkie to know what's going through that mind of yours.'

I pressed my lips together and prayed my gaucheness wouldn't spill.

With a move brimming with confidence, he stepped out of his loafers and dragged off his jeans and briefs.

Cesare was thick. And long.

The prospect of taking all of that inside me made my thighs clench in half dread, half anticipation.

It would hurt. No two ways about it. My past experiences may have been little more than forgettable fumbles in the dark but I'd been present enough to know that none of them had been *this* endowed.

Oh God.

'Maddelena?'

My gaze jerked up to his half smile and crooking finger. I took a step, then stumbled, my heels getting caught in the panties I hadn't fully taken off.

He lunged, he caught me, swung me into his arms.

'It'll fit or I'll fucking die trying,' he rasped in my ear. Then he marched towards the archway leading to an inner suite with a massive king-size bed.

Planting one knee on the bed, he dropped me into the middle, his hooded gaze watching my tits bounce. One large hand closed over his length, caressing from root to tip, as the other trailed down my throat, lingering at my clavicle, the upper slope of my breast, toying with my nipple. When I shuddered again, a thick groan left his throat before he cursed and let go.

'You're so fucking responsive. And those dirty little sounds you make...' He shook his head. 'You were made for fucking, *bedda*, and I'm going to fuck you so hard you'll forget your name as you scream mine.'

He turned away long enough to tug open the nightstand drawer and toss a condom onto the bed. Then he prowled over me, dropped onto his elbows and recaptured my lips.

I lost myself to delirium a second time as he kissed his way down my body. With the last experience fresh in my mind, I thought I knew what to expect.

I was wrong. He took me to the brink repeatedly, making me hiss and cry in bittersweet frustration. And then he plunged two fingers inside me.

The sting of it yanked my head from the pillow. 'Cesare!'

* * *

Cesare

'Damn, you're as tight as a locked vault.'

I paused for a second, sucked in oxygen and control before I blew prematurely. 'What's the key to opening you up, I wonder? Shall I play with your little clit, baby?' I thumbed the swollen nub, revelled in her gasp and shudder, then her slight give as she grew slicker, more relaxed. I pushed in and she tensed up again.

'Fuck, baby. You're gonna kill me before I get in this sweet pussy, aren't you?'

I flicked her bundle of oversensitive nerves again and her mouth gaped as she sucked in desperate breaths. I was confident in that moment that no one else had made her feel like this.

That widening of her eyes? The way they clung to mine with a sheen of wonder? It reeked of inexperience. And while the primal beast inside me roared with outrage for not being her first, I wasn't hypocritical enough to take her to task for it.

But fuck if I didn't vow, here and now, to make sure Maddelena Mancinelli would never be free of the memory of me possessing her body.

'God, it... it hurts.'

'Not my fault,' I gritted out, swooping in for another taste of her delicious wetness. 'It's yours. For being so insanely tight.'

I leaned over her, still keeping the rubbing of her clit going as I caught her nipple between my fingers, and was rewarded with hissed shudders and another glorious inch inside. 'There you go. I've found another key, haven't I? Good girl. Relax for me.'

Sweat beaded on my forehead, dripped down my face.

Pressure collected in the small of my back, and I knew I was almost out of time. Her pussy was fucking magic and I was about to be swept away. Removing my hand from her hot channel, I grabbed her knee and pressed it to her chest, opening her up as wide as possible.

'Sorry, baby, we're out of time.'

Tugging on a condom, I notched myself at her entrance and pushed in. '*Jesus*. Maddelena.' Her name was appropriate. This felt almost spiritual.

My eyes rolled at the sublime friction. She screamed, then immediately countered her protest at the intrusion by clutching my back, her nails digging into my skin.

I couldn't bottom out the way I wanted without hurting her, so I pulled back and thrust again, obsessively drinking in her every reaction.

And what an entrancing picture she made.

Her head thrashed on the pillow, her skin turning a beautiful shade of pink as pleasure rolled over her.

With every stroke she took me deeper with a scream and a tentative push of her hips, until she was swallowing me up in heat and slick so incredible

I knew my obsession wasn't about to diminish any time soon.

'Ah, baby, look how well you take my cock. You love it, don't you?'

'Yes! God, yes. Don't stop.'

As if I could. As if the pressure gathering in the small of my back, along my spine and in my balls would allow me to do anything but pound, pound, pound her into the bed. Guttural, unintelligible sounds hammered from my throat.

It struck me that I wouldn't have a single clue if I was snitching on myself with vital Salvatore secrets.

My only consolation was that she was equally out of it, her gorgeous eyes dazed and her kiss-swollen lips gasping as she begged me to fuck her harder. *Harder.*

The first ripple of her impending climax snatched a long growl from my soul. 'Fuck, baby. I feel you, everywhere. It's insane.'

'Cesare... I'm coming. *Oh God...*'

She scratched the fuck out of my back as with a final scream, she shattered completely, milking me with squeezes so tight I had no choice. No choice.

'Here it comes, baby. Take it. It's all for you. Fuck!'

I exploded like a damn fire hydrant on a hot

summer's day, spewing cum until it spilled between our thighs, and still it wouldn't stop.

My forehead dropped to hers before our mouths fused as we rode the glorious end of the roller-coaster.

* * *

Maddelena

Get up. Get up!
It's time to go.

I tried to drag my eyes open, and failed. To be fair, I wasn't trying very hard. My runaway heartbeat had barely settled and my reeling senses were still scattered to the wind, not interested in being located right now.

Still, I attempted to rally. 'I have to go.'

'Like hell you do,' he grunted. 'You mentioned a three-and-a-half-hour window. We've barely used half of it. And I sure as hell need to fuck you again before you leave my bed.'

At my helpless shiver, he laughed. 'I should spank you for letting me waste my time arguing with you when you want this as much as I do.'

I bit my lip and finally opened my eyes.

He'd recovered much faster. And despite the signs of our vigorous fucking – his slightly flushed cheek, unruly hair and gloriously reddened mouth – he looked ready to go again. A sight that both thrilled and alarmed me.

My body ached, for sure, but it was already priming itself for another round.

And... sweet Jesus, as he rose and prowled to the bathroom without an ounce of self-consciousness – and why the hell should he with a body like Adonis? – I couldn't shut up the voice yelling at me to get up fast enough.

Condom disposed of, he came back into the room and stopped beside the bed. Ferocious eyes traced my body from face to feet and back again, stopping at my pussy. The warm towel he pressed between my legs was a welcome surprise. An alarm-ingly heart-warming act that snatched what little breath I'd regained.

Like his feeding me and catching me when I was dizzy, this felt like an act of a considerate man. Not the vengeance-seeking mobster's heir from the nightclub or the racer hellbent on crushing his enemies.

But weirdly, I didn't even prefer one over the other. They were all tied up in the mystery that had created Cesare Salvatore. And my growing addiction was fiercely worrisome.

Done tending me, he threw the cloth to the floor then, reaching into the drawer, he slid his other hand up my inner thigh.

I watched in awed fascination as his cock began to stir once more.

'Normally, I'd give you a chance to rest, but as you can see, you turn me on like a fucking teenager. And you imposed a timeline on us. So' – he smirked as he gripped my hips and flipped me over onto my stomach, then arranged me onto my hands and knees – 'this, too, is your fault.'

Then he proceeded to pleasure me in the most sublime way.

* * *

'One more thing,' Cesare said as he shifted sideways and gathered my pliant body close.

I groaned, desperately fighting the urge to succumb to the weariness sapping deliciously at my bones. Like most health-conscious individuals, I had a gym membership I used on a semi-regular basis. And when I couldn't go I utilised a semi-disciplined yoga regime.

Sadly, neither of them had prepared me for what Cesare wrung from my body. The result of which was needing every ounce of depleted energy to get up, get dressed.

Leave.

I couldn't fall asleep. Not here. Not now. *Never with him.* 'Seriously?'

There was a reason Bonafacio's plans to marry me off and push his agenda for great-grandchildren had hit a major roadblock five years ago. A reason why in a patriarchal hierarchy where women were low on the totem pole, I ranked even lower.

As a teenager I'd suddenly developed the nasty habit of sleepwalking. And if that wasn't awful enough, I also had a habit of carrying out full-blown conversations with zero recollection of them upon waking.

As a mobster's granddaughter, it was a massive flaw that would've had my tongue cut out in the Old Country half a century ago. Luckily I'd been born in this age, to a grandfather who despised me but thankfully drew the line at murdering his own granddaughter for a flaw that was out of her control.

Small mercies for the win.

But the warning had been drilled into me repeatedly.

Never fall asleep in a presence of anyone untrustworthy.

A warning I was in serious danger of flouting right now.

Getupgetupgetup.

Firm hands brushed back my damp hair from my face, then wrapped around my head to raise my head so he could capture my gaze. 'You need to get dressed.'

I stiffened, distressed to be swinging from an inner pep-talk about leaving to being annoyed and a little hurt that Cesare was pushing for the same thing. 'Why?'

'My doctor is on his way. He's going to draw some blood.'

Doctor? What the hell? Did we do something unsavoury? Or was he now confessing a condition he should've mentioned before? *Oh God.* 'Again, why?'

He dropped his mouth to mine in a quick searing kiss. 'Because the next time we fuck will be without a barrier between us. I'm clean and I know you are too but just for your peace of mind, we'll get fresh tests, *si*?'

My head spun afresh. 'I... don't even know where to start with that.' I shook my head. 'Actually, I do.

How the hell do you know whether I'm clean or not?'

His speaking glance ridiculed my statement. When I kept my eyebrow raised, he chuckled, although the amusement didn't reach his eyes. Sharp grey eyes had returned to predatory alertness. His fingers tightened subtly in my hair.

'The same way I know Matteo has been battling angina for five years, and your uncle Stefano has been making it not so subtly known that he'd love to step into his brother's shoes.'

My breath caught, giving me away before I could hide my astonishment. My father's heart condition had been kept within a very tight circle on pain of death to anyone who dared breathe a word of it. He'd hoped it would all go away via a super-secret operation performed in Sicily two years ago, but the outcome had been less than optimal.

It'd put an even greater strain between the half-brothers, necessitating the need to put a little distance between them. It was also why Bonafacio had put Stefano on overwatch duty within the racing team. It kept him out of New York for the better part of nine months of the year and the friction within the family to a minimum.

'If you know, why...' *Shut up, Maddie. You might not like his answer.*

'Why haven't I used that juicy information?'

My head bobbed before I could throttle my curiosity.

He kissed me again. 'Who says I won't? Everything is about timing, baby.'

'Is it? Because I'm 1,000 per cent sure there will never be the right timing for this if your grandfather... and mine... find out what we did tonight. What you intend to keep doing.'

His face hardened with soul-shaking savagery for a single moment. Before he actively cleared it and shrugged. '*If* being the operative word. I don't intend it to be front page news. Do you?' His gaze probed mine. *Hard.*

It was the right answer. The sensible one. And yet, a bite of hurt pierced my ribcage. Still, I managed to shake my head.

He smacked me lightly on the ass. 'Good. Now get up.' He rose to dispose of the second condom and returned in a silk bathrobe.

'And what if I don't want my blood drawn?'

He paused at the end of the bed, and dear God, his deliciousness was almost unnervingly potent.

He shrugged. 'We keep going as we've started.'

He leaned forward, propped his fists on either side of my feet. 'But go on, lie to my face right now and tell me you wouldn't love for me to fuck you raw?'

Damn him.

I couldn't.

So I didn't.

17

CESARE

The Singapore night race was the most taxing of the whole season. Maybe that was why it was also my favourite. There was something about pushing yourself to the very brink of exhaustion and dehydration in one-hundred-and-four-degree heat that made me feel alive.

Tonight's race was especially sweet. A different kind of exhaustion trailed through my muscles, reminding me of the hours I'd spent fucking Maddelena. My only regret was the hours had sped by far too quickly.

And yeah, the fact that I was starting from pole position, where I rightly belonged, didn't hurt either.

Under the bright floodlights that turned the

track from night to day, I scanned the crowd as Brazzo regurgitated information and scenarios we'd gone over a dozen times already. I nodded and absently absorbed it, reminding myself that keeping him calm would help me in the long run.

Now that I knew where the threat was coming from, I was doing my best to make it up to my team for the hell I'd put them through. Up to a point, anyway. They'd turned themselves inside out this weekend to ensure that while Singapore was always going to favour our humidity-loving engine, every piece of information was kept under lock and key and relayed to our most trusted crew at the very last minute.

It'd made for longer hours in the garage than we'd wanted, but the penalty for working outside parc fermé hours had been worth—

My thoughts screeched to a halt when I saw her.

Unlike the majority of her team, Maddelena didn't wear the team gear.

The gleaming chestnut hair I'd delighted in roping around my fist as I'd banged her from behind last night was layered around her face in stylish waves. I hated that her eyes were covered by designer sunglasses but perhaps it was just as well.

Looking into those blue eyes would remind me

of how she'd looked when she came all over my cock. And springing a boner in this tight race suit with the world's press and several hundred thousand spectators with camera phones thirsting for a scandal would be far from ideal.

But fuck me if she didn't look incredible.

I slid my own shades on so I could watch her without being seen. Then I gritted my teeth when the VIPs she was obviously entertaining surged closer, temporarily blocking my view. When one guy – some CEO of a Malaysian microchip company – placed a hand on the small of her back, a growl rattled up from my diaphragm.

Brazzo froze, his humidity-reddened face growing hotter. 'Uh...'

I waved impatiently at him. 'Keep going, I'm listening.'

He shuffled through his clipboard notes, rattling off wind speed, drag reduction zones, sector times and predicted tyre life as I stared daggers at the meaty hand on my woman's back.

My woman.

Until I decreed otherwise, Maddelena Mancinelli was mine. Not even the perfectly sound argument she'd made of what would happen if our families found out – and my unhinged reaction to it – would sway me now I'd had her.

No fucker would lay a hand on her while I drew breath. I took a step towards them, just as she shifted, dislodging the hand.

Excellent news for both of them.

As if she'd heard me, her head snapped towards me. Her lips parted. I couldn't see her eyes but I knew she was looking at me.

Even from the distance I could almost hear her sucking in oxygen. Knew her nipples were hard beneath the thin gold cropped top she'd worn with a fluttery skirt with a high slit that showed off her spectacular legs. Legs I craved around my waist more than I wanted my next breath. *Soon.* And the next time would be even better since she'd taken the blood test last night and, as expected, the results had come back clean.

A body stepped in front of me, blocking my view of her. Another snarl built in my throat.

'Here, brother. You look like you need to cool down some more.' Rafa held out a fresh ice vest. 'Before all your blood migrates south,' he added.

My growl died. Brazzo mumbled under his breath and retreated several steps. I snatched the vest from

Rafa and tugged it over the perfectly adequate one I had on. I wasn't going to admit he was right, that my little head was in danger of ruling my big one.

When it became clear he wasn't going to shift, I sighed, folded my hands beneath my arms and gave him half my attention, keeping the other half beyond his shoulder in case Maddelena crossed my eye line. 'Anything to report?'

'As it happens, yes,' he said.

My focus snapped to him. 'What?'

He nodded at the concrete-and-chainlink wall that formed the track boundary, and I followed him. 'You said you asked Nightowl for confirmation that Stan was the link, right?'

'Yeah. But as much as I'd love to, kicking the shit out of another driver during race season will be frowned upon. But if he's irrefutably involved...' I shrugged.

He pulled out the phone I'd given to him for safekeeping and showed me the latest message in response to my asking Nightowl for further information after my conversation with Maddelena last night.

Any further links between Willow and Mancinellis?

Nightowl's message was as cryptic as ever.

THE HAMMER IN THE SEA

'*Santo cielo*, I'm not in the mood for more puzzles.'

He glanced around again and leaned closer to whisper in my ear. 'I think this one might be an easier solve. We know The Hammer is the Solynik Clan because they used to be the Molotok Clan, which means hammer. And I'm thinking the sea refers to St Petersburg and the Baltic Sea. Ivanovski is based there, remember?'

I blinked, impressed. 'Fuck, yes.' I saw Brazzo and two other engineers hovering nervously. 'Keep digging. We'll pick this up after the race.'

He clasped the hand I held out. 'Stay safe. Kick ass.'

I nodded and thumped him on the back. The moment he stepped away, Brazzo rushed forward and picked up where he'd left off.

I gave in to the urge and scanned the crowd again.

She was gone.

Just as well. Being buckled into my safety harness by my crew while sporting a hard-on would be embarrassing for all involved.

But for every one of the sixty-two laps and one hundred and ninety miles, I would plan the many and varied ways I'd celebrate my race win between Maddelena's juicy thighs.

She would feel me deep inside her for the next week.

*   *   *

The rousing Italian anthem celebrating my win – I'd fight anyone who didn't agree it was the best in the world – ended to the perfect sync of exploding fireworks along the start-finish straight. My grin threatened to split my face as the crowd and my crew screamed their joy.

Rafa stood with each arm around Bibi's and Dante's shoulders. Beside me, Renzo beamed from the second-place step.

It felt fucking good to be back where we belonged. Even if the driver to my left had given up any semblance of civility.

'Enjoy it while it lasts, old man,' Narciso muttered under the guise of offering congratulations.

I clasped the back of his neck, letting my fingers

dig into his skin. He hissed and tried to back away, but I tightened my hold.

'Keep it up, squirt,' I breathed, my teeth bared in a smile. 'I'm more than happy to teach you one or two things about good manners.'

He looked considerably paler and less petulant when I let him go, and I made sure to aim the Jeroboam-sized champagne spray right in his eyes, then left Renzo to laugh in his face as he sputtered. There was only so much juvenile behaviour I was willing to lower myself to.

Grabbing my trophy after the obligatory photos, I stepped off the podium.

And saw her.

She stood beneath the podium, next to the pit lane wall. Her sunglasses were perched above her head now, and so I snagged her stare easily.

Her crew surrounded her, but none were paying attention. I throttled the urge to wink, torn by the apprehension on her face.

My win meant her loss. Possible repercussions. I didn't – *shouldn't* – care.

They'd made their risky bed, attempted to gain the upper hand with underhanded means. That sucked for her. I was a Salvatore. We *never* let shit like that slide.

Besides, she had nothing to fear as long as I kept her in *my* bed and she kept her mouth shut, right?

I locked eyes and raised the bottle to her as I took another gulp. Anyone watching would think I was taunting her – as was my blood-given right – not imagining spreading her naked on my penthouse terrace, drenching her in champagne and lapping up the bubbles straight from her pussy as the fireworks announcing my victory exploded above our heads.

She hastily broke eye contact when her brother approached where I stood, champagne bottle in his hand. The smile she turned on looked forced, her eyes sombre. My chest tightened but I shrugged that off too, turned and walked away.

No matter.

I planned on putting a much more satisfactory look on her face before the night was over.

Enrico, my personal trainer, approached with a half-gallon bottle of water, holding out his hand for the champagne. 'You need to hydrate.'

'You're no fucking fun.' I grimaced and handed it and the trophy over, then gulped down several mouthfuls of water. He was a hard taskmaster but I had him to thank for my excellent physique.

When he'd satisfied himself that I wasn't about

to collapse into a dried-out husk, he nodded. 'Rafaelle is looking for you. I told him to meet you in the ice bath room after your media interviews. Can I trust you to do your stretches before then?'

I grinned and slapped him on the shoulder. 'Have I ever let you down?'

He smiled. 'No. And it's good to see you in a good mood. It's been a while.'

'Winning always puts me in a good mood, Rico.' The only thing that would top that right now was being balls deep in Maddelena's cunt with nothing between us, but the wait was a sweet torment I could withstand. Barely.

The media interviews were a breeze, my irritation not even rising above a simmer when the usual stupid questions about rivalries with the Mancinellis came up.

I half-unzipped my outer race suit, letting it hang from my waist as I headed to the ice bath room. I fucking hated ice baths but the results were undeniable, so they'd become a necessary evil in my post-race regime.

Rafa looked up with a smirk when I entered, ankle propped upon his knee, phone in hand. 'Congrats, man. Feels good to watch you hand them their asses.'

'Fuck yes, it does.' My eyes slid to my own phone sitting on the table next to him. 'So?'

'Progress.' He slid his phone into his pocket and picked up mine. 'I've established, with some degree of accuracy, that there is indeed a link between Ivanovski and, surprise surprise, the other Mancinelli driver.'

My eyebrows jerked up. 'Stan Paul?'

He nodded and cracked a smile. 'Yup. All-American-Stan with his aww shucks attitude isn't quite so benign.'

'Say more.' I peeled off my race suit and fireproof underlayers and approached the ice bath with gritted teeth.

'For starters, Stan Paul is short for Stanislav Palinski.'

Clad in only boxers, I paused at the edge of the tub and set a four-minute timer on my custom Richard Mille watch. 'Palinski?' I rummaged around my memory banks and came up empty.

'Shadowy figure behind the Aksana Group no one's seen for almost two decades? Rumoured to be in hiding with a not-to-be-sneezed-at army because of a major fall out with a certain dictator?'

'Fuck.' My gut churned for reasons other than the much-detested impending plunge into forty-three-degree Fahrenheit water. Bracing myself, I stepped in and quickly dropped into a crouch, letting the water submerge me up to my armpits. The quicker I got this over with the quicker the ordeal would end. 'How close to 100 per cent is your certainty?'

He held out his hand and toggled it side to side. 'In the ninety-five percentile.'

I clenched my teeth to keep them from shuddering.

'I was thinking we shake the extra 5 per cent out of Dear Old Stan?'

'Agreed.'

His grin widened and he patted his phone. 'I have his itinerary right here. Since he came a lowly ninth in the race and apparently got bitch-slapped for his trouble by the Narc-Fuck, Stan is planning to drown his sorrows in the arms of... get this... six strippers. He's booked into the Sapphire Room at the Golden Empress Club.'

'Is he even old enough to be allowed in there?'

Rafa shrugged. 'If Daddy can afford to toss out a hundred mil on an F1 seat, he sure as fuck can fund a one-man pity party in a club where one lap dance, without extras, costs a cool ten grand, regardless of age.'

I checked my watch. Eighty-two long seconds left. My bones screamed with the need for warmth while my thigh muscles tingled as worn tissues stitched back faster than normal.

To further distract myself, I nodded at my phone. 'Did you verify all this with our helper?'

His good humour dimmed. 'I tried. No response. Whoever this fucker is, they never answer when I ask the questions. They're probably watching us.' His scowl relayed just how much that thought thrilled him.

I made a mental note to be careful where I pointed my phone in future. Especially when I was with Maddelena. Giving an unknown hacker a free show was not my idea of an ideal situation.

'When do we leave?' I asked.

'Bibi and the twins are holding the fort with the sponsors and ass-kissers but Renzo was already complaining.' His grin returned. 'I think one of the Kardashians asked for one too many selfies and he almost lost his shit. Anyway, you're expected to show your face for a bit, shake hands and do the group crew photo thing. So, an hour?'

My timer beeped and I surged out of the frigid water, tugging a towel over my shoulders even before I'd fully stepped out. I peeled off my briefs and was rubbing heat back into my frozen limbs when a knock sounded on the door.

It cracked open at my prompt and Enrico stepped inside with a fresh set of clothes with the Furia Racing insignia and dozens of sponsors' logos, and the stylish dark loafers I preferred to sneakers.

He set them on the table, folded his arms and eyed me when I winced. 'You remembered to stretch before the bath, right?'

Shit. My face twitched with the urge not to grimace. 'Uhh, I—'

'Nah, he didn't,' Rafaelle narked.

I glowered at him. 'You know what happens to snitches, right?'

He held up his hand. 'I'm not about to say "stitches" because this isn't the 90s and I have too much self-respect.'

Enrico sighed and held out a smaller bottle. 'Drink this.'

This was a vile-tasting protein shake, a poor substitute for the juicy steak I craved. But it would hold me over until I was done with Stan. I gulped it down without giving myself a chance to taste it, my mind skipping ahead.

If Maddelena hadn't eaten by then, she could join me.

I crossed over to the table to grab my clothes. Dressed, I finger-combed my hair and snatched up my phone as Enrico left. I followed, texting as I headed for the private hospitality suite within the team motor home.

Have you eaten yet?

The speech bubble rippled for several seconds before she answered.

Just fancy finger food with corporate guests. Why?

Eat enough not to get dizzy but wait for me to eat dinner.

Again, why? Do we need to break bread together? You got all your answers last night.

I'll let you know when I'm satisfied. Also, I like feeding you. 9pm. Lose your minders.

eye roll emoji You think going to the spa twice in two nights is going to fool anyone?

Keep up with the bratty attitude. It makes me want to punish you more. 9pm. Don't be late.

I slid the phone into my pocket, my palm already itching to connect with her lush ass. I could kill two birds with one stone if Stan revealed anything worth pursuing.

Maybe I'd spank her first, then I'd grill her before I drilled her.

'What the fuck are you so happy about?' Rafa griped.

I snapped into focus and nodded at the security guard, who opened and held the door. 'I'm tickled to see if Renzo has survived the Kardashian mob. What else?'

18

MADDELENA

…I like feeding you…

…makes me want to punish you more.

Yep, I was an absolute buffoon for repeatedly reading his texts and a greater one for allowing my heart to skip several beats every time I did.

Sure, after last night I'd be as dumb as a box of rocks not to see that the chemistry between us was irrefutable. Furnace hot with the likelihood of turning volcanic if he stuck to his guns about the no-condom thing.

But it was also glaringly obvious that Cesare was,

at the very least, playing the keep-your-enemies-closer game while admitting he didn't intend anyone to find out. It was a ridiculously hazardous game of chess, but one I couldn't even *contemplate* rejecting without my senses screaming *no*.

Especially since that game came with a hefty side of sublime fucking.

Barring potentially lethal repercussions, it should be as clearcut as that.

And yet...

...I like feeding you...

Four little words that made my heart prance around in my chest like a ditzy Disney princess.

'What's so damn fantastic you look like you're coasting on a thrice of molly?'

I startled, my fingers instinctively clutching my phone harder. 'What?'

Ciso glowered at the phone I was slyly sliding into my pocket. 'You've been staring at your damn phone for the last twenty minutes. While these idiots have been boring me to death. I'm this close to fucking someone up for thinking they can tell me how to drive my fucking car.'

His growl was more than a little slurred and the

shot he tossed back almost missed his mouth. He'd been drinking steadily since the podium ceremony, even before we left the racetrack.

The Gambler, the exclusive bar Stefano booked, cocky that another win was guaranteed, teemed with corporate guests I was stuck with entertaining. He'd brushed aside my objections and invited all our sponsors across Asia with the promise of a wild victory celebration.

I scanned the room for my errant uncle and wasn't surprised when I didn't see him. 'Where's Stefano?'

'Where do you think? Hiding like the weasel he is. He thinks it's your fault, you know?' Ciso muttered.

My head snapped to him, unease crawling up my spine. 'How the hell is this my fault? Correct me if I'm wrong but didn't every projection at the start of the year point to this circuit being the worst for our car?'

Ciso shrugged. 'Yeah, sure, but...' He raised his hand to scratch his neck, then gave up at the last second so it thudded back onto the cushion of the sofa we sat on. 'He was hoping you'd keep... destabilising Salvatore for a bit longer.'

I felt the blood drain from my head. *He didn't*

know. Couldn't know. Too soon. Too soon. Too soon. I'm not ready to give him up. 'Excuse me? What the hell is that supposed to mean?'

'Clearly his losing streak pissed him off and there seemed to be some... friction between you two in Monza. Stefano said it was a good thing. That if you kept doing it we would have an advantage. Even here.'

I tried to swallow around my dry mouth as burning rage warred with relief. 'Did... did he tell Papa and Bona any of this?' *And did they approve that insane call? Was it so insane if it gave me a legitimate in?*

Ciso tried to avoid my gaze but I chased it until he had no choice. 'Maybe. I dunno.'

He knew. So did Sofiya probably.

Hell, it was possible everyone knew what my father and grandfather were plotting but me. I wondered if it was why Roberto hadn't insisted beyond a token objection last night when I dismissed him and the rest of the security team.

I shook my head, wondering why the knowledge seared when I should have been used to this. When being the last to know was par for the course for me despite my supposed status as consigliere.

'Sis, I—'

'So he's off somewhere, throwing me under the bus?'

A wave of pity crossed his face and my anger built. 'He's probably catching heat of his own.'

'What about you? What responsibility do you take for coming third seeing as, oh, I don't know, you were the one driving the damn car?'

He flinched, then his face crumbled into a puppy-dog pout. As the baby of the family and sole male grandchild, it was a well-practised expression that melted hearts and got him out of more shit than I cared to count.

'Fuck, don't get mad at me, sis. I'm only telling you what I heard.'

I sucked in a long sustaining breath, my heart thumping as a different thought blossomed. 'What else have you heard?'

Confusion cut through the pouting. 'What do you mean?'

I wasn't proud of it but I hoped he would be too drunk to remember my questions or level of interest in the morning. 'I know Bona is trying to marry me off. Do you know who to?' I asked, although what the hell I planned on doing with that information was a mystery. Still, forearmed and all that.

His face scrunched, and he reached for his next

shot. 'Some dude from the Old Country. For your sake I hope he's not old as fuck.' He tossed the drink back, slammed the glass down hard enough for it to crack, then patted me on the shoulder. 'You deserve someone born in the last half millennia at the very least,' he said, then chuckled.

I glared. 'I'd like a name, Ciso.'

'You think they'd tell me?' he scoffed. 'Ask Mama. Or maybe Sof?'

Of course Sofiya knew. *Of course.*

'I'm going for a leak.' He staggered upright, stepped away from the table, then careened back, swaying on his feet as he stabbed a thumb over his shoulder. 'Stay away from that fucker with the com-bover. He gives me the creeps. Oh, and from Salva-tore too. It's not really worth it, and I'd hate to give Nonno an excuse to lose his shit on all of us. You know that never ends well.'

As much as I wanted to discard it as drunken rambling, his advice was searingly inescapable.

Bonafacio losing his shit and taking things too far was the reason I hadn't seen Giada in five years. The threat of it was the reason Jacinta had enrolled for post-grad programme after post-grad programme before going back to college one final time to study for the bar exam, then found every reason under the sun to remain in her tiny Manhattan apartment instead of living at home like Sofiya and I were forced to.

Only her breathtaking brilliance with the law had stopped Bonafacio from hauling her home and marrying her off at the first opportunity. And at the tender age of twenty-six and a second-year associate in a prestigious law firm, my sister had already earned what little freedom she'd carved out by defending Mancinelli runners, soldiers and capos from all kinds of charges on a crushing pro-bono schedule.

My insides tightened into impossible knots as I pulled out my phone and brought up the texts.

It's off. I'm not coming tonight.

It felt like an eternity, and no time at all, before Cesare responded.

Like hell you're not. You come to me, bedda. Or I'm coming for you. Your choice.

* * *

Cesare

Her text arriving as we entered the Golden Empress Club put me in a shitty mood.

I'd expected her to baulk at some point because, let's face it, what she was doing was downright hazardous to her wellbeing. Still, when it came, the hollow it left in my belly was deeply unsettling, fouling my mood even further.

Which was good news for the management, and very bad news for Stan Paul.

I waved my Black Card at the sharply dressed man with slicked-back hair who glided towards me like he was one of those Disney villains, on an invisible hoverboard. I half expected his toothy smile to keep going until it spliced his face in two.

'Five figures of your choice, charged to whatever item you're selling in here, for twenty uninterrupted minutes with your guest in...' I glanced at Rafa, brow raised.

'The Sapphire Room,' he supplied. 'Oh, and that figure also covers any unforeseen damage *and* your utmost discretion or my friend Fist here will forget himself and accidentally let slip to the police commissioner that you serve underage customers.'

The man didn't even blink.

He simply cupped one hand in the other and held both out for the card like he was taking holy communion. 'We're very pleased to have you join us, sir. The room you seek is upstairs, last double doors on the right. Enjoy your visit.'

I dropped the card in his palm and he glided away with the easiest money he'd make this week.

I took the stairs two at a time, Rafa, Fist and a trio of soldiers hot on my heels.

The doors in question opened just before we reached it, denying me the satisfaction of kicking it in. For a moment I was furious the fucker downstairs had ratted us out. But it was a scantily clad woman with skyscraper heels and fake tits the size of bowling balls who stepped out.

The keycard discreetly tucked between her fingers suggested she'd been signalled to open the door.

Excellent.

We entered and were halfway into the room before Stan lifted his head from between another pair of outrageously large knockers. His two minders, also busy indulging in the available entertainment, didn't realise what was happening until too late.

The closest one, a steroid-pumped meathead, jumped up and rushed me.

I met his forward moment with a throat punch. He coughed once. And kept coming.

Fuck. Either he was coked out of his mind or his pain tolerance was sky high.

I aimed two rapid-fire lead hooks at his temple, then another jab at his throat. This time something crunched.

He flailed back and dropped to his knees, clutching his broken Adam's apple as he gurgled in pain. I shook out my smarting knuckles. That would bruise and be a little tender for a few days. Good thing I wouldn't be driving for another two weeks.

Fist took care of the other minder even before the two strippers contorting around their respective poles had made it to the floor.

As the downed guards were completely immobilised, Rafa whistled and spun a slow three-sixty. 'You don't hold back when you need a pick me up, do you, son?'

The room was decked out in deep blue velvet sectional sofas along one wall and a long bar with dozens of high-end liquor bottles, several buckets of Dom, multi-hued bottles of pills and two trays with half used lines of coke.

On a low table next to the sofa, several sex toys,

lube and – Jesus, was that a tub of glitter? Why? – sat waiting.

Rafa took a detour to the bar and plinked a fingernail against the coke tray. 'Are race drivers allowed the good stuff, or is our boy here special?'

'I believe he thinks he's special.' I made eye contact with the stripper who'd opened the door and subtly jerked my head towards the exit.

Her serene smile didn't slip as she murmured softly in Mandarin. One by one the ladies stood and calmly vacated the room with zero fuss.

Rafa stared after them with a grin before redirecting his gaze to Stan, who had paled and turned into a statue in his chair. 'You really ticked every item on the menu, didn't you? Still experimenting with finding your type, huh? I respect that.'

'What the fuck is this?' Stan finally unfroze to screech, his dilated gaze bouncing between us before settling on me. 'Look, man, you won fair and square today. I have no beef with that, okay?'

I tilted my head. 'You sure about that? Only I'm not sure you value the true meaning of fair and square. But I appreciate that that may not be up to you. That you're simply caught up in "sins of the father" bullshit. But I'll need some insight into the working of it, just to be sure.'

He gulped audibly when he saw Fist plant himself in front of the closed doors, his thick arms
crossed in front of him. 'What... what are you talking
about? Sins of what father?'

'Yours, Stan. Keep up.'

His confusion deepened. 'W-what do you mean?
My father is back home in... in Chicago. He's an
investment banker. He's a good guy... There is no
sin.'

'Are you sure about that, *Stanislav*? Because I'm
sure your American just took a little detour there.
What do you think, *frate*?'

Rafa nodded. 'Yup, he's definitely giving shades
of deep winters and ushankas. St Petersburg,
maybe?'

Stan had been simply nervous before, but now
naked fear swam in his eyes. He wasn't too far gone
on the booze and coke, and as I prowled closer I felt
the waves of terror rising off him. His fists bunched
and un-bunched on his thighs.

I thought about taking a seat and changed my
mind. High-end club or not, far too many bodies
dripping with heaven knew what had used that sofa.
I wasn't in the mood to catch something.

Not so soon after discovering the delights of
Maddelena's enchanted pussy.

'Interesting that you're not rushing to deny your name is Stanislav, hmm?'

His shoulders curled and it was almost pathetic how easily he folded. I was highly annoyed, but not enough to take out my wrath on a helpless manchild who hadn't had the brains to bring enough security to make it worth my while.

'You are Stanislav Palinski, correct?' I pressed.

He chewed his top lip for several seconds, his eyes darting between his fallen bodyguards, before he gave up any hope of escaping this, and nodded.

Rafa glanced at me, and a pulse of relief passed between us. Finally, a real-life confirmation that wasn't dependent on a mysterious hacker.

'And your real father is...?'

He shook his head, ashen and utterly distraught. 'I cannot... He will... No. You have to... t-to do what you want to me. I cannot...'

I propped one loafer on the cushion next to him and patted him on the shoulder. 'Shhh, it's okay, we don't need to talk about your papa right now. What about Liv Ivanovski?'

Misery crept across his face, sinking in. Then his chin dipped to his chest. 'What about him?' he whispered.

Rafa glanced at me and smirked before stepping

closer to the boy. 'He facilitated your race seat and orchestrated our recent... misfortunes. Yes or no?'

'*Da* – yeah.' The word floated on a shuddering exhale.

I patted him again. 'Good. You know what would really help? The names of everyone Ivanovski co-opted into his little scheme.'

Fear-soaked eyes lifted to me, and I saw remnants of white powder ringing his left nostril. Fucking hell. Maybe I would do a little snitching of my own, let it drop to the authorities about Little Stan's habit. Sliding behind the wheel of a 1,000-horsepower racing car with top speeds of over three hundred miles an hour while coked-up was like screaming 'fuck you' at the Grim Reaper. Even worse was taking others into the afterlife with you. 'What are you going to do to me?'

'You? Nothing. My issue isn't with you. As long as you stay in your lane, literally, and lay off the coke, you get to finish your season unscathed. Names,' I repeated.

He spat the names out like pips from a diseased fruit. Rage billowed in my belly. Two were mid-level people on my crew I trusted. Another two were officials I would be paying a visit to in the next week. The Mancinelli traitors who implemented the ill-gotten info would also be appropriately dealt with.

That might be where things got hairy, but I'd cross that bridge when I came to it.

I straightened up and looked down at the terrified driver. I shouldn't really have thrown him a bone but... 'My advice to you? Lay low for a while. The next couple of weeks are going to be a little... chaotic.'

Surprisingly, he shook his head. 'Liv will not come after me.'

My eyes narrowed. 'Oh no? What makes you sure?'

'He's my second cousin. Plus he's terrified of...' He clamped his jaw shut.

Rafa laughed. 'What, you can't say your own father's name? What is he, Voldemort?'

Stan flinched.

'Ah, so Ivanovski is blood? Are you an only child, Stan?' I asked.

His face creased some more and he nodded.

'Well, that might just save you. That means he probably won't kill you if you're your father's only child. But I can't vouch for how badly he's going to rough you up. He has a trigger-happy temper, I hear.'

Again, he stunned me by shedding a layer of fear and meeting my eyes. 'It's you he wants. He's still angry about you killing his deal with the Mancinellis five years ago.'

Rafa stiffened.

I flicked a glance at him and saw the icy rage building at the back of his eyes. He didn't tolerate the casual mention of the series of incidents that had taken our mother from us.

'That was his first mistake, believing he had the right to make deals with anyone without due respect where needed, but especially doing business with El Topo. The Salvatores own New York. Always have. Always will. Feel free to tell him if he needs a reminder. I'm happy to oblige.'

I swept through the doors Fist held open for me, and seconds later I was back in the foyer.

The manager stood in the same position, hands held out, my card in his palm. 'It was a pleasure to serve you, sir. You're welcome back any time.'

Fist swiped it and handed it to me, casting a lethal glance at the weasel that had Rafaelle smirking.

'Yeah, I bet you would,' he said.

We stepped out of the club and I stopped on the sidewalk to suck in warm air as Fist grabbed the keys from the valet. When the car arrived, a soldier opened the door and we jumped in the back.

'That was almost too easy,' Rafa rasped.

I frowned and rapped twice on the thin, polished wood trim of the Bentley SUV. 'Hey, don't fucking jinx us, man.'

'*Scusa*.' He mimicked my knock. 'So what next?'

'For now we gather the info on our traitors and we make damn sure they never cross us again. And we get everyone capable of doing so to keep track of Ivanovski's movements. Unfortunately, the kid was right. He's not going to take this lying down. And he might be stupid enough to use the Mancinellis again. We need to be ready.'

'Sounds good. I'm starving. Wanna get some dinner?' he asked.

My nostrils flared as I remembered Maddelena's text. And the pointed and ominous silence from my phone since my response. 'Yeah, but not with you, brother. Sorry. I kicked one Mancinelli ass today. Time to go take care of another.'

He stared at me for an age.

But to his credit, he kept whatever he was thinking to himself.

19

CESARE

'What the fuck was that all about?'

She flinched at the sound of my hotel room door being kicked shut after she entered. And even that pissed me off.

Fuck.

I'd won my favourite race and gotten a solid lead on my traitor problem after months of scratching my balls like a schmuck while the Mancinellis and Ivanovski laughed.

I should have been celebrating.

Instead here I was, searching Maddelena's face for clues as to why she'd tried to bail. And yeah, the signs of carefully controlled distress weren't filling me with warm fuzzies.

'What happened to you?' she asked, eyes widening.

I followed her gaze to my bruised hand. A couple of knuckles were busted open and in the hour since my little skirmish, they'd swelled some.

'Nothing a little ice won't fix,' I said, dismissing her concern. 'Answer me, Maddelena.'

She ignored me, crossing the room to the liquor cabinet on four-inch heels that made her legs look miles long and started rummaging around.

My irritation with her didn't mean I couldn't appreciate the view, and when she bent over to scoop ice from an ice bucket, that was exactly what I did. She was wearing the same skirt as before with the slit that showed her creamy thighs, and I was no fucking saint.

The fact that she'd meant to keep that ass from me tonight riled me all over. Still, I waited, curious despite myself, as she finished whatever the fuck she was doing and returned to where I stood. Waiting like a horny, doe-eyed moron.

'Hand.'

I raised a brow at her sass.

She flushed but didn't back down. Fuck, I loved her little bursts of spirit as much as I hated the signs of her distress.

I held out my hand, then snatched it back when she stepped forward to take it. 'You think playing nursemaid gets you off the hook, baby?'

'No, but I'm assuming you intend to fuck me. And I'd rather you didn't touch me with literal blood on your hands.'

Fair enough. Eyes narrowed, I gave her my hand.

She cupped it in her smaller one, and fuck, in one short night, I'd missed the feel of her soft skin against mine. Was damn thirsty for more. 'Are you going to congratulate me on winning or is that something else I have to drag out of you?'

She flicked me a look from beneath her eyelashes and just like that, my dick, which had half-masted when she knocked on the door, jerked to painful life.

I wanted that look when she was on her knees, deep-throating me. Did she even know how? Would I have to teach her? The possibility thrilled me no end.

For now, I let her clean my cracked skin with a wet towel before she pressed the ice-filled napkin over it. When she started to look around, I caught her wrist to stop further delays.

She protested half-heartedly as I walked her to the dining table.

Seeing her startle at the laid-out table threatened to annoy me all over again.

'You ordered dinner even after...?'

'I did. So you better not have gone against my wishes and eaten.'

Her belly gurgled right on cue and, my mood altering with whiplash speed, I laughed at her blushing scowl. 'I'll take that as a no.' I pulled out her chair. 'Sit down, Maddelena.'

She resisted for the briefest moment. Then sat. 'You had almost a quarter million people screaming for you. Wasn't that enough?'

I caught her chin in my hand. 'Nice as that was, one more wouldn't hurt.' Yeah, I was being a bastard, and I could reduce this to petty 'you-started-it' with her trying to cancel on me bullshit, but hell, I couldn't deny I wanted her accolade.

She licked her bottom lip, and I stifled a groan. 'Congratulations.'

I kept hold of her for a little longer. The feel of her skin was intoxicating and I didn't drink nearly enough champagne after the race. 'You watched the race?'

Her nostrils fluttered and she tried to look away, but I loved that she couldn't. 'Yeah.'

I couldn't resist brushing my thumb over her

bottom lip. 'Good.' I jerked my chin at her plate. 'Eat. I don't want you getting dizzy again.'

I rose and went to dispose of the ice towel and wash my hands before rejoining her. She'd spread the napkin on her lap and uncovered the dishes holding two juicy Wagyu steaks and an assortment of vegetables.

At my approach, she turned with the potatoes dish in her hand and a question in her eyes. I nodded, calling myself all sorts of Neanderthal for how much I enjoyed her serving me. Then I shrugged. I was a red-blooded male with an enemy threat hanging over my head. It was right that *some* primal instincts came into play.

But I could be civilised enough to select a bottle of red wine, which she didn't refuse this time, and pour two glasses.

She was a neat but ravenous little eater.

She didn't pick at her food or complain about calories, which was hella refreshing. I wolfed down my steak in record time – Enrico's protein shake had finished doing its job hours ago, and punching out coked-up meatheads took it out of a man.

I sat back and savoured my wine, enjoying the simple act of having Maddelena Mancinelli in my space and within touching distance, the latter of which I intended to do plenty more of.

'Are you going to sit there and watch me eat?' she asked.

'Nah, I'm going to repeat the question you think you've evaded answering. What the fuck was that about tonight?'

She tensed, toyed with the stem of her glass, then sipped the wine. 'I was tired.'

'Bullshit. Your lying skills haven't improved in the twenty-four hours since we last spoke, baby. Try again.'

Her glare was adorable. But it slowly morphed into something else. Something that made the exceptional steak I'd just consumed roil in my gut. 'Did something happen? Someone upset you?'

The homicidal growl in my voice made her startle. Left her unguarded enough to tell me I was on the right track.

'It's fine—'

'Don't fucking do that. Tell me.'

The alpha bark was intentional. It made it known I wasn't fucking around. And it'd worked with enough people for me to be confident of its efficacy.

So no, I wasn't surprised when she responded.

'My uncle is using this' – she waved a hand between us – 'whatever this is, to his advantage.'

'How?' I snapped, already planning how to dis-
member Stefano Mancinelli the first chance I got if
what she said didn't sit well with me.

She licked her lips, and my cock throbbed impatiently. 'He thinks it's a good thing as long as it...
destabilises you.'

I raised my brows, almost amused. 'You mean as
long as he thinks I'm pussy-whipped by your admittedly magnificent cunt, he'll keep believing he has a
chance of winning the championship?'

She winced but nodded. 'Something like that.'

'And if he thinks otherwise?'

A flash of misery darted across her beautiful
face. 'He's already laying the groundwork to throw
me under the bus in case the tide has turned against
us.'

This was where I needed to keep my mouth shut,
let the Mancinelli family destroy each other from
the inside. It would make everything so much easier.

But seeing her distress wasn't sitting right with
me. Scratch that – it fucking *infuriated* me, especially
now I knew the truth. That they were Ivanovski's
willing or unwilling puppets.

'The tide has turned, *bedda*, like it or not. But

your uncle won't be telling tales about you. Not if I have anything to say about it.'

Her eyes locked on mine. A little apprehensive. A little hopeful. 'Tales? So you believe I didn't have anything to do with the sabotage?'

I paused. Whatever this feeling growing inside of me was, I still had a duty to protect my family. She might well learn the truth on her own, but telling her what went down at the strip club wasn't on the table. *Yet.*

'Let's just say I've learned more than I knew last night, and we'll leave it there for now, yeah?'

Hope dimmed into frustration. She started to rise from the table. I caught her wrist and tugged, and she tumbled into my arms.

Catching her, I placed her in my lap. 'I wasn't done talking, baby.'

'Fine,' she said with a hint of sass.

I curbed a grin. 'I was going to say, if that's what Stefano wants to believe, then let him.'

Her gaze snapped to my face. 'What?'

I shrugged. 'We have two weeks before the next race.' I picked up her hand, pulled her pinky into my mouth and sucked on it. She gasped, her hips squirming in my lap. 'Let him believe you've got me wrapped around this little finger.' I sucked again, harder, and she moaned.

'W-why would I go along with that?' My long, steady look made her lips purse. 'Right. More blackmail.'

'Do you want them to find out you're fucking me of your own free will instead of just sassing me every chance you get? That your pretty Mancinelli pussy is already addicted to my Salvatore cock?'

Her head fell forward, but I caught the war of guilt and mutiny on her face before she shook her head.

'Good, then this keeps everyone in the dark and we carry on as we want, agreed?' I might even keep the lid extra tight on rooting out our traitors if it buys me more time with Maddelena and keeps her out of her stupid uncle's crosshairs.

She swallowed. 'Agreed.' She started to get up.

I banded one arm around her waist to keep her immobilised. 'Stay. I have a treat for you. Don't make me take it away.'

With a small flourish, I uncovered the last dish and placed it in front of her. Delighted when her mouth fell open.

'Is that...?'

'Your favourite apple tart from Le Gémir? *Sì,*

bedda,' I crooned in her ear, then flicked my tongue over the delicate spot beneath her lobe.

She shivered, whether at my confirmation that the tart indeed was from the exclusive French bakery in New York she ordered from twice a week, or in delight at my caress, I didn't much care. Watching her face lose its distress made the ache in my chest – which was fucking alarming – dissipate.

'Are you going to eat the thing, or simply eye-fuck it?'

She turned in my lap, a motion that had my dick straining with the need to burrow into her hot slit. 'But... where? How?' Her eyes widened in adorable wonder. 'You didn't have it flown from the States, did you?'

I smiled. 'Not quite. They have a branch right here in Singapore. Besides, you should be lucky I didn't. Having it flown over while you were trying to cancel on me would've made me big mad. And who knows what I would've done then, hmm? Because I know you still haven't told me everything.'

She stiffened. Then wriggled some more.

I picked up the spoon and pressed it into her hand. 'Hurry up and eat your dessert. Or I'm going to fuck you right here while you're still gawking at the fucking tart.'

She took the spoon – with a glare – and dug into the dessert, took the first bite while I pushed her silky hair aside and dropped kisses along her vertebrae.

Her sweet moan made my cock surge against her ass. Made me regret I wasn't deep inside her to feel the sweet percussion all over my dick.

'You know what *gémir* means, baby?' I licked her third vertebrae, and she shuddered.

'No.' Her spoon trembled as she went for another helping.

'It translates as *moan*.'

'Really?'

'They know their audience, I guess.'

She twisted in my lap again and, yeah, I suspected the little minx was milking having me at her mercy.

Well, I was going to remedy that.

The fastening of her skirt was conveniently located at the back, and I made quick work of it, my breath strangling to nothing when I saw the blood-red thong dissecting her firm ass.

Cristu, I was so fucking screwed.

Maddelena was a work of art from every angle, and I couldn't unhitch my belt and lower my zipper fast enough. My stiff cock fell out and surged against her ass as she took another bite.

The moment I managed to shimmy the skirt down her hips and off, I took hold of her smooth thighs and tucked them over my knees. I widened my stance, opening her up to me. Her breathing, which had turned wildly erratic, roughened some more as she waited for my next move.

When I dragged it out, she glanced over her shoulder. A crumb of pastry had caught at the corner of her plump mouth.

I licked it off as my seeking fingers found their prize. She gasped and ground against my hand even as she wrapped her lips around another mouthful. Catching my eye again, she slowly licked the spoon.

And moaned.

'Oh, you're in the mood to tease, huh?'

Sliding beneath the slit of her panties, I flicked her clit. The spoon clattered to the table and she threw her head back against my shoulder with a siren's hiss.

'So fucking wet. So damn needy.' I tortured her little bud until the hissing turned into throaty, desperate moans. Wrapping my arm around her, I pulled her back and nipped at her lobe, her jaw, her throat.

I was leaving teeth marks on her but I didn't care.

Hell, I hoped I marked her in some way so she could remember just who she'd tried to toy with tonight. Who she belonged to.

'If this hungry little cunt wants my cock, you need to lift up for me, *bedda*.'

* * *

Maddelena

My whole body was on fire, the need to come a writhing being inside, screaming for an outlet. Right now, that outlet was his incredible fingers, wreaking havoc on my clit.

But I wanted more. I wanted everything he was promising.

So I used his knees as leverage and hoisted myself up, until I felt his broad head at my heated core. Anticipation seized my breath, froze my whole body. But he didn't drag me down as I hoped. Craved.

'Did you try to talk yourself into believing you don't want me? Is that what happened tonight?' he grated in my ear. His voice was rough with arousal, but it also contained sharp slivers of fury. Cesare was clearly still pissed about me trying to ditch our agreement.

'W-what?'

He rubbed his length up and down my sopping sex. But denied me what I wanted... needed most. *Oh God, he meant to torture me?*

Need tore through me, but I knew better than to take my pleasure when he was in this mood. I would only be prolonging my agony. 'Maybe. Yes. I thought...'

He laughed, low and wicked, his hands digging onto my hips.

Then Cesare yanked me down onto his steel length. I screamed as he filled me to the point of pain.

'You thought you could get me out of your system that easily, babe? Tell that to this pretty cunt strangling my cock like I owe it money.' He bounced me on his shaft, then started fucking me from below like a feral beast.

'I told you you sealed your fate that night in the warehouse. You would've been so much better off running. But you didn't, did you?' He slammed deep, bottomed out inside me so hard, another scream ejected from my throat. The sweet pain of it was chased with so much pleasure, my vision hazed.

'There you go. Why fight when you're already addicted to my cock?'

'I'm... I'm not,' I attempted, desperate to cling to a bit of dignity. To survive this tsunami of pleasure so I could at the very least walk out of here with my head held high.

But already my hips were rolling, chasing him as he withdrew.

'You sure about that? Maybe I should stop then, hmm?'

20

MADDELENA

I accepted in that moment that while Cesare possessed a temper that could turn on a dime, somehow he could also command absolute lethal control when it suited him.

My louder scream of protest only made him laugh again. Then he went one better and stood, his cock still deep inside me. His arm still banding my waist, he marched us to the nearest wall, pulled out, ripped off my panties, and spun me around before hoisting me back onto his rigid length.

Then he went completely still, watching me with deadly focus. Focus that said, at last, he had me where he wanted me.

My fingers dug into his back in a silent plea.

It drew a hiss, then a growl. Then a savage kiss, with gentler ones trailed along my jaw to my ear. But still he pulsed hard and deep inside me, without moving.

Waiting. Waiting.

'Cesare...' I whimpered.

'Yeah, baby?'

I gritted my teeth, desperately trying to keep the word at bay. But it built and built and built. Then, 'Please!'

Dark triumph blazed through his grey eyes, turning them molten silver. 'That's a start. More, baby, I want more.'

My back arched off the wall, clawing arousal running rampant, the desire for satisfaction a drug I was being so viciously denied.

'Please... move!'

'Move where, *cara*?' he taunted. 'Move off? Move sideways?'

Thick amusement didn't disguise his own arousal. Supreme control or not, this was costing him too. A faint tremor shook through him and his nostrils fluttered minutely when I jerked my hips.

That bolstered me enough to shave off a layer of haze. Provide enough clarity to devise a little torture of my own. I blushed at the thought, saw his keen gaze follow the wave of heat sweeping over my cheeks with manic interest.

I didn't even know if this would work but... I drew my hands from his back, threw one arm over my head as I bowed my back deeper, then, clenching my channel hard, I dropped one hand between our sweaty bodies and... touched myself.

He hissed, a deeply animalistic sound that would've terrified me anywhere else but here in his arms, where it seemed I had *some* power.

'Maddelena.' His voice was a growled warning.

But that haze was returning full force, making me reckless. Turning me on so hard and so sharply, I threw caution to the wind. 'What, Cesare? Your little g-game not going your way... after all?'

He captured the fingers sliding dangerously close to my clit, yanking my hand up to join the one above my head, keeping them both trapped with laughable ease.

Then, eyes narrowed into formidable slits, Cesare *moved*.

The first tortuous thrust, pressing me into the wall, was sublime. Bliss rippled through me, tailing off with a deep abiding fear. That he was right. That this could turn into an addiction I couldn't escape.

By his tenth thrust, I was convinced.

Because there was a studied method to Cesare's fucking. With each thrust he gauged my response like a scientist studied the results of an experiment. He gathered the data, stored it away. Then just when I was ready to blow, he slowed down.

Then proceeded to multiply everything he'd learned, deliver it with filthy diatribe that turned me inside out. 'There you go. I feel you getting wetter. You love it when I pound your pretty cunt like this, don't you? You ready to beg some more?'

My head thrashed as he dragged me to the edge one more time. 'Yes! Please, yes!'

He released his death grip from my hip and plucked one painfully budded nipple, then the other, sending wild zings to the inferno building in my sex. 'Will you be a good little slut and come on my cock?'

'God, yes. Just... just don't stop!'

'Open your eyes, Maddelena,' he commanded.

I pried open eyes I didn't remember squeezing shut. Then almost wished I hadn't.

If he'd been feral before, he was absolutely manic now. Sweat on his temples, hair falling onto his eyes, the hard, sensual slash of his mouth. But especially the absolute deadly intent in his eyes. He was a wild beast, and I was ready to surrender to his dominance.

'You get to come, but after we get one small thing out of the way,' he rumbled.

'W-what? Now? Y-you're a fucking monster!' My body couldn't stop thrashing against its denied climax. 'God... please!'

Surprisingly, he lowered his head and kissed me with gentle comfort. 'Trust me, I'm ready to fucking blow too, but this needs taking care of.'

It physically hurt to be denied what my body desperately craved. But he'd locked me in place and since there was nowhere else on earth I'd rather be right in that moment, I sucked in a ragged breath.

'First off, no more trigger-happy plans to bail the second things get hairy, understood?'

I blinked. 'You can... y-you don't get to dictate that. I have more to lose—'

'I can and I will. And we both have something to lose. But this isn't up for debate.'

That savagery from before flashed across his face. A feral threat to anything and anyone who stood in the way of what he wanted. And it seemed, even in the face of danger and the insane risk of a terrifying fallout if our families found out, *I* was what he wanted. I was wrapping my giddy mind around that when he continued.

'Run and I'll find you. Resist and I'll make you regret it. Especially since I have evidence right here that you want this as much as I do. Are we clear?'

I swallowed. 'That sounds suspiciously like a threat, Cesare.'

His eyes darkened. 'I'd prefer it not come to that. And I'd rather not waste time chasing you over something we both want.'

'What if I like being chased?'

'I'd much rather make any chasing required desirable instead of acrimonious.' His head dropped and his mouth covered mine in a filthy kiss that ramped up my already heightened senses and reminded me of all the delicious inches buried inside me. I moaned long and hard like the slut he'd called me. 'Say yes, Maddelena.'

I didn't want to. For a thousand different, *dangerous* reasons.

He was the heir apparent, but for all intents and purposes, he'd already taken control of the Salvatore mafia empire. While I was a mere cog – sure, an important one because my skills ensured the money rolled in the right way and multiplied – but with my grandfather already making plans to snuff out what little freedom I had, my days as a free woman were numbered. And *those* days would disappear completely if he discovered what I was truly doing with his enemy's heir.

I shook my head. 'It's not that easy, Cesare, and you know it.'

His nostrils flared in displeasure. And fraying control. 'If you haven't noticed I'm very good at what I do. I'll take care of the logistics,' he said.

But what happened after we were done?

Would he throw me to the wolves, make our secret tryst public and leave me at the mercy of my father and grandfather? Blood or not, they would flay me alive.

But look where I was right now. I'd already stepped *waaaay* over the line. In Bonafacio's eyes, one sin was as egregious as a dozen. Whichever way I cut it, I was already doomed if he found out.

'And how do I know you won't throw me under the bus when this is all over?' I felt a little horrible asking when he'd surprised me with the plan to thwart Stefano. But Cesare hadn't lost enemy status despite the occasional bouts of consideration. Even kindness.

His eyes darkened and he looked startled, then

offended. Even *hurt*, and my heart lurched. But for some insane reason, his cock thickened inside me, making me gasp.

'Because I told you you're a shit liar.' His gaze pinned mine with untamed intensity. 'Do you still claim innocence?'

'Yes.'

'Then we don't have a problem. You can take my word for it or not.' He watched me for another short stretch. 'Now let's finish our conversation, baby. This requires very little thought because it's not even a negotiation. All it requires is a "Yes, Cesare." Then this pretty, needy cunt gets to milk my cock to your heart's desire.'

Caution scattered to the wind at the throaty promise. For, insanely foolish or not, I believed him that he wouldn't betray me. 'Fine. Yes, Cesare. Now get on with it, damn you!'

'Until this thing ends, you're mine. Anyone comes sniffing around you, you look at another man for longer than two seconds, and they will be put down like a fucking diseased dog, you get me?'

'Yes.' Maybe my response was too quick. Too willing. Whatever. My need reached breaking point five minutes ago. 'Fuck me! Please, fuck me!'

Perhaps it was my imagination, but even as he let

loose another feral smile, Cesare was shattering too. Certainly, the way his neck muscles stood out, his jaw tightly gritted as he started to piston in and out of me like a man possessed, said so.

Incoherent words babbled out of my mouth as I careened back to the precipice. 'Please... Oh God, yes... right there... just like that!'

Then I jumped off. And sweet heaven, the fall was nothing short of spectacular. I came so hard for so long, my spasms flirted with agony but in the best way.

Above me, Cesare's thrusts lost their studied rhythm but not their power. He fucked me through my climax, determination still etched into his face.

'Fuck yeah, strangle me with that tight pussy, baby. Jesus, you feel incredible. I should do this all the time, *si*? Edge you until you're out of your beautiful mind?'

Then he broke completely. '*Fuuuuck!*'

* * *

The transition from wall to shower was seamless and conducted in silence.

But the questions circling like vultures in my head wouldn't be silenced. One slipped free at the tail end of Cesare soaping me up and washing me from head to toe.

'Why were you so pissed off that night in the warehouse? I mean, I know you hated me, but that seemed... next level.'

He stiffened, then glared molten fire at me. 'You really want to do this right now? You're spoiling for a fight that much?'

I spread my arms wide. 'Why the hell not? We've been circling this particular drain for a while now. Why not get it all out in the open?'

His teeth set for several seconds before he exhaled loudly. 'I was fine with leaving you clinging to the lockers or hiding behind your little friend like your life depended on it whenever you saw me coming. Hell, half the time, I forgot you even existed.'

The dent to my pride would've been painful if I didn't know what I knew now. That somehow, Cesare Salvatore was as hooked on me as I was hooked on him. Perhaps there was some truth to my thought about this being some Romeo and Juliet bullshit complex with some macabre twist.

Did Cesare feel that too?

I shook my head to free myself of the voice. 'Only half the time?'

His face darkened with visible displeasure, the

taunt hitting a sore spot. 'You had a very bad habit of following me with those beautiful eyes. They clung just as hard as you clung to the walls.'

My dismissive snort fell a little flat. 'You were... *are* my enemy. I would've been foolish to pretend you didn't exist, as much as I wanted to.'

He laughed, although there was little humour in the conceited sound. 'Yeah, *duci*, let's go with that.'

I huffed in protest. 'So I kept track of you every now and then. So what? You had the same vicious temper then as you do now. Pardon me if I didn't want to be caught in one of your stupid outbursts.'

His eyes blazed and my belly clenched, wondering if I'd taken it too far. But he gained control of himself almost immediately, his caress slow and hypnotic as he continued to wash me.

'So...' I pushed after another minute of silence.

Jaw set, he took my hand, turned it over to examine my fingers with that same ferocious intensity. Then, lifting them to his mouth, he kissed the tips, sending my breathing haywire all over again. His other hand captured my waist, and he dragged me close until my nipples brushed his chest.

Still keeping hold of my fingers, he raised our linked hands to his nape, brushing the skin beneath the curls touching his collar. 'I felt your stare, right here. All the fucking time.' He pressed my fingers into his skin, rubbing back and forth. Back and forth. 'It was annoying... at first.'

My tongue thickened in my mouth, thankfully blocking the trigger-happy questions brimming at the back of my throat from spilling free. *Only at first? What changed? Was it a good thing?*

'But I was willing to chalk it up to our family history.' His mouth twitched again. 'Like you said, an acknowledgement of an enemy or anomaly that didn't belong.'

A sound rumbled from my throat. 'That wasn't what I said. Stop twisting my words.'

'You were beneath my radar,' he continued as if I hadn't spoken. 'But then you went and changed all that, didn't you, *bedda mia*? I touched you and you went and fucking kissed me, stuck that addicting, virgin tongue in my mouth.'

'What makes you think I was a virgin then?' I dared.

It was intentionally provocative. Seeking a reaction. One I got in spades.

His chest swelled with a slow, long inhale as his eyes turned that fascinating molten that said his control was fraying. 'Stop trying to get a rise out of me, baby, or it won't end well for you. You were a virgin,' he insisted. 'I haven't only just recently taken up keeping an eye on the Mancinellis. We knew every breath you lot took, even back then. Granted, one of the few times you slipped away from my spies was that night. If I'd known you'd be there...' He paused, then his mouth flattened. 'We're veering away from what you want to know.

'Which is that you poked the fucking lion that night by indulging in your little game. And you went from here' – he pressed my fingers to his hot skin once more, then dragged them over his shoulder, down his chest... to the packed grouping of muscles above his navel – 'to here.'

It wasn't his... his heart... *Thank God.* I didn't want to be anywhere near Cesare Salvatore's heart. *I absolutely didn't.*

'What are you saying, that I gave you a belly ache? Indigestion?'

He didn't smile. Or chuckle. Or even look mad any more. But his gaze was more direct than it'd ever been. The intent to deliver his message, acute.

'I'm saying you went from an irritant to a hunger, Maddelena. A wild, unquenchable hunger in my gut I haven't been able to shake for almost a decade and a half.' He delivered this with even, deadly intent. 'And that's why, until I do, you will remain mine. Fuck everything and everyone else. Now get on your fucking knees.'

Completely and utterly disarmed by his words, I got on my knees.

Cesare fucked my mouth like he was digging for gold.

Or an extra three-tenths on his favourite racetrack.

'Look at me, Maddelena,' he rumbled. He waited until my watering gaze lifted to meet his. From below, he was a virile, towering inked giant.

A gladiator entirely comfortable in his arena and supremely confident he had his quarry cornered. But his smile was a little strained, his breathing choppy from the way my tongue worked his slit and his shaft, the way I sucked him like my life depended on it.

'You've got everyone fooled, haven't you? You walk around so pious and demure, smiling that serene smile like you're Mona Lisa or your namesake herself. And yet look at you. Here you are, on your knees, swallowing my cock like a dirty little slut.' He pushed inside until his broad head blocked my airways. Held and held and held, then released me with a hoarse shout, the hands braced on the wall curling into fists. 'Fuck, you're too damn good at that.'

The praise, filthy and genuine, went straight to my head. Then reversed direction, lodging with glee between my legs, soaking me and ratcheting my need.

Emboldened, I wrapped one hand around his base and cupped his balls with the other. They were drawn up and tight, ready to blow.

He hissed when I played with them. 'Jesus.' Eyes laced with madness blazed down at me. 'If I ever catch you giving another man this mouth, I'll kill you both. Do you hear me?'

I took my time to suck him deep, then let him pop free. 'As long as I have the same leeway when it comes to another woman.'

The unhinged look intensified. As if the thought of me taking out another woman out of rabid jealousy turned him on. 'You have my permission,' he breathed, his cock astonishingly thickening even fatter.

'Thank you.'

A hint of a smile whispered over his mouth. 'You're welcome. Now make me come, my beautiful slut.'

He drove himself back in. My eyes watered so hard I couldn't make out his features. Obscene noises filled the bathroom as he fucked my mouth roughly.

And I loved every second of it.

21

MADDELENA

I pressed the keycard to the panel and entered my suite, the pulsing aches generously distributed all over my body dragging a lustful sigh. If nothing else, I would sleep like the dead tonight. Hopefully with no—

'Of all the guys in the world, Maddie? Seriously?'

'*Jesus!*'

'Nope, most definitely not him.'

I slapped my hand on the light switch, snatching at the ball of shame building in my gut before it had the chance to erupt. 'First of all, would you stop creeping into my hotel room like some wannabe ninja and just come and knock like a normal person?'

From her position on the end of the living room sofa, she spread her arms wide. She was dressed in a jade-green lounger set that made her hair and eyes pop. 'I did. You weren't here, obviously.'

'So you just broke in and sat in the dark?'

'No, I told the nice receptionist downstairs that we're sharing. And that you'd accidentally taken all keycards with you.'

I snorted. 'Fat chance she believed you. And this room comes with a butler, who also would've known you were lying.'

The corners of her mouth turned down. 'I'm hurt, sis. You don't think we look alike enough to fool people?'

I stared askance at her, then shook my head. Sofiya didn't react well to attention being drawn to her astonishing beauty. More than a few boys had collected bloody noses back in high school just for telling her she was pretty, and I would bet my whole bank balance she'd broken more than one dude's nose since.

'Doesn't matter whether she believed me or not. Your butler took pity on me and let me in, obvs, so...'

'Fine. To what do I owe the pleasure besides your obvious judgement?'

She watched me with eerie stillness. 'What the hell's going on, Mads?'

I swallowed and turned away to ease off my heels. It bought me a laughable ten seconds. 'Should I not be asking you that? Apparently, I'm the last to know everything around here, including the plans being made for my fucking life.'

This time she wasn't quick enough. I caught the tailcoats of guilt as it fled her face.

Her perfect eyebrows arched. 'You're turning this around on me? Nice.'

I tossed my purse on the bed and whirled to face her. 'I love you, Sofiya. But seriously, could you drop the tough girl shit and have some damn compassion for a moment and tell me what the fuck is going on?'

Her expression sobered at the weariness and, yeah, my deep sadness I didn't bother to hide.

'You know what I'd wanted more than anything when we were growing up? For you and me to be best friends. To share everything, from nail polish to how shitty it was growing up in that gilded cage disguised as a home.'

She scowled faintly, taken aback. 'You had Ciara.'

I shrugged. 'Yeah, but her father was our junior lieutenant. I loved her but she had a grass-is-always-greener mentality I couldn't shift. She thought I was lucky to be Bonafacio's first-born granddaughter and had it made.' My laughter seared my throat. 'She had no idea I would've given anything to have a different surname. But you, despite your nothing-can-touch-me-ness and...' I waved a hand at her, and her frown deepened. 'You and I knew how bad things were. *Are.* Just as Giada and Jacinta understood eventually the life we'd been born into. We had zero freedom as women, and complaining got us punished. Or worse, got Mama punished for not doing enough to keep us in our place. I thought you and I...' I shook my head. 'I thought you were a loner, but I know you're not. Not with Ciso.'

She winced and her jaw set. 'So I was a shitty sister who disappointed you because I didn't want to be besties?'

I sighed. 'I don't... Look, I'm not sure why you don't like me—'

She blinked. 'What? Of course I like you. You're my sister.'

'And yet you've never had my back. And you've never needed me to have yours. Why's that?'

She reached up and tugged on a lock of hair at her nape. My eyes widened. I hadn't seen her do that since she was about fifteen. 'Maddie...'

'It's fine, Sof.'

'Obviously it's not or you wouldn't be bringing it up,' she griped under her breath. 'Look, I just wasn't... I had a different way of handling my shit, okay? And I... I didn't know you wanted... that. You seem tight with Ciara. And Bona warned me not to get close because of...' She cringed.

My heart bled. 'Because I could blurt out family secrets on any given night?' Having my suspicions confirmed hurt like the devil. But I crossed to the room to perch on the end of the bed. 'Are you going to tell me why you're really here? Why you came to my hotel room in Baku City, too?'

Her gaze swept to the side, and she stared out of the window for a long stretch. When she looked back at me, I spotted uncertainty on her face.

'Sof?'

'Yes. I wanted to warn you...'

My heart jumped into my throat, blocking any effort to speak until I forcefully cleared it and leaving the space in my chest a little numb. 'About what?'

'I think you know. Bonafacio has plans for you.'

The numbness was spreading like ice over a wound. But the thing was, it was temporary. Once the ice thawed, the devastation would wreck me. 'But you didn't tell me. Why?'

Her nose twitched with a thwarted grimace. 'Because I wanted to buy you some time by dragging things out a little. I managed, by the way. Barely.'

My head felt too heavy to nod. But the question blazed in my eyes.

'You and the heir have a history.' She shrugged, crossed and recrossed her legs. 'I thought maybe you wanted to have a little fun with him first, while everyone still thinks you're working him to our advantage,' she said, her eyes locked on my face. 'Did you?'

Heat built, fast and furious, cutting through the numbness with a vivid replay of the filthy decadence Cesare had visited on me, and the eager abandon with which I'd welcomed it.

It was my turn to drop my gaze, to corral my fracturing composure. An almost impossible task when even now, I felt the insistent throb deep inside me at his rough possession. The screams he'd dragged from my soul.

'And here I thought you wanted to be besties,' Sofiya huffed after a minute, mistaking my silence for reluctance to answer. 'Don't besties share that sort of thing?' she asked, her tone attempting humour that fell flat. Probably because she still hadn't fully divulged what she'd come here to say. What I feared would shatter me.

'I...' I glanced down at my hand and grimaced. 'Fun wouldn't be how I'd describe it.'

Her sharp inhale snapped my head up. 'He fucking hurt you?'

'No! It wasn't like that at all,' I hastened to tell her. Then I cringed inwardly at my rabid defence of Cesare.

'Okay. So then what was it like?' she pressed, probably not realising she was leaning forward in her chair. Or that her eyes were sparkling with wild curiosity, not the judgement she'd first levelled on me when I entered.

My eyes widened. 'You really want to know, don't you?'

She tried to shrug it off, but her face pinked. And she fluttered her hand.

I smirked, absurdly happy to see my unflappable sister so flustered. And yes, I realised I was also grasping at any reason to delay opening the black door and confronting the bottomless chasm that awaited me in the form of an arranged, unwanted marriage.

'Yeah, fine. So?'

My eyes widened further. 'Sofiya... are you a virgin?'

She jumped to her feet, rushed to the French doors, threw them open and stepped out.

Laughing, I followed. 'What, you'd rather throw yourself off the fifty-second floor than answer my question?'

She gripped the railing and peered over it. 'Definitely thinking about it, yeah.'

I gently took her wrist and steered her around to face me. 'I'm not a virgin, obviously. But if it helps, up until a couple of nights ago I was as good as one. And considering our background, I think it's entirely understandable. There's no judgement here, okay?'

She nodded after a few seconds.

I led her back into the suite.

Crossing over to the wine selection the butler had arranged on the cabinet, I plucked the first red – Sicilian, of course – and grabbed the electric opener.

It whined, then gave a satisfying pop. I let it breathe for all of a minute while Sofiya grabbed two glasses.

I poured and she raised her glass, eyeing me as she took a large gulp. 'The night has taken a definite turn for the unexpected. So, spill.'

I cast around for appropriate words to describe

my experience without divulging sordid details. Because yes, I intended to jealously guard them.

Leaning a hip against the cabinet, I winced when the movement reminded me just how sordid my night had been. 'I can definitely say he is as much of a hotshot in the bedroom as he is on the racetrack. Pole position all the way.'

Her eyes searched mine and I didn't mind the bite of jealousy I saw in her eyes. Sofiya was the prettiest Mancinelli granddaughter, after all. 'It was that good?'

I smiled, knowing she would never admit Cesare's talent in public, and especially not to Ciso. Recalling his hands, his teeth, his tongue, his delicious cock, I caught my bottom lip between my teeth to stifle a moan and nodded. 'Better than good.'

She kept on staring for a stretch longer, then transferred her gaze to her glass. 'He's not my favourite person for obvious reasons, but... I'm glad he was good to you.'

And just like that, the reprieve was gone. I stopped my fingers from curling too tight around my glass. Lifting it, I drained it in three large gulps and set it down with a hard click. 'Tell me, Sof.'

She braced one shoulder against the pillar next to the cabinet, running one finger along the glass rim, her gaze actively avoiding mine. 'He's found a husband for you. He plans to get you hitched by Christmas.'

I reached out to brace my hand on the cabinet.

Why now? Why didn't you tell me? Why do you know and I don't? Why, why—

'Why?' I hated that my voice wobbled a little, and I blamed it on the wine I'd consumed tonight. Shame it wasn't doing a damn thing to make my head fuzzy enough to fool me that this was some twisted Kubrick dream. No, I was fully compos mentis in this nightmare.

'It's been coming for years. You know that. And lately, he's been talking about great-grandchildren. He thinks you're getting too old. That people are beginning to talk.'

I shook my head in dismay. 'Of course. How long have you known?'

She shut her eyes and exhaled. 'About a year.'

Something hard and brittle cracked in my chest. It probably wasn't my heart because that was still lodged in my throat. My soul? Maybe. 'Jesus. Sofiya.'

She set her glass down and grabbed my upper arms. 'Trust me, this is far more time than I thought I'd be able to buy you.'

My breath stuttered. 'Really?'

She nodded. 'Yeah. He asked me to look into the candidate. To see if there was some leverage to be had considering your... issue.'

My small issue of sleepwalking and spilling family secrets.

'I dragged my feet. Until I couldn't.'

A borderline hysterical laugh left my throat. 'The *candidate*? Does he have a name, or shall I just call him that as and when I'm deemed worthy enough to meet the stranger my grandfather has picked to saddle me to?'

Her mouth firmed at my caustic tone. 'Bonafacio wants to tell you himself.'

I snatched myself out of her arms. 'I'm asking you! I guess it's down to who you love more, Sofiya. Or is that a redundant question? After all, you've been running around helping him plot the rest of my life behind my back! Is that where you've been disappearing to?'

Her face hardened. 'Mostly. And that's not fair. You fucking know why we – every single one of us – jump to Bonafacio's tune. And FYI, I dragged things out because yeah, I wanted to buy you time to... I don't know, maybe enjoy life for a second. And because I knew the second you were hitched, it would be my turn. So yeah, I was being both selfish and selfless. You fought tooth and nail to join the racing crew, but every time I've seen you, you've looked unhappy. Sombre. But now it looks like you've found some excitement. You've got some colour in your cheeks. You're welcome!'

Uneasy silence rang through the suite, like the eerie echo left behind after the mistimed clang of a tuning fork.

After another minute, she exhaled heavily, flicked me a glance and tugged on another lock of hair.

I sighed. 'Thank you. I guess.'

She glared at me for a fistful of heartbeats. Then her mouth twitched. But sobering reality soon threatened to suffocate us.

I licked my lip, despising the question I wished I didn't have to ask. 'When is he planning on telling me?'

'He's heard that Orazio plans on announcing his eightieth birthday plans soon. Nonno wants to steal his thunder. Wedding trumps birthday.'

'Seriously? Why the hell am I surprised by the infuriating pettiness of it any more?'

I opened my mouth to tell her what Cesare asked about the Russian connection, but the words wouldn't come out. Because... because...

I couldn't quite bring myself to admit the reason so I pushed it away. Besides... 'You said mostly.'

She stiffened. 'What?'

'When I asked, just now... you said "mostly". Why else have you been disappearing, Sof?'

She crossed the room and briskly pushed her feet into her sneakers. When she looked up, the carefully neutral expression was back in place. 'It's private, Maddie.'

Maybe it was, but I sensed it was more than just privacy shoving her guard back up. My heart thudded. 'Is it Giada?' I whispered. *Hoping.* Very few people knew the whereabouts of our little sister and it hurt deeply that she was being kept from us. Because no matter how ridiculously dysfunctional it was, our family wasn't whole without her.

Bonafacio near enough lost his mind anytime any of us dared to ask, so we mostly never did. And with every week, month, year, I desperately feared my baby sister risked becoming a hazy memory. An abandoned and forgotten inconvenience.

Sofiya's expression fractured for a moment before she snatched back control. 'No, it's not. I have to go.' She approached long enough to brush a kiss on my cheek before hurrying to the door. There, she paused. 'I'll just say this though. While Bona and the other men think you're disrupting the enemy rather than just getting laid, you're good.' She eyed me solemnly. 'But that window is fast closing, so you need to come up with a helluva good explanation before they find out otherwise.'

Fear and savage rejection warred in my chest at the thought of losing what I'd just discovered with Cesare.

Juliet. Anna. Isolde. *Now Maddelena?*

I'd only indulged in the forbidden twice with Cesare and already I was crazed at the idea of it ending. At the idea of lying down and letting life – and other *men's* will – just happen to me.

'Will you be heading back home with Ciso?' Sofiya asked when I remained silent.

The gaze I lifted to her felt heavy. My soul was shattering. 'Do I have a choice?'

She left without answering.

But it turned out I had a choice. A sleepless night and restless pacing churned out one option.

It was a stupidly dangerous one.

But a *choice* nonetheless.

22

CESARE

'I'm taking the plane,' I announced as I pulled out the dining chair and sat down. I placed my phone face down so I wouldn't be tempted to look at the screen, only to pick it back up ten seconds later.

Crap, I should've left it in the bedroom. But I didn't want to miss Maddelena's next text. Especially if it showed signs of her changing her mind.

I was learning she had a habit of second-guessing herself and attempting to wriggle out of agreements hours after they'd been made.

Well, there was no light of day remorse and definitely no take-backsies on the eye-raising text she'd hit me with two hours after she left my hotel room last night.

Am I still in your crosshairs?

Is that impatience or surrender?

It's a desire to disappear... for a while.

Are you asking me to take you somewhere, bedda?

A long pause before...

Would you?

Hell, yeah.

Yes. But a time, location and duration of my choosing. Agreed?

A shorter pause.

Agreed.

The euphoria that filled me then rivalled every race win so far.

> Pack your bags. We leave in the morning.

I'd immediately put the plans in place. Hence the shocked faces staring back at me at the breakfast table.

'What do you mean, you're taking the plane?' Dante asked.

'I mean you'll need to find your own transport home. You were going to have to anyway, since Rafa's taking the other plane.'

'But we were hoping to catch a ride with you,' he replied, exchanging a horrified look with his twin.

'So you want us to, like... fly *commercial*?' Renzo said that like it was a dirty word the nuns at Sunday school would've boxed his ears for as a kid.

'That or take a fucking boat. Don't give a fuck. You're grown men. I'm sure you can work it out.'

Rafa, who hadn't taken his eyes off me since my announcement, twirled his coffee cup. 'And where exactly will you be taking the plane, if you don't mind my asking?'

Compulsion dragged my eyes to the phone, then I met his gaze. 'I do mind you asking, as a matter of fact.'

He tensed, his usually steady gaze sharpening as he tried to read me.

His eyes flicked to the twins, and I knew he was dying to get me alone so he could grill me. I reached for a fat croissant, slathered it with butter and bit into it, relishing the decadence. It tasted nowhere near as incredible as Maddelena's pussy, but I planned on reacquainting myself with that sublime taste before noon.

I blocked out the twins' grumbling about the inconvenience I'd dumped in their laps, pretty sure one of them would call Bibi within the next five minutes to whine about the injustice.

Rafaelle, however...

Sure enough, the second the twins leapt from the table to chase down our sister, he leaned back in his seat, propping one ankle on his knee. 'What the fuck is going on?' he asked with deceptive calm.

'I'm taking a little detour before heading home.'

'With her?'

My nostrils flared. 'You know the answer to that so why are you bothering to ask?'

He exhaled audibly and stared into the middle distance for several beats before he glanced back at me. 'What I'm about to say are words I thought would never cross my lips but... aren't you worried that all this... *trysting* will draw attention to her? Have you thought at all about the danger you're putting her in? El Topo won't take kindly to discovering you're banging his granddaughter. And that unhinged fucker will not hesitate to take his fury out on her as much as on you.'

My gut clenched. Hard. Because it *had* crossed my mind. More than a few times. And my knee-jerk response to that was becoming set in stone. Which was that I couldn't... *wouldn't* let her go. And I would ensure she remained safe... while she was with me.

My shrug felt stiff and starchy. 'They think it's the other way around, that she's leading me around by my dick. For now we... I'm letting them believe that.'

His brows spiked. 'And then what?'

'Let it go, brother. I'll handle it. But keep the rounding up of the traitors quiet, would you? I don't want the Mancinellis to know we're onto them just yet.'

He frowned. 'I'm a miracle worker, sure, but you're assuming Stan Paul hasn't blabbed by now.'

'He's a fucking coward. He'll hunker down until the ship starts sinking.'

'You're basing a lot on assumptions, *frate*—'

'And you're bordering on disrespect. So enough

already.' Yeah, I was pulling rank just so I didn't have to hear the truth of what he was saying, which was that this particular racing car was headed straight for a concrete wall. That at best I had a matter of weeks before it all unravelled. Because I sure as shit wasn't going to lose a race just so the Mancinellis would believe their moles were still in place.

And once Stefano realised Maddelena wasn't the saboteur they wanted her to be, shit would truly hit the fan.

Rafa sighed. 'Tell me you're at a least bringing Fist with you?'

My mouth twitched into a grin. 'He'll hunt me down and smother me to death with those baseball-mitt fists if I don't.'

* * *

Maddelena

I double-checked the hotel room out of habit for anything I'd left behind, even though the butler had been exceptional in his duties, including getting my things packed within half an hour of my informing him I would be checking out a day early.

The text I'd sent to Cesare on a desperate whim last night had set a wild chain of events in motion. I didn't realise the sheer lunacy of it or whether he would even be on board with it until he'd replied thirty seconds later, and my breath whooshed out before I burst out laughing with the hysteria trapped in my chest.

Even before the echo of Sofiya's footsteps had faded I knew I wasn't on board with simply handing myself over to my grandfather's whims.

Not after what I'd learned.

Not after what Cesare had made me feel.

Whatever fate awaited me after this interlude of *sui generis*, I would either accept or rebel some more. Funny, I hadn't quite made up my mind which way I'd go. But if Bonafacio was this blasé about losing the services of his moneywoman, reducing me to a faceless stranger's housewife only good for breeding the next generation of Mancinellis, then he deserved a taster of what life would be like without me.

'Your bags have been loaded and the car is ready for you downstairs, Miss.'

I examined my reflection in the giant living room mirror, checking for signs of the terror lurking within.

Outwardly, I looked calm and collected, my bold gold and white Dolce & Gabbana sundress showing off my lightly tanned shoulders, arms, and a respectable amount of cleavage. I straightened the tasteful hoop earrings and slid on oversized Celine sunglasses.

My shaky breath seemed to burrow all the way to my heels, and when I exhaled, out came a layer or two of fear.

Last night, Cesare had as much as admitted Liv Ivanovski was behind the sabotage, possibly with the full blessing of Bonafacio.

In a moment of panic, I'd wondered if that would be the end of his interest in me. Having him fall on me straight after, and gorging himself on me for hours after that, had allayed my panic.

But then he'd accepted my departure with zero complaint, merely lying back in bed, his powerful biceps flexing as he tucked his hands behind his head and watched me dress. Hell, he hadn't even asked me when I intended to leave Singapore.

Was that why I made the insane proposal? Or had I played perfectly into his hands?

What the hell did it matter?

'Thank you, Sam.' I smiled, tucked my yellow Birkin into the crook of my elbow and followed him into the lift. If he was surprised my minders weren't shadowing me, he didn't show it.

I'd texted Sofiya an hour ago with a request for her to take care of them. I didn't know how she had but I was grateful.

I plucked out my phone when I reached the ground floor. What I was doing was pure insanity but while I had a crumb of common sense left, I'd at least put some precautions in place.

When I spotted Cesare outside, leaning against his Bentley SUV, my footsteps faltered to a stop. He looked menacingly *divine* in a black shirt opened at the throat and sleeves folded back to reveal those brawny hair-dusted arms that had pinned me so deliciously to his bed last night. Black slacks and his customary Italian loafers completed the look.

Despite the busy foyer, his fierce gaze zeroed in on me. He clocked my hesitation, and his jaw rippled. *Come to me*, his gaze growled. *Now*.

One foot moved, the compulsion irresistible.

Shit, I was really doing this.

Resuming walking, I typed quickly before I lost my nerve.

I've decided not to head straight home.

I'm taking the week. Be in touch when I can.

Love you. Mx

With his sunglasses dangling from his fingers, he watched me with predatory focus, nodding at the phone I was slotting back into my purse when I reached touching distance. 'Who was that?' he growled.

'I was texting my sister.'

One corner of his mouth tilted. 'What's the point? You don't know where I'm taking you. And I'm thinking you've either turned off your phone or are about to, so you can't be reached?'

It was scary how intuitive he was. But then I shouldn't have been surprised. That single-minded precision and instinct had won him two championships. And if he'd indeed succeeded in flushing out his traitors, he could win a third. 'No comment,' I quipped.

He straightened, waved Fist away and opened the back door himself. 'Get in the fucking car,' he rasped. His hand slid from the small of my back to my ass when I didn't move fast enough, squeezing the flesh he'd spanked before helping me up. 'Now, *bedda.*' My gasp earned me a wicked grin. 'That's for sassing me.'

He slid in after me, slammed the door and immediately yanked me onto his lap, unbalancing me. He ignored my yelp and spanked my bottom again as his head descended to brush the tip of my nose with his. 'And that was for not saying hello properly.'

'I didn't say it at all,' I corrected.

'Exactly.'

The mechanical whine of the privacy partition didn't even distract me. I crawled over him, threw one leg over his lap, and braced my knees on either side of his hips.

His hands immediately cupped my ass and yanked me down onto the straining erection behind his fly. My hands landed on his shoulders and I almost groaned at the volcanic arousal in his eyes. I was growing irreparably addicted to that look. It made me feel more powerful than I had in a long time. *If ever.*

'How far to the airport?' I asked, my fingers delving into the hair at his nape.

A shiver coursed through him when my nails scraped his scalp. 'Doesn't matter. The plane takes off when I say so. And the doors to this vehicle open when

I want them to. Whatever you want to start, sweetheart, go right ahead.' His voice was strained and hoarse, his gaze pinging between my tits and mouth like he wasn't sure which body part he wanted to devour first.

Another wave of drugging power swept through me. I didn't fool myself into thinking it would tip the balance. Cesare's dominance was merely taking a backseat. But I intended to revel in this sweet reign for as long as I could.

Leaning closer, I rubbed my chest against him, knowing he could feel the hardened peaks. 'Good morning, Cesare,' I crooned, adding a slow roll of my hips over his stiff rod.

He groaned, his eyes dropping to my cleavage. 'Hey, beautiful. Did you miss me?'

'I don't know. Can't you tell for yourself?'

His nails dug into my ass and my pussy dampened, shamelessly and eagerly. 'Nah. I'm gonna need a little more evidence.'

Without preamble, I smashed my mouth to his, moaning when he immediately parted my lips to stroke his tongue against mine. It was sinful how quickly he could drag me under his spell, turn me into putty.

Arms locked around his neck, I met him stroke

for stroke, taste for taste, until the need to come up for air drove us apart.

His heated eyes immediately delved back to my chest. One hand left my ass to slide one thin sleeve down one arm, then the other, his mouth dropping open when he saw I wasn't wearing a bra.

'Fuck. I love that I don't know whether I'm getting the demure Catholic girl who barely knows the wonders of her pussy or the siren who confidently walks around with her beautiful tits one flimsy layer away from my mouth.'

'Which do you prefer?'

'Do you even need to ask? I'm a greedy motherfucker. I'm all in for both.'

'You are?'

He tweaked both nipples. I gasped as delight jerked through me.

'I'm a jaded man, Maddelena. The pleasures of the world are mine to command at my fingertips. But this... Fuck, I can't work out why the fuck you fascinate me so much and I'm discovering, maybe I don't need to. Maybe the magic is in the surprise.'

Last night he'd talked about keys and unlocking my secrets.

I had a feeling Cesare was a lot closer than he knew.

Because while his words were skewed towards sex, their meaning travelled higher than my pussy, bypassing the hunger in my gut to lodge alarmingly close to my heart.

The thought was unbearable.

It was dangerous. Forbidden.

It was foolish.

He was my enemy.

I couldn't fall for him.

We were risking a fresh, all-out family war that would leave countless casualties and broken souls, like the last skirmish did to Giada.

Yet I craved him with every fibre of my being so desperately in that moment, I seriously considered if there was anything I wouldn't do for it.

Luckily, Cesare had other plans that didn't include me examining my feelings too closely. Still toying with my nipples, plucking and tweaking, he grunted, 'Unzip me, baby. Take me out.'

I rushed to unzip him and reach inside for my prize. We both groaned when I wrapped my hand around him. Just about. I'd barely managed to stroke him a few times, spread his pre-cum over his wide crown, before he issued the next instruction.

'Now lift up your dress, baby. And I swear, you better be wearing fucking panties.'

'Or what?' I sassed, then gasped when he pinched my nipples. *Hard.*

But I was learning I wasn't averse to a bit of pain. So it was no surprise when I grew even wetter.

'It's a long flight. You want to be able to sit down at some point, although there are alternatives to that. But it's totally up to you if you want to board my plane with a spanked ass.'

I was wearing panties, because that Catholic upbringing allowed rebellion only to a point, and strolling through a busy hotel with dozens of guests while totally naked beneath my dress was too sinful for my blood.

What about what you're doing now?

My heart squeezed painfully at the question, but that too I stuffed into the 'to be examined later' box.

Still stroking him because he was beautiful and I was addicted, I tugged up the hem of my dress, arranged it high up so he could see the silk lace I had on underneath.

He drew a knuckle along my seam. 'Look at you, already soaked for me. You walked across that hotel lobby like this, didn't you, hungry for my cock?'

'Yes,' I moaned.

His head dropped and he flicked his tongue across one nipple, then sucked it into his mouth.

'Oh God.'

He toyed it with his teeth, then released it for a second. 'Good?'

'So good,' I cried.

'Are you sore from last night?' he asked, and that foolish, dangerous sensation swelled higher at his tender consideration.

'A little,' I replied, ignoring the heat consuming my face. 'But I can take it. I want it.'

'Then let's make it even better. Push your panties to the side, baby. Show me how well you can take my cock.'

I was a simpering fool by the time I raised my hips and notched him at my core. My fingers digging into his nape to steady myself in the swaying car, I held my breath. And sank down onto him.

His head snapped up long enough to catch my tiny scream as he surged deep to bottom out in the best possible way.

God, it felt so, so good!

'Fuck!' His choppy breathing played like a symphony to my ears. 'I'm growing seriously addicted to you, you know that?'

Did I say I needed to throttle my power? Be sensible about celebrating it? Because right in this moment I wanted to dance in the deluge until I was soaked to the marrow. *Fuck the danger.*

I forgot I was in a moving car, that a simple pane of possible soundproof glass separated us from an audience. I was utterly consumed by Cesare Salvatore and not a single bone in my body was sorry.

And needless to say I didn't take in a single sight of the scenery until we arrived at the private hangar where his jet waited, ready to whisk us to our dangerous, forbidden adventure.

23

MADDELENA

'The Maldives?'

'Yes. It's a four-and-a-half-hour flight. Minimum interruptions. And best of all, we'll be surrounded by water so you can't get away from me that easily,' Cesare said.

The hand gliding down my naked back was lazy but his gaze was anything but. Since our heated exchange in the shower last night, his intensity – already head-wrecking – had increased.

He probably sensed I wasn't telling him everything, and hell, I wasn't sure he was entitled to know. Or perhaps more accurately, I wasn't sure how he would react so I was holding on to the fact that my grandfather had all but given me away to some Sicilian stranger like a sack of grain.

'I see.'

One eyebrow quirked. 'Not even a token protest? You're slipping, *bedda*.'

I shrugged, my muscles protesting languidly at the exercise they'd been put through for the last few hours.

I'd officially joined the mile high club. And yes, there was something wildly decadent about fucking at thirty-five thousand feet.

After boarding, and with a cursory greeting to his pilot and crew, Cesare had bundled me into the back of his jet, where the king-sized bed had been put to vigorous use.

We'd surfaced in the last hour to eat and hydrate at his insistence so I didn't pass out. Only after eating had he finally divulged our destination.

A four-and-a-half-hour flight was good. There was no risk of falling asleep. No risk of exposing flaws and family secrets. 'Why protest, when it's one of my favourite places in the world?'

Scepticism lingered but it was soon overtaken by approval. Satisfaction, even. Before his eyes narrowed and his grip tightened on my ass. 'When and who with?' he growled.

Delight shivered through me, and yup, I was accepting that the primal and possessive jealousy Cesare wasn't bothering to hide any more since the debauched incident in the bathroom last night turned me on. That any sign that he was as deeply into me as I was into him made my chest fizz with joy. Made all this rebellion worth it.

No, I wasn't going to think about that.

'A clutch of siblings and far too much security taking over a resort for my twenty-fifth birthday.' A handful of months before the deadly incident that had locked the Mancinellis down in our Connecticut compound for the better part of a year, while the Salvatores went on a vengeance rampage. One of the last times I'd seen Giada smile and laugh and be carefree before she'd been decimated by trauma.

A layer of intensity eased from his face, and Cesare's caress resumed. He lowered his head and dropped a kiss on my shoulder. 'I'll make sure this one is equally memorable.'

I was humming with delight when he asked, 'Does your uncle make a habit of throwing you under the bus?'

I stiffened at the curveball change of subject. 'Why do you ask?'

'Because he seems like the type. And because I'm not going to allow it.'

Yeah, he was wrecking me systematically with these displays of violence-tinged chivalry – an act I would've never have seen myself endorsing, but go figure...

I squeezed my eyes shut as his fingers slid between my cheeks, the destination my sopping centre. If he meant to make me melt, bend me to his will, well, he was succeeding. And I was plenty pissed with Stefano to say, 'He hates that I'm consigliere. I'm a woman and I'm younger than he is. As Bonafacio's son, he believes the role should've gone to him. So, yes. Throwing me under the bus when it suits him doesn't cause him too much heartache.' I was also fairly sure he would've fully endorsed Bonafacio's plans to have me shackled and bred by next year just to get me out of the way.

'But why would you want to save me from my *pazzo* uncle?' I pushed when maybe I should've shut up. Enjoyed the next impending orgasm sweetly and slowly winding towards me. 'Letting Stefano take his wrecking ball to me is to your advantage, isn't it?'

A flicker of menacing rage washed over his face, but he didn't stop his caress. 'If you deserved it, absolutely. Do you deserve it, *bedda*?'

My heart lurched and I squeezed my eyes shut so the excess emotions overwhelming me didn't show. 'Stop playing knight in shining armour, Cesare. It confuses me.'

Again, he froze. Long enough that I opened my eyes, met his sizzling stare.

'What?' I prompted, my heart picking up its rollercoaster pace.

'I just tried that on for size. And while I want to say fuck no, I'm no one's knight... I'm not averse to making an exception. This once. For you.'

Oh. God. 'Why?'

The corner of his mouth twitched. 'Fuck if I know, baby.' His fingers delved deep, curled until I saw stars. Then he shook his head. 'That's a lie. The hunger is still there. Hell, it's grown. It's infuriating as hell, but... I also like it. Like this.' His fingers resumed their torture, curling and scissoring, seeking and finding pleasure spots only he could. 'I love watching you melt into your pleasure, knowing I'm the one to give it to you. It's a fucking addicting power I'm not ready to relinquish. So yes, for as long as I need you fully participant in it, anyone who distresses you feels the full force of my wrath. No exceptions.'

I was climbing him even before his words were

complete. Rolling him onto his back and planting my hands on his shoulders.

He didn't laugh or mock my voracious hunger, the overwhelming emotions driving me to the brink of insanity. Instead his eyes blazed with unhinged hunger of his own, his nails digging into my hips as I positioned him at my entrance and plunged with a feral scream.

The pace I set was blistering, stunning the hell out of myself, knowing I would be sore as fuck when this was over, and not caring a single iota.

'That's it. Ride me, baby. Take your pleasure.'

Hoarse cries echoed around the cabin, my madness overtaking me as I bounced on his rock-hard cock with a deliriousness that felt out of this world. And right when I was on the brink, I wasn't surprised at all when he shackled me with both arms, dragged me low until my breasts were plastered on his chest.

'I own you, Maddelena. Don't I?'

Yes. God above, yes. He did. 'Yes!'

'I own this cunt? This mouth? This insanely beautiful body? It's mine to do with as I please, isn't it?'

'Yes! Yes, yes!'

'Do you want to come?'

'Please! Yes!'

'On the count of three. One. Two... Now!'

I exploded.

Triggering his low, animalistic growl that built until it culminated in 'Mine!' as he found his own release.

As I struggled to catch my breath, I heard the echo of his claim in the deranged sprint of my heart.

His. His. His.

* * *

My nerves were devouring me alive.

I'd banked on the destination resort having more than a suite or chalet and to my relief, it did. Just about. Because the private two-storey, three-bed-room overwater residence was set apart from the main resort and had two smaller chalets attached, presumably for staff.

And even before I opened my mouth to make my request, I knew I'd have a battle on my hands. But exhaustion was seeping at me, so I had no choice.

'Something bothering you, *bedda*?' Cesare asked. His stare had grown increasingly demanding over the last hour, after a sublime sunset dinner where I wore the tiniest bikini known to man and he wore briefs that broadcasted how turned on he was. The residence faced the sea and his staff had been banished to one of the smaller chalets. 'Need another ride on my dick?' he half-joked with a smile that set my heart racing for a different reason.

That addiction he'd talked about on the plane was in no way one-sided. Hell, I feared I was more addicted than he was. It would've been the most perfect completion to the day to give in, knowing I could fall asleep in his arms after.

But I forced a head shake. 'No. I mean yeah, but...' I bit my tongue, cursing my stupid blush as he laughed and rose from his seat. Going to the extensive bar, he mixed another pina colada for me and poured himself another MacCallan 21.

Taking it, I murmured my thanks, then cleared my throat and bit the bullet. 'I want a separate chalet.'

He froze on his way back to his chair. 'Over my fucking dead body is that happen—'

'That's my one request, Cesare. I mean it. I know what I agreed to. And it didn't include me sleeping in your bed twenty-four-seven.'

His eyes narrowed, and that unique way of single-mindedly focusing on me made my pulse skip. 'Let me get this straight. You'll jump on my plane with me to the middle of the Indian Ocean, fuck me whenever you please, share meals with me. But you won't sleep in my fucking bed? Is this some independence thing? Do you turn into a crone at night or something?'

I shrugged. 'Or something,' I said, then forced a huff. 'Look, I don't like anyone sharing my space for extended periods, all right?'

Something flashed across his face. Like I'd offended him. Upset him. Which was absurd, right?

'No, not fucking all right. What are you not telling me, Maddelena?' he murmured, low and seductive, but deadly serious with it.

'Nothing. It's just... what I want.'

'Look at me,' he commanded.

I forced my gaze up to hold his, praying I passed this test. Because if I didn't...

Two fingers trailed over my jaw, his face still hard. Over to the centre of my chin before rising to rub over my pursed lips. When he applied a little pressure, I opened up for him. His gaze dropped to watch his fingers slide over my teeth to flick over my tongue.

'Suck,' he ordered.

With a helpless moan, I closed my mouth over his digits, sucked on them like they were my favourite dessert.

I barely heard the clunk of his glass as he set it on the table, but I definitely felt the insistent tug of my bikini top as he bared my breast. Caught my nipple between his fingers. And set me on another road to nirvana.

But just when I thought the subject I'd been dreading was over, he kissed the corner of my still-sucking mouth. 'You're lying. Tell me the truth, Maddelena,' he whispered.

I tried to jerk free. The move pulled on my captured nipple, and incredibly, shamefully, sent a fresh wave of need straight between my legs. 'Uhmm... nnn.'

He watched me with almost unfeeling eyes, then slowly pulled his fingers from between my lips. 'Speak.'

'I'm not...' I repeated, fervently hoping he blamed the heat in my face for outrage. 'We've been going at it quite a lot. I'm... sore,' I plucked out of thin air. It was only partly true and, Jesus, given the choice, I would've ignored my throbbing pussy and the uncomfortable chafing I felt whenever I moved, just for the chance of sleeping in Cesare's arms.

But I couldn't.

He released his vicious grip on my nipple, his nostrils flaring. 'You're sore. And you think I'm such a monster I would insist on fucking you when you're in pain?'

Shame doused my heat, making me squirm in my seat. 'I didn't... say that.'

Ice and disappointment slowly tightened his face, and my heart dropped through the floor. 'Even if you thought that, we have a perfectly adequate second bedroom. But you want your own chalet.' His tone was flat. Cold.

'Cesare... I—'

He surged to his feet, snatched his glass off the table and turned his back on me. 'Fist will have your things moved.' He strolled over to the edge of the terrace, planted his elbows onto the railing, and fixed his gaze on the orange and purple sunset.

I'd been dismissed. This was what I wanted, right?

Except my feet were lead stumps that weighed me down with each step to scoop up my beach coverup and glasses.

As ever, Fist, with his weird bat signal radar, was waiting for me when I reached the hallway leading to the bedroom. He held out my purse, his dead eyes resting steadily on me. My dainty Birkin looked so ridiculous in his meaty fist it was funny. But I couldn't summon humour.

'The boys will vacate the place next door. You should be all good there. We'll bring your stuff in ten minutes.'

The thing with Fist was that you could never tell if he was happy or sad about a situation. So I didn't even bother to read which way he swung in this particular one. With my heart thudding in protest like I was dragging it through a lake of sticky molasses, I nodded, took my purse and headed for the front door.

* * *

Cesare

It was a little thing.

Inconsequential.

Something I'd done myself to countless faceless women in the past when I was done fucking them. And yet, I was equal parts furious and... *Cristu*, was I actually *hurt*? The very idea of it made me gulp down a mouthful of cognac and immediately return for a refill.

My eyes fell to the glass of frilly pina colada she'd left untouched, and my mood face-planted all over again. What the fuck?

My head whipped around when I heard movement, my heart doing an actual fucking leap at the thought it was her, changing her mind. Coming back to me. I had a flash of wicked gratification where I made her make amends for her little bullshit stunt by sucking me off right here on the deck, for all the fish and stars to see.

But it was Fist who appeared. 'She's gone,' he announced.

My jaw clenched. As if I didn't know. As if I couldn't tell the marked difference with the absence because the light breeze washing over me didn't carry her alluring scent. She was only next door and yet with the aching hollow in my middle, she could've been ten thousand miles away.

What the hell was happening to me? How had I gone from scratching a long-awaited itch to being pathetically upset she refused to spend the night with me? From feeling like I couldn't quite catch my breath because she wasn't within touching distance.

Fist was still watching me. Rare curiosity in his gaze. 'Anything else?' I snapped. Did she seem unhappy? Was she regretting her decision? Begging to come back?

'No, Boss. Goodnight, Boss.'

I waved him away, then drank some more. Because apparently it was my only recourse since I wouldn't be fucking Maddelena tonight. Or talking to Maddelena. Or falling asleep next to Maddelena on our first night as a... what? A couple? A short-to-medium-term-flirting-with-danger-and-death hook-up?

Jesus.

Shaking my head, I threw myself into the nearest lounger, glad Rafa wasn't here. He would be laughing his head off until I threatened to drown him in the ocean.

My phone pinged. I debated ignoring it. But with everything going on, that wasn't wise. And helluva a thing if it wasn't the devil speaking.

> Heads up. Orazio is on the
> warpath. So enjoy that pussy while
> it lasts.

Fuuuuuck! Two weeks had whittled down to days. Days Maddelena was wasting with her bullshit.

> Grazii, I plan to. Anything transpire from our conversation with our little cokehead friend?

Nope. But our heads remain on a swivel.

> Good.

I tossed my phone away and discarded my glass in favour of drinking straight from the bottle. Admitting I wanted to get drunk as quickly as possible to fill the stupid ache inside felt even more pathetic. But did I stop? Nah.

And when the familiar haze descended, I was far too eager to embrace it. Even though I suspected the reprieve would be woefully short.

* * *

I'm not sure exactly what woke me.

It was still night. And with minimal light filtering through from the living room, the blanket of stars above my head was even more spectacular. The kind poets wrote reams about. I was no fucking poet. And my head throbbed like a motherfucker. Joining the ache that was still... yep... gnawing at my middle.

I sighed, dropped my feet to the cool polished wood and stood. The haze had cleared, leaving dry-mouth and regret behind.

Striding inside, I grabbed a bottle of water, downed half, and sipped at the remainder. The prospect of going downstairs to the glass underwater bedroom – the pricey as fuck novelty which made this particular overwater bungalow eye-wateringly pricey but which had drawn sexy little appreciative gasps of delight from Maddelena – now annoyed the hell out of me. But sleeping on the sofa seemed like something a pathetic chump would do. So I headed back out to the terrace.

And saw her.

I froze, wondering what the hell I was seeing. The water bottle halfway to my lips slowly lowered to my side as first bewilderment, then fury, resurged.

Her lingerie, clinging to the dangerous curves and valleys of her body, was the sort of lace and de-bauchery concoction filthy men like me paid for-tunes for the chance to rip off a woman's body, desperate for the treasure underneath. The kind that should sure as fuck not be on display for public con-sumption.

Yet there she was, right in the open. Doing what exactly?

She was staring into the distance as she walked towards the edge of the deck next door.

'Maddelena?' Savagery, naked and primal, bled through my voice.

She didn't answer.

Was this a fucking joke?

I tossed the bottle away and stalked closer. There was no way to get to her from here without jumping in the water and swimming over. In that time any waiter, butler or guest out walking could set eyes on what was mine. Like hell that was happening.

'Maddelena.'

Her lips moved but I couldn't hear her. And why the hell was she ignoring me?

Her pacing hastened and her hand shot out, as if warding off an invisible attack. As I watched, her movements grew more agitated, her lips moving faster. She bumped into the railing and about-faced, rushing towards the other end, *away* from me.

What the fuck? 'Maddelena!'

I was moving as I called out, dropping into the cool ocean beneath the deck and striking out towards hers. With powerful strokes, I reached her deck in less than a minute. Water sluiced off my body as I clambered up the steps.

She'd reached the end and had turned, coming right at me.

Looking straight at me... and yet... not.

'Giada, no! What did you do? No! Oh God, is that... that's *Isabella Salvatore*!'

My blood ran cold, my feet turning to ice. A roar started in my head and I couldn't breathe. Could only watch as her shins bumped the nearest lounger, slowing her down for a moment. But the terror-glazed conversation she was replaying, lost in her sleepwalking nightmare, continued.

'Giada, did you...? Oh please, God, no. No, no, no!' Her hands, trembling like leaves in a tornado, cupped her mouth, her eyes wide with the horror that had unfolded one random Tuesday afternoon five years ago, when my mother decided to go for confession at our local parish church before shopping in Manhattan.

Not knowing it would be her last.

Not knowing that Ivanovski, furious with our fucking up his months-long attempts to encroach on our New York territory, with the full backing of the Mancinellis, was intent on revenge. The unscrupulous fucker had targeted the innocent, striking down my mother and the handful of wives and cousins she'd been out with that day in a deadly and cow-ardly attack.

We'd struck back ten times harder of course, after the asshole had dared to crow about slaughtering our loved ones, and before he'd had the good sense to flee back to Mother Russia, we'd massacred three dozen of his crew. Fist, who'd lost his mother that day too, had personally killed at least fifteen men.

I shook my head now, unable to wrap my brain around the shocking, unwitting confession un-folding before my eyes. Had Liv lied about who'd pulled the trigger that killed Mama?

Had it been Giada Mancinelli?

My fingers clawed through my hair, pulling at strands in the hopes of yanking me out of this night-mare. Or if not, finding an alternative explanation that made sense.

But what was there to understand?

Maddelena had known all along and covered up for her sister. The hollow in my chest turned into a block of ice.

She approached where I stood, stared me straight in the eye. 'Give me the gun,' she whispered fervently.

I shook my head, words locked within the ice.

Cristu. Pi favori. No.

'The gun, Giada. Please! Run!'

Her agitation drilled a hole through the ice, enough for me to drop my hands. To reach for her. But... My fists bunched. I couldn't.

I paused. Swallowed. The burn from thinking she'd believed me to be a horny monster who couldn't keep his hands off her – borderline true to be fair – necessitating the need for her own bed, was almost laughable now. If I'd thought my feelings were hurt then, they were fucking mincemeat now.

'Run, run, run, run...' Her voice was wreathed in hopeless terror and despair, trailing off in hoarse rasps as tears dripped from her eyes.

Sucking in a breath, I reached for her.

She flinched. Attempted to dislodge my grip. It occurred to me that I needed to snap her out of it. Wake her up.

But that would mean engaging with her. Confirming what I'd heard. And fuck it all to hell, I wasn't ready for that. Not when I was reeling like fucking tumbleweed in a desert storm.

She was quietly sobbing when I led her through the living room and into the bedroom. And dammit, hearing it thawed the numbing ice, replacing it with a ball of grief mixed with... fear?

What the hell did I have to fear? *Her* family had gravely wronged *mine*. As the underboss and heir, I had every right to exact retribution.

To demand an eye for an eye... or the equivalent. Demand that she...

My insides congealed just as the thought stalled, unable to complete any thought or scenario that involved hurting Maddelena.

Fuck. The full connotations of this revelation threatened to chop me off at the knees. But her quiet sobs were wrecking me harder.

When we reached it, I paused in shock at the state of her room. The bed was severely rumpled and she'd left a minor trail of destruction in her path. The lamp near the door was overturned, as were the cushions, pillows and sheets. A couple of drawers were half and fully drawn, as if she'd been looking for something.

Something like... a key? I blinked.

She'd tried to lock herself in, knowing the risks. And she'd failed.

Cursing under my breath, I pulled her into my arms, freakishly alarmed when the ache in my middle immediately subsided. With one final sob, she crumpled against me. Sweeping her up, I returned her to bed, remained until her breathing evened out in deep sleep.

Then I rose, shutting drawers, righting the lamp and returning pillows to the bed. I rescued the cushion from the floor to the chair and sat down.

And as I guarded her through the night, I accepted that if I'd needed proof that I was oceans deep for Maddelena Mancinelli, I now had full, irrevocable confirmation.

24

MADDELENA

Those precious few seconds in between waking and complete wakefulness where troubles, big and small, were suspended in a bubble and you could pretend they didn't exist? As the firstborn granddaughter of a mobster, I was desperately protective of those seconds where the world was full of non-threatening possibilities.

But, always, the bubble burst.

I groaned, opening my eyes as reality surged in like a rogue wave. My fight with Cesare last night. His dismissal. Trying to contain my distress as I showered and, for the hell of it, slid on the lace lingerie set I'd planned to wear for him when I saw him today.

Locking the door, tossing the key into the back of the bathroom cabinet so I couldn't find it eas—

Locking the door.

So why was it wide open?

Oh God. *No, no, no!*

I jerked upright.

Cesare occupied the armchair near the window, his eyes feverishly fixed on me. Something in his quiet watchfulness, the dark shadows in his eyes, locked my breath in my lungs. While I was in no way an expert, I was learning Cesare's myriad expressions.

This one... wasn't good.

'Good morning,' I said hesitantly, dragging my tousled hair from my face.

He followed the move, then chased it across my arm, my shoulders. My breasts. Searing every inch of flesh it touched.

A deep, long exhale expanded his chest, and one hand dropped between his legs to adjust himself. But if I thought the sight of my body would alter the turbulent electricity careening around the room, I was wrong. Hell, it almost felt like his arousal was an afterthought to a more significant subject.

I slicked my tongue over dry, swollen lips, wondering whether to stall or meet whatever this was head on.

He decided for me with one simple sentence. 'I found you sleepwalking last night.'

Shitshitshit.

I tried to swallow and nearly choked. I disguised it with a throat clearing as I dragged my fingers through my hair again to buy myself time. 'You did?'

His look of fury mocked my efforts. 'First of all, you didn't think to mention it before I booked us into a fucking overwater bungalow? You're lucky I was the one who found you before... *Cristu*, Maddelena. You could've fallen into the ocean, been badly hurt. Or worse.' He spiked his fingers through his dishevelled hair, and I caught a haunted look in his eyes.

My heart lurched, then carried on lurching some more as my brain supplied the possibility that Cesare cared about me. Perhaps beyond temporary hot-enemy-fucking-it-out-of-our-system basis. 'But I wasn't,' I pointed out a little sheepishly.

He levelled a searing glare at me. 'For that there will be consequences, trust me.' He took a beat, a few breaths, then ploughed on. 'How long has it been going on?'

I suspected he could put two and two together if

I answered with a precise timeframe. But there was an off-chance that sleepwalking was all I'd done. That the even worse flaw that had triggered both loathing from my father and grandfather but had given them no choice but to protect me – until recently it seemed – hadn't been revealed. So I dragged my gaze from his and shrugged. 'A few years.'

He studied me for a minute, then his hand dropped back between his knees, and that look I'd first seen on waking up settled over his face. This time when my heart dipped, it kept going, charting a path of terror all the way to my toes. I drew my knees up and wrapped my arms around them, as if it would protect me from the grenade he was about to throw at my feet.

'That wasn't all that happened.'

My breath froze in my chest.

'You also talked in your sleep last night.'

No. Please God no. 'W-what... what did I say?' I whispered, my lips numb.

His eyes had darkened until the grey was barely discernible from his pupils. The skin around his mouth was tight with fury. Grief. Regret. Disappointment.

For the darkest, most horrifying secret locked within my soul.

'I think you know exactly what you said, *bedda mia.*'

* * *

Fear chiselled chunks out of my heart.

This was the reason Bonafacio had forbidden me from going to confession and downright laughed in my mother's face when she'd hesitantly broached the subject of therapy.

Perhaps if that had been the end of it, the burden would've been manageable. Instead, the third time I'd been caught sleepwalking and obliviously muttering the full-blown exchange I'd had with Giada about the night Isabella Salvatore died, and exactly who had pulled the trigger that ended her life, he'd summoned the three most terrifying capos in his hierarchy. And between them I'd been left in no doubt what would happen to me if I ever divulged the biggest secret in the Mancinelli family.

The roar in my head that said I was about to pass out intensified. I barely clocked Cesare surging to his feet and striding across the room. In the next moment, a glass was being pushed into my hand.

Orange juice.

It was almost laughable, and deeply puzzling,

how even now he was taking care of me. He should have hated me with the fire of a thousand suns. I drank half of the contents, almost regretting it when the noise in my head receded. Because then I had to make room for what came next. And I knew it wasn't going to be good.

He perched on the bed, never taking his arctic eyes off me. 'Did your sister kill my mother, Maddelena?' he grated out.

The chiselling ripped another chunk. 'The real truth is I didn't see it happen. So I don't know.'

'What does that mean?'

'It means my sister never confirmed or denied it.'

A curse ripped from him.

'Tell me everything that happened. Do not leave anything out.'

I didn't. I recited memories locked in my brain for five years, and he listened with a frozen expression. Then stared at me for the longest time when I was done.

'So what now?' I whispered.

Mouth pursed, he exhaled audibly. 'This is too big to let it go, Maddelena.' Solemn. Grave. *Final.*

He'd never used that tone before and it scared the crap out of me.

'Not even to protect me?' I tried, lilting my voice in a sorry attempt to be jovial.

His expression didn't waver. 'No. My family deserves to know.'

Fear resurged, locking in my heart. Most people pondered at some point or another when and how they would die. Those from violence-mongering families like mine risked it becoming a preoccupation.

Knowing that I could sign my own death warrant by revealing my flaws was why I hadn't fought Bonafacio's ban on me having relationships.

It was the reason he and my father hadn't pushed me into marrying until they could find a husband they could fully control. The hands I raised to my face shook uncontrollably, the tears I was trying to hide unstoppable.

'When?' I whispered, abstractly noting the macabre peace in knowing when I would die.

He didn't reply immediately. To my surprise, he captured my trembling hands and drew them down from my face. 'That's to be decided. But probably not before Orazio's birthday.' He must have read the question in my face because he added, 'He's turning eighty next month.'

He surged to his feet and prowled across the

room, digging his fingers through his hair. As he turned, I caught the anguish on his face. And my belly dipped in alarm. He might not have relished turning me over to the firing squad that was his family but Cesare planned on doing it anyway.

I drew the duvet off me, planted my feet on the floor, relieved to find the weakness from before had receded. I rose and headed for the clothes strewn at the bottom of the bed. 'So I have until then?'

Eyes so dark they were almost black narrowed at me. 'What the fuck do you think you're doing?'

I froze. 'L-leaving. You can't... you can't expect me to stay.'

'I fucking can and you fucking will.'

My bewildered gaze darted to the bed. 'You can't possibly want to... to keep doing this...?'

'Why the hell not? You haven't stopped being beautiful just because you're carrying a horrifying secret.' He ignored my flinch, a rough fury building in his face as he closed the gap between us. 'And I sure as fuck haven't stopped craving you.' He dragged his fingers through his hair once more. 'And even if I had...' He exhaled, the same bewilderment ploughing through me, visible on his face. 'I don't think I can let you go.'

'What are you s-saying, Cesare?'

'I'm saying that once this comes out, the best protection you're going to find is with me.'

I swallowed. 'What?'

'A few things are falling into place, *bedda*. Correct me if I'm wrong. You've been forced to carry this on your own, haven't you?'

There was no point lying, so I nodded. 'Sofiya and Giada know, but I don't think Jacinta or Ciso do. And my mom, obviously.'

'And I'm guessing nothing's been done medically about it?'

I laughed. 'What do you think? All I got was a warning from my grandfather about the consequences if I...'

His jaw rippled with fury. 'I get the picture.'

Again, my heart lurched at his reaction. 'You seem angry on my behalf. Why aren't you more angry *with* me?'

The question seemed to take him aback. Then another wave of pain swept across his face. I wanted to step to him, pull his hand to my chest and soothe. I also wanted, desperately, to take back the question. But I pursed my lips tight and waited.

'I am. You knew the truth and you didn't tell me, but I also get that with our history, confession wasn't the best option for you. Also... you didn't pull the trigger.' He shrugged, dragged his hands down his face. 'It could be the way I'm wired but... she's gone. I wasn't around when it happened and I've made a certain peace with it. But Rafaelle...' He stopped again and winced. 'He was there. Amongst all of us, he was the most affected.' His eyes met mine in clear warning. 'He won't take this well.'

Fear sloshing through me like a drunken sailor on a storm-tossed boat, I nodded.

'I think in some ways, the story of our feud prepared all of us. And at the time, we took down enough of the people he thought responsible for everyone to feel somewhat... avenged.'

Horror moved through me at the cold way he discussed his family's way of grieving. It was mine's too, but it still didn't stop the surge of dismay. Of recalling how many soldiers from my family and other smaller outfits across the United States and around the world had been slaughtered in payback for Isabella Salvatore's murder.

The question boiling at the back of my throat seemed almost nonsensical, but I asked anyway. 'And now? Aren't you... Are you okay with re-igniting the war? Because you know as well as I do that Bonafacio isn't going to let you take me or... my sister without retaliation. Many more people are going to die when this comes out, Cesare.'

His nostrils flared and for a moment he looked positively livid at the obvious truth. Then his face settled in cold calculation. 'Like I said, some outcomes are inevitable. But I have a couple of weeks to see how I proceed with this.'

'And what am I supposed to do in that time? Be at your beck and call?' My insides jumped in confused elation, in direct opposition and in mockery of the dissent I tried to project.

His hand curled around my nape, used the hold to propel me closer. 'Nothing has changed, *bedda*. You will do exactly what I want when I want.' His words said one thing, but there was an undertone within it. A... *pleading*.

Cesare wanted me to comply... *because he feared for me.*

'And then what?' I murmured. 'You hand me to your executioner in two weeks' time?'

He fused his mouth to mine, and I sank into the kiss, eager for the relief from fear. From grappling with the repercussions of what I'd done. And, Jesus, they were endless. I hadn't just thrown myself into the lion's den. My carelessness had dragged my sweet, fragile sister in too.

My brain threatened to dissolve beneath the on-slaught of his rough passion. Only when I was breathless and clinging to him did Cesare raise his head.

Fierce charcoal-grey eyes pierced into me. 'You're mine, *bedda*. No one lays a hand on you.'

Until I decide otherwise.

The unsaid words rattled in my brain long after he'd ripped off the lace I'd put on with seduction in mind and pushed me back on the bed. Long after I'd spread my thighs and he'd dropped to his knees to feast on me like a starving man at a banquet.

And much, much longer after he'd fucked me into the mattress and roared his most frenzied and agonised release yet.

25

CESARE

Keeping this secret would be like loading an anvil and two anchors around my neck and attempting to breathe and walk and talk like normal.

Rafaelle knew something was up within the first day of the US Grand Prix. Thankfully, he attributed it to woman trouble and I didn't disabuse him of that. There would be hell to pay when I finally came clean. I knew that. The new ache in my chest burned with a feverish hope that hell wouldn't be apocalyptic.

Orazio would lose his mind. Pops would be homicidal. War would be declared, no doubt.

But Rafaelle was my main worry.

I couldn't lose my brother.

My guilt intensified when he caught me instructing Fist to double Maddelena's security.

She'd turned on her phone halfway through the week to a dozen messages from Stefano, her father and El Topo, all demanding to know where she was, why she'd ditched her security.

She'd looked stricken for a moment, then with a face set in gorgeous mutiny I was getting familiar with, she'd quickly typed a long message. She'd turned the screen to me before hitting send and I'd been shocked and hella impressed at her boldness.

> I need some time to myself. I'm safe. Give me space to get the results we need or accidents might happen. Nobody wants that, do we?

Her message had worked – apparently – because no one had stormed the island.

We'd decided to come straight to Austin after leaving the Maldives. Buy ourselves a little more time before she needed to face El Topo's wrath in light of her little rebellion. Since we were the only two who knew I was now privy to her secret, and I wasn't on a tearing, bloodthirsty rampage, her grandfather would be more inclined to believe she hadn't let any dirty family secrets slip. That I might still be in her thrall.

So what if the last part was true enough?

Rafa weighing in with which soldiers to fly in from New York to Austin and the best way to go about secretly watching her without tipping off her own security who'd returned to her side made me feel like the worst fucking shit.

Even worse was when I left the team meeting early so I could slide my keycard over my suite door, every atom in my body jumping to feel that first glide of my skin against hers when I slid between the sheets. Her helpless moan as she spread her thighs in welcome or dropped to her knees, her eager hands and greedy mouth ready to swallow me whole and dissolve my brain.

When my tongue curled around hers and I growled, '*Mine*,' and the voice that warned me that my addiction to her was getting way out of control wouldn't be quieted.

'Congrats on winning another race,' she said when we'd caught our breaths. 'And thanks for not strangling my brother even though he caused your puncture.'

'I don't have to drag congrats out of you this time,

huh?' I grinned and dragged her pliant body closer.
'As for your brother, he got the penalty he deserved.
And I didn't get backtalk on the podium. His neck is
safe.'

Her hand slid up my chest as my gaze coasted
the room to the open laptop on the desk. 'Got any
work done?'

'Some. This is the first race I've missed all season
so it's not raising eyebrows. Yet. As long as the
money gets where it needs to go and salaries are
paid, I'm fine.'

'Anything else?'

Her lips pursed and anxiety darted across her
face. 'More messages from my father and Bonafacio
telling me to come home. I didn't reply,' she murmured, then sucked in a breath. 'I don't think he believes any more that I have you wrapped around my
finger. He sees this for what it is – his granddaughter
rebelling.'

Shit.

We were watching the last dregs of sand drip
through an hourglass. The reckoning was coming.

A caustic little laughter drew my frowning attention back to her. 'At least now I don't have to hide
that I know he plans to marry me off to some crusty

old coot with a mandate to put as many babies in me as possible before he kicks the bucket.'

My head filled with static.

I suspected it was my body's defence mechanism, a fierce and visceral reaction to what I was hearing. I shook it once. But it didn't dissipate, which was why I roared the words, 'What the fuck did you just say?'

Her eyes goggled. 'I said... well, as bullets go, it might not seem like much but if you're going to tell your family about what I know, then my grandfather can't marry me off at Christmas if I'm not around, can he?'

A kind of madness washed over me. A tsunami of fear and rage. It'd been a handful of weeks. I shouldn't have been this gone over any woman, never mind this one. Or... had I been kidding myself all along? Was this far from an irritant in my chest or an itch waiting to be scratched? Because that sensation had spread like a virus, sneaking up on the slipstream of my lust and hubris and overtaking me before I even realised it was happening.

'Bonafacio plans to marry you off... this Christmas. *And you fucking knew?*'

Her eyelids fluttered down, but the rest of her face gave her away. Like I said, shit liar. 'It was why I wanted you to take me away. I couldn't face going back home.'

My breath shuddered out as the implications moved, calibrated. Realigned themselves into a new, undeniable state. I didn't want Maddelena for a short time, for the handful of races left, to teach her a lesson or to triumph over my enemies. I wanted her... forever.

And she was... she was... 'You're...'

'...marrying him at the end of the season. Possibly before Christmas.'

The roar in my head ripped free as I flung myself out of bed, then whirled to face her.

She didn't cower. Didn't react. Just stared with a heavy sadness that terrified me even more. Because that look said she'd accepted her fate. Either death by my family's hand or reconciliation to belonging to someone else. *After* El Topo had punished her for her little rebellion.

'Over my dead, rotting fucking corpse.'

'Cesare—'

'No!'

Now she reacted. Fire ignited in her eyes, burning away the sadness and acceptance.

Great. About fucking time.

'You think you can stop any of what's coming?'

'I *know* I fucking can. And I dare any fucker to stand in my way—'

'No.'

I froze. 'What did you say?' I demanded for a second time.

'I said no.'

The static returned, bringing with it an icy fog threatening to swallow me whole. A debilitating weakness attacked my knees and I fucking stumbled. Thankfully the wall was right there. The wall I'd fucked her against last night. While she bliss-sobbed and screamed my name. Was it a lie? Did she really not... 'You don't want me?'

Bullshit, my brain scream.

Fuck that shit, my heart echoed. She does this, remember? Pulls back before she gives in. But my eyes were latched on to her beautiful face, craving confirmation that it wasn't true.

She licked her lips and rose onto her knees, shaking her head. 'I meant no to violence, Cesare. Not no to wanting you. Have you forgotten who we are? Not a single person is going to accept this beyond this handful of weeks. Hell, they're plotting punishment now! You know as well as I do this isn't hyperbole or melodrama. Genuine fucking war will break out. Again. I can't... can't have that. Not in my name.'

Her words crashed through my head, but I was staggering from the wall to the bed, shoving my fingers into her hair to direct her gaze to mine.

'Say that again. That part about you wanting me. The rest can get fucked but I... I need to be 100 per cent sure we're on the same page.' My voice felt and sounded like gravel. Hell, my whole body felt as if I was being dragged through a woodchipper. Backwards.

'I want you. Badly. Desperately. But without bloodshed. However this... if this happens—'

'It's fucking happening, *bedda*. Accept it.'

Her eyes clung to mine for an age before she asked, 'How?'

I dragged her close, closer, and when she wrapped her arms around me, I kissed her long and deep, desperately infusing strength and purpose. We were going to need both.

'Carefully, baby. And while I can't promise no violence' – I tightened my grip when she started to protest – 'I will not instigate it. You have my word on that. But I *will* do whatever it takes to protect and keep what is mine. Do you understand?'

* * *

Maddelena

Orazio lost patience with his grandson's avoiding tactics the evening after he won the Brazilian Grand Prix.

Sofiya – against every security protocol put in place by a meticulous Cesare and his team – managed to get through with a message from Bonafacio.

'He's out of patience. He wants you home. Now, sis. He's willing to forgive if you come back with me. Today.'

I stared at her from across yet another hotel room. 'I don't believe that and I know you don't,' I replied flatly.

She'd barely hesitated before she shook her head. 'No, I don't. He knows something's up. We're back to not winning races. But you knew there would be some consequences. So what are you thinking—?' She stopped when her phone rang. With a flash of alarm, her eyes darted to me.

I sucked in a shaky breath and held out my hand. Pressed the answer button. 'Nonno.'

'I don't know what in God's name you think

you're doing but you will finish it now and come home.'

'So you can marry me off?'

Sofiya's eyes widened.

Bona's breath hissed in fury. 'Is that what this is about? You heard a rumour—'

'A rumour? Or a fact?'

'Do not interrupt me, child.'

'I'm not a child, Nonno. I'm a grown woman.'

He scoffed. 'Are you sure? Because with the way you've been behaving lately it's debatable.'

'What way? I thought I was meant to be spying for you? Collecting information so we can beat our enemy?'

'And have you done any of that? Or merely indulged in other wayward activities?'

Sofiya winced.

'I've learned a few things, yes. But you didn't answer my question. Do you intend to marry me off to some stranger?'

He fell silent but his fury surged like a rogue wave. Had I been in his presence, I would be on the floor by now, reeling from a backhand. Or worse.

'This impertinence will not go unpunished. You know that, don't you?'

Even though I knew after what I'd let slip to Cesare there was no chance of going home anyway, my heart still cracked. 'I know. Which is why I'm taking more time for myself. I'll come home when I'm ready. Goodbye, Nonno.'

Sofiya was frowning when she took her phone back. 'What the fuck's going on, sis?'

Since I couldn't tell *her* I'd slept-walked and spilled my guts to Cesare, I chose to answer her earlier question.

'You were asking what I was thinking?' I smiled sadly. 'I was thinking I wanted to live life on my terms. For once. Wasn't that what you advocated? For me to get some colour in my cheeks?'

A sliver of distress slipped through her expression before she sighed. 'Yes. But will it be worth it in the long run?'

There was a seeking in that question. Even a hope? I smiled. 'I hope you find out, Sof. Maybe not in this exact way but... yeah.'

She nodded. Strode across the room and covered me in a long, tight hug.

I was fighting tears when she left as silently as she'd arrived. Still holding back sobs when Cesare rushed in, his eyes darting around the room for the long-gone threat.

'What did she want?'

'To deliver a message from Bonafacio. Come home. All will be forgiven.'

He rushed across and yanked me into his arms. As if my uttering the words would magically whisk me away from him. 'Bullshit.'

I nodded against his chest. 'I know.'

He pulled away to peer into my eyes. 'You're not thinking of going, are you? Because you're fucking forbidden.'

My smile touched the sides of my soul, then dropped away. 'I know.'

Unease flitted across his face. He shook me gently. 'You're scaring me a little, *bedda*. What are you thinking?'

'I spoke to him. Told him I won't be coming home yet. But... I think we're out of time. And I'm scared,' I whispered.

A feral sound left his throat and my arms wrapped tighter around his waist as we held each other. 'You belong to me, Maddelena. No one else gets to have you, you hear me?'

I squeezed my eyes shut as words I'd longed to hear what felt like my entire life rushed tears to my eyes. 'I hear you.'

His chest rose. Held. And fell. 'Marry me.'

I yanked my head off his chest. 'What?' Heaven

and hell were created and destroyed in my heart in the space of a second.

And even he looked a little shellshocked by his words.

But I still had enough time to live every single fantasy of being Cesare's wife. The mother of his children. Then I was forced to accept reality. Shake my head free of the fantasy. 'You don't mean that.'

His expression morphed into titanium resolution. 'The hell I don't.'

He walked me back and I wasn't surprised at all when I found myself pinned to the wall, my hands above my head.

'You're taking this knight in shining armour thing too far, don't you think?' I ignored the hitch in my voice that screamed I wanted this too. Now he'd tossed it out into being, *I wanted it*. With a savage need that went beyond every rational thought I'd ever possessed.

'You're mine. You've always been mine. Marry me,' he repeated, serious as a speeding bullet.

On every level imaginable, this was pulling the pins off a million grenades, tossing them into our lives and flipping a nuclear switch on top. Forget decimating families. This was potentially world-ending.

But for three decades I'd done as I was told. Smothered my every want and need in the name of family. Maybe if there'd been a hope that I could chalk this side trip as a little inconsequential me-time jaunt that would be laughed off once I returned to New York, I would've thought twice.

But knowing what awaited me? What Bonafacio planned for me...?

This was supposed to be a last hurrah of sorts, to experience the thrilling magic of Cesare's touch after years of yearning for him. His focused dedication to my pleasure. And yes, those bouts of tenderness I'd never experienced and grown addicted to.

Now I had, I couldn't see myself letting it go.

'Answer me, Maddelena,' he breathed against my mouth, his grey eyes drilling hard and true. Exposing my heart. My need.

'You're insane. *We're* insane. But...' I gasped and sucked in a breath and released it. 'Yes.'

His eyes blazed with volcanic triumph. And pleasure. And deep, deep satisfaction. And I didn't even care.

Because he was yanking up my thighs around his waist. Pounding me like his sanity depended entirely on achieving his next high. Imprinting his possession like he would die without it. And with each shout of 'Mine', I knew I was exactly where I belonged.

* * *

Cesare

I asked Maddelena to marry me because I wanted her with a desperation and obsession I was done trying to fathom. But yeah, as much as I hated to admit it, I was also marrying her because I needed to give her another layer of protection from her family and mine. From Rafaelle. To make her an Untouchable. Because once the truth came out...

I dragged my hands down my face. I loved him and didn't want to fight. But if it came down to it, I knew who I would choose. And I sure as fuck didn't want it to come to that. Ever.

Glancing over to make sure she was still sleeping, I stepped out onto the terrace, shut the French door behind me and hit the dial button.

Luckily the US-Brazil time difference was just two hours so I could kill the proverbial two birds with one stone. I grimaced at the metaphor and tightened my hold on the phone as my grandfather answered.

'The last time I checked I was still head of this family, true or false?'

I gritted my teeth. 'True.'

A pissed-off grunt. 'So explain to me why I gotta chase you around like a schmuck offering a three-dollar shoeshine?'

'There's been a development, Nonno.'

'Oh, I know that much, *nupito*. You've developed a serious case of what-the-fuck-itis, is what you've done. I don't even know where to begin. I mean, of all the places to stick your dipstick you choose—'

'Nonno,' I interrupted before he used slurs I'd have no choice but to call out. Because nobody insulted my woman on my watch. 'My involvement with Maddelena isn't why I called. Well, not entirely.'

Orazio cursed under his breath. 'I'm listening. And this better be good.'

'I'm patching in Rafaelle. You both need to hear this.'

I sensed his heightened tension, but he waited as I dialled. Rafa had missed the last two races, citing having his hands full dealing with the Turks, who kept demanding more and more shipments from us. The money was good but we were having to bend over backwards to accommodate their level of need.

Yalcin was also hella sore over having his consignment cut. And yeah, I'd been secretly glad not to deal with Rafa on a day-to-day basis.

That was all about to change.

'You're calling me after a race win, *frate*? The only reason you'd do that instead of being balls-deep in—'

'Rafa, Nonno is on the call. Behave.'

Dead silence for three seconds. Then he cleared his throat. 'Hey, Nonno.'

'Rafaelle,' Orazio impatiently acknowledged his grandson. 'Tell us why you called, Cesare.'

'I'm flying back tomorrow. I need you both to meet me at my place. Bring Pops too.'

'Why? You better not have done something stupid—'

'Maddelena was there the night Mama died,' I interrupted. 'Other members of her family too.'

Dead silence turned deadlier. Longer. The breath locked in my throat screamed for release.

'What did you say?' Rafa whispered, the words like ice daggers.

'I... We will explain everything tomorrow. Six o'clock. My place.'

'You don't get to dictate where and when,' Orazio

snapped. 'Bring her home. We'll have the meeting here.'

'With respect, no.'

His shock slammed into me from thousands of miles away. Rafa's too. But I held my ground.

'How long have you known this?' Rafa demanded.

The question I was most dreading. I squeezed my eyes shut. 'A little while.'

'Since your little trip?' he pressed.

'Doesn't matter. Tomorrow, six o'clock. *Si?*'

Neither objected, but they didn't say anything either.

I hung up with the stone churning in my gut. The cat was well and truly amongst the pig—

A sharp cry had me striding back inside.

'No! Giada, no! Give me the gun. Run, Giada.'

The words congealed my blood, turned me inside out as I tossed the phone away. On the one hand I absolutely loathed hearing them. Having to relive the night my mother died. On the other, it killed me that she was haunted. That her fucker of a grandfather had put her and her sisters in the position in the first place.

It made me want to hunt him down and drag him into a very, very deep hole filled with molten tar.

'Run, Giada!'

Rushing to the bed, I flipped her over. Her eyes were scrunched shut, her breath choppy as she neared hyperventilation.

'Wake up, Maddelena.' I cupped her chin but she resisted, almost wrenching from my hold. I held her still, brushed a kiss over her mouth. 'You're having a nightmare, *bedda*. Wake up,' I ordered.

'Please! Go!'

The naked terror in her voice chilled my heart, her struggling nearly toppling me off her.

Fuck it.

Yanking down my boxers, I freed my cock, pumped it twice and slid inside her.

She stilled immediately, her eyes fluttering open. 'Cesare,' she whispered.

'*Sì*, it's me. You were dreaming.'

She was awake now. And as much as it killed me, I moved to leave the haven of her pussy. But her legs flew around my waist, her heels digging into my ass.

'No. Stay. Please,' she begged.

I thickened inside her because, yup, I was a fucking bastard. A horny one, too. 'You sure?'

She nodded. Slid her tongue over her lower lip, making me harder. She felt it and trembled delightfully. 'I wish every nightmare ended this way.'

I couldn't help it; I laughed and kissed her gorgeous lips. 'Yeah?'

'Hmm. Definitely.'

'While I'm happy to oblige, I would prefer you didn't have them at all.'

Her eyes dimmed and she exhaled. 'Me too. But you're here. And I want nothing more.'

26

CESARE

'Is she here? I want to talk to her.' Rafaelle stalked down the entryway to my Lower Manhattan condo, his icily furious eyes searching.

'Yes, she is. And no, you will not.'

His eyes narrowed to murderous slits. 'You planning on denying me?'

My heart twisted with anguish for him. 'That's not what's happening here and you know it.'

'I know nothing of the sort. Do not stand in my way, Cesare.' His gaze sliced to the hallway leading to my bedroom, and his mouth twisted. 'Let me guess – you have Fist guarding her? Does he even know who he's guarding?' he taunted.

I stepped up to him until our noses were an inch

apart. 'This is where I pull rank, soldier. Fall in line or I will fucking make you.'

He stared at me for an eternity, emotions cycling through his eyes. Disappointment. Shock. Deadly malice. An ocean of pain. The last one wrecked me but I had to stand my ground. I looked over to my father and grandfather, and they were equally tense.

'Are you really doing this, son?' my father murmured. 'Have you lost your fucking mind?'

Orazio glared at me. 'Bring her out. I want to hear what she has to say.'

'I will, after we've had a conversation.'

'What's there to talk about?' Rafa asked, one brow raised. 'Unless it's to discuss getting you help for this cesspool of stupidity you seem to have fallen into. She must have a gold-plated—'

'Finish that sentence and I will cut out your tongue.' The vicious intent in my voice made him catch his breath.

For the first time in our lives, my brother stared at me like he didn't know who I was. I prayed he would eventually. That the love he had for our mother would pave the way to him understanding a fraction of what I felt for Maddelena.

And if not? What then?

I shook my head, refusing to believe there was no way through this. There had to be.

His laughter was frozen acid rain filled with spikes. 'You really have lost your fucking mind.'

'Maybe I have. But this is where we are right now.' I looked each of them in the eye. 'This is what I want, and I need you to accept it. I'll bring her out but not a single hair on her head will be harmed. By your hand or anyone else's. Agreed?'

My father shook his head, bewildered, as my grandfather watched me with furious eyes. 'Give me a good reason why we should agree.'

'Because she's the means by which we have leverage.'

'What, a granddaughter who's as good as dead if she even thinks about stepping foot back in Bonafacio's house?' Rafa taunted.

Last fucking straw, my gaze warned him.

'Leverage in that El Topo has known all along that it was his granddaughter who had something to do with Mama's death, but he sat back and let Ivanovski take all the damage. Sure he lost some men, but we know that the beating Ivanovski took he's still recovering from. How do you think he'll react if we let slip that it was the granddaughter who did it?'

Orazio's head tilted. 'And you'll do that? Burn her to that Russian fucker?'

He wanted me to say yes. I could see it in his eyes. But he also knew I couldn't. Maddelena would never forgive me if I endangered her sister, and until I knew the full truth it wasn't a risk I was prepared to take. 'The threat of it will be enough,' I said.

'You can't hide her forever, *nupito*. Bring her out here. I want to look her in the eye and hear what she's got to say.'

My heart pounded so hard in my ears I was hard pressed to hear my footsteps on the wooden floor as I walked down the hall to my bedroom.

Fist stood at attention, his eyes holding the same flat, dead stare. If he'd overheard anything we talked about, he gave no indication.

I owed him an explanation. At some point.

Once I dealt with this powder keg rolling towards the fucking bonfire in my living room. Sucking in a breath, I pushed the door open.

Her off-white power suit screamed sexy and in control. But the saucer-wide blue eyes that met mine, holding equal parts fear and trust, slashed up my heart. Shutting the door, I caught her in my arms, tilting her face up to mine. I kissed her until a layer of tension eased out of her.

'It's going that bad, huh?' she half joked, her eyes searching mine.

'It went... about as well as I expected.'

She went a shade paler, but she managed a brisk nod. 'So what now?'

I gripped her elbows, infusing as much strength as I could. I'd taken my stance and laid down the law, but I still couldn't predict the final outcome of this. 'My grandfather wants to see you.'

She swallowed audibly and her shoulders trembled beneath my hands.

'Hey? No one is fucking touching you. You hear me?'

Her nostrils fluttered delicately. Her gentle stare said they were my family. That she wouldn't blame me if I was blowing smoke up her ass. For that, I would probably take that ass tonight, remind her who owned her, body and soul. For now though... 'Do you trust me?'

She nodded. More tension eased from her. 'Yes. I do.'

My heart jumped. I held out my hand.

She took it, and we walked out to face the firing squad.

* * *

Three sets of eyes swivelled our way on our return.

A peculiar look momentarily filled my grandfather's eyes.

It wasn't hate, for which I was thankful. And then it occurred to me that this was the first time he was meeting the progeny of El Topo – the man who had once been his best friend – in the flesh. However he felt about that, he controlled it very quickly, his eyes hardening.

'I hear you have something important to tell us, young lady.'

She stiffened. To her credit, she didn't drop her head or lower her gaze. Hell, she lifted it the tiniest notch.

Pride mingled with apprehension as I watched three of the most important men closest to my heart like a hawk, ready to inflict damage should they harm my woman.

'Yes. I... was there... in the church the day your... Isabella—'

'Do. Not. Fucking. Speak her name.'

She flinched.

'Rafa.'

'Why were you there? To kill her?' This came from my father, his eyes sharper than I'd seen in years.

'No! Of course not,' replied Maddelena, horrified.

'Then why?' he pressed.

She swallowed, years of sadness pinching her face. 'It was a stupid, horrible coincidence. My mom wanted to go. She'd heard her childhood priest was visiting from Napoli.'

Orazio smirked. 'Ah, yes, your mama. A pious little thing, afraid of her own shadow. It's a miracle she birthed someone like you with a little spirit. And the other odd one, what's her name?' He snapped his fingers.

'Sofiya,' Rafaelle supplied, a weird little glint lighting his eyes before they turned that deadly shade of unhinged fury again.

'Yeah. I don't know much about the other two but—'

'Nonno...'

The old man glanced at Rafaelle, then nodded and waved for her to continue.

She cleared her throat. 'Anyway, she wanted to see him, ask him to hear her confession. And she brought me and Giada with her.'

'Why?'

Her gaze darted to me, pained embarrassment in her eyes. She saw her sleepwalking as a flaw.

Probably even more than the dangerous sleep talking.

'It's not important why,' I answered for her. 'It was just one of El Topo's bullshit rules to make the women in his house fall in line that they couldn't confess to anyone he didn't approve of.'

Orazio's eyes narrowed. 'And this priest wasn't one of them?'

She shook her head. 'He wasn't on the top of his list, no.'

'What was his name?' my father asked.

Her gaze swung to him. 'Father Calogero.'

We all locked the name tight in our memory banks.

'So she went for confession, then what?'

'It was my turn. Mom and Giada were waiting in the vestibule when I heard the gunshots... and the screaming.' Her beautiful face twisted with the memory. 'Father Calogero asked me to stay in the booth, and I did at first, but I was scared something would happen to Mom and Giada. So I went looking for them.' She sucked in a shaky breath. 'That's when I saw... them.'

'Them who?' Rafa barked.

She jumped. I squeezed her hand while glaring

ineffectually at my brother. His entire focus was pinned on Maddelena.

'My mom and Giada were kneeling over... over your mom. I thought Giada had been shot. She had so much blood...' She shook her head. 'But it was your mom who'd been shot.'

'By your sister?'

Maddelena paled, and I growled under my breath. This was fucking torture. For her. For me. But she had to get through it. Once. I was never putting her through this again.

'I... don't know. She was holding a gun. Another of my grandfather's rules is that we weren't allowed to leave home without security or our own guns. We learned to shoot when we were thirteen.'

Orazio's eyebrow went up at that. Then he scowled.

Rafa stepped closer. 'Did your sister shoot my mother. Or not?'

'I don't know,' she answered. 'And that's the truth. I took the gun from her and told her and Mom to run because I was terrified of... of...'

She didn't need to say it.

'If she didn't shoot, what the fuck was she doing next to her?' Rafa gritted out. He was moments away from losing it.

'I think your mother was saying something to her, or Giada was trying to stop the bleeding.'

'You think? All this bullshit guessing is to cover your sister's ass—'

'You're saying your sister heard my wife's last words?' my father asked through lips gone white with tension and renewed grief.

A horrifying sound leapt from Rafa's throat, and he turned abruptly, striding over to the kitchen island. From the corner of my eye, I watched him hunch over, breathing through his mouth.

'Y-yes. Maybe,' Maddelena replied.

'What did she say?' Papa pressed.

Misery etched deeper into her face and every bone in my body wanted to pull her close. But I couldn't risk it with the tension in the room. 'I don't know. Giada never said. She hasn't spoken a single word since the shooting.'

'Where is she? Where's your sister?' Rafa demanded, voice as deadly as a viper's venom.

She shifted her attention to him, eyes bold despite the pulse racing at her throat. I stabbed another warning look at him, but he ignored me.

'I don't know,' she said. 'I haven't seen or spoken to her since that night. My grandfather took her away in the middle of the night and he refuses to tell us where she is. But even if I did, I wouldn't tell you.'

Fuck.

Rafaelle's chest expanded, his tattoos writhing as his breathing grew erratic. My brother rarely lost his cool. It was always a little terrifying and a lot disturbing watching it happen. They stared each other down for an age. Then, probably guessing she meant every word, his eyes flicked to me. Then to the phone sitting on the coffee table.

'Have you asked?' he hissed.

Her head swivelled my way. 'Asked who? Who's he talking about?'

I kept my gaze on him. 'No, I haven't. And I'm not going to. Just yet.'

'I'm interested to know who this person is too, *nupito*. Have you been holding out on us?' Orazio asked.

Tell him or I will, Rafa's gaze blasted.

'He means the source who helped us find the moles in the team.'

Orazio's gaze sharpened, ever hungry for an advantage. 'Who is this source? Are they an asset we can cultivate long term?'

'There's been no contact since the Singapore race.'

Orazio tsked. 'You sound like a girl waiting to be picked for prom. What's stopping you from initiating contact?'

'Because I haven't needed to. Still don't.' This was directed at my brother. Whose fists bunched at his side.

'Are you fucking serious right now?'

'Giada was off-limits before this conversation started. She's staying off-limits until I say otherwise.' I squeezed Maddelena's hand, lifted it to my mouth and kissed her knuckles, delighting in her hitched breath. 'And fyi, that won't be anytime soon because Maddelena is going to be my wife. Which makes her – if it needs spelling out – an Untouchable. Are we all clear on that?'

Pain and bewilderment writhed through his eyes. Then with a searing look at Maddelena, Rafa stormed out.

Silence throbbed.

Giacomo stumbled over to where Rafa had just vacated and braced himself on the counter.

Orazio's gaze darted back and forth between me and Maddelena. 'Explain this madness, Cesare. Because I'm lost here.'

'It's very simple. She's mine. I'm keeping her.

And she agreed to have me in return. If El Topo has a problem with it, he can suck it.'

My grandfather's eyes widened. And a bout of sheer delight blazed his eyes before he dimmed it. I knew I'd scored a valuable point.

He turned his weighty focus on Maddelena. 'Is this true? You want my grandson? This isn't some misguided attempt to tear my family apart?' He bared his hundred-thousand-dollar Park Avenue dentist teeth. 'Because if it is, you're in for a substantial amount of—'

'It's true.' She dove closer to me, and I caught her to my side. 'I want to marry Cesare. For me. No one else.'

I loved the blush that crept up her cheeks. Nonno saw it too, and a layer of savagery left his eyes.

'Are you pregnant?' he barked, a thin layer of hope in his voice.

Maddelena's gaze darted to mine. It'd been one of the outside options we'd discussed, whether to float the idea of a possible pregnancy in the hopes that it might soften El Topo. But we'd discarded it.

Secretly, I didn't care if she never spoke to her asshole grandparent again. Things were all sorts of fucked now but I held out hope that she would gain a new family once she was a Salvatore.

'N-no. Not yet.'

My heart jumped, absurdly pleased with that 'not yet'. Then suddenly, it was all I could think about. Breeding Maddelena.

Fuck yes.

I glanced at my father. He was watching us with a peculiar look in his eyes. 'We would like your blessing,' I said.

Pain twisted his face, but he breathed out. And looked at his own father.

'We will announce your engagement at my party. And you will wed the day after you win the championship,' Orazio said abruptly.

With measured strides, he approached where we stood.

Maddelena's hand trembled in mine, but heaven bless her, she held her head up admirably. 'And if you're not pregnant right now, you better work harder on it. I want the damn trifecta of wedding, championship and great-grandbaby to rub in that *stronzu's* face before the year is out. *Capisci?*'

I transferred my hold to her shoulders, pulling her into my body. 'We'll work on it, Nonno.'

He stared us down for another full minute.

'Then you have my blessing. Mine, and your father's,' he said, then walked out the door.

My father's gaze met mine, still full of pain. But lurking beneath it was a measure of understanding. Nodding after a minute, he too left.

I exhaled long and deep. Then dragged Maddelena closer, dropping my chin on her head. 'Fuck.'

Her arms wrapped tight around me. 'Rafaelle is furious.'

'I know.'

'Is he going to be all right?' Worry husked her voice.

I kissed her crown. 'I'll make sure he is.'

We held each other, basking in the aftermath of an avoided catastrophe.

'So... we'll work on it?' She echoed my words, eyebrows raised.

I shrugged. 'You were thinking of telling El Topo you're pregnant. Orazio's frothing at the mouth at the thought of a great-grandkid. We're just bringing the timeline forward a little.' I tilted her head so I could stare deeper into her eyes. 'You do want my baby, don't you?'

Yearning, sweet and powerful, darkened her eyes. 'Yes. More than anything.'

'There you go. I can't wait to breed you, *bedda mia*.'

Some of her sass evaporated. 'You don't think we're tempting fate with all this?'

I kissed her long and deep. 'If she won't be tempted to our side, then we make our own fate, baby. But I have a feeling with the amount of effort we'll need to put into making everyone we care about happy, she'll have no choice.'

Wrapping my hands around her trim waist, I picked her up and flung her over my shoulder. She shrieked. 'Wait, what... Where are we going?'

I slapped her ass. Enjoyed it bounce against my cheek. 'First, I'm going to take this ass as payment for your earlier near-insubordination. Then we're going shopping for the fattest diamond on Fifth Avenue. We're good for now, Fist. Be ready to head out in an hour.'

She groaned at the reminder that Fist was seeing her slung over my shoulder on the way to getting reamed.

I grinned as I stepped back into my bedroom and kicked the door shut.

Things had been hairy for a second – and would probably remain tricky for a while – but for now, I was going to enjoy my woman in all the ways God had intended. And in some of the ways he didn't.

27

CESARE

It helped that the woman I was planning on marrying hadn't pulled the trigger that had killed our mother. But it was inconvenient as fuck that her last name was Mancinelli. And that her little sister may or may not be directly responsible for my mother no longer being alive.

I would've been highly entertained if I'd have been watching this on a big screen with popcorn and not living every second of this heaven and hell myself.

Every day until Orazio's eightieth birthday was like navigating a landmine with clowns on my heels. I fucking hated clowns. The only highlights being the nights I spent between Maddelena's thighs.

In four races, I'd closed the championship gap to Narciso to within seven measly points. And with three more races to go, the championship was back within reach. The sponsors were less angsty, the Turks were happy with our level of supply and service, although I wasn't holding my breath on that lasting, and an alternative pipeline was developing with the Armenians. All our clubs, casinos, warehouse and trucking concerns that served as the perfect cover for moving product hadn't needed serious oversight for a while.

Everything was ticking along as smoothly as could be expected. Except there was a calm-before-the-storm vibe in the air that made me angsty as fuck.

Or maybe it was Rafaelle's continued cold shoulder. I gave him three days to cool off after Maddelena's bombshell revelations before I reached out. He'd agreed to turn up to the family meeting in Fallbrook only after Orazio threatened to throw his collection of guns into the Potomac.

Breaking the news of my impending marriage to Maddelena to the wider family, after telling them of her sister's role in my mother's demise, produced fresh outrage and more speculation as to whether I'd lost my mind, but thankfully, the temperature had died down quickly.

Giacomo had absented himself from the meeting, with Orazio's blessing, and to my relief. The haunted grief in his eyes still devastated me. And now I'd found a woman of my own, I was beginning to understand the depths of his loss and heartache.

My grandfather shutting everyone up by reiterating his blessing had calmed things down quickly. For which I was grateful. Although the twins looked sullen and pissed off, and Bibi looked pained when she approached me after.

'This isn't a joke, is it? You really have a thing for the Mancinelli girl?'

'It's more than a thing, *soru*.' That heady feeling moved in my chest with the admission. I hadn't quite found the words to describe it yet, but it was a living, breathing thing inside me.

'I ought to be shocked as hell but considering what this family is capable of...' She shrugged, then her gaze shifted to Rafaelle, who sat brooding in the corner with a glass of cognac in his hand. He'd remained silent all meeting, but he didn't look like he wanted to tear my head off, which was something. 'Is he going to be okay about this?'

I nodded. '*Sì*. I'll make sure of it.'

She kissed my cheek and left. And by silent signal from Orazio, everyone filed out, leaving him, me and Rafa.

I got straight to the point. 'I think Father Calogero is worth looking into. I'd like to hear his version of things.' And to thank him for keeping Maddelena safe that day.

Orazio nodded approval. 'I had the same thought. Which was why I put out some feelers.'

My brows shot up. 'Already?'

His scathing look told me what he thought of my reaction. 'You think I sit around all day waiting for you to come up with all the pearls of wisdom?'

I showed respectful contrition. '*Scusa.*'

He nodded, then turned his focus on Rafa. Who stared at me for a long moment – making my gut clench hard – before dragging his phone from his pocket.

'I had the same thought too, surprisingly. So I started digging. With a little help from our friend.'

My brows went up for the second time. 'Nightowl is talking to you?' I wasn't jealous, exactly. I was just a little sceptical of someone I thought was *my* person switching allegiances.

He shrugged. 'Guess you're not the only one needing answers.'

My spine stiffened. 'Rafa.'

He held up a hand. 'I'm toeing the line, as ordered. That doesn't mean I can't set the groundwork for when you finally come to your senses.'

'So you haven't been looking for her?' I pushed.

His jaw gritted once. 'No.'

'*Grazii.*'

He exhaled, then nodded at my pocket. 'You should check your phone,' he muttered. 'Looks like they've been talking to you too, so no need to get your panties in a bunch,' he added.

I glanced at my screen and frowned at the message.

Ponder Papal Positions

'Great. We're into alliterations now.'

'From the looks of things, we're on the right track.'

'*Positions*, plural? So more than one priest?' I asked.

Orazio hummed. 'I'm sending your father to Sicily, to see what he can dig up with Calogero.'

My surprise was reflected in Rafa's eyes. 'You are?'

'This concerns your mother. He's motivated. If

there's something there, he'll find it,' Orazio stated with complete confidence.

I couldn't argue with that. So I didn't.

And it turned out, there was. Something none of us expected.

* * *

Maddelena

'Are you sure you don't want me to talk to him first?' I asked.

A week had passed since the tense meeting with Cesare and his family. A lot had happened since then, most of which I was still in the dark about, but not Cesare's plan to meet with my grandfather.

He shook his head, then grinned fondly when he saw my gaze stray for the thousandth time to the ring glistening on my finger. The emerald cut, 15.2 carat Harry Winston diamond, bordered with platinum-mounted smaller diamonds was a cool seven figures, a part of a bridal set that came with a mid-seven-figure price tag. It was the most expensive thing I owned and I was very thankful I wasn't allowed out without a small army or I would be terrified of being mugged.

Having my first anal experience right before an appointment at Harry Winston was... eye-opening.

Cesare had been as patient and gentle as he could be... up to a point. But eventually he'd broken, cursing loudly that my *culu stritti biddicchiu* – cute little ass – was too much for any sane man to withstand.

Which was why I'd spent the entire two-hour appointment guzzling champagne to soften the edges of my embarrassment and balancing sideways on one ass-cheek, glaring at Cesare every time his shoulders shook in silent laughter.

He was deadly serious now as he shook his head. 'I can't risk him doing anything stupid, baby. Let me gauge the temperature first, yeah?'

I wasn't thrilled about Cesare facing him without me, but it made sense. After my call to Bonafacio and my flat refusal to come home, I wasn't looking forward to talking to him anyway. And the news we planned to drop on him would send him into orbit. It was a little disconcerting that I was in the midst of what might be my last ever interaction with my grandfather, possibly my father. The rest of my family was debatable, but I didn't plan to let my siblings go without a fight.

The agreement was for Cesare to meet my grandfather on neutral ground, like the hotel I didn't know the Salvatores owned a massive chunk of on the Lower East Side. Or the Sicilian restaurant Bonafacio believed was owned by a celebrity chef but was in fact fully funded by Cesare's uncle Pietro's wife. It didn't gladden my heart that the Salvatores laughed at my grandfather every time he dined there and probably had something sketchy put into his food, but since I knew to my cost his level of hubris and cruelty, I wasn't in a hurry to spring to his defence.

'Hey.'

I moaned softly when Cesare's hand coasted down my back. God, I loved it when he touched me. 'Hmm?'

He dropped a kiss at my temple. 'It'll be fine.'

It wouldn't. Not for a while. Not while my mom, sisters and brother believed I'd gone over to the dark side. But I had to be patient, let things play out and settle before I could make my case.

I sighed when his hand dropped and he picked up his keys. 'You're leaving already?'

'If I stay here much longer, you get fucked again. And you need a long bath to relax and rest for when I get back.'

I sighed again, then immediately got distracted

by the sunlight refracting through my gorgeous ring. His low, pleased laughter drew me from my bling infatuation. 'You're taking Fist with you, right?'

His grin widened, and my heart galloped with pure happiness. The road ahead was all sorts of rocky, but Cesare Salvatore was *mine*.

'I'll let him know you're a fan.'

I pouted. 'He'll still look through me like I don't exist.'

'You exist for me, *bedda*. That's all that matters.'

28

CESARE

The meeting with Bonafacio was set at Tero's in Midtown.

Few people knew about my history with Charlie Nicotero. Even fewer knew the Salvatores were silent partners in all eleven of his world-renowned restaurants.

I had a brief thing with his sister back in the day. He'd been all set for a flashy debut in Formula Two when he'd face-planted in cocaine. His sister begged me to kick him straight before he lost a promising career.

Long story short, he never made it into racing. But in my attempt to help him out, he'd introduced me to the sexiest motor racing on earth. And to the best *busiate alla trapenese* outside of my mother's kitchen.

He got his act together long enough to take my advice about opening a restaurant, then promptly lost it all to drugs. I dug him out of his dark hole a second time with the condition I fronted his business and the threat to slit his throat if he so much as lost me a penny.

He'd made us both millions in the ten years we'd been partners.

I slid into the backseat after leaving Maddelena and met Fist's gaze in the rearview. It'd been a week, and I still hadn't spoken to him.

Now was as good a chance as any. 'You know what's going on.' It wasn't a question.

He hesitated, then nodded. 'Yes, Boss.'

'Do you have feelings about it I should be concerned about?'

He'd eyed me for a stupidly long stretch, making my nape itch. 'No, Boss. You'll do what's right, when it's right,' he replied in his usual monotone.

One of the many knots in my gut untangled. 'Good man.'

I slapped him on the arm, eased back in my seat, and texted Rafa.

On my way. 15 minutes.

At his prompt response, I slotted my phone back in my jacket pocket, next to the virtual grenade I intended to win this particular battle with.

I still couldn't believe what my father had uncovered in Sicily. All for the low, low price of a full refurbishment of an old crumbling sixteenth-century church and direct access to Orazio and me when needed. I agreed immediately. Orazio, being the ornery bastard he was, had held out for a day.

I patted my pocket, unable to stop my grin from spreading as we arrived at Tero's.

My grin disappeared on seeing Rafa, his face set in coldly furious lines, waiting on the curb, which in itself was surprising considering Bonafacio would be arriving with a small army like we had, and the last thing I needed was for him to be caught in some stupid drive-by by a runner with twitchy fingers.

'What the fuck are you—'

'El Topo's not coming.'

My own fury sparked. 'He cancelled?'

His lips thinned. 'Correction. He's not coming here. He wants *you* to come to him. Alone. I told him to fuck off.'

My teeth gritted hard enough to hurt my jaw. 'Call his people. Tell them I'm on my way.'

Fury turned to shock. 'Like fuck you are. *Frate*, this is a trap—'

'He probably thinks so, but he won't after he learns what we have.' At his mutinous look, I sighed. 'I have three back-to-back races starting in a few days plus Orazio's birthday party thrown in there. I'm not letting this hang over us for another three weeks. It gets settled today.'

His fists bunched hard, but after several beats they unclenched. 'I'll call. But I'm following. And so are our men. Anything happens, we kill them all. *Capisci?*'

As a sign that he didn't totally hate my guts, it was touching enough to bring a lump to my throat. Bumping fists with him, I let him slam the door.

Fist, who'd heard everything, put the vehicle in drive.

And we were off.

* * *

I'd seen pictures of the home Maddelena had grown up in. At a fifth of its size, it would never meet the majesty of Fallbrook, but it was impressive nonetheless. In a Westchester look-how-fucking-rich-I-am kind of way.

I had little time to admire the architecture though.

At the end of the short drive, twelve men in two rows of six, armed to the teeth, formed a beefy receiving line to the imposing front doors.

I hid a grin and waited for Fist to open my door.

Behind me, the single SUV they'd allowed through the gates let out the six soldiers I'd brought. Another forty lined the streets surrounding the Mancinelli property in case hell broke loose.

Stepping out, I buttoned my jacket and strode in measured steps towards the thin, hawk-nosed man framed in the door.

Like Orazio, El Topo was showing his age of a life lived on the edge of constant danger. But with thinning hair and a sickly complexion, he looked slightly worse for wear than my grandfather. I searched his features for signs of Maddelena, and to my relief I saw very little.

She'd clung hard to her grandmother's and mother's DNA.

'I told you to come alone.'

I smiled. 'You didn't tell me shit. We had a meeting which you pulled out of at the last minute.

Besides, I'm a terrible dancer when the tune isn't to my liking.'

His eyes narrowed. 'It's clear nobody bothered to teach you respect, boy.'

'Oh, I know respect. So I know it's earned. You haven't earned mine. And you're already in a deficit by calling me "boy".'

From the corner of my eye, I saw his men fidget at my lack of deference. But I was starting as I meant to go on. 'Now, I can leave if you want, but then so does any chance you have to make the right choices.'

His eyes narrowed. Assessing my level of bullshit. Then he looked over my shoulder.

'Where's my granddaughter?'

'Not here.' I shook my head. 'Did you seriously think I would bring her with me?'

Unholy rage sizzled to life in his eyes, and I was glad Maddelena was safe and sound in my bed.

'Shall we?'

His gaze shifted to Fist and the two soldiers flanking me. Then to the lieutenant closest to him before turning to head inside.

The armed man stepped up to me. 'Just you.'

I raised my hand at the slow hiss emanating from Fist. 'It's fine.'

I felt his silent protest drilling into me, but I

didn't look back as I followed El Topo. Hopefully, the ticking bomb tucked into my pocket would make him behave.

The inside of the mansion was just like the outside – showy, expensive but altogether unremarkable. My feet ate up yards of polished floors as I followed another soldier to a large study with all the antique bells and whistles.

Bonafacio was seated behind a massive desk that almost swallowed his slight figure. I hid my surprise that his son, Maddelena's father, wasn't present.

I waited till the door shut behind the soldier to approach.

'May I sit?' I asked evenly.

A flash of surprise lit his watery blue eyes. Then he waved permission.

I released my jacket button and sat down. 'First things first. I'm marrying your granddaughter, most likely by the end of the year. If it's a rumour you were hoping was false, sorry to disappoint you. I'm also here to advise that doing anything other than giving your wholehearted blessing will be viewed very unfavourably.'

His eyes slitted. 'Let me get this straight. You're keeping my Maddelena hostage, no doubt blackmailing her into your bed, and you have the balls to come here to ask for my blessing?'

It would've probably been less volatile to allow him to believe that. But I had to take every crumb of suspicion off Maddelena. Because sooner or later, he'd work out that blackmail or not, his grand-daughter and I were seriously into each other. Hell, even I got a little embarrassed for us for our inability to keep our hands off each other.

When that happened, El Topo's tiny brain would explode all over my Maddelena. So I needed to play this right.

'The only blackmail going on here is mine. On you.'

'There you go, showing your balls again. Why should I not send you back to your grandfather in several tiny pieces?'

'Because the outcome will be the same. A pile of shit on your doorstep.'

His beady eyes flashed pure loathing. Then he bared his capped teeth. 'This should be interesting.'

'I know the identity of the person who killed my mother.'

His smile switched off. 'Be very careful what you say to me next, boy.'

I nodded solemnly, like I was taking his advice

seriously. 'I don't want nor need your blessing. I'm with your granddaughter now. What I came here to say is that if you do anything that even hints at you attempting some sort of retribution for the fact that Maddelena is now for all intents and purposes an Untouchable and a Salvatore...' I paused to savour the sight of his face contorting with rage at the very thought. 'If you do that, I will take immediate steps to put you down.'

He grinned, a mirthless display of too-large teeth. 'You've clearly been inhaling too many engine fumes from your piece of shit car.'

'And you, unfortunately, are giving gangsters a bad name by not knowing when to keep your mouth shut. Especially after doing something as sacrilegious as having your rival's wife gunned down in broad daylight.' I reached into my pocket for the tiny pen drive, watching him closely. Sure enough, his smile slipped once more and he micro-shifted in his seat. 'At your age it's probably a waste of time to teach an old dog the trick of not making the mistake of confessing to murder to a priest you then murdered too, huh? Poor Father Sanguinetti, God rest his soul.'

He lost a shade of colour, but his eyes didn't shift from the drive.

'What you didn't know was that after your first confession, Sanguinetti told Patri Calogero he feared for his life. That he feared exactly what you ended up doing to him. So he took precautions. We have you on tape, literally confessing to murder. And implicating your granddaughters and several other people who would be very upset to be named.' I tapped my forefinger on the drive a few times, just to taunt him. Then tossed it back into my pocket and rose.

'I'll say this once. Stay away from my family. From today onward that includes Maddelena. Her mother and siblings will be welcome at our wedding if she wants them to. You and your son, however, are not. I'll leave it to your imagination what the consequences of defying this request will be.'

I turned and headed for the door. The creak of his chair reached me just before he snarled, 'You will not get away with this.' His agitation thickened his accent, but I heard him loud and clear.

It was my turn to smile. 'We both know I already have.'

Outside, my men re-flanked me.

And yeah, outwardly I may have looked calm, but facing the enemy in his territory was anything but a walk in the park. All it took was a tiny spark to start a conflagration. Whatever my past temperament, Maddelena deserved not to be left alone to face our families with news of my demise.

We made it to the car in one piece, Fist's more uncanny-than-usual hovering telling me the big man was just as eager to leave the Mancinelli compound in his rearview. I breathed a little easier when he shut the bulletproof door, but I waited until we were on the highway to answer the silent buzzing of my phone. "Hey, *cara*."

'Cesare? I thought you'd be back by now. Are you okay?'

A wave of tenderness swept through me at the proof of her worry and concern. 'Easy, baby, I'm fine.'

Her hitched breath told me she'd either been crying or on the brink of tears. Another, stronger wave doused me.

'You're on your way home?'

I smiled, loving that she already considered my condo her home. 'After a couple of pit stops, yeah.'

A throb of silence told me she wasn't pleased with that answer. 'How did it go?'

I loosened my tie and sprawled back in the seat, letting the sound of her husky voice wash over me. The only thing that would've been better was feeling her soothe me in person. I planned to remedy that soon enough. Sagging against the headrest, I answered, 'He called me some choice names. Threatened me a few times. But I think the message got through.' *Fuck, I hope so.*

Carnage might be inevitable but I wanted some things to go smoothly. For fucking once. The sound of slow-moving water reached my ears. 'What are you doing?'

'Having a bath. I was hoping you'd come back and join me.'

I squeezed my eyes tight as lust unravelled through me. Reaching out, I hit the privacy button, waited impatiently as it rose. 'Switch to video, *bedda*.'

'Hmm, I'm not sure I want to.' I heard the pout in her voice. 'I don't know that you deserve it.'

My breath whistled through my teeth as my cock jerked to painful life. 'You want me to beg?'

'I mean, that's a start, I guess.'

'Baby,' I cajoled. 'I just spent a whole half hour in the last place I wanted to be, just for you.'

'Are you calling the home I grew up in a hellscape, Salvatore?'

Nah, I knew better. 'No, *bedda*. Just a very small faction of your relatives who live there.' The sound of moving water increased, churning my imagination. 'Come on, baby. Please.'

She made me wait, breathing softly. 'Since you begged...' A soft ping announced the change of medium.

I pulled the phone from my ear just in time to see her fill up my screen.

Her hair was piled up on top of her head in a messy bun my fingers itched to release. But what drew my every focus was the glow of her skin and the hint of glorious tits above the suds. Her face was make-up free, her clamped eyelashes and slightly rosy eyelids telling me it wasn't just water dampening her face.

She'd been crying. Even still, *Cristu*, she was gorgeous.

'Fuck,' I breathed, tackling my belt with uncouth haste. Pre-cum was already beading from my slit by the time I freed myself. My dick surged then slapped against my abs. 'You're so fucking pretty.'

'You're not so bad your—' She stopped, eyes widening when she caught a peek of what I was doing. 'Are you jerking off?' she whispered, cutely scandalised.

I laughed. Considering everything we'd done to each other in the last few weeks, it blew my mind that she could still blush. 'Not yet. But that's the plan.'

She did that mouth twisting thing that told me she was biting her inner cheek. 'Can I watch?' she asked, her cheeks reddening even more.

'On two conditions.'

'Cesare,' she protested.

'Hear me out before you say no. You might like it.'

'Doubt it,' she tossed back, but her eyes glittered, and the tightness in my chest eased a bit to know I'd distracted her from her concerns. 'Okay, what?' she said, unable to resist the lure.

'First, you show me those beautiful tits. Show me what I'm missing.'

She drew out her compliance for several long seconds, then leaned forward and propped up the phone on the bath caddy. Reclining against the head cushion, she scooped out a handful of suds and tossed it over the side. Two more revealed the tops of her breasts. Then, lifting both arms, she tucked them behind her head.

'Fuck!' I scrambled for a worthy description, but my brain was short-circuiting. So I fell back on the simple but utterly befitting word. 'Beautiful. God, you're so beautiful.'

A soft moan puffed through her parted lips, drawing my attention to the cupid's bow I wanted wrapped around my cock more than I wanted to breathe. I released my death grip from my shaft and pumped my fist up and down, groaning at the dirty delight of it.

'My turn. Show me, Cesare,' she whispered. The surface of the water rippled with her restlessness. Her tits bounced and my vision hazed as hunger tore through me.

'In a moment,' I managed to get out. 'There's another condition, remember?'

'What is it?'

'That you go to bed naked tonight.' Normally, she wore one of her decadent sets of lingerie that drove me insane. Tonight I had something different in mind. Something she might not go for. 'Naked and wet.'

She watched me from lust-drugged eyes. 'Why?'

'I want to slide inside you while you're sleeping.' The very thought of it made me leak some more.

Her breath hitched. But the scandalised expression didn't return. Instead, her nipples slowly hardened. Fuck yes, my little minx wasn't against the idea.

'Will you do that for me, baby?'

The slightest hesitation, then she nodded. 'Yes.'

Her gaze dropped, searching the bottom of the screen.

I dutifully angled it. 'See how hard you've made me, *bedda*?'

Her moan was louder, longer. My hand moved faster, jacking myself off for both our pleasure. When her right hand started to lower, I paused long enough to catch her attention. 'One last thing, Maddelena.'

'Oh God. What?' she whined.

'You're not allowed to come.'

Her open-mouthed outrage and upright surge, displaying her glorious tits, was all I needed to nut all over my hand. After I cleaned up, I lifted the phone.

'Sleep well. I'll wake you up in the best way, baby,' I said, blowing her a kiss. 'Count on it.'

29

MADDELENA

From the poolside of the Nevada canyon mansion we'd rented for the race weekend, I tracked Cesare as he readied to leave for the racetrack.

I'd been nervous-cooking all morning, much to the quiet horror of the chef who came with the house. Eventually, I'd taken pity on the poor man and returned his domain to him, choosing to sit out in the sunshine, tearing my freshly made croissants to little pieces.

'Hey, baby, what's wrong?'

I startled and looked up.

He was dressed and the fleet of SUVs were waiting to drive him to the track. 'I have a bad feeling I can't shake.'

He was already peeved at having to leave me behind, and his mood turned darker. 'I know. So do I.'

'You do?' My fear surged, but I liked that he didn't try to dismiss or minimise my concerns.

He wrapped his arms around me and brushed a kiss on my forehead. 'Yeah, I've had it for a while.' He tilted my head up and looked deep into my eyes. 'But I'm doubling down on every precaution, you hear me? I'm not taking chances. With you or with myself. Okay?'

The ball of terror shrunk a little as I nodded. 'Thank you.'

He kissed me. Long and deep and slow. Then reluctantly stepped back. 'Gotta go, *bedda*. Miss me, please.'

'I already do.'

And as he walked out, I wondered why I didn't say the other most important thing of all.

That I loved him.

* * *

Cesare

The glitziest race of them all. Las Vegas.

I still preferred the classic elegance of Monaco, but the sponsors creamed themselves over coming out on top in Sin City.

My gut churned as the clock counted down. Ten minutes to lights out.

'You know what to do?'

Renzo nodded, face pinched with pre-race nerves and the reality I'd thrust on him of having to deal with a riled Narciso Mancinelli.

'Guard your six at the start, do everything I can to stop him sliding into your slipstream.'

I gripped his shoulder to focus his attention. 'Everything but putting yourself in a shitty position. *Capisci?*'

'*Capisci.*'

'We have a faster car and DRS at our disposal. If things don't go according to plan at the start, we still have options.'

His pinched scowl deepened. 'You think I'll fail you?'

I switched my grip to his nape. 'No, I don't. But I think he's going to be rash and ruthless because he's fucking pissed. So we need to keep our heads. Yes?'

'Okay. He lifts a little too soon at Turn 12. If I'm in the drag reduction system zone, I can catch him after the pig's snout,' he said, referring to the layout of the circuit which resembled an upside-down pig.

Relief barely glanced off the surface of my anxiety. From pole position, I had the greatest chance of a clean start, whereas Renzo, in third place, was caught between Narciso and Stan Paul in second and fourth.

If they chose to go after him...

I shook my head of the crippling thought, scanned the crowd even though she wasn't here. The itchy resonance in my chest was constant now, aching when she wasn't with me, exhilarating when she was.

In my cheesy moments, I was accepting that Maddelena had stolen a piece of my soul that day in the warehouse. And slowly, relentlessly, she'd been claiming the rest, piece by piece. And fuck if I had any objection to it any more.

I shoved my helmet on and stepped into my cockpit. I barely registered the team's last-minute prep, my eyes pinned on the start lights.

Narciso positioning himself far too close during the warm-up lap was the first sign of trouble. Beneath the glaring lights, he fixed me with a gimlet stare for three long seconds until the rules forced him to ease back. When he pointed his front wheel towards me on the start grid, I flexed my fingers on the wheel.

Future brother-in-law or not, the little shit was about to get a spanking.

I blocked out the roar of the crowd and engines when the lights winked out, flooring the most powerful race engine on earth.

I shot towards the first turn. Only to feel my belly drop to my toes when I saw Renzo was nowhere near where I needed him to be. He'd dropped back to fourth, leaving me to punch a hole in the air for my two nemeses. Who used it to dart into place alongside me as we steered Turn 1.

I clocked Narciso's maniacal grin just before I flipped my attention to Paul. His gaze was equally determined. More malicious.

Teeth gritted, I accepted their game plan. Neither of them planned to back out. They meant to pincer me into bailing, allowing one of them to take the lead.

Fuck that.

At the last possible moment, I tapped on my brakes.

They were so focused on me doing the opposite,

speeding up and losing control into the turn, that they didn't realise I'd fallen back by half a car length until it was too late.

For all three of us.

Their side pods slammed into each other in a jarring mangle of carbon fibre, which flung debris into my path. I heard my tyre blow a millisecond before my race car launched into the air. Flipped over in a kaleidoscope of whirling lights.

Maddelena.

Fuck.

The shoe had dropped.

Bonafacio had delivered on his threat.

If I survived this, I guess we were going to war after all.

*　*　*

Maddelena

There was a special kind of horror in watching your brother attempt to kill the man you loved on a racetrack. A terrifying moment when you were frozen on a cliff edge, torn straight down the middle as to who you loved more.

I was ferociously aware of alien sounds rippling from my throat.

Of Fist rushing into the room. Of him staring at the TV without reacting.

Then of him catching me around the waist as we watched Cesare's race car flip over, once, twice, three times, as my legs gave way.

I didn't need to whisper or bellow commands. Didn't need to race to my phone or yell for help. The second Narciso stumbled away from the wreckage on his own two legs and, *please God, please God, please God,* Cesare was cut free from his upside down position by the marshals and rushed into the ambulance, Fist was manhandling me out the door.

Into the fleet of SUVs.

The only sounds in the dark interior as we sped towards Vegas were the keening from my throat and the unruffled conversation Fist was having on his phone.

We arrived in a screech of tyres and swarm of black-suited mafiosi storming the hospital.

Rafa was prowling the fifth-floor corridor when I stumbled in, every frantic atom praying to every saint I could conjure up.

'Ishh... I... peeease...' Every word tasted wrong.

'He's fine,' he rasped. 'They're checking him out but he's awake and talking.'

I sagged against the wall, the tremor coursing through me showing no signs of abating. 'Arhhh... gggghhh...'

Rafa blinked and shot a glance at Fist.

'Yeah, she's been pretty much incoherent.'

I licked desert-dry lips, my heart still skewered on spikes. 'C-cnnn s-he...'

'I think she wants to see him,' Fist monotoned.

'Yeah, I got that, Fist,' Rafa returned dryly.

He nodded, retreated a few steps, and planted himself in the middle of the hallway, a human roadblock.

'Come on,' Rafa murmured.

I slanted a grateful glance at him, but when I tried to walk, I stumbled. He caught my elbow, his eyes watchful as he led me towards the double doors.

'You're really gone for him, aren't you?'

I should've loathed his amazed tone but seeing as he didn't exactly sneer the revelation, I contented myself with a nod. 'Y-yes. I... mm.'

His gaze speculated for several more seconds.

Then he pushed open the door.

And I lurched towards the man laid out on the bed.

* * *

Cesare

'I'm okay, *bedda*. I promise. Fuck, don't cry. I'm fine. Promise.'

'Y-you're not. You... you... God, it was horrible, Cesare,' she rasped.

Maddelena was hoarse from crying, and it was killing me. More than the injuries I'd suffered.

A dislocated shoulder and two sprained ribs. Possible concussion. And the unrivalled memory of barrel-rolling before hanging upside down from a Formula One race car caught in a chainlink wall.

It hurt like a motherfucker, but I was thankful for small mercies. A rib fracture or break would've ended my season. Pain from a sprain was fakeable. Another small mercy was that the two assholes had taken each other out and Renzo had ended up winning the race, a big score for the constructors' championship.

I only needed one more race win to secure the drivers' championship.

We looked up as Rafa re-entered. His eyes darted to Maddelena, who was stretched out beside me on the hospital bed. She tensed but there was no malice in his eyes.

'Update?'

He'd left an hour ago after confirmation I was fine, heading back to the paddock after the race ended, on a lethal warpath.

His lips curled. 'The stewards are still deliberating. As if there's any other way to see this. Those two fuckers deliberately put you in that wall.' His gaze darted back to Maddelena. 'Your baby brother is a little shit.'

To my surprise, she nodded, fury brimming her eyes. 'Agreed.'

Something glimmered in Rafa's eyes. Respect maybe? 'But from my initial... probing, he wasn't primed for it. Just took advantage of it. Not so much our other friend.'

Maddelena twisted in my arms. 'Are you saying Stan deliberately targeted Cesare?' she demanded.

'Yes.' He met my gaze. 'I had a quiet word with him. The *stronzu* caved even faster this time. He was under orders from his cousin to do whatever it takes to make sure you didn't finish the race.'

I cursed. 'Just his cousin?'

Rafa's gaze rested for a beat on Maddelena. I pulled her close, felt her screaming tension. Her worry. Her resignation.

'It's okay. You can say it.' Her voice broke a little.

Rafa softened. Barely. 'No, he wasn't acting on Ivanovski's sole command. Your grandfather endorsed it too.'

A choked sob escaped, and she tucked her face into my shoulder.

Dropping a hard kiss on her temple, I pinned my livid gaze on my brother. 'Go get the doctor to hurry the fuck up with my release papers. We're going to pay Stan a little visit.'

Ivanovski and, unfortunately, El Topo were next on my shit list, but that would need careful planning.

A growl started in my throat when Rafa shook his head. 'No need, *frate*. He broke his leg in two places stepping out of the shower after he returned to his dressing room. Initial assessment is it'll take three months to heal. He's out for the season.' He shrugged. 'Maybe out of racing altogether.'

Against my throat, Maddelena muttered, 'It's the fucking least he deserves.'

It reminded me that beneath all that gorgeous

sexiness lurked the heart of a mobster's grand-daughter.

A mobster who'd tried to have me killed.

* * *

'The fucking bastard had the balls to try it a second time. We can't let this slide. I hope you know that, *nupito*.'

Vegas was nine days ago. I won the Qatar Grand Prix two days ago.

In that time, Bonafacio, on learning his grandson had received a one-race ban for causing an accident and that Stan Paul was out of commission for the rest of the season, had lost his mind. His soldiers had attempted to burn down one of our casinos, targeted three of our trucks and two strip clubs. We'd lost two runners and a lieutenant, and a few hostesses had been roughed up.

He'd stopped for all of two days when we snuffed out two of his lieutenants and sent one minus his left hand with a clear warning.

Stop. Or else.

El Topo's response? He would quit his shenanigans if I called off the wedding and Maddelena returned home.

As *fucking* if.

The proverbial straw was Sofiya's call to Maddelena last night. Their sister Jacinta had been yanked back home. And El Topo was laying vicious hands on the women in his household. My woman was going out of her mind, starting to toy with falling in line, attempting to placate El Topo.

He'd zeroed in on her one weakness – her siblings.

Sheets of ice fought with white-hot rage. The next words out of my mouth would either doom me in my family's hearts or end the life of my future wife's grandfather. There was no hiding from either.

'Cesare.' Orazio rarely used my name. When he did, he meant business.

I looked up. Three sets of eyes watched me. My father, brother and grandfather.

Orazio wanted my compliance but didn't need my permission. This was happening with or without my consent.

A part of me was relieved. The other part braced for Maddelena's heartache. No matter the fallout, I knew she'd hoped it wouldn't come to this. But here we were.

I sucked in a breath. Released it. '*Sì.*'

Orazio slammed his palm on the table to seal the mandate. 'It is done.'

The date chosen was the day after our wedding day.

Bonafacio Mancinelli wouldn't die at my hand because it turned out there were some lines my grandfather wouldn't cross, one of them being having El Topo's blood on my hands.

The burden of confessing the impending deed to Maddelena, however, he had no problem tossing on my shoulders.

30

CESARE

She knew something was up.

If nothing else, my bundling her into the chopper and flying her to Fallbrook straight after the arson attack on the casino clued her in.

Keeping her distracted with wedding planning and away from Orazio and Giacomo for the time being had become a full-time job.

But I was thrilled she fell in love with Fallbrook at first sight. She might be spending more time here than she'd anticipated if this thing with Bonafacio went sideways.

She'd been doing her best to hide her unhappiness at not being able to see her sisters. Narciso she'd called from my hospital room, and it'd been glorious listening to her ripping him a new one for the dangerous stunt he'd pulled.

Hell, I got hard watching her pace, worried, angry and raining down hell on my behalf. She would make a great mama bear when the time came. I couldn't fucking wait.

Last night, I treated her to extra special fucking, not stopping until she was blissed out with a smile on her face.

Today I had another surprise in mind. It'd taken careful logistics orchestrating, which Rafa, Bibi and Fist excelled at, and the promise of blowing up shit, which the twins, the uncles and a bunch of trusted senior lieutenants were all too eager to helm.

When my five-minute heads-up text arrived, I went looking for her, navigating a sea of event-planner minions bearing giant vases of flowers that had some sentimental connection to the Old Country for Orazio. Another group were setting up extra lighting along a strip of red carpet that would form the receiving line in the foyer. After a five-minute search I gave up and wandered into the kitchen.

'Where's my wife?' I asked the busy room at large.

Fabiana looked up from a gaggle of apron-clad

helpers with a mock-stern frown. 'She's not your wife yet, *caru*. Don't test Him.'

I half-smiled but kept my eyebrows raised. I wasn't going to apologise for that. *Fiancée* had felt inadequate right from the jump. The second I asked Maddelena to marry me, she'd become my better half. My soul.

'She might be in the chapel with the wedding planners?' one starry-eyed maid offered with a blush.

I nodded my thanks, went out the side door and jumped into a golf cart.

Capos, lieutenants and staff had taken the news of the Salvatore heir marrying a Mancinelli with the expected shock and wariness, which had slowly dissolved into grudging acceptance then well-wishes as some understood the method to the madness. They didn't need to know the ins and outs of their Don's and Underboss's reasoning.

So I was gratified by the extra security guarding the paved lane from the house to the chapel, where another army of planners were hard at work prepping for two big events.

In a little over a week I would be a married man.

A reality I would've laughed raucously at three

short months ago. I was shaking my head in silent wonder when I saw her.

Dressed in cream leggings and a chunky white cashmere sweater to ward off the cold, she was leaning up to touch the top of a six-foot floral and candle stand. The winter sun slanting through arched windows bathed her in light, making her chestnut hair glint. My gaze ate her up, my breath locked in my throat.

Fuck, she was beautiful.

Sensing me, she turned around. 'Cesare? I thought you were in the city with Rafa and the others until tonight?' Her eyes frantically searched mine for bad news. Reassurance I wouldn't be able to provide for another week.

Pushing that from my mind, I walked up, sliding my arms around to cup her luscious ass. 'Not just yet. I wanted to see you first.'

'Well, here I am,' she said softly. Her own arms crept around my neck, and we kissed until the need to breathe and *not* be struck down for dry-humping in church pulled us apart.

'I have a surprise for you. Come with me?'

Her eyes searched deeper. 'Of course.'

I took her hand, led her outside and into the buggy.

From the corner of my eye, I saw her head swivelling back and forth, attempting to uncover my secret. Smiling inwardly, I drove past the main house and swimming pool to the second of the five guest lodges.

Her eyes narrowed when I stepped out. 'I hope you're not trying to flirt your way into seeing my dress before the wedding?'

'You think I can't?' I challenged.

She pouted. 'I hope you won't. Cesare, I don't—'

I kissed her silent. 'It's fine, baby, I'm not coming in. Your surprise is inside.'

She looked from the lodge to me, flustered and a little wary. 'What did you do?'

I didn't get the chance to answer. The door bust open.

'Can you two grope each other in your own time? We're on a timer here.'

Maddelena glanced past me and gasped. 'Jac? Oh my God!'

The third Mancinelli sister stood on the wide porch, hands at her sides. She sent me a wary glance as Maddelena flew up the steps.

I exhaled, content as the sisters hugged.

A second later, Maddelena gasped again when first Sofiya, then a middle-aged woman joined them.

Vittoria Mancinelli's gaze was equally wary, softening only when it fell on her daughters.

I watched them greet each other with easy affection, Jacinta earning the most attention from her big sister before Maddelena hugged her mother.

Then she glanced over her shoulder. 'Thank you.'

I nodded. I didn't really expect thanks from the other women. Old enmities aside, the men in their lives had created this shitty situation and they were right to be pissed about it.

As long as my Maddelena was happy, that was all I cared about.

'You have an hour, *bedda*,' I said, earning myself a fleet of glares. Which made me grin as I turned towards the buggy.

'Wait.' Maddelena hurried down, her eyes shining with happiness, unshed tears and a hint of worry. 'How...?'

I brushed my knuckles down her cheek. 'I've made sure your grandfather is occupied for the next few hours. As long as your sisters and mama don't blab—'

'They won't,' she reassured firmly. Then she leaned close, pressed her mouth to mine. 'Thank you,' she repeated.

'Sure thing. Go, have a good time.'

* * *

Maddelena

I watched him leave, my heart still racing.

Was there a time when I'd thought him a monster? Well, I knew there was a feral beast lurking beneath his Brioni suit; that came out when needed, but...

God, I loved him.

So why hadn't I told—

A throat cleared behind me. I turned to three expressions.

Jacinta's was more curious than wary. Sofiya's held the usual edgy scepticism.

My mother's was an ocean of worry. Multiplied by a hundred. Her hand delved into the pocket of her stylish grey pants worn with her pink twinset, and I knew she was twisting her rosary, probably reciting a silent prayer.

Swallowing, I joined them, sighing when Jacinta slid her arm around my waist.

'So you've gone all the way over to the dark side,

huh?' The half-joke came with the killer stare that had made her a force in the courtroom.

We stepped into the living room of the lodge that had become the hub of the Sicilian wedding dress designer who'd descended on me a week ago. Pia, a fireball as short and fierce as her name, had understood her assignment and executed it with aplomb, delivering my dream wedding dress within seventy-two hours.

That concoction was under heavy-duty guard within the closets of the master suite.

I pushed away the swell of sadness at the reminder that a week from today I would be walking down the aisle to Cesare, with no family support.

'I guess I have,' I responded belatedly to Jacinta.

On the coffee table was a spread of savoury and sweet dishes, including desserts from Le Gémir. All untouched.

Sofiya followed my gaze. 'We weren't sure if it was safe to eat.'

'Sof,' Jacinta berated under her breath.

She grimaced. 'What? Can you blame me?'

'No, I can't,' I replied before she and Jac got into it. 'But I'm happy you're here.' My gaze encompassed Mom, who'd been staring at me like she couldn't work out what was going on with me.

'Mom?' I prompted.

She shook her head. 'Despite all this turmoil, you seem... happy.' The last word held a hint of wonder. As if the concept of happiness was beyond her. That saddened me. But deep inside, I also felt deep gratitude that I'd got to experience this all-encompassing, forbidden, balls-to-the-wall *love*.

My heart squeezed. Sitting down next to her, I took her hand. 'I am, Mom. I didn't think I'd get to be happy, and I know it's not under great circumstances.' I stopped as Sofiya snorted, and Jacinta glared her silent. 'But I've accepted that I can't go back and change how this unfolded.' And I wasn't sure I wanted to. 'All I can do is move forward.'

'I've accepted His mysterious ways but... this?' Her dark brown eyes searched mine, her hand flipping over to grip mine, hard. 'Maddelena, are you sure?' she whispered fervently.

Even if I wasn't, I couldn't go back home, and we both knew it. My *Romeo and Juliet* musings had come true, but hopefully without all the awful dying. I nodded. 'I am.'

Silence fell for several awkward seconds before Jacinta reached for the nearest platter. 'I don't care what's in this. It looks too good to waste. I'm eating.'

I side-eyed her. 'There's nothing in it. Help yourself.' I looked at Mom, but she shook her head. Sofiya glared at a square of decadent brownie before snagging it. We ate in silence until Jacinta looked over.

'So you know we won't be here for the day, right?' she said softly.

Suppressing rising dejection, I nodded. 'Yeah. I understand.'

'So is it nice playing queen of the castle?' Sofiya muttered around a bite of brownie.

'I'm not. I don't want to be.'

'You're marrying the heir. You might not have a choice.'

It was one more thing I didn't want to think about. Hell, I hadn't even spoken to Orazio since I arrived. Deliberate planning on Cesare's part, I guessed. 'What's the temperature like at home?' I asked nervously, changing the subject.

'What do you think?' Sofiya tossed back.

'Armageddon had a baby with Dante's seventh circle of hell?'

'You said it,' Jacinta said. 'It's Eggshell Central, so I guess, thanks?'

I examined her face for signs of more. But if there was, she was hiding it well. 'Cesare said you've had to leave your apartment? Take a leave of absence from work? I never meant for any of this to happen.'

Sofiya dumped her half-eaten brownie and wiped her hand on a pristine napkin. 'Mads, whatever the heir said to Nonno or threatened him with... he's pissed. Worse than I've ever seen him. And it's the cornered, burn-it-all-down type of pissed.'

Terror squeezed my throat. 'Has he hurt you?'

Mom paled. Jacinta avoided my gaze. *Oh God.*

'He acted out a couple of times,' Sofiya confirmed, and my heart dropped through the floor. They were suffering while I was tucked away, approving candle stands and flower arrangements. 'I'm sure as hell not going to let Mom or the rest of us be caught in the shitstorm, but you need to understand there's only so much I can do.'

I cupped a hand over my mouth to stop the sob forming, and when I managed to swallow it down, I said, 'I'm sorry. And thank you.'

Silence stretched before she exhaled. 'We kinda get why you did what you had to do. But you also need to know that your rebellion won't come without a price.'

Ominous words that grew heavier and heavier, staying with me long after I'd given in to Jacinta's coaxing to see my wedding dress, and I showed it to them with a quiet excitement I'd buried deep. Afterwards, Mom, on learning I was getting married at the private chapel on the grounds, asked to see it, so we'd walked over, and she'd stood at the altar, staring up at the man-sized crucifix with tears in her eyes.

The heavy feeling was there, long after Cesare arrived with a trio of SUVs to drive them back to the City. Long after my heart broke when I hugged Jacinta tight and she flinched and I saw both Cesare and Sofiya look furious, confirming my worst fear that my father or grandfather had doled out physical abuse.

I was waiting up in bed, reading Sofiya's text when Cesare walked in just after midnight.

'What's up, *bedda*?' he asked evenly, although his eyes bore hard into me. 'I thought you'd be asleep.' I knew him well enough now to spot the wariness buried deep beneath his casual tone.

'I wanted to thank you again for today.'

He shrugged off his jacket and tossed it on the armchair. 'Anything for you, *bedda*. You know that.'

I nodded, then waved my phone. 'Got a text from Sofiya.'

He stiffened, ever so slightly. 'Oh yeah? Anything interesting?'

I tossed the phone aside, rose to my knees. His gaze instantly rushed all over me. 'Hmm. She says six of Bonafacio's warehouses in White Plains and New Rochelle were hit this afternoon. Bonafacio is now over twenty-five million in the hole with the Russians.'

He fought hard to hide the triumph that ghosted over his face and shrugged. 'I'm sorry, baby. I want to say it sucks but I can't.'

I nodded solemnly, crawling towards the end of the bed on my hands and knees. His breathing grew choppy, the bulge in his pants growing with every feverish second. 'She also says they were expecting him home, but my father just told them Bonafacio will be away for a while. That he's gone into hiding?'

He reached me in two long strides, his gaze frantically searching mine. 'Ivanovski will be wanting answers, and that fucker isn't known for being rational. Are you mad, *cara*?'

'Mad that my grandfather won't be around to beat up on my sisters while I'm not there to protect them? I should be, very mad that you Salvatores have won, again. But' – I kissed him, my heart squeezing with everything I felt for him – 'I absolutely cannot find it in myself to be. Not when my mother and the girls are safe.'

'Good. I'm glad.' He deepened the kiss.

This was by no means over.

But when Cesare pulled me close in bed an hour later, I fell asleep with a happy smile on my face.

31

CESARE

My third Formula One drivers' and constructors' championships were in the bag.

We had one hundred and forty million dollars to develop next year's car.

In two days, I was marrying the most beautiful woman in the world. And the other secret project I'd been working on was rolling along nicely.

With Bonafacio scrambling to liquidate assets to appease Ivanovski before he was literally liquidated in a vat of sulphuric acid – ostensibly one of Liv's preferred methods of dealing with his enemies – Maddelena had insisted on joining me in Qatar for the last race. I'd given in, of course.

I thought she would be wicked mad at me for the

unapologetic hand I'd played in fucking shit up for her family, but hell if she hadn't flipped the script and thanked me in the sweetest way possible.

And with every day her grandfather stayed away, every day her mother and siblings remained un-harmed, her eyes grew brighter, her smile wider and layers of tension dissipated.

I would puff my chest out with pride like a fucking peacock for protecting my woman if that stone in my gut wasn't growing heavier by the day.

Standing on the top podium for my last race win, I fixed my smile in place. Hell, I even managed a wink in her direction, making her blush when a mil-lion gazes swung her way and the whispering started.

Eyes on me, bedda.

We hadn't exactly publicised our intentions, but she was wearing my ring – proudly – and fuck if that didn't fill me with even more pride. And if she was nervous about being acknowledged as publicly mine for the first time, she hid it well.

The anthem finished playing. I was handed the trophy and hoisted up by Renzo and the third-place guy – not Narciso, thank fuck – and something clicked into place inside me.

I'd done it.

I'd achieved my goals. Wrestled my dream into reality. With three championships I was already in an elite group. I would probably never achieve super-elite Lewis Hamilton or Michael Schumacher status, but I'd launched the Salvatore name into Italian racing history books.

Orazio wouldn't have a leg to stand on now.

Not when I presented him with the next Salvatore dream project I had cooking up.

I pushed the ball of dread churning inside and allowed the team's euphoria to carry me all the way to when I opened my dressing room door an hour later and saw what awaited me.

'Oh... fuck. *Bedda*.'

'Hey, champ.'

I fumbled for the door handle behind me and opened it a crack. 'Fist. I do not want to be disturbed for the next hour. *Capisci?*'

'Yes, Boss.'

I slammed the door shut and inhaled, but it was no use. All my blood had rushed south.

Maddelena was spread out on my small bed, decked out in the racing green and black colours of my team. I couldn't make heads or tails of the leather and lace concoction, nor did I want to.

I tugged off my suit, grimaced at the sweat and champagne stickiness of my skin. 'I need a shower.'

She shook her head vehemently. 'Absolutely not. I want to lick the victory and hard work off your hot body.'

What man could argue with that? What sane man tried?

Five minutes was all I needed to recover after I'd come down her throat, and she'd swallowed every drop with a vixen's gleam in her eyes.

Then I put her on her knees, poured more champagne down her arched back and watched it drench her pussy as I rammed her to a screaming climax.

'I can't wait to make you my wife,' I said afterwards in the shower.

'I can't wait to be yours,' she replied, her arms sliding around my neck.

And if that knot in my belly continued to grow? No one needed to know.

Yet.

* * *

Maddelena

In less than an hour I would no longer be a Mancinelli. I would be swapping one volatile heritage for another. And yet I couldn't be happier.

The only fly in the ointment was the marked absence of my family. In anticipation of that, Cesare and I had agreed to ditch the tradition of designating family areas in the chapel.

Salvatores occupied pews on both sides of the beautifully decorated chapel, with honoured guests spread out behind them.

Three hundred of Orazio's nearest and dearest had cleaned out Tom Ford, Brioni, Valentino and Prada.

I was walking down the aisle on my own.

There'd been a few minutes of tension last night when Orazio had announced he would like to do the honours. As much as I'd craved the support, my suspicion that he was doing it more to fuck with Bonafacio than with my needs in mind had firmed my refusal.

His thunderous glare had quaked my insides for a full minute before he'd backed down. Cesare's gruff '*Brava, bedda*' a moment later when Orazio turned away had warmed me up very quickly.

As had Bibiana Salvatore's unexpected visit ten minutes ago.

She'd arrived just after I'd been helped into my wedding dress, looking effortlessly stunning and elegant in a Dolce & Gabbana gold satin sheath overlayed with silver tulle as she held out a large black jewellery box.

At my wary look, she'd done that half-smile thing I was realising was a family trait. 'Don't worry, it's not the family jewels. It was just delivered for you.'

The hard ball of tension lingered as she'd dismissed my attendants with a jerk of her head. Door shut, she'd blatantly stood there in my bedroom as I opened the box.

To find an exquisite pair of antique chandelier diamond earrings. And a handwritten note from my mother.

This was always meant to be yours, figghia. *It wasn't how I wished to present it to you but your* nonna *and I would be honoured if you wore it today. I will pray for you.* Ti vogghiu beni. *Mama. X*

Bibiana's eyes had softened a little as I dashed away tears, her arms folded as she watched me. 'I'm glad you said no to Orazio.'

'You are?'

'You've drawn a hell of a line by changing lanes to this side of the war zone. Buckling under the thumb of the men in this family now will only set you back. I suggest you go on as you've started.'

'Noted. Thanks.'

She'd nodded, then cast my wedding dress a beleaguered little look, reminding me that she had a murky past with another crime family.

'Good luck. I hope you won't need it,' she'd murmured.

Before I could think up an appropriate response, she was gone and my attendants were back, buzzing around me like overexcited bees, muttering about being late to church.

I was fifteen minutes late on account of reading my mother's note for a second time with a fuller heart and more tears, and needing my make-up touched up.

It may as well have been hours by the rabid look on Cesare's face when the doors swung open, and the fact that he was halfway down the aisle, storming towards me. He stumbled to a halt for a split second, then charged even faster, renewed, savage need etched into his face.

Sweet Lord, he was a sight.

I stopped in my own tracks, unable to move as my heart pranced in my chest like the pistons of Cesare's racing car.

Pia, my dress designer, and Cesare's stylist had coordinated, so it came as no surprise to see the silk cravat he'd worn with the navy three-piece morning suit was the exact dark ivory colour as my dress. His hair was slicked back, his clean-shaven jaw highlighting the wicked dark ink crawling up his neck.

He was danger and sophistication. Wicked control and feral hunger.

He was mine.

My breath stuttered as he reached me. 'Maddelena,' he breathed. As if he couldn't help but say my name.

'You couldn't wait?' I whispered shakily, my gaze devouring him.

He caught my hand, brought it to his lips and kissed my knuckles. 'No, *bedda*. Another second would've killed me,' he rasped fervently. 'You look magnificent.'

My heart sang at the reverence in his voice. The very public claiming, not as a trophy but as someone he wanted to spend the rest of his life with. So much so he couldn't wait a second longer at the altar.

'Shall we do this?' I whispered when the murmurs rose.

Behind him, Rafa stood equally suave in a similar three-piece suit, a ghost of bemusement on his face as he watched us.

Father Calogero, another surprising revelation, waited at the altar, a sort of stern fondness on his face as he waited.

A deep breath shuddered through Cesare, and he nodded. '*Sì*.'

He walked me up the aisle, ignoring Orazio's mildly disapproving frown.

Once there, he bluntly refused to let me go, and we stood hand in hand, in the presence of all of his family and none of mine and said our vows.

* * *

'I'm so fucking glad I blackmailed you.'

My soft laugh held echoes of a sob, and I blinked back tears of joy as I glanced up into the face of my husband.

My husband.

The hand wearing the exquisite platinum band matching my gorgeous engagement ring rested on his shoulder as Cesare swayed me across the dancefloor. Hundreds of eyes watched us, but I only had eyes for him.

'Technically, you asked me to produce something I didn't have. Or else.'

He shrugged. 'Potato-pot-aa-to. I had you. And I never intend to let you go.'

He pressed a kiss to my forehead, and I sighed. It was a little scary how happy I was. How complete I felt. Did that mean I wasn't going to squeeze the joy out of every second of this feeling? Hell no.

'Rafa and the twins treat you right?' he murmured.

I smiled. Cesare had ordered his brothers to dance with me after our first official dance. Rafa still remained a little stiff with me, but he'd done his duty without complaint. Renzo had flirted with me all through the four-minute dance. Dante had mostly grilled me about my family.

It was early days yet, but I couldn't wait to uncover their unique personalities.

'They were perfect gentlemen,' I replied.

He grunted, just as the music trailed off and a mic was tapped for attention.

Cesare turned me so my back was to his front, his arms wrapped around me as his grandfather stepped up to the podium.

'Here we go,' Cesare muttered.

I hid a grin.

'On any other day, someone would pay dearly for upstaging me,' Orazio started, to a smattering of forced and nervous laughter. 'But for the wedding of my grandson to Maddelena – yes, his choice of bride shocked me too at first, but' – he paused, casting a curiously nostalgic look at us – 'sometimes the heart must have what it wants. So for the sake of love alone, I must step aside, let them have their day. With my blessing.'

A loud cheer went up. And when Cesare turned to me, the fiercest blaze yet lighting his eyes, the last ball of apprehension melted away.

'That went better than I thought it would,' he said.

'You expected him to misbehave?'

'With Orazio, you never know. At the very least, I was expecting a quip about that great-grandchild he mentioned.'

My eyes widened. I'd clean forgotten about that.

Cesare frowned. 'You still want my babies, don't you, *bedda*?'

'More than anything, *caru*.'

His face transformed from civil to feral in a heartbeat as he stared at me for the longest, nerve-shredding stretch. 'Take a walk with me, baby?' he murmured in my ear.

I nodded readily, needing a reprieve from the cloying attention of guests and Cesare's family alike. To them, I was still very much an unknown quantity. A decades-long enemy had suddenly become an ally. Morbid curiosity vied with open wariness.

It hadn't strayed into open hostility, for which I suspected I had my new husband to thank.

He took my hand and I caught the dull flash of his ring. Matte black platinum embedded with a ring of black diamonds. It blended into his inked flesh as if it was always meant to be there.

Hand in hand, we stepped outside, past the brightly lit terrace strewn with guests, many of whom had spilled onto the many paths that led to relaxation areas around the garden.

Seats were set out in large and small groupings for the fireworks planned later, and extensive bars manned by sharply dressed waitstaff were dotted around to keep the drinks flowing.

We reached the grand gazebo decked out in fresh flowers and ambient lighting, and I breathed crisp cold air into my lungs.

'How are you feeling, *bedda*?' he asked, pulling me close.

'A little overwhelmed.'

'But happy?' he pressed. His eyes, as ever, dissected my every expression. And I caught a frantic edge in his gaze. Almost as if he was... nervous?

I slid my arms around him. 'Yes, very happy, Cesare.'

'*Bonu*.' He stopped for a moment. Then exhaled. 'Our path has been far from conventional. You know I desire you, that you've worked your way into my soul. You know this life we lead. You know the road isn't always smooth. But know that I will protect you with my last breath. *Si*?'

My heart attempted to hammer itself out of my ribs as I blinked back tears. 'Yes.'

He unmeshed our fingers, placed mine where he had three short months ago. At that intersection of muscles just above his belly button. Then, eyes latched fiercely onto mine, he drew my fingers up the landscape of his tattooed torso. To rest on his heart. 'You were always going to find your way here. Your rightful place. This heart beats for you, *amuri miu*.' He left my hand there, where his heart thumped strong and steady and mine, to wrap one hand around my waist and the other over my nape.

He pulled me close until my hand was smooshed between our bodies. Then looking deep into my

eyes, he said, 'I love you, Maddelena. With everything I am, *t'amu.*'

I knew then why'd I'd waited. Any other time
wouldn't have been as perfect as this. He was right;
we'd done things upside down. So confessing my
heart long after we'd made our vows felt right.

'I loved you in secret and in the dark. I loved you
in danger and through opposition. All my yester-
days, todays and tomorrows belong to you, Cesare.
With everything I am, I love you.'

A long, holy shudder moved through him. I suspected I saw a telltale sheen in his eyes too, but his
head was swooping down, claiming my mouth with
a deep groan as we kissed as true loves for the first
time.

Then, foreheads pressed together, we breathed.
Laughed. Kissed. *Loved*.

* * *

The first *pop* deceived me. I looked up, expecting
fireworks.

My head was still tilted up when the second
arrived.

The sky remained dark. Then carnage descended.

Screams ripped through the air, some abruptly silenced in a way that meant only one thing.

We were under attack.

'Fuck!' Cesare yanked me into his body and dropped to the deck, wrapping his body around me. Protecting me. Leaving himself wide open to flying bullets.

'Cesare!'

'Stay down, Maddelena! Do. Not. Fucking. Move.' The command was raw. Lethal. Totally belied by the single tremble that went through him, before he grew statue still.

Pops turned into a spray. I yelped when a staccato round landed far too close.

I felt Cesare move, assess. Then press down tighter on me.

'Boss.'

Fist. As ever close by.

'What's the situation?' Cesare snapped as I heard a gun cock close to my head. Squeezing eyes I didn't remember shutting open, I saw Fist crouched next to us, his gaze scanning as he passed a gun to Cesare.

'They entered through the west gate where the catering trucks were parked. Dressed as fucking waiters,' he reported flatly. Then just as blandly, he shot off three rounds. A shout nearby preceded the heavy thud of a body dropping.

'We need to move from here, Boss. I'll take her—'

'No. I have her,' Cesare interrupted.

Springing up, he swept me off my feet and into a full sprint.

'I've got you, baby,' he repeated.

My head bobbed as I curled into his arms.

More blood-curdling screams tore through the air, soldiers sprinting past us as Cesare raced us inside.

The ballroom, festive just minutes ago, was a scene of chaos. Tables were overturned, the cake I never got to cut a giant mess on the floor.

Cesare tensed as another round of gunfire shattered a window.

'Bibi and the women?'

'They're safe in place. They're waiting for your missus before they lock down.'

Waiting for your missus?

'Tell me you don't mean what I think you mean?'

Livid eyes bore down on me. I knew the emotion wasn't directed at me, but it still made me shiver.

'It means exactly that,' he rasped. 'You can take

any unhappiness you feel about that out on me later.'

I'd lost sight of where he was taking me, but when I saw the reinforced double doors, my blood went cold.

He'd just declared he would protect me with his last breath. What if fate had decided he should make good on that promise tonight?

I clung onto his lapels when the doors opened and he walked through it. And I saw that, indeed, the room held all women, children and the elderly.

He was leaving me here, going back out into a firefight. As the underboss, it was his duty. His destiny.

But I gripped him tighter. 'Cesare, do not make me a fucking widow before we've even had our wedding night.'

The blaze that I saw now, which had been there since high school, at times merely simmering, often-times mislabelled but always, always there, flared higher than ever. Consuming me. Protecting me. 'I make a second promise, then,' he replied, his voice hoarse. 'You will not lose me tonight, Maddelena Salvatore. I'm the fucking greedy *bastardo* who will put fat babies in that belly and demand you love me and my children for decades before I draw my last breath.' He yanked me close and planted a short, hard kiss on my quivering mouth. 'Agreed?'

'Agreed,' I whispered shakily.

With one last searing look, Cesare tore off his wedding jacket, placed it gently over my shoulders.

Then, gun in hand, he stalked out of the bunker.

Leaving me to count every excruciating second.

* * *

Cesare

The good thing about the other shoe finally dropping – if there was one to be found while embroiled in a gunfight at your own wedding – was that the immovable stone in my gut was gone.

It left me clear-headed, sharp-eyed and thirsting for vengeance on those who'd dared to harm my family. *My wife.*

I sprinted up from the underground bunker into the hallway and froze for a moment at the carnage. The dancefloor and walls were spattered with blood and broken furniture.

A sickening number of our soldiers were down

but more 'waiters' had met their end. Guests who hadn't made it out cowered behind tables and doors.

A shellshocked junior congressman was cradling his sidepiece – crap, from the look of it, the woman was either dead or near death. He would need careful handling and a fat bribe to keep this under wraps. But the good thing was, he would be even deeper in our pockets. I clicked my fingers at a passing lieutenant and pointed at the congressman. He nodded and changed course, dragging the man and his girlfriend to safety.

I followed the sound of the heaviest gunfire, arriving in the darkened hallway leading to the west exit to find Dante, Rafa and several of our soldiers crouched behind a wall of bulletproof shields. Yup, someone had broken out Orazio's prized armoury. Rafa glanced over his shoulder, and I saw his evil smirk.

I approached him in a crouch just as he jumped up and fired off a shot, catching one between the eyes.

'What the fuck are we pissing around in the hallway for?' I snarled.

Rafa pointed to my left. Renzo, hidden in the doorway to the pantry, was holding a gadget in his hand.

At my frown, he murmured, 'Drone. Outside. There's a truck coming with more of the fuckers.'

'Show me.'

He angled the screen and I saw more men dressed as waiters jumping out of the small truck. I counted twenty, half sporting handguns, the other heavier artillery. My jaw clenched. 'Orazio? Pops?'

'In the nest with thirty of our men. They're picking off any strays coming in from the east and south.' The nest was the heavily fortified highest level of the residence with panoramic views. A great vantage point.

Satisfied they were safe, I holstered my Beretta and reached for the machinegun propped next to the wall. 'We're not fucking waiting for them to come in.'

Dante's head whipped towards me. 'You sure? They're easy to pick off if we let them come in.'

But Rafa was reaching for another automatic, as did Fist. Around the grounds, the gunfire was dying down. I fucking hoped it meant our men were winning.

Rafa caught my arm as I stepped out of the hallway. '*Frate*, wait.'

I turned to him, jaw tighter than concrete. 'He sent them into *our home*, on this day, Rafa,' I seethed.

His eyes burned into mine. Whatever he was searching for he found, and he nodded. 'Let's go.'

I glanced back at Renzo. 'Shout if you see more coming.' To my men, I said, 'Keep a couple alive for questioning.' I was pretty damn sure this was Bonafacio's doing, but I wanted verification all the same. Any last shred of mercy I may have harboured was gone, so I wanted that cherry on top of his grave.

A red haze washed over my eyes, shrinking the ball of fear to a pebble deep in my gut.

The first wave of enemies was gunned down within seconds, my finger never leaving the trigger. The second was more cagey. I took the decision out of their hands by prowling forward, meeting every tentative approach with a bullet. Fist kept a steady head count until three remained.

The first I shot in the legs while Dante disarmed him.

The second Rafa caught in the throat with a shuriken he'd produced from fuck knows where, killing him instantly. 'Oops, my bad.'

The third was scurrying back to the truck when I pulled out my Beretta and shot him in the spine, disabling him.

One hour later, the compound was free of guests,

and the two soldiers had squealed that indeed, they'd been sent here by Bonafacio Mancinelli.

Another hour later, the chopper holding Orazio's high-level FBI inside man landed. I handed over the pen drive of El Topo's confession and one mil in bit-coin, and a warrant for Bonafacio's arrest was issued immediately.

It was the legit cover for our illegal manhunt to end Mancinelli once and for all. But if the FBI did our job for us beforehand, that was fine too.

Bloodied and arms folded, I watched the chopper take off.

'Helluva fucking night,' Renzo rasped.

'But an excuse to have another party, eh?' Orazio said from my left.

I said nothing.

He could have as many parties as he wanted.

I had married the love of my life tonight, no matter how it ended. That was all I needed.

As the last of the red haze disappeared, a deep, ravenous hunger took its place.

The hunger to see her face. To touch my Maddelena.

Still without speaking, I turned from the helipad, my strides lengthening as I headed for the bunker.

'Hey, Cesare, wait.'

'Fuck no,' I growled at Rafa.

'*Frate*, you're covered in blood. Maybe wash up first?'

I looked down at myself. My vest and shirt were ruined beyond repair. My knuckles, arms and face were covered in blood spatter. But the need clawing through me was greater. Besides, I was proud to let her see how I'd protected her.

So I kept walking.

The soldiers guarding the door took one look and sprang into action, throwing the bolts securing the bunker.

She was the first thing I saw.

In the middle of my nearest and dearest. She was the jewel of my heart.

I stopped in the doorway as her eyes darted frantically over me.

'Not my blood.' I answered her silent, screaming question.

She nodded once, then threw herself into my arms. I caught her tight. Tighter. Breathed her in. Took her mouth. Revelled in my naked adoration and obsession.

When we broke apart, I whispered against her mouth, 'I love you, and I will always come back to you. Do you hear me, *bedda*?'

'I hear you, my love.' She pulled back, looked deep into my eyes. 'But it's over for now, yes?'

'It's over,' I echoed. 'Shall we begin our beautiful, crazy life now?'

'Yes. Absolutely yes.'

EPILOGUE
SEVEN MONTHS LATER

'Where are we going?'

'Are you going to be patient or do I have to pull over and pound that gorgeous pussy until you pass out so I can get us there in peace?'

I produced a fake pout that made my husband's grin widen. 'Are you calling me a brat?'

'Oh, most definitely. And brats get spanked on top of what I just promised. So what's it going to be?'

I squirmed in my seat and his grin widened. He knew exactly what his sexy threats did to me. And he knew exactly when to sprinkle them.

Lately, they'd been arriving more frequently.

At six months pregnant, my horny hormones showed no signs of slowing down. Cesare loved it.

He was stoked to be on call for my every little need, just as he was obsessed with every tiny change in my body.

He reached over and spread his large hand over my swollen belly. 'Do you need me, baby?'

Biting my lip, I whimpered and nodded.

'Five minutes. I promise it'll be worth it.'

I dragged my gaze from his face which, now that he smiled more, had gone from stupidly hot to cardiac-threateningly magnificent.

I looked out the window just to get some reprieve from said hotness, then as I concentrated on my surroundings, my eyes widened. 'Oh my God, is this...'

'The warehouse where we first officially met? Yeah. I bought the surrounding land and buildings around it ten years ago. But I didn't settle on the true purpose of what to do with it until last year.'

A lot had happened since our fateful wedding night.

My grandfather had disappeared, the combination of being hunted down by Cesare, the FBI and the Russians sending him deep underground. The last we'd heard he was back in the Old Country, but our sources hadn't been verified. Yet.

His soldiers confirming that they'd been offered a bonus to kill both Cesare and me on my wedding day had killed any dregs of loyalty for my grandfather.

It hurt, a lot. But I'd learned to live with it.

His disappearance also meant I was free to spend time with my mother and sisters, although I wasn't allowed in the Mancinelli home by my father's decree. Not that I much cared.

In three short months, I was going to be a mother. I couldn't wait. The joy in my heart outweighed the rejection from some factions of my family.

'Wait for me to open the door, baby,' Cesare instructed when he stopped the car in front of a building with soaring glass windows. My eyes widened when I saw the massive signage at the top.

Furia Motor Sport.

'This is what you've been not-so-secretly excited about the past few months, isn't it?' I asked as he helped me out.

He grinned. 'Guilty.'

'So your car design is finally done?'

Much to my surprise, and secret relief, Cesare gave up his racing seat to Dante the day we found out I was pregnant. The dangers of being an underboss was one we would live with until he passed on that mantle to the son I was carrying, but having achieved his dream of being a racing driver, he'd wanted a different, exciting challenge.

And my clever husband had found that challenge.

'*Sì.*' He dropped a quick kiss on my mouth. 'The manufacturing plant itself will be in Sicily but this is where the ideas will be born. Because this is where the most profound feeling I didn't recognise as the true purpose of my life started.'

I was lost for words. It was only when his fingers brushed my cheek and he murmured in husky Sicilian did I realise I was weeping tears of joy. I stumbled into his arms, knowing he would catch me. Always.

After a full three minutes where we simply basked in the deep, embracing warmth of our love, he pulled back. 'Would you like to see it?'

'Yes, please.'

He took my hand, held it all through the tour, until we reached a giant door. Then he released me to throw it wide open.

The space was cavernous. And empty. Except for the large spotlit object in the middle of the warehouse.

A few steps in and I recognised the shape.

I gasped. 'Is this what I think it is?'

Without answering he walked me to it, then reached for the heavy dark gold cloth covering it.

Cesare unveiled it with a flourish and tossed the cloth away. 'Meet the final prototype of Furia "Elena".'

My hand darted to my mouth, whether to cover my quivering lips or my shocked delight, I wasn't sure. 'Elena?'

'Maddelena felt too long and naming it after myself felt entirely too pompous...' he said with a grin.

I walked around the supercar, my eyes growing wider until I was scared it would pop out of my head. Every line and feature was exquisite.

'Congratulations. It's utterly gorgeous, Cesare.'

His head dipped in a momentary motion of modesty. '*Grazii, bedda.*'

I joined him at the front, laying my hands on his chest. 'And thank you for naming her after me. I'm hopelessly honoured.' Rising on my tiptoes, I touched my mouth to his.

And just like that, the arousal that had taken a temporary backseat beneath the awe of his words and deeds came roaring back.

'I would very much like to celebrate your introduction to your namesake.'

My eyebrows shot up and I glanced from the car

to his face and back, thrilling to the idea with shameless haste. 'Wait, we're not going to damage it, are we?' It would be a shame to wreck his beautiful creation.

'It's much sturdier than it looks. Besides, it's a prototype. That's what it's here for, to test its resilience.'

I giggled. 'So I'm really a crash test dummy of sorts?'

He winked. 'The most beautiful one I've ever seen.' He kissed the corner of my mouth as he tugged on the tie to my wraparound dress. It shimmied off my shoulders with barely a wriggle, pooling at my feet.

Stepping back, he stared down at me and groaned. '*Cristu*. You get impossibly more beautiful every day.'

The squirming returned too.

I wanted him, desperately, *everywhere*. His eyes turned inferno hot as he accurately read my urgent need. With the deft flick of his hand, my bra was unhooked and on the floor. 'Hard and fast, *caru meu*?'

'*Pi favuri*,' I answered.

Predictably, his eyes darkened at my answer. Cesare loved me speaking the language of our heritage, especially in moments like this.

He caught my hands and gently nudged me back until my calves touched the low bumper of the sports car. Another nudge and I perched on the hood.

The carbon fibre was cool against my ass but the goosebumps it spread over my skin felt delicious, plus it cooled me down long enough for me not to climb my husband like a tree.

'Lie back, baby. Let me drink in this incredible sight.'

I propped one hand behind me and he groaned when my breasts thrust up. Every inch of my body was Cesare's playground, but my breasts remained his personal obsession. Once I was settled on the black hood, I waited for the next instruction.

'Arms above your head,' he croaked.

'Like this?' I rested my wrists on the glass, one above the other. I was on full display to my husband, and he looked as if he was seconds from losing his mind.

'Oh fuck! I love you, Maddelena.'

'I love you too. Now get over here and put your cock in me. I need you.'

He tore his clothes off then, grabbing my ankles, he gave me exactly what I needed. Did we make dents in his hideously expensive prototype sports car? Most likely. Did I care? Absolutely not.

When we were done and I was wearing Cesare's shirt because I was too lust-drunk to leave the comfort of his arms to put my own clothes back on, I tucked my face into his neck and breathed him in. 'Did the car survive?'

'Looks like it,' he said, amusement trailing his voice. 'But just to be sure, we'll test out all twelve.'

'Hmm? Twelve prototypes?'

'Nah, the Elena collection will comprise twelve original super-exclusive editions. I invited bids and have already selected their owners.' He dropped his head to my ear as he carried me to the door. 'What they don't know is that I intend to christen each car with my wife before I send it off.'

'Oh my God.'

His laughter was rich and free, and it wrapped me up like the warmest blanket. 'You like the sound of that, don't you?'

'I shouldn't but... damn it, I do.' I wrapped my arms around his neck. 'I can't wait to get started. *T'amu* Cesare.'

His face transformed as it did every time I confessed the simple truth in my heart. 'One last stop before we go.'

He crossed the room and stopped next to a pillar.

I focused long enough to read the simple inscription on the wall he'd pinned me to the night of my seventeenth birthday. The first time he kissed me.

Attruvau pi sempri ccà. I found forever here.

I placed my hand on his chest, felt his heart beat fierce and true. 'Cesare.'

He brushed his lips over mine. 'I love you, *caru meu*.'

* * *

MORE FROM ZARA COX

The next book in the Mafia Rivals series from Zara Cox, *The Enforcer*, is available to order now here: https://mybook.to/TheEnforcerBackAd

ACKNOWLEDGEMENTS

First of all to my brilliant editor Megan Haslam, whose first and enthusiastic response to my email about writing a gritty, mafia-formula-one mashup with hot guys and fast cars, was "this is exactly what I'm looking for!" Your enthusiasm for this book and series has been priceless and made this book an absolute joy to write. Through you, I'm perpetuating my love for all things Formula One and sexy book boyfriends, and I couldn't be happier!

As ever, to Sally and Jo, my two-woman cheering squad. I struck gold with you two as friends and writing partners. So happy to have you both in my life.

For the readers who've been patiently waiting for a new Zara Cox book, I hope this one was worth the wait. I promise the next wait will be way shorter.

Finally to my family, for knowing exactly what I mean when I say "it's going to be one of those days/weeks, guys." Thank you for your support and for indulging a writer's mad process. This journey wouldn't be possible without you.

Much love,

Zara xo

ABOUT THE AUTHOR

Zara Cox is the writer of spicy contemporary romance, she writes intense, spicy billionaire romances for Boldwood, including the Indigo Lounge series.

Sign up to Zara Cox's mailing list for news, competitions and updates on future books.

Follow Zara on social media here:

f facebook.com/zara.cox.98

X x.com/zcoxbooks

O instagram.com/zaracoxwriter

BB bookbub.com/authors/zara-cox

ALSO BY ZARA COX

The Indigo Lounge Series

Mile High Addiction

Sky High Obsession

Seven Night Stopover

Million Dollar High

High Sea Seduction

Mafia Rivals Series

The Mastermind

The Enforcer

Boldwood

EVER AFTER

x♡x♡

JOIN BOLDWOOD'S
ROMANCE
COMMUNITY
FOR SWEET AND
SPICY BOOK RECS
WITH ALL YOUR
FAVOURITE
TROPES!

SIGN UP TO OUR
NEWSLETTER

HTTPS://BIT.LY/BOLDWOODEVERAFTER

Boldwood

Boldwood Books is an award-winning fiction publishing company seeking out the best stories from around the world.

Find out more at www.boldwoodbooks.com

Join our reader community for brilliant books, competitions and offers!

Follow us
@BoldwoodBooks
@TheBoldBookClub

Sign up to our weekly deals newsletter

https://bit.ly/BoldwoodBNewsletter

www.ingramcontent.com/pod-product-compliance
Lightning Source LLC
Chambersburg PA
CBHW010656100726
47900CB00010B/2683